DARKHUNT

DARKLIGHT 9

BELLA FORREST

1

Lyra

*M*iami's muggy air was a shock after leaving the frigid snow in Chicago. When the pilot opened the door of our private plane, sunshine greeted us with blinding intensity, even in March. I squinted against the glare.

"I already saw a mosquito," Bryce said in disbelief. "Bloody bloodsuckers."

His Scottish brogue made me laugh. Nicholas Bryce, my co-captain in our new business, had a certain way with words, and they were usually blunt.

"I resent that remark," Dorian said. My husband was, of course, a bloodsucker himself.

Bryce elbowed Dorian. "And make sure you tell us if that human makeup smudges," he reminded him.

We all disembarked with our bags and the rest of our team in tow. The vampires, whose skin tones were far different than those of humans—because of the dancing shadows beneath the surface—sported full makeup to cover up the anomaly.

It wasn't just Callanish and monsters we would be dealing with this time, so we would all have to be extra careful not to reveal to the public, or anyone else sensitive for that matter, that a group of vampires was in their midst.

Cam, Bryce's young nephew who had a penchant for religiously sticking to the rules, followed immediately behind Dorian. His furry companion, a squirrel-like critter from our first mission, quietly poked its head out of his backpack.

The redheaded ex-soldier had left his life in Scotland to join our ranks, and he'd proven himself very useful on our adventure through the Pocket Space. He'd slowly started to loosen up over time. He used to button his shirts up to the top in a rigid style, but now the collar of his uniform shirt hung slightly open.

Behind Cam, Sike laughed with Chandry. They were both vampires, and fairly unusual, as neither had been trained as a warrior like many of their kind's survivors. Sike looked more like a human than a darkness-draining vampire with the bright Florida sun hitting his olive complexion.

Chandry was as bubbly as ever as she commented on the sprawling airstrip around us. She wanted more experience in the Mortal Plane, and so, Arlonne agreed to Chandry joining our team for the moment. Her acrobatic and healing skills would likely come in handy for this mission. She was also excellent with sensing the gates, but with the nature of this particular mission, I wasn't sure that would be necessary.

Cam had to file a special vampire license for Chandry before our mission, making her our newest addition to Callanish. Humans still thought vampires were under strict government regulation.

The Bureau and the government had worked together to issue a few licenses for vampires to move around freely if any unfamiliar Bureau members caught them. My own husband was one of these licensed vampires; he'd obtained the highest level of permission to be allowed to work with Callanish.

The largest stipulation for vampires required them to stick to The Bureau's human members at all times. So our plan was to continue using makeup to camouflage the vampires' skin, although we also planned to limit the view of our vampire members through accommodation by the local Bureau office, just in case.

It was a bit annoying that the vampires couldn't use their skills in front of random people. The restriction would be something the vampires had to keep in mind constantly, but I hoped everything would go well. We were still brainstorming ideas to address this frustrating problem. I hated that it was an issue in the first place, since vampires were the only reason that we'd saved the universe months ago.

But, alas, I'm just a young woman trying to keep the government happy. After all, the Department of Homeland Security was funding this particular mission.

As I moved with the rest of my team, a nervous energy fell over me. Being back in the field and doing something useful was great, but I worried about my abilities to lead us to a successful mission after the last one ended abruptly without full resolution. And this case was different than anything we'd handled in the past.

It involved humans more than it did monsters. Though, sometimes, those two could be one and the same.

A black van slowly pulled up on the tarmac. I pulled off my outer jacket, which had been necessary in Chicago but was utterly unnecessary here. I could understand why people retired down here after working their entire lives up north, though I couldn't say I was looking forward to being out in this kind of heat for any length of time.

A handsome Bureau official emerged from the vehicle. He was tall and tan, his dark hair smoothed back with gel. He held himself with a strict military posture and gave off an air of chilly politeness that was hard to read.

I pegged him as the same age as Bryce, despite the guy's sun-kissed glow.

Bryce and I stepped forward to greet him.

"Munroe and Bryce, good to meet you," the man said, extending his hand for a polite handshake. His honey eyes searched us with the analytical gaze that often came with power. "I'm William Torres, your contact for the mission."

The levity Bryce had showcased earlier dimmed slightly. His jaw tightened but he said, "Nice to meet you."

His short, gruff response made me wonder what he thought of this man, but I merely put my hand forward and gave Torres a firm handshake. It was best to let military men know that a woman meant business from the beginning.

Immediately, Torres looked past me and nodded at our vampire companions. Cam stood next to them, looking reserved.

"I'll take you to our Miami office," Torres said a bit stiffly. He gestured to the sleek black van behind us that had dark tinted windows—perfectly average for any kind of business transport.

The vampires and Cam piled into the back while Bryce, Dorian, and I sat in the middle seat. The driver guided our car out of the airport, and we merged into moderate traffic. Chandry whistled as she looked out the window at all the cars.

"People sure love to eat and drive at the same time," she marveled.

Bryce let out a humorous snort, but it wasn't his typical boisterous laugh. He'd seemed preoccupied on the way over as well, as if he weren't as excited about this mission as he typically would be. I didn't know the reason, but if it continued, I'd have to pry. I cared about my team; not just as soldiers, but as human beings.

I settled into the seat, sending a silent *thank you* to whoever had invented air-conditioning.

The building we pulled up to was simple and unassuming, nothing like the other larger Bureau offices I had seen. As soon as we entered the office, Torres got right down to business. We settled in a boardroom with tinted windows, Torres standing up front next to a small projector screen. One of the fluorescent lights in the corner had a burned-out bulb.

Budget cuts looked like they had made their way over here... Odd. I'd always thought our partner for this mission, The Bureau—my old organization and the leading guard against all things supernatural in the Mortal Plane—had virtually unlimited funds.

I was glad Homeland Security was the one providing the funding for this, then. And maybe it was why we had been asked to help The Bureau out in the first place. Beyond the Leftovers' issue, I speculated it was also about equipment and maybe even manpower.

Torres angled toward Bryce and me, as if the others weren't even in the room, and his voice came out flat as he began. "We've called you here to help us deal with a new criminal group that has been taking advantage of the Leftovers to commit illegal activity."

He clicked a button on his remote and glanced up at the large screen on the wall. An image appeared of a man in his forties. He clicked again, and another image popped up beside the first to show a woman around the same age. The man had piercing green eyes and a tiny burn the size of a quarter on his left cheek, and the woman had dyed blonde hair with dark roots that flanked either side of her oval face in messy waves. Neither was smiling.

"These are our current suspects," Torres announced. "We believe they are involved in the recent kidnappings of local teenagers. The Miami police got CCTV footage of them outside a gas station near where one of the kids went missing, and a witness placed them in range of two other abductions. The witness works as a delivery man and noticed the suspects more than once when making drop-offs at convenience stores in the area. They stuck out to him for some reason, so he called in and said the guy gave him a creepy vibe."

Bryce spoke up. "Are they random abductions, like the kids were out trying to have some fun but met trouble?"

Torres shook his head. "Unfortunately, these two individuals are very organized. They use occult websites and forums to entice their victims, and they seem to focus on teenagers. We can track at least three cases back to a particular website called *Occult Geeks*. It's geared to the current trends of youth using tarot cards and astrological signs, but they also have a forum that's very popular in Florida thanks to the Leftovers carving out a large area of the Everglades."

I exchanged a glance with the others. What did the Leftovers have to do with teens obsessed with the Occult?

Torres gave Dorian an uncomfortable glance which set me on high alert but then cleared his throat and kept going. "We've linked several social media accounts, mostly from teenagers who have tagged this site in supposedly supernatural videos. I've watched them. For the most part, they seem to include viral challenges like running through abandoned buildings with friends on the outskirts of the Leftovers."

Social media and teens are always cooking up some dangerous things, but shouldn't the Leftovers be an obvious threat by now?

I shook my head and wondered who owned the website in question. Surely, we could check, or perhaps the police had already obtained user information from the webmaster through a warrant.

Cam typed away on his sleek laptop and brought up the website for us to look at. Torres clicked his remote again to show a smiling, dark-skinned teenager with braces. Next to her photo, her details were written as Alicia

Smith, aged fourteen, and a member of the *Occult Geeks* forum. She wore a skull T-shirt that Roxy would've loved. As for the website, it looked like every other fringe interest site to me. An animated ghost danced at the top of the forum page as Cam made an account to look at the posts.

On the surface, the whole thing looked harmless, but it might be a scheme in and of itself to lure in the most vulnerable. Humans were predators too sometimes, just as much as crazy monsters in the Leftovers.

"Alicia's is the strongest case we have at the moment," Torres went on. "We believe, based on her story and several others that we've pieced together, that the suspects are finding teenagers online and asking them to meet on the outskirts of the Leftovers. After the meetings, the kids disappear."

Alarm bells went off in my head at that.

Torres sighed as if the weight of it all rested too heavy on him. "Alicia rode her bike all the way to the eastern part of the Leftovers, which must have taken hours. She is an interesting case because she told her best friend about the meeting. The friend advised her against it, but Alicia believed the strangers to be in possession of some valuable information. She wouldn't say anything about what sort of information it was. Her friend waited for a text from Alicia to confirm her safety after the meeting, but never received it. The next day, she came to the station with a picture that Alicia had sent her just before the meeting of a license plate in an abandoned parking lot."

Torres pressed the remote again, revealing a blurry but readable photo of a license plate on the back of what appeared to be a boxy sedan.

"The license plate is a fake. Alicia hasn't been seen since." Talking about the case had relaxed Torres some, loosening some of the rigidness in his shoulders. His worry for the kids made him look less like a department-store mannequin and more alive.

"Any problems at home with the kids?" Bryce asked. It was a factor that always had to be considered in the case of missing children. The idea grounded me in reality, the kind of reality that existed in the past, before the Leftovers and the Immortal Plane.

Not all crimes and horrors were because of a supernatural entity. Some came from right under a person's nose.

"Negative," Torres confirmed. "Most of the parents reported good relationships with their kids—well, as good as they can be when the kid is that age."

Fair enough.

"The parents seemed genuinely confused about the occult sites and that their children would willingly meet strangers from online. We also talked to the victims' friends to corroborate that these weren't kids running away from abusive homes. Even their friends thought it was unusual for their friends to run away, but they couldn't offer anything else. Alicia was the only one who said she was actually meeting someone."

I remembered being a teenager. Those years had come with the moody certainty that I knew better than anyone else and a driving need for independence, but The Bureau's strict lifestyle ensured that phase didn't last long.

I tried to imagine myself in these teenagers' shoes. They were part of a generation who'd grown up with constant warnings about cyber-safety, so why would they run out and meet a stranger from a creepy website?

"The Miami police realized they were in over their heads when the count of missing teenagers started to rise. They recognized it was happening too close to the Leftovers and handed things over to us." Torres cleared his throat. "We are... Well, we aren't as used to supernatural issues in this branch anymore. I never thought the Leftovers would pop up here. Even with all of the case files the Miami police handed over, nothing can be proven with the evidence we have."

"The photos," I pressed, "of the adults. From the CCTV footage. Do you have any leads on their identities?"

"They likely have various usernames and retire them for new ones after a successful abduction. We know all the kids' usernames, though."

At least they had something.

"As far as the suspects," Torres added, "a Miami beat cop actually recognized their faces after the chief circulated the footage. Unfortunately, the cop couldn't remember where he'd seen them, and he didn't know their names. It lends to our theory, though, that these two are local. Maybe they're innocent, maybe they've just got terrible timing at gas stations. But it's only a matter of time before we identify them. The webmaster wanted to issue a safety warning on his forum after he found out about the investigation, but we worry that scaring them off will cause them to start over somewhere else. He did publish a *strong* statement reminding others to be cautious about sharing personal information, citing spamming threats and phishing scams."

Torres paused and twisted his wedding ring around his finger. "We're in a pretty tight spot."

Cam gave his computer screen a lopsided frown. "It looks like many of these forum posts are about the Leftovers. A few threads have been locked, but it seems that a bunch are talking about their cell phones and radios jamming around the Leftovers area. Do you have any information about the effects of the local Leftovers?"

Torres gave a firm nod. "My next few slides, actually." He clicked forward past more bright, young faces. I saw names like Jones, Rodriguez, Brown, and Lopez. *So many kids taken, but why?* Finally, Torres landed on a display of four scans from the Leftovers' regions. Increased electromagnetic activity in certain areas definitely showed something odd going on. It was like what we'd experienced in Utah.

"And how much progress have you made with researching the area?" Bryce asked. He lifted one eyebrow when Torres shifted uncomfortably.

"To be honest, we don't have the manpower," Torres explained with an unreadable expression. "The Bureau in the Southeast is understaffed. We don't have as much experience with monsters as the Midwest and Southwest offices, and our region's staff was reduced when vampires supposedly went extinct."

That explained it. They'd been vampire hunters and not much more.

Torres gestured broadly to the room at large. "I've worked in the Miami branch all my life, in a strong network with the other southeastern offices. We used to be strong during our vampire hunting days, but that's simply not the case anymore. On the whole, we don't have much experience with the supernatural, outside of our vampire history."

Torres had been an expert vampire hunter. Without vampires around as the ultimate enemy, his office's funds had dried up like the desert. Now, I understood. His coldness, the state of the office, everything...

Dorian's jaw clenched uneasily. Sike lowered his eyes to the table as Chandry placed her chin in her hands to listen intently. As far as I knew, she had very little experience among humans, but on the surface, she didn't seem overly disturbed.

Torres cleared his throat. Despite their expert makeup, he knew which ones were vampires. Had he noticed their faster movements? The tension was explainable now. His past dealings with vampires had all been negative; all he had known were the monsters even *I* had assumed vampires were.

An odd, charged silence fell over the room before he spoke again.

"We believe the suspects are working with revenant vampires, but we've been unable to find them officially. Our resources are limited."

It was the same thing that my contact for this job had said. I doubted that theory. We'd destroyed the revenant system. There was no ability to control them anymore.

But if a guy like Torres read about revenant vampires in The Bureau-wide briefings for chiefs, then maybe he wanted to believe in it.

Torres pushed on. "So we don't have the personnel to explore the Leftovers, as I've explained to you. We don't have funds like we did in the glory days."

I exchanged a look with Dorian. His face was lined with tension, though he remained silent. It was hard to hear that Torres harbored some complicated feelings about his branch's downgrade at the end of those vampire hunting days, like the fact he might have enjoyed the way things were before.

He could at least try to hide it.

Bryce crossed his arms and nodded, which I suspected was intended to hurry the conversation along rather than struggling in this tense pause.

"Do you have all the evidence for us to review?" I asked, hurrying to break the silence. "I'd like to go over it in more detail. Our tech members will tackle the websites." That task would fall to Cam and Sike.

Torres pointed to the corner, where a stack of four evidence boxes waited on a plastic table. I hoped some of them had external drives, and it wouldn't all be paper to sort through.

"I have a meeting to attend," Torres informed us. "So I'll leave this in your care. We can discuss your accommodation details and transport when I get back."

I thanked him as he left, while Bryce pulled the first box off the stack and brought it over to the conference table. When I was sure Torres was gone, I allowed myself to relax.

"He's happy about us vampires," Dorian muttered sarcastically as he watched Bryce page through a thick pile of documents. Bryce distributed different things for us to check out. I glanced over a map from the Miami police, noting that the disappearances were largely spread out around the edges of the Leftovers. A footnote mentioned they were based on cell tower connections, so who knew how accurate that was. I frowned, worried. Our suspects were clever, even if they looked like rough company.

"Anything on the website?" I asked as Cam and Sike hunched over the computer together.

"I could tell you more if you gave me a list of usernames," Cam said. I nodded and started going through a box of flash drives. The label attached to the box said it had various archives and long lists of usernames of interest on certain drives. It was going to be a mountain of research to go through. I wished this office had a coffee machine in it. Could that be arranged in our accommodation?

"We should investigate the website and then head after those weird signatures in the Leftovers to see if there's a hideout of some kind," Bryce said confidently. "It won't be revenants, but it might be something." As far as we knew, all the revenants were back in the Immortal Plane under Reshi's guidance. Some of them were making good recoveries like Kreya. I peered over his shoulder at the maps he'd pulled from the box. According to one, that area was mostly the northern part of the Everglades and encompassed part of Big Cypress National preserve, about an hour away.

"Sounds good," I told Bryce. "Tomorrow morning?"

Bryce smirked dryly. "Assuming we can get transport from our friendly contacts here."

It couldn't come soon enough. The faster we could get out into the Leftovers, the sooner I would feel like we were making some progress. Alicia's face haunted me. I wanted to find her—alive.

2

Roxy

*I*f there was anything that made me happy, it was sweating and beating someone up. If there was anything that made me *extra* happy, it was doing it to my siblings.

Sweat coated every inch of me, while a fist flew at me from the side.

It was Jordan, being characteristically sloppy with his punches. I easily executed some footwork to trip up his feet while dodging his blow. He yelped as my hand clapped onto his forearm. All it took was a yank to pull him down like a tree falling in the forest. He unleashed a string of curses as he fell to the mat. I threw my head back and laughed.

It was my right as the older sibling, and it was their fault for not practicing. They were good, but not that good. I'd picked up a few moves from Kane when we used to grapple.

A heavy weight hit my chest that had nothing to do with Jessie throwing herself at me.

My siblings were like spider monkeys with their energy levels, but luckily they came with all the grace of a two-year-old. This was an old trick in the twin playbook. While Jordan distracted me, Jessie would sneak up on me. I neatly stepped out of the path of Jessie's leap, and she landed beside her brother, groaning.

"When did you get so fast?" she moaned. "When we were kids, we always beat you."

I smirked wickedly at her. "Oh, you thought that was for real? I was letting you guys win."

The twins exchanged looks of consternation, and then Jordan snorted with laughter.

"Wow, I really thought I was the strongest kid ever because we used to win against you," he said, and then did air quotes as he repeated, "'Win.' Okay, now that I say it out loud, I realize how dumb we were."

"How are we giving ourselves away?" Jessie asked, her voice sharp as she eyed me. "I don't mean that playful move. You've been countering us on every serious attempt, too."

The twins were the newest additions to the Hellraisers, the monster hunting squad I led for The Bureau. They were sometimes cocky, but always ready to learn if it meant besting someone. They needed more discipline, though, something my supervisor, Hindley, liked to remind me of.

On our days and evenings off, I bribed them into sparring with me by promising to buy them lunch afterwards. After their first successful mission in the Sierra mountains with me, I felt confident that they were on the right track, but... I still worried. *And what's twenty bucks to get them some extra practice?*

Jessie was in for a good lesson. Before I met the vampires—Kane, specifically—I'd sparred just like the twins.

"You're fighting like humans trained by The Bureau," I told them bluntly. "It's what I did before the vampires came along, and I got to spar outside of my comfort zone. The Bureau has taught you mixed martial arts in a variety of styles, and basic defense. It's great for when you're dealing with other humans, but it has limits when wrestling with monsters."

"Like what?" Jordan asked as he pulled himself off the mat. Nobody else was in the gym today. Nobody in their right mind would waste their precious extra hours sparring, unless they were crazy like my family. The Taylor name had a certain reputation.

I pointed to their feet. "When I first started sparring with vampires—"

"Your brain infestation," Jessie cut in with a smirk.

"My friend, Kane," I pushed back, ignoring the teasing. They knew about my mental link with Kane, which worked as well as a shoddy cell phone connection some days. I never knew when his voice was going to suddenly come to me in the middle of the day, but we talked most days after my work was done.

The connection was clearer in the evening for some reason. Maybe I was more relaxed after practice, and it was easier to talk when I knew that I would be alone.

"I've learned to watch my opponent's body for the smallest micromovements and anticipate their thought processes. That's how I knew where you were going, Jessie. You saw Jordan fail with a punch and figured you'd go all in with your weight, since you're fast enough. It might've worked on a more overwhelmed fighter, but no dice with me."

Kane was part of the original vampire group that I worked with in The Bureau. Even back then, he'd been handsome and intimidating, like a cold wall of ice that I couldn't chip my way through. How many times had Kane kicked my ass? Several, but he'd made me good enough to return the favor a few times.

"Don't let your emotions cloud you," I told the twins. "You're changing just like I did when I began with The Bureau."

Jordan whistled. "When did you get so wise?"

Somewhere in between my first day at The Bureau and my stumbling into a captain position? They would follow a similar path. I licked my cracked lips, parched from the workout.

"You learn as you go, if you're willing to." I tapped my head. "We just have to make sure that the signature stubborn, dogged Taylor nature works in our favor instead of against us."

Jessie's eyes sparked with understanding, and she grinned. I could already see new ideas for training exercises popping off in her head. She was the mastermind and schemer of the two. Although the twins hated assigned training, they adored working out their own ideas.

"Let's go again," Jessie said and smacked her fist into her palm. She shot a knowing look at Jordan who wore a goofy smile as they both flanked me. My skin pricked with that sixth-sense of knowing my ass was about to be handed to me. The twins were working together now, instead of trying to attack me separately.

"Is Kane your boyfriend?" Jordan blurted. The question knocked me off guard for a moment. As he stared at me earnestly, Jessie tried to put me in a headlock. I narrowly evaded her, but my brief delay caused me to miss Jordan's attack. He tackled me to the ground, and Jessie succeeded in securing my head in a perfect lock.

"That's dirty," I accused with a howling laugh. *Leave it to my siblings.* Jordan slapped the blue mat underneath us, calling out numbers like a wrestling referee.

"And that's a defeat for Captain Taylor," he cried. "The crowd goes wild."

We erupted into laughter as I pulled myself from Jessie's grip. "Good job working together," I told them, "although you won't always have each other to depend on. It's important to work with your other teammates just as well."

"Holt we get along with," Jessie said. "We'll rope in Evans and Jones soon enough. It's great now that Jones has stopped being such an asshead."

That was one way to describe it. Jones had given me some trouble earlier in our work together, but he had mostly settled down now. I had a feeling he and the twins would be a good match, in terms of Jones wiping the floor with them. It would do a lot for their learning and for their cocky attitudes.

"We get along with Colin, too, even if he doesn't talk much," Jordan added.

It was true that Colin, our resident sniper, was quiet, but he was extremely intelligent. I hoped he was enjoying his day off. He once told me he had a collection of bonsai trees that The Bureau apartment manager had agreed to water when he left for missions. Odd to think one of our best marksmen was into gardening, but I was all for my team having their own lives. He was going on leave soon because his mother was ill.

And speaking of our own lives...

"How is party prep going?" I asked my siblings as we toweled off our sweat. Jessie brought over the disinfectant spray to clean the mats.

"Good. Have you given any thought to a playlist?" Jordan demanded. "You promised to make us one, like the old days."

I bit my tongue to hold back a warning against getting their hopes up. It was possible that we wouldn't even get to celebrate the twins' upcoming birthday if we got called away. They were amped, ready to celebrate in their apartment near The Bureau campus with all our family and friends.

"I'll make a playlist," I promised.

When the twins were kids, I used to burn CDs for them to share in their clunky secondhand boombox. Money was tight when we were young, but now, the twins earned respectable incomes from The Bureau as special soldiers. Their barbecue was top-notch, and they had a long list of groceries to buy for the planned day.

With the three of us out of the house and working a new job in The Bureau mailroom, my mother was also looking forward to the party. She was in a much better financial position and planned to spoil the twins, no doubt. And since The Bureau offered childcare for our younger siblings during the day, she was more well-rested than ever.

My mother had raised seven children in all, in part because I'd helped. My dad split when he felt like it until finally, he just stopped coming home altogether. I suspected some of my younger siblings were actually my half-siblings, but my mother would never own up to that.

I guess we're all better off now. It had been years since I'd had to count pennies the way I had as a kid.

"Will you wear a dress?" Jessie asked with a smirk. "A big poofy one, like a prom dress."

I snorted. "No way."

I never went to prom as a teenager since I'd enlisted in The Bureau's high school training program. I was able to complete my high school diploma alongside soldier training, but there had been no time for dances. My entire life was dedicated to fighting—and now helping—the supernatural.

"I'm aging the beef as we speak," Jordan informed us proudly. "Don't ask me about the process, 'cuz you don't want to know. It will be delicious, though."

I grimaced. "I'll tell my stomach to prepare for food poisoning, just in case." Jordan playfully punched my arm as we headed to the locker room. Jessie and I went to the women's section to shower, while he split off to the men's.

Tomorrow, it was back to work for them, but I had more to do tonight after dinner. Hindley and I were meeting up to go over next week's schedule.

As I showered, I couldn't help but smile and reminisce on how far the twins had come. They'd worked hard to set up their own lives, and I wanted them to be excited about their birthdays and barbecue. I just hoped they actually got to celebrate.

On our way out of the gym a few minutes later, I warned them, "Just prepare yourselves, in case we end up having to go on a mission. Mom and the others might end up eating all the food."

"Then we'll barbecue monster meat," he suggested. Jessie and I gagged at the thought. Eating a monster from the Leftovers would only be done as a last resort, before we ate one another. For all I knew, the meat was poisonous or radioactive.

I said goodbye to the twins and made my way down the block. Their apartment was just off The Bureau campus, but I had special accommodations as a captain. It was cheaper than a regular apartment, and I preferred to be closer to the action. After all, I thrived on it.

You there, yet? I threw out my thoughts into the world, though I always felt the tiniest bit silly as I did. Kane and I usually started our chats by just making sure that the other was free.

There was no reply as I unlocked my apartment door and made my way inside. Everything was pristine, save for a few jackets I'd thrown on the couch and been too lazy to hang up. *Not all of my old habits are gone.* Sometimes, that annoyed me, but other times, it made me smile. I liked that there was still a wildness inside me somewhere.

"Are you talking about your messy organization skills?" Kane asked, his sudden question startling me as it broke the quiet around me.

During my childhood, there was always noise. I could never have a moment alone; I just lived for the smack of pans on stovetops and the shrill laughter of tickle fights that turned into wrestling matches. After I moved into the barracks, there were always other people around, laughing and arguing. I still wasn't used to the quiet that came with living alone, and sudden noises just made that phobia worse.

You scared me. I thought you weren't listening. This was how it went with us now. We called and teased each other. Even when I felt like it was flirty sometimes, I never thought it went beyond friendship... not even after that kiss. Or at least, neither of us had said as much.

Get kidnapped by any monsters today?

"Very funny," Kane said with a throaty chuckle. I froze as a shiver ran down my spine. In my mind, it sounded as though he was right beside my ear. "I'm not in need of saving right now."

He had *also* kissed me when I rescued him, but he either didn't remember or refused to acknowledge it. I had feelings for him, but I'd decided that I wasn't going to set our friendship on fire for it. Perhaps this was better. Maybe he wasn't ready. *Or maybe I'm imagining everything and there was no meaning in that.*

After the meld, I'd thought he'd gone back to the Immortal Plane, but he'd somehow gotten lost in the Pocket Space with the strange Ghost monster we'd dealt with on our last mission. He was back in the Immortal Plane now, healing up after nearly dying. I was happy to hear him sounding stronger every day.

"No meaning in what?"

I swallowed hard. *Oops.* Sometimes, it was hard to control what went to him and what stayed with me. I had gotten better with practice, but the occasional stray thought slipped away.

Nothing. How are you? I've got a planning session in a few hours.

"You sound about as fun as Lyra and Dorian," he said dryly. "I'm fine. The healers are annoyingly present. Every time I turn around, they're lying in wait for me."

They want to make sure you're getting better, and not taxing yourself by doing something stupid. Kane was anything but a good patient, and he'd well-earned the healers' suspicions.

I smirked to myself as I began heating up some leftover—Chinese noodles that I'd ordered the other night. I wasn't much of a cook, but I sure loved to eat, and Chicago had plenty of takeout places.

I sparred with the twins earlier. They're getting better. Smarter, too.

"They have a good teacher," Kane said.

I shifted my weight from foot to foot as I waited for the microwave to heat my food. Kane was hard to read. One minute, he was cheerfully dissing me, and the next, he was making my heart slam against my chest while I searched for a soy sauce packet.

Thanks. I can't wait to throw them your way. You'll love wiping the floor with them, and they'll be better off for it. They're a bit cocky, but they're learning.

"Your family sounds interesting," Kane said. "I can't wait to see what kind of secrets the twins will tell me. They've probably got loads of dirt on you, as you humans say."

The microwave dinged, but food was barely on my mind. I wanted to spar mentally—possibly emotionally—with him. I wanted to try to test our communication technique. We'd talked about it before, but Kane had been recovering from his time in the Pocket Space and hadn't felt up to the task. But last night he'd told me that he felt recovered, and we were ready to give it a try. We had the time today, and I could eat on autopilot while we tested our mental connection.

Are you ready for some mental sparring?

I could practically see Kane's confident smile. It made me warm all over.

"When have I ever backed down from a challenge?" he asked.

The answer was never. *Let's do this.*

3
Lyra

"Are you ready to see your accommodations?" Torres asked.

In the balmy evening air, I looked around the parking lot of the Miami branch. Our Bureau contact was standing proud as a peacock in the midst of the few vehicles scattered throughout the lot and a ridiculous RV parked in the corner. I looked at the van he'd used to bring us here from the airport, thinking perhaps he was going to hand over the keys to that. The only other options were a few boxy sedans that wouldn't fit our entire team.

Bryce clicked his tongue with a sound of recognition just before Torres gestured grandly to the motorhome in the corner of the lot. I kept my mouth firmly closed, even though my jaw wanted to drop at the sight of the twenty-five-foot-long beast of a vehicle. It had a beach sunset and dolphins airbrushed onto the back, and on the side, a cartoon alligator opened its jaws wide as if to eat the front door of the RV.

"The Paradise Palace," Sike read uncertainly off the painted title on the motorhome. 'Paradise' and 'palace' were both a long stretch. I was expecting tinted windows and bullet-proof off-road SUVs, not... Mom and Dad taking the kids camping.

"Brilliant," Bryce said, a touch more cheerful now. I shot him a skeptical look behind Torres's back. "We're going to fit right in with the tourists."

Torres turned to aim a megawatt smile at us. He was clearly proud of himself. "You'll be a tourist bus, basically. Nobody will give you a second look."

With these paint decals, I highly doubt that. The bumper sticker on the back said, *I'd rather be fishing!*

"I guess it won't be that strange to see outside of the Leftovers," I mused slowly, trying to work out where we could park this mammoth thing. Perhaps it was best to hide in plain sight, like Torres clearly thought we should.

Unless he was purposefully trying to humiliate us. Given his history with vampires, that also seemed likely.

"The green animal looks interesting," Chandry said merrily.

We'd have to give her a quick zoology lesson along the way. I held back a sigh and glanced at Bryce who nodded contently at the motorhome.

"Back in my day, before I was as wrinkly and dry as the gator on that RV, I wanted to live in a motorhome like this and explore the country. It was my dream to have adventures, especially after watching movies all about life in America," Bryce explained. He turned to Torres with a grin, and our Bureau contact raised his eyebrows with a touch of surprise.

So he was expecting us to protest. Interesting.

"It'll suit your needs?" Torres asked.

"Certainly. If we can get the generator working and fill the water tanks, I think we can all sleep in the RV tonight," Bryce said. "We don't have to budget for hotel rooms. We can also use your internet from the parking lot if needed."

Cam whipped out his cell phone and gave a thumbs up. "I arranged a hotspot for us."

Torres ran a hand over his sleek hair. "I—well, you're right. That'll be fine. I can get someone to prepare it for you."

Bryce had him flustered, which gave the older man a victorious air. While the prospect of sleeping all together in an RV sounded less pleasant than separate hotel rooms, I was happy if we were saving money. We had a decent budget, but I'd rather spend it on weapons and supplies... especially seeing the bare minimum that Torres had to offer from his own Bureau stock.

I simultaneously marveled that a painted alligator could look so happy and yet so terrifying at the same time.

"We'll take it," Bryce said firmly. "Can your staff bring us the equipment that we brought?"

We hadn't been able to fit everything in the trunk of the van.

Torres looked over to a white moving truck in the parking lot. A man had walked out from The Bureau office and was headed to the truck, waving at Torres. "That will be them right now. I'll go check in." He was quick to trot off. Bryce's sneaky smile remained.

I was glad to see him in better spirits, although I had no idea what had caused his earlier mood.

Was he angry that Torres had treated us coldly because of the vampires? It was hard to say, but Bryce went back further than I did in Bureau history. Perhaps he knew the Miami branch.

I fell into work mode, trying to ignore the occasional bug zipping annoyingly past my ear. We unloaded our equipment into the motorhome, which smelled strongly of artificial vanilla. Dorian made a disgusted face as he searched for the culprit of the sickly-sweet smell. It turned out to be a wax air-freshener, which he promptly threw out the window. Torres left us to our own devices, though he promised to arrange the plumbing and energy accommodations Bryce had asked for.

Chandry was poking around in the small kitchenette, getting Sike to help her clean with some old rags they'd found under the sink.

Cam set up his computer and pulled a file from one of the evidence boxes. "The Bureau and Miami police already set up some dummy accounts, so we can use those for our investigation." He connected his computer to a large monitor for Bryce and me to look at.

The same website flashed on screen. Now, Cam separated his display into three windows on his screen with a quick keyboard shortcut. One was the *Occult Geeks* site, but there were two others. They looked just as cheesy as the first, with an old-school forum design that looked like it had come directly out of a nineties' web design class. I read the other websites as Cam slowly scrolled down.

Each looked as hokey as I expected, especially after having seen *real* supernatural things. Dorian shook his head as Cam clicked on a forum post about vampires. The first image that it brought up in the thread was a badly photoshopped image. It was clearly supposed to be a "real" photo taken at VAMPS camp, where most of our vampire allies who remained in the Mortal Plane were located.

A vampire, in grainy pixels, bit the neck of an equally pixelated figure, presumably a human. It was all behind the fence that surrounded the camp in Scotland. Underneath, the poster claimed that this was a real photo captured from outside the premises.

"As if my mom would ever let anyone get that close," Cam said with a disbelieving scoff. "You can see where they edited in fangs on this guy. It's way too in-focus on the grain and far too white."

Bryce shrugged. "People will do anything for drama."

Cam went back to the main forums, and we looked through them. Our suspects, the man with the burn and the woman with the bad dye job, had supposedly met all their victims there.

"The new celebrities of Scotland?" Dorian asked, reading another post. To his visible horror, when Cam clicked the link, a picture of Dorian with hearts drawn around it popped up. I rubbed my temples in disbelief. I knew there was an audience for this thing, but why did my husband have to be at the center of it?

We had been so busy with our... Well, saving the entire world and keeping it saved, we'd neglected to check in with what was going on in social media, for the most part. But I was both annoyed at the ridiculousness of it and a little jealous about others going goo-goo over my hot vampire husband.

I side-eyed him warily, wondering what he thought, and he shrugged. I rolled my eyes, earning a saucy wink while he slid his hand over my back in response. Of course, I had nothing to worry about. I supposed newlyweds had sensitivities and trouble whether the couple was human, vampire, or both.

We moved on to read a few conspiracy theories involving gamma radiation and twins born with strange abnormalities, which Cam marked to peruse later. We knew Jessica had exhibited some kind of power. The meld had done something to the world. It might be worth looking into possible effects on recent births near the Leftovers.

There were also several stories about monster attacks, some of which made for grim reading. For us, monster attacks were our job, but we often missed the trauma and grief that came afterwards. It was easy to get caught up in the action and excitement of my job, but this served as a sobering reminder of my true purpose. I wanted to protect people from this.

My stomach roiled with guilt at our recent failure. We hadn't saved the people we'd set out for on the last mission, and now it was stagnant. I had no clue where my parents or the other missing people and Bureau members might be.

I had no plans of failing this new mission.

Finn scampered down the main section of the RV, Chandry in hot pursuit. The little guy had stolen her towel, possibly to make a nest with.

"We're going to need a full pot of coffee tonight," Bryce muttered as we continued our search of the websites. Three more laptops had come out, but I stuck to Cam's. We read at virtually the same pace.

My eyes were dancing across the third screen as Cam scrolled down, when something about "powers" caught my attention.

"Cam, can you go back?" I asked, pointing to the screen. "This one."

"Oh, good catch," he said, bringing the forum up full-screen. The post in question was entitled *Developing Superpowers?*

Dorian drummed his fingers on the table and raised an interested brow. He was content to listen to our findings since vampires weren't great with technology—besides maybe Sike. "Well, it could be interesting. What do you think it is? Abilities to talk to redbills, super strength, invisibility?"

I shrugged as Cam navigated to the full thread. "It's anyone's guess. It didn't seem like Jessica really had a *super*power, though. It was more like she had heightened senses."

Bryce grunted in agreement as we looked over the post. It was mainly discussing how forum members had noticed new powers after the appearance of the Leftovers.

Sike joined us. "TruthHolder88," he read, referring to the original poster. "That seems a bit grandiose, don't you think?"

Definitely.

I read aloud to my team, hoping it might give us some idea of what kind of people were on these forums. "'I was scared and shocked when things began happening to me. I felt like I couldn't turn to anyone. Luckily, I discovered some shocking truths about the strange phenomena associated with this area. The government doesn't want you to know the truth, but I do. You might be scared, but I can promise you what you've been looking for. I will give you the truth.'" An icy sensation darted down my back, because the tone sounded all too familiar. It was even more sinister since I knew what was really going on, despite the promise of "help" embedded in the post.

Bryce put my thoughts into words. "Sounds like a criminal ring preying on impressionable youths if I've ever heard one. They're promising the truth, but not offering anything publicly. Who in their ruddy mind would be taken in by this stuff?"

"Teenagers," Sike supplied and glanced at me. "That's who they're going after."

Cam sniffed as he read another user's reply to the original post. "'You have no idea how happy you've made me. I've suffered. Nobody believes anything I say. My parents told me that I'm imagining things. They want me to take anti-depressants. I'm not depressed, I've changed.'" He frowned worriedly. "Sounds like a teenager who read too many young adult novels promising a dazzling destiny. From the look of these posts, most of the kids seem to be having headaches or hearing voices out of thin air. That's really strange."

I leaned back and ran a hand through my hair, feeling frustrated. These suspects were preying on young people who wanted answers because they thought they were changed by the Leftovers. *Are they truly changing, though?* The promise of the truth reminded me of the way Jessica had been desperate for the same kind of information.

"*I haz powers* in big bold text alongside a cat image," Dorian said, reading a graphic. "I don't get it. What's this got to do with a cat? What is *haz*?"

"You won't get it. It's the internet," I told him bluntly. "Obviously, this is a treasure trove of victims for our TruthHolder88. All they have to do is post vague promises, like those hooded figures from the Pocket Space. Of course, they're telling people to private message them because the public forum isn't secure enough."

"It does sound like those cloaked guys," Bryce mumbled.

Everything Dan had told us about Jessica's changes was suddenly of interest. "Dan said Jessica was really secretive when she started experiencing her changes. He said that she hid things." I paused. Jessica had loved Dan, but she'd wanted answers even more than she had wanted to be with him.

Even after we'd rescued him in the Pocket Space, she'd stayed behind with those cloaked creeps to get her answers. She was *that* desperate.

"Something was happening to her," I went on, "even if it was initially only Jessica who believed it. There was definitely something to her claims, I just didn't completely understand it."

Cam saved the entire thread for further examination and added, "Jessica was pretty young, too, but her drive was scary intense."

"If only she'd used it for good instead of getting involved with those guys," I muttered. Jessica's attitude had left a bad taste in my mouth, but part of me wished I had tried harder to dig beneath what I'd assumed was a shallow exterior. "Still, we did fail her. She wanted help and couldn't get it from us."

Bryce looked thoughtfully at the website. "I'm not sure anyone could really give her what she wanted. Look at these commenters. They're desperate for answers, and they don't know who to turn to. I remember being young and a lot stupider than this."

I'd never had many opportunities to be stupid as a kid. My parents were fairly strict, and I'd followed the rules even in the darkest depths of my teenage angst. I felt out of my comfort zone since I couldn't relate, and I didn't like feeling so out of control and with no answers. That just wasn't me.

I sighed and looked over the sites as Cam scrolled through them. Any information we could pluck from these pages could turn out to be useful, but what were we looking for? What kind of truth were these guys selling?

"It comes down to whether they do have information or they don't," Dorian mused. "Seems like these criminals just happened to see a vulnerable group online and used the group's weakness to their advantage for their criminal activities."

I hated that we knew these teens were gone, and yet had no idea what had pushed them to such desperate lengths to agree to meet complete strangers.

To be fair, I reminded myself, *I also grew up in a Bureau family with safety talks on the daily.*

Torres suspected revenants were involved, but that made no sense. We had taken out the mind-controlled vampires, and they no longer had handlers to be controlled by. This case sounded more and more confusing as we delved deeper into the situation.

I reviewed the post again with Cam. There were the mentions of headaches and strange senses, although many of them seemed purposefully vague. Someone said they could move water, but I highly doubted that... right? I expected to see a video for proof, but the poster stopped commenting after someone responded to him or her.

Cam was right about it potentially being hysteria among teens, but it could be an actual widespread phenomenon. We had to consider all possibilities, including that at least *some* of the claims were legitimate.

Bryce met my gaze with his wise, blue eyes. "We'll probably have to interview witnesses again, depending on what we find in the Leftovers."

I agreed whole-heartedly. The police had been out of their depth and so, it seemed, had The Bureau branch down here. We needed to attack this from all angles, like Dorian suggested, but we wouldn't know anything for sure until we actually saw what was going on.

Sike spoke up, a smile in his voice. "Lyra's got her motivated face on."

I paused in my reading, surprised to find my brows knitted tightly and my face inches from the screen. I guessed I was feeling the fire of the mission.

"I want to find those kids and bring them home," I said, feeling the words light the determination inside me. "As soon as we can get going tomorrow, I want to be out in those Leftovers." Dorian swatted a mosquito on his arm, killing it. "Preferably with industrial-strength bug spray."

After the sun set for the day, we humans settled down with a few takeout pizzas and the RV fully stocked with everything we needed. There were quite a few places to sleep in the big motor home. Dorian and I thankfully got the master bed in the back bedroom. Bryce and Cam took the foldout sofa. If it was too stuffy, Cam volunteered to just pitch a sleeping bag in the hallway.

There was a loft above the driver's seat that could fit two people. Chandry smacked Sike's arm.

"Want to tell me stories about weird human stuff to get me up to speed?" she asked. Either she didn't realize she was flirting, or she didn't care that we'd heard. Sike stumbled over his *yes*.

I bit back a chuckle, but nobody said anything. It might be interesting to see where that would go, but part of me worried that Sike would get hurt again, like he had with Louise. I pushed the worry away as I followed Dorian to the back of the motorhome. Sike was an adult and could make his own decisions.

Even though it was only nine, I was wiped after our day of travel. I pulled off my fatigues to change into pajamas, since Cam and Bryce were taking the first showers. Dorian smiled as I rolled into bed, and he pulled me close to him. He still had his Callanish uniform pants on instead of the sweatpants I'd convinced him to start sleeping in.

"Everything okay?" he asked gently. I shrugged and snuggled into him, planting a kiss on his cheek.

Alicia's face flashed in my mind.

"I'm thinking about the kids," I admitted. He gave me an understanding look and tucked my head beneath his chin. "I'm worried for them."

More so, I was determined to save them.

"Let's rest up," Dorian whispered. "We'll be more useful if we're well-rested."

I knew he was right. In his arms, I felt safe and warm. Outside, the occasional car headlights passed, casting light into the room.

Was Alicia able to sleep where she was? Cold fear gripped my heart. Was she even alive?

I shut my eyes. I would feel better tomorrow with a fresh perspective on the data.

Somewhere nearby, the Leftovers lurked with the potential promise of answers.

4
Roxy

Okay, I'm thinking of a playing card. Can you tell what kind?

"What's a playing card, again?" Kane asked, his voice a bit strained. "Hold on, I'm walking away from the city. It's easier if I stare off into space elsewhere; the medics won't think I'm having a freak out."

I leaned against my couch cushions and inhaled my early noodle dinner while I waited. *Okay, the playing card bit wasn't fair. I'm imagining an apple. You've seen those before.* Vampires were surprisingly good with human stuff, but they had their blind spots.

To test our communication, I had hoped to picture an image in my mind for him to see, but words seemed like the only way we could communicate. Minutes ticked by. *Did I lose you?*

No answer. I flicked on the TV, and an infomercial for a vegetable-chopping contraption popped up on screen. A woman with bright white teeth smiled at me as she pointed down to a stack of freshly chopped onions. How was she not crying, and why was this on? I thought I'd left it on the mixed martial arts channel, which didn't usually show cooking commercials.

"I'm here," Kane said after a moment. I eased back into the couch.

Good. What's up?

"Well, I've made it to the outskirts of Aclathe and—"

Agathe. Ac—what now?

Kane sighed wearily. "The grass wildlings won the contest for naming the new Coalition city. They say Aclathe means something close to 'new beginnings' in their language. It's supposed to represent the concept of eternal springtime or something. I don't know, it's all too flowery for me. I mean, Vanim was a proper name." It was the name of the ruined vampire city, a destruction from their old enemies which decimated the vampire populations in the Immortal Plane.

I smiled to myself. *You sound awfully tuned-in for someone who's spent most of his time in the healing tent.*

"You try relaxing with a bunch of medics watching you like you're about to fall apart any second. I can't help but hear everything going on," he shot back. I nodded, even though he couldn't see it. It was fair, although at least he didn't have Hindley. My supervisor had the perceptive abilities of a hawk and a bloodhound, and the iron will of a true commander. I hoped my meeting with her in the late afternoon would go well.

Where are you outside the city? How is the construction going?

"It looks good," Kane admitted gruffly, as if it pained him to do so. "I'm in a secluded area. There's a series of natural pools that the wildlings expanded on the outskirts. This one never has people around it. Apparently, if you dig deep, the wildlings can draw up water from way underground. It's interesting... kind of neon-blue looking. Never thought there would be water like this around here. It looks too pretty for the Immortal Plane."

I tried to picture it in my mind, but all my thoughts could focus on was him. I cleared my throat. *Are you near the water?*

"Getting up in a tree overlooking it, actually," he said. "I like to come here for some privacy, which can be hard to find when the whole city is in motion. The makers don't hang around much in this area—they're working on the other side of the city. The wildlings made quick work of the landscape. The fall of the Immortal Council and their city really motivated them. They've been at it for months."

I fondly recalled Lyra's beautiful wedding, which Kane hadn't been able to attend since he was missing at the time. The wildlings had done a beautiful job of cultivating the plants around the area. I had no doubt that whatever Kane was looking at was just as wondrous.

I bet it's pretty. Are you ready to chat now? I looked forward to talking with

Kane. I could just imagine him, settled into his spot on the tree. His voice soothed me in the way few things could. The twins had definitely noticed me tuning out more in the evenings if we were on duty for something. I was always rushing back to my apartment when things wrapped up for the day. I wondered if the medics had noticed Kane doing the same. They were probably frustrated about having to look after such a stubborn, contrary vampire all the time.

They're taking care of you, right? And you'd better not be at the highest branch or something.

"I'm not a weakling," Kane said with a snort. "And I'm safe, thank you very much. Looking at the souls drifting through the sky, actually. It's good to see them going the right way," he mused, sounding far off in thought.

"Anyway, whose side are you on? The healers are more annoying than helpful." His pride would be the death of him, but I heard the note of humor in his voice. He was just a tough talker.

And now, we were back in our delicate dance of not-really-flirting and friendship. Kane had made zero mention of that moment in the Pocket Space after Colin and I rescued him.

Ready?

"Born ready," Kane replied.

Okay, I'm going to focus on the sound of this noisy TV commercial. Let me know if you get anything. I wanted to test how sensitive our connection could be. He could overhear my thoughts, but what about my perception of my current reality?

I focused hard on the commercial, which now switched to advertising a giant sprinkler system. The voice was loud and annoying but I turned up the volume. My thoughts, which I didn't direct necessarily toward Kane, flooded with images of sprinklers. I concentrated on the water splashing across the screen onto lush green grass outside a suburban home.

"Nothing," Kane said.

Not even the bit about it saving water?

He chuckled. "I have no idea what you're talking about. Are you watching something about those human shower cubes?"

Stalls, I corrected him. *It seems like we can't really talk to each other unless we're focused on directly saying something. Do you want to try on your end?* I turned off the TV.

"Let me know if you hear the distinct shrill cry of an angry redbill in the distance. I suspect one of the makers accidentally got too close to a nest on the outskirts of the forest across the city. I hope a wildling or vampire arrives in time."

I chewed my bottom lip anxiously as I listened. Nothing. *I can't hear a thing. Can you try to focus on the sound again?*

"I can hear in the distance that the bird is calming down. Maybe try some more indirect thoughts," Kane suggested. Thoughts could be dangerous right now... thoughts that he wasn't meant to hear, that is.

A lump of tension settled in my throat, and I looked toward the TV, searching for ideas that wouldn't be about Kane's handsome face or my complicated feelings. In the background of my frantic thoughts, I registered some noise from the low volume TV... a fight between Brian Ortega and Yari Rodriguez. Yari was getting his ass handed to him.

I landed on a picture of the twins at their cadet graduation. It was hung above my TV in a crooked frame. They both looked ecstatic. Jordan had a baby beard on his face, which he'd been so proud of at the time. I'd blinked, and they'd suddenly become adults right before my eyes.

I'm proud of them. It wasn't a thought I truly meant for Kane to hear. It just came up.

"Who?"

The twins. I guess our connection wasn't perfect yet. Maybe it would grow stronger as we worked on it. *Should we try to "disconnect" from one another? We can see if we can make sure to block out things that we don't want to share.* We had already been in that murky territory before.

"Why not?" he suggested. I twirled my hair nervously and then resented myself for such a silly move, even though he couldn't see me. "Okay, I'll call out to you in a minute after purposefully cutting you out. I'll be shouting my thoughts to the sky while I'm trying to shut you out. Try to break in, I guess."

I'll count. I stared at my watch to count down the seconds. It was an onboarding gift from when I'd come back to The Bureau as a captain, waterproof with fancy detailing and clocks set to three different time zones. I tried to focus on Kane and call for him. A minute passed with flying thoughts.

"This whole new city stinks of idealistic dreams. I'm not really sure

I believe in them, even if it's a beautiful sight," Kane muttered. Was he talking to himself or me? That sounded like a personal reflection.

I pulled myself up from the couch and stretched. *Kane?* There was no answer. I walked back and forth in my small living room and called out his name after another minute.

"I just feel like there's always going to be an enemy lurking around the corner," Kane continued with an aggravated sigh. "I wish all the bad guys would just show up at once so I could pound their faces into the dirt."

Now, there was Kane.

I can hear you. Listen to me!

"Ah, so you're there," he finally said. "You could hear me?"

Disappointment twisted my heart in my chest. *Yes, but you couldn't hear me.*

I grabbed all of my stuff from dinner and took it to the kitchen, disposing of the trash and rinsing off the dishes. I didn't have the time or patience for massive chores, so I cleaned up after every meal instead.

"I guess it is like a phone connection, like you said," Kane muttered. "I feel like it only started working when I let my thoughts focus on you again. When I was reflecting to myself, it was harder to notice you calling. I felt like... an itch on the back of my neck, but nothing much."

Had he been upset that he couldn't stop his thoughts? I stared out the window at the evening skyline outside my apartment. I had also worried, when our connection finally came through. The last time I'd needed to hear from Kane, I'd called out to him in desperation, too.

I wonder if our emotions help our connection. Maybe we could try exploring feelings.

"You've officially lost it, *and* me." Kane was probably rolling his eyes. I pushed on.

I know it sounds ridiculous, but let's try. We were connected when I was searching for you. It made sense when I thought about it, so he could at least help me test my theory. *What do you feel when we make contact?* The question flew out before I realized how it sounded. For a moment, I thought our connection dropped again until Kane came back.

"I feel... relieved." He trailed off. "Well, it's nice to talk to someone who isn't a worried medic."

Relief is interesting. I paused. I was disappointed that he hadn't said more. I wanted to hear things from his perspective, but sometimes that felt like it was still wedged behind a brick wall. *I feel relieved, too. I'm glad you're doing well. Sometimes, I get worried that you won't be there when I call out at night. I know this connection doesn't always work, but it's nice to be able to talk to you like this while I'm in the Mortal Plane.*

"It'd be nice if we could make it work consistently," Kane agreed. His rugged voice made me miss him terribly. Could he feel that longing? "I was relieved when you rescued me, for sure. It makes me think... You said you were focused on me, and the Ghost was. Maybe, if we replicate the feeling of trying to rescue one another..."

I wondered if we could, given that I knew he was safe. The Ghost, the monster who was able to travel between the planes to the Pocket Space, only found Kane after I focused on him *and* worried about him during that mission. "Can you try to worry for me?"

I nearly choked on my spit. Of course, I could if I thought about all the things that could happen to him. *Can you be worried for me at a moment's notice?*

Another pause. "I'm never exactly *worried* about you. I know you can handle yourself. It's more like... an itch that I feel until I've talked to you." His honesty bowled me over, and I leaned my forehead against the window. I wanted him to tell me more about that feeling, but I was afraid to ask. It might disrupt... whatever this was.

Then I'll tell you how I feel when you call for me. I'm not sure if I can fake worry right now. I drew circles on the glass, gathering my courage. A furnace-like heat of excitement and happiness spread through me. *There's a warmth in my chest when we talk, like finally getting to speak to a friend after a long time, even if it's only been a day.* I never knew where the boundaries stood. Sometimes, it felt like there was a vast ocean between us, while other days were more like a teasing session back and forth without pause.

"That's good to know." His charged voice made my skin jump.

Can you feel the heat? I'm sure even someone like you feels it, too, when they think about friends... I was teasing.

Kane hesitated. "I can't tell, to be honest. It's good to know that you want to hear my voice, obviously. What can I say? I'm a glutton for compliments."

As if we needed your head to grow any bigger. I sighed, wishing he was here to grapple with. We always communicated better with light-hearted punches. It was easier to express affection—this friendship and bond—through our rough personalities with playful fighting. *I guess we'll keep finding ways to deepen our connection.*

A light, but warm spark lit in my chest. Was it me or Kane?

I couldn't tell if we could feel one another's emotions, or if we were limited to thoughts. Perhaps that was too much for right now. I wasn't sure I could handle it... or that Kane could.

"Yes, well, I'm sure we'll come up with something." Kane sounded flustered. I shook my head in disbelief as he stumbled to his next point, completely changing the subject. "I mean, I'm sure we'll make progress on controlling our connection. Maybe that's enough for today. The medics will kill me if I look tired."

Sure, sure. Want to tell me about the glorious city of... Aclanthe, was it? I was curious about the new city. I hadn't been to the Immortal Plane since Lyra's wedding, but I'd bet the progress was considerable on the new city.

"It's sprawling. The makers are strict with their schedule. I never expected such a unified system between all these creatures after living in banished secrecy on the fringe of society with the rest of the vampires. Reshi and Charrek figured out a fool-proof organization to have this city completely done in a few years of your human time," Kane explained.

I listened fondly to his words, painting a picture in my head as best as I could. "They've got most of one side of the city's framework almost finished. The wildlings, makers, and even ex-rulers who have proven trustworthy are working well with the vampires. No complaints there. It's nice." Charrek was another maker who was highly gifted in technology, and old friends with Reshi before they joined our cause.

Nice, huh? Sounds like a freaking paradise compared to the set-up at Itzarriol. A regular utopia for anyone in that terrible caste contract system.

Kane cackled. "Not a utopia with Reshi's strict nature. She's got a bell she likes to wake the city with at the beginning of the day, but everybody is reasonably happy. The combined technologies are moving things along really fast. These buildings are nothing like I was used to in Vanim as a kid. It's impressive to see what they're doing."

When I first started hearing Kane's voice, it had been by accident. He'd reflected about his tough childhood and his time in Vanim without realizing I was accidentally intruding on those personal thoughts. My heart hurt just hearing about it, but I couldn't imagine what he felt when he reflected on it.

For him, this was just one casual line in our conversation, but I remembered every second of the stories I heard by accident from him about his childhood. Now, he was easily talking about the new city even if he had worries about enemies around the corner.

You seem in good spirits.

"I am. I actually saw Kreya and Rhome today with the kids."

I grinned. Detra and Carwin were Kreya and Rhome's two children. I loved those kids and had spent a lot of time with them, especially after their rough time as hostages of the now-fallen Immortal Council. Kreya had been turned into a revenant vampire, but she was healing slowly but surely. We weren't sure if she would ever go back to being fully herself again, and her relationship with her husband was still rocky, the last I'd heard.

Is she talking more?

"A bit," Kane said. "The kids are still partial to Rhome, naturally. They get a bit nervous around Kreya since she's not always... present. Kono comes around to play with them a lot. I'm not really sure what the deal is with Kreya and Rhome, to be honest. If I were him, I might push Kreya more in her healing with the medic who specializes in some kind of spiritual magic. I don't understand it; the old woman helps her emotions or something, but Kreya only goes once a week."

I hummed in thought. *Well, once a week is strenuous enough after having your mind pummeled into submission by power-hungry rulers.*

"Fair." I heard a dry smile in his voice. "Your humor is sorely missed here. The kids say they miss Uncle Dorian and Aunt Lyra, and especially you."

I cheered inwardly. *Heck yea, they do. They know who the coolest adult is.*

"In your dreams," Kane shot back. "I chatted with Oz a bit about the scouting that's been going on, but Kono nearly dragged him away from me by the collar. I guess nobody is allowed to talk to me about interesting missions, since they're scared that I'll go off and try to work on them. The medics want me to wait around for at least two more weeks." His voice was laced with a sharp edge of impatience, which I understood completely. For people like us, waiting around feeling useless was worse than the injury itself.

Are you worried about anything in particular? After the fall of Itzarriol, I hoped the Coalition would find some peace. The Pocket Space wasn't a problem for them yet, but Kane had experienced it like nobody else.

"I'm worried about the kids I left behind," Kane said slowly. He had joined a group of young survivors in the Pocket Space, until the cloaked weirdos and starvation had forced him to abandon the kids. He exhaled, long and slow, and I heard every bit of the sadness in it. Our connection felt electric in this moment. "I have no idea how to get back there."

He wasn't thinking about going back already, was he? I gritted my teeth. *Kane, you're not healed yet.*

"I mean when I'm at full strength. I'll try to find a way back there." Kane stifled a yawn, and suddenly, his voice faded as I heard the last bits of his voice saying, "Roxy, you know, I've been—"

He cut out like a bad radio connection. I sighed. *Are you there? Hello?*

I stared at my reflection in the glass of the window. It was late. Our connection tended to die after a certain point when we became too tired to maintain it. I rubbed my hand against my tired face, realizing how much energy it took to focus on these chats with Kane.

He hadn't "hung up" on me, that was for sure. Kane liked these chats as much as I did, even if he inevitably turned awkward. *Not that I'm much better.* I listened, but nothing came, even after several minutes. That was unusual; he usually reached out after we disconnected to say goodbye.

He could've passed out again. I held my breath as that anxious thought made me heavy all over. Even if he had lost consciousness, he was on the outskirts of the Coalition city, so he should be in good hands. Even if he'd passed out near the pools, someone would find him. Surely, there were patrols to protect the city.

He was probably fine, and I'd hear from him in the morning. Like we thought, we had to work on our connection like any other skill.

I took a deep breath and wiped a speck of dust off an all-women's pro-wrestling team poster hanging by my window. I really should have retired the *Lady Brawlers* posters by now. They weren't quite 'me' anymore, but I left them up because I didn't have anything to replace them with.

Kane's face flitted through my mind once more. I firmly set it aside. I needed to get ready for my meeting with Hindley, and I couldn't be preoccupied with irrational worries about Kane. She would smell distraction coming off me a mile away, and he was like a treacherously addictive thought that I couldn't ignore.

Our relationship was something different—something changed—but I wasn't sure exactly how to label it.

Maybe I didn't need to.

5

Lyra

I had slept fitfully last night, with Alicia's face running through my mind. Now, I wondered what surprises awaited us in these swamps. Apparently, the landscape was different than what we'd experienced in Utah.

I can tell that from the humidity here alone. There was talk of "burning" water, which I was especially keen to learn more about.

We made our way to the shabby office building to find Torres in the same conference room as yesterday. The blinking overhead light had been fixed. Four fresh faces sat on one side of the massive table, while two grizzled men shot me skeptical looks from the other.

I met their gazes easily, despite the persistent chilly disposition leftover from yesterday. It was just like Torres. The two men were probably in their fifties, older than Torres himself, and their attention immediately went to Dorian behind me after noticing him.

We sat down at the other end of the table. The younger employees were a mix of young women and men, and I could tell they were new because they hardly hid their shock when the vampires walked in, regardless that the vampires had their makeup on.

It didn't help that the vampires had their licenses pinned to their collars. It was a formality, a requirement from The Bureau.

Two of the younger employees had computers in front of them—much sleeker models than the clunky thing Torres had used for his presentation.

The older employees had the good grace to direct their attention to Torres as he opened the meeting. Were they the only senior members in this branch assigned to this mission? This place had had massive budget cuts from what Torres implied, so I imagined their turnover must be high, hence the youth of the majority of members on such an important case.

Bryce snuck a curious glance at me. Perhaps he was trying to piece it together as well. Bureau investigations usually had a lot more seniority. The newer employees couldn't keep their eyes off the vampires.

Awkward, but at least they're not glaring?

"I hope you had a pleasant stay in the camper last night," Torres said. One of the older guys—burly with a classic crew cut—let out a snort. I ignored that. To be fair, the RV *was* laughable.

"I've prepared some photos of the Leftovers for you so that you can see what you'll be working with. As I understand it, the Utah Leftovers have much less water contamination. I've also heard that the trees are particularly spooky up north. I'm sorry to say that I think this area will be worse."

I sat up straighter in my seat as he clicked to the next slide. Three images of swamps with glowing green water appeared on screen. They looked unreal, like doctored photos. In some spots, the water was purple and mottled brown, and the Spanish moss, rotten and red, had long, bizarre thorns growing from the tendrils.

Creepy. It looked like a blast of nightmare-inducing energy had shocked the southern area.

As the next slide appeared, labeled with the appropriate geographical location, Torres explained, "We call the region at the southern tip of Florida the Everglades, but there are some distinct nature reserves within this area. These photos represent the northwest zone, the Big Cypress region, but the water extends into the Everglades National Park farther south. The effects of the Leftovers have been devastating for locals and animals, and have caused a major hit to tourism."

I had seen pictures of this area before, but the amount of water truly astounded me. The significantly smaller proportion of land made me nervous, the veins of water creating a web that I had little experience with.

"The water is reported to be toxic to humans," Torres continued. "It can cause burns and unexpected rashes if it touches unprotected skin, and the damage gets progressively worse with prolonged exposure. A few minutes won't kill you, but you definitely don't want to stand in it unprotected."

Toxic water awaited us in these Leftovers. We had been spoiled with our murderous trees and dry land in Utah.

The crew-cut man held out his hand and tapped a pink burn next to his watch. "I got that when I didn't notice my sleeve slipping down. I couldn't find fresh water for a few minutes, unfortunately. We weren't able to venture deep into this place, except in protected vehicles, but such equipment is hard to come by for our branch. We've been working with Fish and Wildlife to map the landscape, but nobody wants to set foot in that water."

Bryce grunted. "Can't say I blame them."

"Additionally, firearms don't always work in the Leftovers. They're prone to corrosion with the humid air, although we have a few special ones to take," Torres explained.

In our last foray in the Leftovers in Utah, all of Callanish had an obstacle. For the vampires, it was their senses being off in the Leftovers while our human equipment didn't always function properly.

Bryce and I would have to go over our supplies to ensure everything we brought would suffice for this toxic environment. We had one more person on this trip than last time. It was probably best to skimp on the hotels and utilize our RV in case we needed to buy extra supplies. We wouldn't risk any burns.

"As Patrick said, we've mapped what we could." Torres gestured to his next slide indicating the same map he'd displayed yesterday. In this map, though, there were a few sections shaded in with red. "The red zones represent the places you *really* want to avoid. These watery eastern areas appear more toxic than others. We managed to do a few flyovers in a chopper with scanners. For some reason, these parts read as the most dangerous, or at least they had the most signatures. Additionally, there are some spots where the water appears to have greatly deepened. Our swamps usually average between four and five feet of water, but some places are now showing up as deep as twenty feet. I have no idea how it happened, since those depths just simply shouldn't be there."

I leaned my chin against my hand. If the waters were toxic and virtually everywhere, how was our criminal duo merrily skipping through this area? Perhaps they already had experience smuggling in the wetlands or were working with someone who knew the region.

"Do you have any idea how the criminals are navigating these dangers?" I asked.

Torres frowned, his brow knitting together with a somber air. "Unfortunately, we believe that the criminals are receiving supernatural help to avoid the toxic water and violent creatures in the environment. We strongly suspect that they've established a hideout in the Leftovers away from the cops, since it's virtually impenetrable thanks to the hostile conditions."

Dorian gave a slight frown of skepticism. Perhaps he was in tune with me and thinking about Torres's claim that the revenants were behind this.

"What makes you suspect revenants?" Bryce asked. Patrick, the crew-cut man, stared at Bryce in surprise.

"You see those energy signatures?" Patrick said, nodding to the ones they believed to be revenant vampires, no doubt. "We only find them an hour's hike into the swamp, maybe more. A normal human without help would be dead after more than half an hour in this area."

Torres nodded enthusiastically. "Absolutely. There's a section with some more solid ground in the midst of this, perhaps on one of the small islands. It seems like the ideal place to set up a hideout, but they would definitely need help to reach it."

If he thought they'd had help, I was inclined to believe him, but I doubted that it was coming from revenant vampires.

Torres studied my face for a beat and must've seen the resistance under my calm expression because his eyebrow twitched upward with a frustrated tick that burst through his composed façade. I didn't want to start any arguments that we didn't need. I held my tongue, hoping he would interpret my silence as a sign I was simply mulling over the evidence.

"I'm aware that your team is unique," Torres said, dancing carefully with his words. "But here, we remember the vampires' more violent history. Who else could it be? After seeing and hearing about the revenants, I'm convinced they are the ones responsible for aiding these criminals."

I shifted in my seat and tried not to loudly sigh at the clear prejudice going on here. I'd held the same beliefs once myself.

"They're intelligent enough to do it, right?" Torres said. "I saw them in the media and The Bureau's surveillance. They were organized. We believe that such a strong signature has to be coming from a creature like that. Perhaps they're using their mind-control powers to order regular people to kidnap children, especially given what they managed to do to average citizens during the crime spree across the world."

His words were confident, but they caused an instant spark of frustration inside me that I had to force down.

It wasn't exactly mind-control from the vampires but their immortal handlers. Unfortunately, that was hard to explain to this small team who didn't seem to be in the loop—nor did they seem to care, in all honesty.

I gestured to our vampire allies. "We have strong reason to doubt the presence of revenants. The revenants were being controlled by other beings in the Immortal Plane who no longer exist."

"How can you be so sure?" Torres asked, prodding gently. "Sounds like a revenant vampire might just be someone who gets a little overwhelmed."

"Basically, they were controlled by a chip in their head. Normal vampires will never feed on the innocent. There's nothing there for them. For vampires, feeding is entirely for the basis of nutrition, like our food. They can actually sense the evil within a human. They cleanse a soul. I know it sounds wild, but The Bureau itself has slowly come to terms with this. I realize that things are a bit tense right now, but the vampires you saw in those broadcasts were being controlled, and they don't exist anymore."

Torres pressed his lips together hesitantly. "The Board told us everything in one measly document that they circulated internally. How can you be sure? Do you have proof that they don't exist? We've been through this before with the vampires. Maybe they're allies now, but we once thought they were all gone and..." He gestured to the vampires in our group, making them shift uncomfortably.

This was getting out of hand. I could let a differing opinion go, but this one could affect the entire mission.

Pain squeezed me for a beat when I thought of poor Kreya, united with her kids but not quite the same. At the same time, I was frustrated. I just wanted to be believed for once without having to do a song and dance to convince people about our experiences.

To be fair, Torres wasn't a fool, but he was used to older vampire propaganda within The Bureau. He was right to bring up the revenants as probable potential suspects, but he needed to know that it was impossible. Which I got the feeling he *would* know had he truly read Bureau briefings involving the revenants. His opinions had likely gotten in the way of doing more than scanning. He formed his own ideas.

It was an educated guess, I could give him that, but it simply didn't shake out when I thought about it seriously.

"Proof by witness testimonies," I said slowly, knowing that it might sound weak to Torres. "You'll find the current board will confirm those events. We have the surviving revenant vampires, without their control systems, back in the Immortal Plane."

Bryce jumped in to back me up. "Aye. The vampires are the only reason we were able to stop the world from ending. We certainly don't have pictures or videos from our time. The revenants needed a handler to operate them. The controllers only had their power of persuasion thanks to a magical device, and our team destroyed it."

Torres processed our words. His gaze flickered back and forth between Bryce and me. *He's still skeptical.* I couldn't blame the guy, with our wild stories about the Immortal Plane, but he needed to understand that revenant vampires were very unlikely to be the culprits here. Besides, we currently had evidence that pinpointed to some human involvement.

I wished we had a way to show Torres the extent of all the rulers and creatures in the Immortal Plane, but that might be too much information. Most humans didn't do well knowing that there was a powerful, malicious species of magical giants in an alternate plane of reality.

For the first time, Torres crossed his arms tight across his chest. He looked older and more serious with his rigid posture, and he clearly wasn't about to give up his argument.

"I'm not trying to offend you, but I find it hard to believe that the revenants are all that different from regular vampires." His tone was composed, but blunt. Patrick gave a satisfied smirk. "You have to understand that I've been hunting vampires since the old days, just like Patrick and Donald here. Our junior members don't know what it was like to live in fear of the vampire menace, but I do. I was a high-ranking soldier in terms of vampire hunting, which is why The Bureau put me in charge here. And then, suddenly, The Bureau decides that vampires are okay?"

I grinded my teeth together. How had this team skated under the radar when they were kicking up dirt at the very thing The Bureau was doing now? Yes, it was secretive, and yes they had less tech and money here, but they were in the loop all the same. It felt to me like he *wanted* to believe the revenants were involved, and I didn't like the way he was talking about everyday vampires. The ones sitting with us at this very moment.

Torres forged ahead. "I told the board that I was wary of your initial experiment, and there's been nothing but trouble since then. Yes, I've read the reports about the corruption of the original board. I recognized your uncle among them, Munroe, and I know that must've been hard. You had guts to go against him, but I remember my years of fighting vampires. I saw the bodies they left behind. I had to call home for soldiers lost in combat and listen to their grieving families."

The mention of my corrupt uncle, Alan, who'd tried to stop us from saving the world, made me sick to my stomach with frustration. There was so much Torres and his men didn't know. How could I possibly explain to them in a way that didn't make me seem like a soldier who had just gone off the deep end due to my romantic involvement with a vampire?

Before Dorian kidnapped me on that fateful day, I'd thought vampires were absolute monsters. Now, I was married to one and counted many vampires as some of my closest friends.

Bryce shifted in his seat with purpose. It was amazing how one could draw eyes with just a subtle movement. He was another member of the older Bureau ranks, albeit an ex-member, and therefore, he might have more pull with these people.

I'll let him jump in to hook the old dudes and then follow up. We were each other's backup, and it was our job to make sure Torres understood us.

"While I can understand your frustration, I invite you to keep an open mind and focus on the mission," Bryce said. "I was fighting among you with the vampires. I'm sorry to say that I used to hate vampires as much as the next Bureau soldier, and Munroe was the same. We learned and grew, though, when we were given new information and met some of our colleagues here. We may not agree on this, but I promise you that the vampires with us have come only to help."

I nodded. "We can focus on the mission, Torres. We're not here to try to brainwash you into anything. We just want to do this job, and our vampire allies are here to help." I hesitated, debating on whether or not to continue, then added, "I will remind you that you *knew* that we were bringing vampires on this mission. They're here risking their lives as much as we are. I hope you'll treat them with respect, out of consideration for that."

How awkward was it to do this in front of everyone? It was better for the junior members to see this, though, even if they looked partially terrified. One redhead with freckles looked like there was a permanent frown on his face as he stared at Torres and the other older members, waiting for their response.

This job came with confrontation, but that had never scared me. I was here to get things done. *But it'll be a cold day in hell before you insult my husband while he's sitting right next to me.*

Dorian never faltered in his gaze on Torres and the older soldiers. He was used to this kind of thinking, but I was glad that it looked like we were ending things civilly.

Sike and Chandry weren't as composed. Chandry cocked her head to the side with genuine curiosity, while Sike was chillier. He had his arms crossed over his chest and a dark expression on his face. He had worked so hard at VAMPS camp to garner support for vampires, and it must've been very difficult for him to see that he had to start all over here.

"I'm aware that vampires are helping you—" Torres started.

"They speak English," I reminded him, unable to keep the tiny bit of shortness in my tone under wraps. "They can communicate with several species, by the way."

Patrick cocked a curious eyebrow, but he said nothing. Torres folded his hands in front of him, his posture as stiff as ever.

"Do they want to tell me that they won't kill innocent people? What about the children that we're hoping to find?" Torres asked. The question visibly struck the vampires, landing like a slap in the face.

Sike sucked in an angry breath, and Chandry let out a stunned gasp.

"We don't," Chandry blurted. "And are you anyone to talk? I saw your little crime statistics posted on your weird board thing in the hall. It sure seemed like a lot of homicides were listed. Humans kill one another all the time."

"Why insult us when we're here to help?" Sike asked. He shook his head in disbelief. "You can't lump every single vampire together after such a limited experience. It's like if I judged you for eating, isn't it? We didn't ask to be made this way, and our numbers dwindled because of the old Bureau's corrupt scheme as opposed to the noble campaign that they paraded."

Dorian cleared his throat loudly, successfully garnering everyone's attention. He lifted his hands in a placating gesture. "As the leader of the biggest clan of vampires who came to the Mortal Plane to seek shelter and a new chance at life, I have no interest in changing your mind, Torres." He looked directly at the man without a drop of calm slipping from his face. His tone was perfectly stern.

I loved him more than anyone. If there was anyone who could change Torres's mind, it was Dorian.

"I could plead the case for vampires all day long, but this isn't the time for debate. We came here to do a job. There are teenagers missing out there." Dorian pointed to the map and added, "Alicia may still be alive. She's scared somewhere. We need to help her."

Torres's stony face faltered a fraction. "Yes, of course."

"We're here to work with you, but we need you to tolerate us," Dorian said flatly. "We need your support in keeping us out of the public eye. We didn't come here to change your minds about vampires—we came here to stop whatever is going on in the Leftovers."

Pride swelled inside me. *This is why I married this guy.*

He was right, we needed to keep it professional and not lose sight of what was important. Sike and Chandry simmered down, but I wanted to apologize to them later for what had happened. It was troubling for me to recall how I used to be as ignorant as Torres, but I hoped we could find a place of compromise to work from.

Patrick actually looked impressed by Dorian's words. That was a small start.

Torres sighed shortly. "Yes, I suppose you're right." We obviously hadn't swayed him, but I didn't care. He gave a tiny nod in the direction of the vampires, but then focused on Bryce and me. "Still, this is the *human* justice system. I won't stand by if you guys try to kill anybody. We're not doing this in any supernatural way, killing without trial or jury. We're doing it the human way."

The air was tense in the conference room as we agreed to an uncomfortable truce.

"We need to get going," I told Torres. "Dorian is right. The sooner we get out there, the sooner we can find Alicia and the others."

And the sooner we could get out of Florida.

6

Lyra

$\mathcal{M}$y impatience to get started was edging out the low-level tension I felt with Torres and his team. We headed out immediately once we ensured that our team had the proper suits for wading in toxic water. As Bryce drove the RV to the location near the Leftovers, muttering under his breath about driving and who else knew what, we all strapped on our special boots and wetsuits that The Bureau had provided us. I wanted gloves, but it would be impossible to use them with our delicate scanner equipment and our firearms if we needed them. *I guess we'll just have to be careful.*

Torres and his team led the way. Bryce followed behind them with the occasional grumble about other drivers. I didn't have a chance to talk to Dorian or the others as they suited up, but they were still markedly quiet, which made me worry that the talk with Torres had affected them more than I'd thought.

Sike and Cam were busy checking over the scanners. I had a feeling that the models we were bringing into the area would fare better than what Torres was working with, but we had to expect that the scanners would occasionally fail due to fluctuations. It had happened to us the last time we were in the Leftovers.

Bryce pulled into an abandoned gas station alongside The Bureau's tinted van. I scanned the surroundings, noting the beginnings of the marshy section that Torres had shown us on screen. The gas station was a stone's throw from the park entrance. An old souvenir keychain with a palm tree on it crunched under my foot as I took a step in the parking lot. Tree knobs and roots had pushed up against the pavement, disturbing it in many spots. The Leftovers were definitely close, from the looks of it.

"Cypress knees from the trees. That's what you call the roots coming up from cypress trees. The roots can come up really high," Cam said as he snapped a picture of the parking lot. He lowered the camera and pointed to the path leading to the park. "Their underground root system has spread quite a lot, from the looks of it."

"This used to be part of the tourist section," Torres explained. He was a little calmer out in the field, but when he paused, there was an awkward tension. "It's been closed off since it leads directly into the Leftovers. We'll have to travel by airboat from here."

Cam clapped his hands together. "Great. I've always wanted to try the traditional transportation of the wetlands." Clearly, he intended to make this a decent outing whether the Miami branch was in a good mood or not.

Torres led the way down the road, explaining that it wasn't safe to leave the cars any closer to the edges of the Leftovers. Already, I smelled a certain tangy odor that I couldn't place. Something like sour old lemons. I wrinkled my nose and stared down at my wetsuit. The suits were supposed to protect us from contact with the water. The sleek goggles we wore made us look like futuristic insects.

We'd also donned breathing masks to help filter the hostile atmosphere. They were black and sleek, covering our mouths and just over our noses. No one knew what was in the air but, given the humidity and the effects of the local water, it was likely to have undesirable properties.

Torres stopped at the official entrance to the park. A metal sign arced above the deteriorating sidewalk and boasted a welcome message, but the words had been worn away. Like our experience in Utah with objects corroding faster, but worse, the metal looked truly rusted.

One of the younger techs hopped over to check out our scanners so Cam and Sike could make sure everything was calibrated. Maps blipped on the scanners, and Torres gave us a sharp nod. We were ready to head in.

Walking into the park gave me a sense of unease. It was strange. I felt as if I were moving through diluted molasses. The air was syrupy and quickly took on a yellow tint, like toxic pollen was floating through the air. The mask and suit were too hot, but it was better than getting burns. As we walked, I glanced down the paths we passed. Originally, this place appeared to have been used as a recreational stop where families could picnic or use the restroom. Wooden tables had been reduced to piles of rotting wood. A massive dragonfly flitted past my face, reminding me more of a scene out of a prehistoric film than the Mortal Plane. *Is this truly my home world?*

Down the path, it looked like the route diverged. There were two trails, according to the maps Torres had, but the water lay in the short distance ahead of us. The water here was not as neon as in the photos we'd seen, but it was ugly, with a disturbing lemony color. Torres waved us along but held out a finger of caution as we moved. Twenty yards away, the body of a giant alligator sat to the left of us on the path. It was dead, with bones jutting out from decaying skin, but it was *massive.*

"There are a lot of mutated animals here, unfortunately," Torres explained, his voice sounding stiff and strained through his mask. It took me a moment to adjust to hearing him through the air filter. "We're going to see a lot of alligators. Normal ones usually leave humans alone, although people shouldn't leave small children or dogs out near the water. But the Leftovers completely changed the game. They're massive now. We took that one out with three soldiers on our last excursion. Their skin is even thicker after their mutation. Forget running zigzag from these guys. Shoot first, ask questions later."

Cam's eyes lit up behind his goggles. "That thing is huge, like a dinosaur."

"And they get aggressive without *any* provocation," Torres said grimly.

Finn was tucked safely away in Cam's backpack, and I hoped his smell wouldn't attract any of the hungry creatures... or our smell, for that matter.

"The mutated gators are extremely deadly," Torres continued. "Once you get into the boat, I advise you to be ready for an attack at all times. We have to be very vigilant now. The creatures that lived in and out of the water have all changed here." He gestured ahead toward a misshapen tree hanging over the path. What I mistook for Spanish moss was in fact the dried skin of something enormous. It was no alligator.

"Burmese python?" Cam guessed. Torres nodded. "Wow, I knew they were an invasive species. This place makes a remote, tropical jungle look like a children's playground."

"The pythons get huge," Patrick called over from beside Torres. "Their size is unreal, although we haven't tangled with one yet. We speculate that these creatures survived here because they're at home in the water and out. The land animals mostly deserted this place before becoming too mutated. Of course, that meant we had a few of our Florida panthers fleeing the area if they were quick enough to get out before being mutated. Luckily, Fish and Wildlife caught several of them and relocated them to safer territories. We're devastated over the loss of our local wildlife."

In Utah, the wildlife populations in the Leftovers hadn't been as large or diverse. We had mostly dealt with birds and creatures like Finn. I didn't count the Ghost, the monster who could travel to the Pocket Space, since I wasn't sure that creature even came from the Leftovers.

The mossy grass was slick underneath my feet as the sidewalk gave way to powerful tree roots and vegetation. An airboat waited for us ahead, oddly pristine among trees that were covered in red, weepy moss.

"How did you manage to keep it in such good shape?" I asked, genuinely curious.

"I brought it out on the trailer this morning with the assistants," Patrick said. "Torres will lead you guys in with one of our techs. We try not to leave the airboat out too much since we're afraid it'll get eaten or deteriorate in the water. The Bureau sent us some kind of special polish that seems to be helping with the accelerated rust issue."

I was glad that he'd noted that. He and one of the techs were likely going to stay behind in case of emergency, staying close to our vehicles, while keeping a lookout and being able to run for help if we needed it.

"Here's hoping the gators aren't hungry today," Bryce muttered, staring at the ground with a scowl. His foul attitude was on the brink of returning. Picking up on someone's moods was almost a sixth sense after working with someone for so long, especially when Bryce was not a scowler on the whole. Still, Bryce was good at his job, bad mood or not. *I'm sure it's not fun for him to have to remember his old days as one of these guys.* Torres hadn't so much as looked at any of the vampires.

We explored the airboat's surroundings. Chandry kept close to Sike, eyeing his scanner curiously. I walked with Dorian, stooping down to check out some nearby tracks in the muddy, sloped shore. Larger-than-normal frog tracks littered the ground. I grimaced at the thought of a toddler-sized frog jumping into the boat.

A faded decal on the hull told me that The Bureau had repurposed it from a tour company. A thick, shiny gloss coated the outside, presumably the polish that Patrick had mentioned.

My team boarded the airboat, adjusting to the strangeness of it. I'd never been on one before. Nervously, I watched the water slosh against the boat, jostled by our motion. *What could go wrong with giant gators and pythons to keep us company?*

It was a large airboat with enough seats to fit twice as many people—we had our team and Torres, so there was plenty of room. Dorian took a seat in one of the plastic chairs. Sike and Cam settled in the middle with their scanners between them. The tech who boarded with us was a petite young woman with bright brown eyes behind her goggles. She happily chatted with both Sike and Cam, although her body language, with her shoulders up a few inches, told me she was nervous.

Younger people are easier to deal with when it comes to vampires. I rested my hand on the pistol at my waist, watching the water warily. It was unnerving to think something might be lurking underneath the surface to grab us. There were insects here the size of apples lazily flying through the air.

Torres took off. The fan operated surprisingly quietly, pushing us through the water.

The tech caught me staring and explained, "We modified the fan, since noise can be a pull for the animals."

We moved through shallow channels of water at first, between small islands covered in bright green vegetation with an unnatural shimmer to the color. Some of the land masses were larger than others.

"These little islands have a strange energy," Bryce grumbled next to me.

"This whole place has a strange energy," Dorian said, and he flicked his face mask. "I hate these stupid things. I feel as delicate as—"

"Humans?" I asked, smirking from behind my own mask. Dorian shrugged, acknowledging the point. In the Leftovers, we were on a more even playing field, like we were in the Higher Plane. Vampires still had their superior powers of speed and strength, but the Leftovers often messed with their senses.

I glanced over the edge of the boat, watching the strange current fighting us. It was like the water was pushing and pulling us at the same time, but Torres gunned the boat engine against the flow. Murky colors lurked beneath our boat like a sinister watery mosaic. We passed from green into purple into splotches of red and then all over again. I prayed the blurry colors weren't baby alligators going to get their giant mothers.

"We're getting into the real Leftovers now," Torres warned us.

Cam took a picture of a large pelican up ahead. It had sharp teeth in its bill and regarded us with a wary eye, but did nothing. The birds in Utah had been one of our biggest problems, since they'd sought us out as food. The water rippled in front of us. Sometimes, a large tadpole-shaped creature would leap across our path and plop back down into the murk. Even the splashes here sounded strange, like the creatures were hitting thick mud instead of the liquid that I could see.

The water grew greener and darker. I would've preferred the neon color from the picture, so we could've seen more animal shapes as the water seemed to grow deeper. Now, we would just have to rely on our senses as best as we could.

"Do you feel anything?" I asked Dorian, and he shook his head. Cam confirmed that there was nothing on the scanner, either.

Spindly, reed-shaped plants snatched at our boat as we moved along. Torres pushed us through. The leaves seemed to shiver but didn't attempt to crowd us like the trees had near Black Rock. We passed a sculpture of a beheaded man. Something from the Immortal Plane? The figure had a humanoid bipedal stature, but everything else had been worn away by the Leftovers and time.

I unconsciously inched closer to Dorian. We moved quietly and steadily. Black slippery eels, as thick as my forearm, slithered past us. Chandry waved her hand at them, causing the human tech to giggle. Torres grunted in an annoyed fashion, returning us all back to our tension. After our argument back in the conference room, things continued to feel strained.

A large alligator sunned itself lazily on a nearby rock. I glanced at Torres, surprised to see one of that size since it was long, but not as massive as I would have expected.

"It's a baby," he explained.

Oh, geez. That's the baby?

"Something coming from behind us," Chandry piped up. "It's rather big."

We turned to see a dark shape following us beneath the water. It stayed several yards away, but that was less than reassuring. It was enormous, easily pushing through the invasive plants. Whatever could move the stubborn reeds so quietly unsettled me. Dorian watched it warily as we sailed into a shallower area and the shape stayed behind. Eventually, it broke off our trail and disappeared around the corner of another island, going back to swim in the deep.

"I've got some gas readings. Bubbles coming up," the tech said to Torres, who then grabbed his binoculars as he drove to look ahead of us.

The air here grew thicker with yellow particles floating around. Some settled into my hair with a tiny weight, the sensation like a small ghostly hand had just brushed over my head. A thin stream of green erupted from the water ahead in the distance. Bubbles floated into the air like they'd come from a kid's toy, but these bubbles looked nasty. They popped around us as we did our best to avoid them. When the bubbles exploded, they released more of the yellow substance into the air.

"Whatever is in the air isn't good," Torres grumbled. I was sure that he was equally frustrated that he didn't have anything clear to tell us from his previous work in this place. There were no real answers about what was here beyond the mutant alligators and, possibly, a cove of criminals. Florida had taken the Leftovers and ramped it up several notches.

Chandry settled herself on my other side as Bryce went up to the front of the boat. "This place feels stuffy," she said, shivering. "It's like the vegetation and water are pressing down on us."

The boat groaned as if in agreement.

"Hopefully, we'll find something soon," I said. Nervous anticipation had my blood pumping. I was anxious to get to wherever Torres suspected these kidnappers might be. He looked like he knew where he was going, but the eerie swamp continued to pass by us. Had they ever made it this far in?

Cam and Sike worked with the tech, mapping out various things and pointing out differences between our modified scanners and The Bureau ones. We had small readings of supernatural signatures on our scanners, but it could easily be nearby creatures. It was too hard to see in the water.

Eventually, we clocked in our third hour. I had seen one more "baby" alligator by the time Dorian stood up from his seat.

"Up ahead on the left," he said. "On that branch."

Torres guided us to a fork in the waterway and went left. A snapped tree branch hung at head height, and an abandoned bottle sat on the bank of one island. Up ahead, more broken branches dotted the path in front of us.

"There's something on one of these branches up ahead, too," Chandry said excitedly. "A scrap of cloth?"

We neared it and, indeed, Chandry was right. A torn piece of white fabric was wrapped around a low-hanging branch right beside another snapped one. Someone had been coming through here.

"Another," Sike called out. "Up ahead."

I was excited now. We followed the flags like a trail of breadcrumbs. The kidnappers must have needed markers to get back to their hideout, if Torres and his people were right about this place.

"We're coming up to a significant land mass," Torres reported. It was a larger island than the small ones we'd been passing, with trees lining the rim of it like a natural fortress. The last white flag led up to the shore. Trees bent, by man or by nature's response to the meld, out of our way as we pulled up in the boat. When we rested at the shore, I looked up to realize that this island was much higher than the rest of the marshes by a few feet, thanks to a mound of mud covered in slick grass. *Possibly a byproduct of the meld.*

After waiting a few minutes to ensure there was nothing around, we slowly got off the boat and into the water. My boots squelched on the muddy shore. Although the water was only a few inches deep, it smelled terribly like rotten eggs even through the mask.

I held back a gag and took a step forward, Dorian and Bryce beside me. The white flags gave way to faint footprints. Cam took photos while the tech noted the coordinates on a small recording device.

"This is where the supernatural signatures came from recently," Torres said. His eyes went to Dorian. Did he think Dorian could sense vampires around here?

"The scanners aren't picking much up," Sike confirmed. "Just the regular fluctuations and noise present throughout all of the wetlands."

We climbed to the top of the island and looked out.

A larger island with thick vegetation and trees was right in front of us. My pulse spiked with excitement. I hadn't seen it past the rim of trees, but now I had a good look from the top of this mound.

"That looks promising," I said, until I stepped a bit closer to see that something was different about this island. Deep, dark purple water surrounded the land mass, the edges tinged green where it met with the surrounding waters. The area around it seemed suspiciously groomed. The nearest neighboring spots of vegetation were tidy. Here, there were no reeds.

I frowned. If I leaned my head back, it almost looked like... someone had built a deeper trench around this island. It was too perfect in its shape, completely surrounding the island from the looks of it.

Chandry sighed and put her hands on her hips. "Well, how the heck are we supposed to get over there?"

"Airboat," Torres said, but his voice was laced with hesitation. "I've never seen that kind of water before..."

Bryce sniffed. "Excellent. Let's check it out."

We headed back to the airboat. If we could make it through the deep water, then we could explore the island. Something caught my eye as we made our way through to the muddy shore. Further down the small island, something white protruded from behind a half-dead tree. I made a beeline for it, with Dorian hot on my trail. The material and shape were clear as I got closer.

"It's a boat," I said, my heart pounding in my chest. Dorian helped me pull it gently out into the water so that the others could see. A gasp lodged itself in my throat when I saw what lay inside.

In the small rowboat, there were restraints—nylon ropes and metal. Something pink rested at the bottom of the beaten-up boat. It was a hair tie... one I recognized from Alicia's picture. My heart plummeted in my chest.

"Lyra," Dorian breathed, "I smell blood. It's not fresh, but it's here."

We had found our first piece of evidence.

7

Roxy

"I swear it was a redbill," Captain Koenig said, raising his arms to indicate a massive wingspan. "This big."

At the other end of the conference table, Hindley shook her head. "Koenig, we've been over this. There are no sizable redbill populations in the Mortal Plane except at the VAMPS camp. I'm sure it was a large non-supernatural bird. Advise your team to look less to the sky and more to the streets for monsters, since your region currently has no Leftovers."

We were stuck in our weekly meeting between the captains. Hindley and I had met yesterday to go over things. Something I didn't anticipate about becoming captain was the sheer volume of what felt like useless meetings.

The room was hotter than I liked, with the aggressive heating on in the Chicago HQ. I was tired after my unsettling disconnect from Kane the night before, since he hadn't offered even a morning message that he was okay, and from trying to keep my eyes on Hindley. We were in a group of captains who focused on the monster hunting initiative The Bureau had started. Our Chicago branch was the strongest one, next to the Los Angeles branch.

On the computer screen, a Bureau representative from LA was in a small square at the bottom of our projector. The rest of the screen was filled with newscasts from this week reporting various supernatural phenomena. Honestly, it was all the same junk each week. *Little girl spots a two-headed kitten and screams the whole way home. Elderly man reports vampires around his trash cans.* Some of the stories were definitely just wild rumors and probably bad eyesight at play.

I resisted the urge to chew on the end of my pen. My nerves were all over the place, and my head was in the clouds when it should have been in this room, focusing on my career. Usually, I would've poked fun at Koenig for his exaggerated stories about supposed sightings, but he somehow managed the best team of techs that our task force had seen. He was a good person to have on our side.

Today, I was off my game, and I sincerely hoped nobody had noticed.

Kane, can you hear me? Silence greeted me as Hindley moved on to our next order of business.

We had some updates about the VAMPS camp situation, where many vampires who didn't feel safe going back to the Immortal Plane were taking refuge. The current illegality of vampires in most jurisdictions made the refugee hotspot a contentious situation in Scotland. In the international debate around vampires, many countries wanted to completely ban them. Members of my own government were peeved that the US had zero legal jurisdiction there and, therefore, no legal say in any decisions that Scotland was making.

Kane would've been furious at the situation. He would've pointed out how many times vampires had helped save the day...

Maybe I could contact someone in the Immortal Plane with one of the comms, or call Lyra to ask her if she'd heard anything about Kane. She was in Florida, if I remembered correctly, although I had no idea where, thanks to the secrecy of the mission.

"A red-eyed deer nearly ate the finger off a kid," Hindley announced wearily. "He wandered away from his campsite near the northern end of the Sierra Leftovers. He'd gone out to take photos of the area. I'm thinking we might have to expand our patrols to make sure people aren't taking late winter vacations near the Leftovers' zones."

The Sierras was my last assignment, and it had been dangerous. "We should," I agreed, shaking off my internal worries and snapping back to attention. "I understand some people are stubbornly staying, but after the last mission, I think the creatures are growing bolder."

Koenig snapped his fingers and grinned at me. "Like the redbills?"

"*No*," Hindley said, exasperated. "There are no redbills in our area. Maybe some lone ones making their nests near the Leftovers, but I highly doubt you saw one in Greektown. Now, we have the budget we need for more patrols, but we'll have to decide where we want to concentrate The Bureau troops." A map appeared on screen with red dots to signify claims that had been verified by The Bureau as legitimate complaints from citizens. The US government wanted us to do whatever it took to make people feel safe again. It was a tall order, if you asked me.

Kane's confident face was all I could focus on. *He usually throws out at least one line if we disconnect to say he's going. Isn't that strange?*

I tapped my pen against the page in front of me, the schedule for our meeting. Why did organizations print out outlines for meetings, anyway? It seemed like such a waste. Kane would've hated it. He would've seen this whole meeting as a useless waste of time, and I usually agreed with him, even though Hindley always had something interesting to say.

Kane had said he wanted to go after the kids. What if he broke off from the medics and went to try to find a way back into the Pocket Space? It should have been impossible after the Ghost's death, but the Ghost's mere existence suggested the slim possibility that there might be other ways to get there.

I bounced my knee up and down underneath the table as Hindley talked about the Utah Leftovers. Lyra had already given me the rundown, so my brain fully tuned out. Was Kane hurt?

Halla lived in Aclathe, now, with him. She would be keeping an eye out for him in case something happened. It was Halla's way of life... hovering over her precious son and hating anyone who came near him. She was also one of the reasons that I couldn't see myself with Kane, because Halla had it out for humans.

I bit the inside of my lip to keep from groaning in frustration. This was so irritating. *Kane, talk to me.* Silence, again. I might have been the only one who knew something was wrong with Kane—if he was hurt, or passed out at the bottom of a tree somewhere.

"Roxy," Hindley said sharply. Her eyes narrowed, and my skin pricked with despair as I realized she had just called my name for the second time.

Someone stifled a chuckle.

I had tuned out staring at the map, so I hoped I still looked halfway engrossed.

"Again," she said sternly, "can you give us your official brief from your last mission with the Hellraisers?"

I recovered quickly. "Sorry. I was just thinking about a connection the Sierras had with the Utah Leftovers. I've noticed a lot of red markers on the maps of both regions. It seems to show an increase in both areas, whereas others have remained fairly consistent." I hadn't been paying attention, and now I was trying to cover for it with what felt like one functioning brain cell.

Hindley pressed her lips tight together, but the others seemed neutral. It wasn't any worse than Koenig's claim of a redbill in Chicago. *Oops.* I covertly looked around the room to gauge each officer's reaction. I doubted anyone on my team had told them about my lovely brain connection with a vampire, but one never knew.

I can't slip in my duties now... not after coming this far.

"The Sierras were an interesting mission." I had practiced my brief last night in my room after I'd been disconnected from Kane. I detailed the events of the mission and displayed some pictures we'd taken. I'd had a rough start with Jones and Evans, who were older Bureau members, but I'd won them over in the end. As I talked, I felt Hindley's eyes on me. Hopefully, she wouldn't give me a lecture about paying attention during meetings after this was over.

To my surprise, my briefing went well even after the initial gaffe. The other captains asked questions and seemed genuinely curious about my experiences without nitpicking how I'd handled things. It was a nice pat on the back in the end. As the meeting wrapped up and we moved on to talks of future meetings, I eased back in my chair. Finally, Hindley called the meeting to a close and left without speaking to me.

It was a good sign, although I almost wished she'd called me out. It might've been nice to confess to her what was happening with Kane. The room emptied out, and I was the last to leave. I made a show of stacking my papers and organizing my notes, but my mind was just wrecked.

Training was up next. Before I was a captain, it was a nice way to forget my troubles when I was a mere soldier since I could just throw myself into drills without having to think. When I got to the training area for my team, Holt and the twins were the first ones to greet me. I gave everyone brief instructions. Thankfully, we weren't deviating much from our standard practice protocol. I tasked Holt with watching the first few drills, citing the need to do a few laps to warm up and clear my mind of the meeting.

"Bureau meetings are torture," Holt said with a laugh. "I'm glad I'm not a captain at the moment."

I thanked him, changed, and started trotting around the indoor track. I loved moving my body and exercising my muscles. It allowed me to escape whatever struggles I was facing. For the sake of my day, I needed to push Kane far from my mind... but I didn't want to. Worry slowed my pace as I began my second lap. My anger grew inside myself. Why hadn't I tried harder to contact him this morning? If I had acted earlier, I could've gotten in touch with Lyra already, or alerted someone in the Immortal Plane. Kane had sounded so confident in his healing, though... He had to be okay, even if he had randomly cut out.

By my third lap, my sweat and worry were drowning me. I hadn't slept well or even downed my usual amount of water, so I was struggling to keep my regular pace. My distracted thoughts weren't helping. Hell, if I was distracted, I might as well dive into it.

Maybe he was listening, but he couldn't respond.

Are you there, Kane? It's Roxy, duh. I'm training with my team. We disconnected last night, and I can't focus thanks to you because you've got me worried. Contact me when you can. I just want to make sure you didn't fall out of that tree and break your neck, since it was a secluded area.

It was a reasonable worry.

Maybe he'd been distracted by something he saw from the tree. Or worse... he could've fallen to the ground after passing out. What if he broke his neck and died while cursing his choice of tree? He'd never said how high the branch was.

"Hey, Captain," Jessie called as I finished my warmup. "Ready?"

I ran up to them and immediately dove into the drills with the team. If I exhausted myself physically, maybe I could push past the gnawing anxiety. Worrying like this wouldn't help Kane. The smart thing would be to be patient, perform my duties, and contact someone as soon as the day ended. I had responsibilities as a captain. *I want to help him... maybe he doesn't need help, though.*

After our showers, I met with the Hellraisers. I was never one for energy drinks, but I bought one from a vending machine and chugged it right before the meeting to see if it would help. My elevated energy made the meeting go by more easily, but the twins made fun of me for resorting to desperate measures. It was harder to hide my connection to Kane when I was with them, but I hadn't expected it to be equally hard to hide my inability to connect with him.

"Any idea what our upcoming mission will be?" Jones asked toward the end of our meeting.

My empty stomach rioted with a loud growl, and my head pulsed with a sugar rush from the energy drink. I never drank stuff like that.

"Honestly, not yet," I replied, trying to keep myself together. "I'm just here to brief you on the news we got about the Leftovers. Our training schedule remains unchanged, although there might be a chance that we get a visiting Krav Maga expert to do a workshop if anyone's interested. We'll see what gets handed down the command chain as far as missions go, but right now, we just need to focus on our training. Everyone is doing great work."

I didn't add, *"Except me."*

Kane, are you there? I made my way down the hallway to return some reports to Hindley's mailbox. There was nobody in the gray corridor. I hated the silences that followed after I called out to Kane. After dropping off the files, I sighed and stared into the mailbox as if it might contain a message from Kane.

You've got thirty seconds to tell me something, or I'm contacting people.

Again, my grief and anxiety multiplied as no reply came. That was it. I had to do something. He could be passed out, or *worse*, so I was done waiting for him to reach out. My restless energy propelled me toward the supply room until I remembered that Lyra had said she was taking all the interplanar comms with her on her mission, due to Miami's lack of supplies. I paused in the hallway outside the supply wing and mumbled a curse. Okay, I couldn't access a comm, but there had to be another option.

I'm calling Lyra, Kane. It sounded like a threat a mother might make to her child, but I figured the last-ditch effort was to tell Kane something that he would automatically argue against. He would never want Dorian and Lyra running to help him. *Too bad, cupcake, you're getting some kind of checkup.*

I immediately dialed Lyra on my phone. It rang and rang, finally going to her voicemail. I cursed to myself and left a message. After a few more minutes, I tried to call again. I was starving, but worry overwhelmed every other instinct and desire. There was so little I could do from here. I tried calling Bryce, as well, but got a busy tone. Were they in the Florida Leftovers already? I had no idea who the contact in Miami was, and if I asked Hindley, she would immediately suspect something.

Great. Fantastic. Utterly wonderful. Do you see what you're doing to me?

My chats with Kane had become a nightly ritual that I'd never planned to give up. Imagining not talking to him tonight was sad... sadder than it should have been.

What would my life be like if I found out he'd been seriously injured, and I could do nothing about it? I had already lost him once in the Pocket Space, but had been given a rare chance to rescue him. I refused to lose him again.

I didn't do powerless.

As I made my way to my apartment, on fire with energy and grief, I spotted my own flustered reflection in a mirrored window. I looked like a woman in love.

The realization brought me to a startled halt in the middle of the sidewalk. A Bureau man in a suit passed me, paying no mind to the captain who was slowly coming to terms with herself.

I was really falling for Kane. I hadn't seen him in weeks. There was no guarantee that I would ever see him again. This was the *worst* timing.

I hope you're happy, I cried to an absent Kane. *I'm going to help you somehow. Somehow, I'll save you, even if this thing between us can't ever grow.*

8
Lyra

An eerie air had fallen over our group. The criminals were using this waterway like Torres had suspected, but were they still here? We might just stumble upon them at this moment, unless something with scales managed to slither out from the water and snatch us up first.

"I don't sense anything at all," Dorian growled.

I got closer to the boat and bent down toward the vessel. With the air filter and our protective suits, I didn't risk contaminating much, but the Leftovers might pose more of a threat to us if we uncovered something and exposed it to the toxic air.

If the boat was planted here, did that mean the kidnappers were using this island and maybe the next as their headquarters? I didn't see any structures suggesting a hideout. And why leave the boat here? Saving victims was our first priority if there were children over on the island, but we also had to preserve evidence.

Torres saw me hovering over the boat but said nothing about me contaminating anything. *Guess it's okay with the brass.* I jumped inside, making sure to gently pick up Alicia's hair tie and drop it in a sample bag. I only hoped the natural harsh conditions of the air wouldn't destroy any DNA evidence. We had no idea what this swamp could do. What if a piece of fiber or hair exposed to this air couldn't be used as evidence because of degradation?

Assuming that we catch these guys, and they actually go through the justice system like Torres wants. I understood Torres wanted to stick to rules, but after doing whatever we could to stop evil in the Immortal Plane, I hoped his rule-abiding nature wouldn't hamper any rescues.

The tech worked quickly to bag the scraps of rope restraints left in the boat. She wrinkled her nose with disgust as she looked at them in the sample bag, holding it up to the light. A hazy fog was rolling in, a cloudier white that diffused the sun. It made me feel like we were in a horror movie. *Please let there be no giant alligators hiding in the mist.* The tech brought out a UV light, but I wasn't sure that was going to do much good in this environment. Still, she could try. Torres would insist on it.

"Do we have kits for fingerprint dusting?" I asked her. She nodded, then explained that she would have to do it to keep the evidence in proper condition for legal purposes. The tech dusted the oars for prints. We were clearly too late to catch the criminal in action. I wondered how long this boat had been here.

Frustrated, I turned back to Dorian as he leaned down to the boat, sniffing. Although his senses were strong, he'd always been especially sensitive with auras and smells. The tech bagged the evidence as Dorian used his vampire senses to pick up information about the boat. It could be a potential crime scene, given the likely presence of blood.

"I can't say for sure if there's blood here. Sometimes, the amount is very faint, and you really can't tell until you're in the lab," she said uncertainly. "I won't know anything until the crime lab does their diagnostics on the evidence we collected."

Torres was watching Dorian like a hawk. Torres wasn't used to the vampires and their senses, but he had a lot to learn if he expected us to succeed in the Leftovers. The vampires were a vital part of this team.

"He's using his sense of smell," I explained to him. "Dorian smells old blood here. We've used vampire senses to collect evidence before, in a case with the FBI." I relayed our experiments working with vampires to identify criminal activity. The stories involved our old FBI contact, Jim, who was a close friend to Bryce.

I spoke as gently as I could with Bryce around. We had found Jim murdered at The Bureau's own hand thanks to the ex-board's corruption.

Would Torres have had anything to say about that, if I told him the full extent of what the very human old board used to do?

I fought the urge. He would have to see reason by looking at our successful work. I only hoped he would get over his prejudices in time to make our jobs easier.

"Something's here," Dorian said suddenly. He'd found a compartment in the bottom of the inner boat. It was completely white, blending in easily with the surrounding material. He flipped a door open and tugged out a cooler from the compartment. Inside the cooler, there were a few water bottles, a towel, a packet of old antiseptic wipes, and a bloody knife. My heart seized with dread at the sight of the knife.

The tech scooped up the knife before we could examine it further, moving quickly underneath Torres's critical gaze. I had a faint idea that their employee turnover might be high at his office if he was always watching them like that. The younger members probably came in excited to join the cause, only to find old grizzled members lamenting their glory days.

The mist lightened a bit, and the diffused sunlight gave way to a more somber shade. Torres glanced up, citing a forecast for light rain today. A disturbing chill ran through my body. I looked around the area, wondering what had caused the abrupt sensation, but nobody seemed bothered by anything but the presence of the boat. I pushed the feeling away.

Maybe we could use the boat to cross the channel with less noise. If the smugglers had left it here, it was presumably important. Perhaps there was a lookout or some kind of scout who trusted the sight of *this* particular boat. It was worth a chance if Alicia was still nearby.

"Can we use the boat to cross?" I asked Torres.

After a short pause, he gave a shrug. "We're not going to be able to take it out of here. If Claire got all the evidence she needs, it's fine." He glanced over my shoulder to the dark, shadowy depths of the underwater trench around the island. "You should be careful."

"We'll manage," I promised, because we had to. We had to explore the area. If Dorian and I went together, that ensured we had one human with good firearm aim and a vampire, in case something happened. It seemed better to pair off to increase our strengths.

Bryce gave me an approving nod as I climbed into the boat with Dorian. It was only large enough for three people, but Dorian was tall. Our combined statures were just enough for the small craft. I gripped the oars with sweaty palms, anger coursing through me when I realized it was also the perfect fit for two adults and a tied-up teenager. *What are these creeps doing with these kids?*

"I'll keep an eye on the water," Dorian said when he saw my white knuckles around the oars.

Sike and Cam gently pushed against our craft to launch us off the muddy shore. Clouds of dark green mud filled the water underneath us. Another tadpole darted by, and I sincerely hoped that would be the only fish I saw in the water.

"Can you smell anything else?" I asked Dorian as he took up the head of the boat. The mask probably blocked some of his senses, but Dorian had always been excellent with smells. There could be a trail of human scent somewhere.

He shook his head and glanced back at me.

"The scent of old blood and the swamp air are blocking me," he admitted gravely. We were out far enough from the others that he could slip in, "Torres thinks I'm a mad bloodhound."

I sighed. "He's not used to vampires. I hope we can change his mind, although I guess his behavior is fine for us to get by on the mission. As long as he doesn't get worse, we can keep going without problems."

"I appreciate you trying to speak with him about it," Dorian said. He stiffened abruptly. "There's something odd about this water."

"The current?" I guessed. The water fought against my rowing, but I pushed on. The sour smell of the water was stronger here. This channel was extremely wide compared to the other waterways we'd navigated through—at least 100 yards across. The distance to the island would take us a few minutes to cross.

The prow rocked to the side an inch, and I frowned, fighting to counter the stubborn current. Dorian sucked in a breath.

"Lyra, the shape from earlier—" Dorian's voice cut off as Torres yelled from the shore.

"Watch out," he cried. "That thing is coming after you!"

I looked to see the huge shape that had followed us earlier swooping around us in the water. It had shot off from somewhere on the left side of the island's trench ahead of us. It was moving faster than its previous lazy pace, swerving like a race car on a course beneath the waves. I froze for a moment, wondering if tentacles or fins would shoot out of the water, but the giant shadow never broke the surface.

Adrenaline surged through me. I threw myself into desperately rowing backwards as fast as possible. The boat jerked to the side, and I lurched back, halfway falling off the seat.

"It's not surfacing, but it's doing something," Dorian said.

The water sloshed upward from the force of the creature's movements. I steadied myself and hauled on the oars. The underwater trench churned with frenzied movement, rocking our boat back and forth. I kept us as steady as possible, but treacherous whirlpools were trying to swamp our little boat. The creature wasn't trying to attack us by smashing into the boat, but trying to sink us by creating the whirlpools. It had to be insanely powerful to be able to do this.

"What is this thing?" I shouted. I fought the current as much as possible, but my left oar went flying. I stood up and drew my gun, lining up a shot into the whirlpool below us. All I could see was the barest hint of black scales beneath the murky, moving water. I fired into the center as Dorian narrowed his eyes.

"I have no idea, but I'm useless if it doesn't come up here. I'm going to find us a way back," Dorian said, and we switched sides. I fired again, the water momentarily stilling as the dark creature let out a gurgle of pain. The water came back up around the beast, shielding it from any fire. My bullets wouldn't go into the water unless the creature drained the area around it. At least, my gun was working at the moment. Would it be dumb enough to let me fire again?

Water flew over the sides as a groan from below the boat shook me to the core. It sounded like a massive whale was just beneath us. I hissed as some of the water splashed on my face, hitting exposed skin between my mask and goggles. The Bureau hadn't prepared us for more than wading through the water. The burns hurt, but we had to try to escape. The suits, at least, deflected most of the gross toxic liquid.

"It's starting again," Sike yelled with warning. *Oh, great.*

How were these criminals getting across the water? Did they have a trick to get around this beast? The whirlpools started up again as Dorian tried desperately to use the oar to propel us back. He made a few feet of progress toward the shore, closer to our shouting friends.

Chandry weaved around Torres and sprang into a tree, the branches of which stretched over the water. She reached her hand toward Dorian, who could just touch the tips of her fingers. He grabbed her hand and she yanked, but the whirlpool kicked up another notch with even faster speeds. The boat pulled away from her for a brief harrowing second. I couldn't fire another shot because, now, the creature had the sense to go deeper.

We had two options, with Chandry in the tree and the others on the bank, but the latter meant crossing more territory. Could she carry both of us? She was strong, but her position in the tree swayed.

Torres was right beside Chandry, close enough now to grab Dorian's arm.

"Forget the boat!" Bryce bellowed. I leapt to the other side with Dorian. Instead of reaching out toward Dorian, who was closer, Torres grabbed for me. His hand wrapped around my forearm while Bryce leapt forward to grab both my arm and Dorian's. The boat was sucked beneath the water, the wood splitting and chipping as the monster crushed it with what looked like giant tentacles. It was hard to see in the blur of shadowy movements.

Stings burning on my cheeks, I gritted my teeth as I stumbled forward onto the muddy shore with Torres and Bryce. Chandry yanked on Dorian from the tree, much harder since he was further out than I had been. Whirling around, I watched as a few remaining bubbles popped on the water's surface. The dark shape sank deeper into the water and vanished into the depths of the channel. My emotions hit me all at once.

I was pissed at Torres for not grabbing Dorian in the split-second chance he had, horrified at the monster, and disappointed that we'd lost the boat.

I hissed as the light breeze stung my face.

"We need to get your burns looked at," Chandry said to Dorian and me. She had no problem meeting my gaze, unlike Torres, who looked flustered. I was about to open my mouth to ask if we had a towel as I dripped the rest of the excess water onto the ground, when something buzzed in my equipment belt.

My head buzzed. On autopilot, my limbs moved.

I pawed at the pouch on my belt for my phone. "Hello?"

"Lyra," Roxy breathed. My heart rate spiked with worry. "I need your help."

I shook the water from my boots as best as I could as we walked farther up the island, just in case the monster decided to come ashore. "Is something wrong?"

The panic in her voice was uncharacteristic. She wasn't on a mission, unless something had changed in the last twenty-four hours.

"It's Kane. I usually talk with him, but he disconnected yesterday." I listened to Roxy while watching the awkward face-off between Torres and the vampires. Sike had turned his entire back away from the man, saying something in hushed tones to Chandry.

"He was right there," Chandry said fervently. Their discussion fell into a hush as they caught sight of my face.

"Kane," I croaked to my team. My head was still spinning. "Roxy called. I think he's passed out and hurt somewhere. I need you to try to get ahold of Arlonne or someone else in the Immortal Plane to see if they can find him."

Kane might be hurt. He was already injured from his time in the Pocket Space. We couldn't risk not calling in to ask for a check-up on him.

"Bryce, I need you to call Arlonne to ask her to check on Kane," I called out. Bryce froze at my request, then threw his hands up.

"I can't," he pushed back. I couldn't hold back the scoff. He had just been happily flirting with her over the comms a few days ago, and now he suddenly had a problem? I knew they had progressed to the point where Bryce passed out due to their feelings for one another.

"Is he doing it? He was on the edge of town, near some pools or something. He was in a tree," Roxy explained after a beat of silent disbelief. She must've heard us on the line.

"Bryce, call her," I snapped. Anger crawled up my throat. Torres had already ticked me off, but now I was going to lose it if my co-leader didn't get his act together.

"I can't," Bryce insisted. His cheeks were red. Even Sike and Cam stared at him, confounded.

"Then *someone* call her. Kane might be in trouble. They need to check on him," I said, and directed my attention back to the phone. I was grumpier than Bryce now. "Look, Roxy, we're going to get someone to call her and check on Kane."

Roxy let out a relieved sigh. "Okay. Thanks, Lyra. Sorry to interrupt." She ended the call, and I pocketed my phone, sighing in frustration as I turned back around on the group. The vampires stood at odds with Bryce and Torres now, looking at them both incredulously—save for Dorian, who stared at the lake. Sike tapped his comm, calling Arlonne. It was giving him trouble. My frustrations doubled.

Why wouldn't Bryce call, and was Kane really hurt?

I looked to the water. The boat was sunk, along with any physical evidence other than what we'd managed to grab for Torres and his techs. We'd lost our only connection to that island. Dorian and I needed medical attention. A giant monster lurked at the bottom of the lake, making it impossible to get to where the criminals likely were, and... they would soon know that someone had been here.

They would know we'd found their trail.

9
Lyra

*A*t this point, I almost wished I'd gone down with the boat. At least I would've escaped this awkward ride back to Miami HQ in the RV.

Cam sat in the back with the vampires while I manned the front next to Bryce. My co-captain drove with his shoulders pinched up to his ears, and the vibe from the back was even tenser. They were discussing Torres, understandably.

My heart was heavy for the vampires, especially Dorian. He had dealt with prejudice before, like being led into the old Bureau office in a muzzle before the old board had been ousted. He was no stranger to hatred of vampires, and he was probably the best one to discuss how to de-escalate situations. He had more experience than the others, even Sike, thanks to all of our extra work with human organizations in the past. Dorian would be able to guide the others on human prejudice and how to handle people like Torres.

My greater concern at the moment was Bryce, as he blared his horn at a minivan going too slow in the fast lane. We were in an RV—what were we even doing in the fast lane? In the end, Bryce had been the one to contact the Immortal Plane after Sike's comm had failed from a fluctuation. Bryce had specifically called into Reshi.

Not Arlonne. How interesting.

She must have had something to do with his bad mood.

"What did you hear about Kane?" I asked him gently.

Bryce's hand gripped the steering wheel tightly, and he scowled at the road ahead. "Reshi sent the others to check. Turns out some wildlings already found him earlier today. He was passed out under a tree, but he's back with the healers. Sounds like Roxy was right about him. He hasn't woken up yet, though."

I settled back into my seat, unsure whether I should broach the topic of his mood.

This mission was already hard enough, with Torres being a stubborn bull about vampires, but something was obviously upsetting Bryce. We needed to discuss it, but first I needed to answer Roxy.

I dug out my phone and saw that I had missed six calls from her before she'd eventually gotten a hold of me in the Leftovers. I swiped her number immediately, and she picked up on the first ring.

"Hello?" Her voice was a taut tightrope. I had never heard her like this. Her usual attitude was simultaneously rough, warm, and unbothered.

I told her everything Bryce had relayed to me, hoping Dorian was also hearing it from the back since he and Kane were close. Roxy let out a relieved sigh.

"Thank goodness," she muttered.

I asked her as discreetly as I could about the six calls. There might've been something she hadn't told me in the Leftovers about why she was so concerned. Roxy and Kane had always had an interesting relationship, but it wasn't one that I understood. I'd seen them kiss once, but perhaps things were on the rocks. A relationship between a vampire and a human was destined to be hard.

"Oh, that," Roxy said and cleared her throat. "I was *really* worried. It just... it felt like he was dying in the Pocket Space all over again." She paused, and in the background, I heard a rustling like shuffling papers. Was she still working, doing Bureau paperwork, in the midst of all her worry? I was impressed.

Finally, she added, "I know that I have to deal with this." She didn't elaborate on what "this" was, but I had a strong suspicion that it had to do with her complex feelings about Kane. Perhaps those feelings were more serious than she'd ever realized.

As someone who had fallen for a vampire myself, I knew the difficulties that such a life could present. There was the curse, first and foremost, never mind the logistics of everything else.

"I'm here for you if you need anything," I assured her, although Roxy's characteristic stubbornness often meant that she felt as if she had to do everything by herself... not unlike a certain moody vampire named Kane.

"I'm fine for the moment," she assured me. "Thank you."

We hung up, and I stared at my phone for a moment, contemplating her words. I wondered how she was going to deal with her feelings. If she was worried enough about Kane to call me several times while I was on an official mission, she obviously cared for him a lot.

I was just grateful that the wildlings had found him. The fact that he hadn't woken up yet concerned me, but Kane always needed a bit more time to heal compared to the other vampires. I often chalked that up to the fact that he was built like a tank and pushed himself too hard.

In many ways, those two are perfect for each other, if they can just learn to live in harmony.

It was easier said than done, but I wouldn't pry any more than Roxy allowed me to. Kane would roll over into an early grave if he knew anyone was discussing his private emotional life.

Or probably just say that he doesn't actually have emotions.

Bryce glowered at the traffic in front of us. We were stuck in a bit of a jam; maybe it was a good chance to talk. A small child waved at us excitedly from the back of an SUV, but Bryce was too focused on the road ahead and the cars moving inch by inch. I gave the kid a wave back since Bryce was in no mood.

"You want to talk?" I asked softly, stealing a glance behind us. The vampires and Cam were completely engrossed in conversation. I turned up the radio for good measure. I might as well be everyone's therapist today; maybe it would do some good.

"About what?" Bryce asked. He eased his shoulders down, as if he'd just realized I was actually right beside him. He was playing dumb, and he had trained me better than that.

"What the deal is," I pressed, unwilling to give up. "I can see that something is going on."

Bryce sighed sharply and turned his head to the side for a moment. "I don't want to drag personal emotions into work."

I shrugged sympathetically. "You know, I was dragging my emotions into work with Dorian. Call it payback. This work isn't without emotion, Bryce. You taught me that."

Bryce's hands eased on the steering wheel. We rolled forward a few more feet. "I know... I just... Arlonne and I discussed things. We're taking a break from talking at all this week."

A whole week-long break? I sat up straighter in my seat.

He went on. "Our future is looking bleak, I'm sorry to say. We admitted to having feelings for each other. I mean, it was obvious after the fainting bit, but I wanted to talk to her openly about it. So... we did. I was amazed to find that she felt the same way for me. Even with the fainting, I couldn't really believe it, you know?"

He spoke with such a wonder that I had to hide the sudden smile on my face, knowing that bad news was soon to follow. Clearly, something had soured between them if they were taking a break.

Although Dorian and I did something similar, once upon a time.

"What happened?" I asked.

"The conversation was like a happy dream, but also a nightmare," Bryce admitted. "It was hard. Arlonne seemed distressed in a way that I'd never seen her. I was so bowled over that she liked me that I couldn't realize what was happening. Things seemed like they might work out, until she brought up our age. We're older. She wants a lasting relationship, and we don't have as much time to work out the difficult bits of such a relationship."

And long-lasting was hard when it came to vampires and humans, unless one was ready to make some sacrifices.

"Arlonne is technically older than me," Bryce mumbled. "She wants to settle down, and she deserves to be with someone who can give her what she wants right away. I thought I could convince her. I told her I didn't want a fling, but... she doesn't think we can make it work, in the end, with the curse. We thought of going back to Scotland, where Arlonne would willingly starve herself while living in the Mortal Plane. She would never go for that, the warrior that she is. The other option is—" He cut himself off to honk at someone who'd pulled in front of him without signaling. I leaned forward.

"Is what?" I asked.

"The other option is to see if Reshi can look at your necklaces to research them. She might be able to replicate them for us. I used to be excited for that idea, but then Arlonne told me that Reshi had already looked over the necklaces, covertly, at the wedding. I guess she'd been interested in them ever since you showed up with them. The maker thinks they're quite complicated, and if replicating them is even possible, she would have to have them in her possession for a substantial amount of time to work up a model. And then you guys would have to deal with the curse again, yourselves. You wouldn't be able to work together in Callanish for that time, either... Arlonne and I agreed that we couldn't ask a happily married couple to do this. You guys are our friends, and there's only a chance that Arlonne and I would work out, even assuming Reshi could pull it off. It wouldn't be fair."

Reshi needed our necklaces, but my work and marriage required them at the moment. It wasn't out of the question in the future... but the length of time scared me. And what if she couldn't get them back on? Where would Dorian go if I stuck with Callanish? Still, I would do anything to help Bryce and Arlonne. They had already done so much to fight evil together, they should get the same chance as Dorian and me. Dorian and I weren't special, in terms of love. Everyone deserved a chance at being with the one they loved, even with this awful curse.

"Just forget about it. I see that face you're making, lass," Bryce said warningly. "You and Dorian deserve your happiness. Don't try to help two old folks when you should be having the time of your lives in your prime."

I raised an eyebrow and gestured to the RV around us. "You mean like traveling around in a giant motorhome in muggy air to solve some kidnappings? That's evidently our idea of a good time. Dorian and I are used to dealing with the curse." It would take a lot from us—like our ability to be together if we let Reshi have the necklaces. Obviously, not on this mission, but once it was over...

Bryce caught my look and shook his head furiously. "I said no. Don't worry about it."

And yet, there was a sad look in his eye. I couldn't ignore that.

I would have to talk to Dorian first, to float actual timelines. But it *was* possible.

"We understand how hard it is," I told Bryce gently. "We'd be willing to do it, with the right timing.I can talk to Dorian about it later. You guys worked around us constantly when we were figuring out the curse. It seems fair that we pay it back to our teammates."

Although Dorian and I had discussed it once before, I didn't want Bryce to think we were conspiring behind his back.

"No, not happening. Don't worry yourself, Lyra. I'll figure something out. Eventually. It's just that Arlonne is not very optimistic at the moment. And sorry for my mood lately. I'll try to keep it under wraps." All Bryce's attention went back to the road.

Behind us, the light conversation between the vampires and Cam told me that they were all still discussing the ongoing situation with Torres. I couldn't hear them much over the radio, which now blasted smooth jazz.

Bryce was going to feel worse the more I tried to persuade him. It was better I didn't push the subject too much.

"I'm going to bring this up again," I promised him. After the mission, we would talk about this further. For now, I would grant him peace while he escaped the dreaded traffic jam.

Finally, our RV flew down the highway back to The Bureau office. I was dreading seeing Torres and his team, but there was no helping that. We had to do hard things if we wanted to find those kids, and Dorian was right: It was the kidnappings that mattered the most.

10

Lyra

*B*ack at the Miami HQ building, it was time to chat with Torres. It would just be him and our team, and he looked as relaxed as when we'd left him—stiff as a wooden board with a cup of coffee beside him at the head of the table. He had the evidence laid out with printed signs that said not to touch the evidence bags in front of us.

Okay, so he either thought we were stupid, or this was a power trip after his performance in the Leftovers.

"Glad you didn't get lost in traffic," Torres said with a sharp nod in my direction. He was still only looking at Bryce and me.

Oh, boy. This is going to be interesting.

We took our seats. Naturally, the vampires installed themselves at the other end of the table, away from Torres. Dorian snagged a seat beside me, while Bryce sat closest to Torres. Silently, our own little war was brewing.

Suffer through the awkward tension for Alicia.

And I would.

"We have the fingerprints from the oars. It should be interesting to see if we get any hits from our criminal database," Torres said, pointing to the kit in question. "I'm thinking that if these guys are so organized, they might already be in the system somewhere. The DNA from the knife should be promising. It'd be nice if one of the kids cut one of the kidnappers in a struggle."

It was equally possible one of the kidnappers had stabbed a victim, and my stomach turned at the thought. The memory of those restraints haunted me.

I wanted to go back immediately and try using the airboat to get to the island, but Bryce had talked me down, and rightfully so, after the monster moment. I was just so desperate to keep our lead on the kidnappers.

I looked at the fiber cords collected by the tech. How many victims had been fastened inside those restraints?

"We'll work with the Miami police to use their DNA database to see if we can find any matches with the evidence," Torres explained. It was sensible, but I wanted to talk about our next steps, beyond just evidence collection. "With any luck, we'll get a lead there."

"How long does the crime lab usually take here?" I asked him. Every state had different times depending on their backlogs.

"It might be a while, even if I put a rush on it," Torres said with a frown.

My hope was slowly fading that anything would be done about this case quickly. Hell, I could call Fenton, a rich and well-connected member of the new Bureau board, if I needed to get some strings pulled in that crime lab.

"The state crime labs are quite busy at the moment, but who knows?" Torres added with an uncharacteristic air of positivity. "This is a special case, and *maybe* we can put a rush on it. It might not be up to my demands, though. The governor has kept the whole Leftovers story hushed up as much as possible, so I'm not sure whether he wants it solved quickly or just quietly."

Of course they had. Well, we could use that information to our advantage if we had to.

In the meantime, one way to make some headway in the mission would be to interview the suspects by tracking them down and pretending to ask for their help in an investigation.

I broached the idea with Torres.

"We can act like they're the good guys," I told him as the idea took shape in my head. "We just ask them to help us in an investigation with a website that they're linked to. They don't have to know anything beyond that. The Bureau has given us some training on investigative work. Often, the bad guy tries to cover their tracks by acting like a good citizen."

Torres laced his fingers together with a pensive look. "Wouldn't that give us away?"

"They probably use multiple sites, right?" Bryce asked. "They'll find plenty of ways to get to teens, no matter what. If they get spooked off that *Geeks* site, then they'll be on another one."

Dorian nodded. "I can also be nearby to assess the darkness of the suspects. It would support that we're on the right track if I have a reaction to them," he explained for Torres's benefit.

At this, Torres's eyes widened fractionally. "I'm not sure I like that idea."

"You're not sure, or you don't like it?" Bryce challenged him. "Because we need direct information about how we can proceed to save those kids."

I hid a proud smile behind my hand. Bryce was back on board; his bad mood about Arlonne had turned into a take-no-prisoners foul mood.

That I can deal with.

Torres scowled. "Fine, I'll put it another way. You shouldn't do it this way. I suspect that you'll be putting the entire case on the line. A defense attorney can easily sink their claws into this and cry foul about vampires targeting humans. In the current climate of opinion, that'll be difficult. You risk putting the public in danger. We could lose the case *and* the children if something happens." He darted a look to me. "What if the vampires can't control themselves and end up feeding on our own case leads?"

A hot spike of anger hit me before I even fully processed what he'd said. He was suggesting that one of the vampires would accidentally attack people. Which was ridiculous—they weren't monsters.

"They don't do that," I fired back, but Torres made no movement to back down. He met my gaze with a defiant stare. "They don't hurt innocent people or lose control like wild animals." *Not unless they're starving and pushed to the breaking point.* What did he not understand about that?

The conversation had lurched from professional to tense in a matter of seconds. *Fantastic. Torres is really showing his worst side right now.* His prejudice against vampires was going to hurt our mission, and worse, the kids. We needed to get these kidnappers into custody to stop more teenagers from being taken.

To my surprise, Chandry rocketed up from her seat, her usual calm and sunny demeanor gone. "I've sat here through all of your rudeness toward us since the beginning. When I came to the Mortal Plane, nobody told me that the humans asking for our help were going to be so cruel. In vampire culture, you'd never see someone ask for assistance and then insult those who offered it. You didn't even try to save Dorian, when he was closer to you than Lyra, during the boat fiasco."

She was right, but this was the first time I'd seen the free-spirited Chandry get upset about something. Sike stared at her, his eyebrows up to his hair with shock. Out of all the people in our group, nobody had expected this reaction... even if she was well within her right to be offended.

I motioned for her to sit, nudging Dorian underneath the table as I did. I needed him to be prepared to calm things down if it got to the point where a true conflict arose... a conflict that we might not be able to come back from.

"Chandry, I hear you, and I'd like to ask Torres to trust the vampires." I turned my burning stare on him. "At the very least, you can trust the judgment of the humans who are proven soldiers with a great reputation for getting things done. It makes zero sense not to trust us. The vampires haven't attacked you, and we've been more than cordial."

Torres didn't miss a beat. "With no disrespect, Munroe, I have to take an objective view on this as the head of the Miami branch. I'm not sure that I can completely trust people who regularly deal with vampires, since you're naturally biased. I mean, I can't expect a logical perspective from someone married to a vampire."

The remark hit me like a slap. I was stunned, but Torres pressed further as my teammates went deadly silent.

"I lost good men and women out in the field, back in the days of vampire hunting," Torres said. His voice swelled into a wave of anger. "I have a history of fighting these creatures, and I remember them as bloodthirsty from a distance. I watched them stalk their prey and attack people. How could I feel anything other than anger after watching my men and women get killed out there? They fought with their lives, and many of them lost. We never felt safe down here. We had a particularly nasty nest of them in this area. I don't know how they got here, but they were deadly cruel."

"Chandry is right to be upset," Dorian said. His tone was laced with a dangerous edge, but he spoke calmly. Torres was playing a contentious game. "We understand that you can't put those memories aside, but neither can we put aside the memories of being hunted by humans when we only targeted the worst parts of your society for feeding. Those vampires you're talking about could have been desperate to survive and fighting back in self-defense, or they could have been evil, just like there are evil humans in this world. You don't seem to trust half of this team, and that's going to be a big problem if you expect this mission to succeed."

Adrenaline rocketed through my body. *Calm down*, I warned myself. Yelling at him, like I wanted to do, wasn't going to get us anywhere.

Torres crossed his arms stubbornly and a tight muscle in his jaw flexed. His chin pointed high as he said, "You say they don't attack innocent people, but there's no way to prove you're right."

I grunted. I could understand all sides in this room, but I wanted Torres to trust that we were here to do good work and save the kids.

"Look," I said tightly, "I had the same concerns when I first met Dorian, but we were both fed a certain propaganda when it comes to vampires, Torres. I tested many of the same ideas that you're talking about, trying to understand why the vampires needed to feed. When we hid out from the old Bureau, my teammates were there with me watching these things take place. It wasn't an easy task for both parties to trust each other, and there were many arguments over the ethics of it. But the fact is that they *only* attack evil humans filled with darkness. They're not completely overtaken by the urge unless they're starving. Our vampires aren't starving. They're trying to help you. The biggest thing I can ask of you is to trust your superiors at The Bureau. The board hands out licenses to vampires for a reason."

"And the least you could do is be decent in return," Chandry seethed with narrowed eyes.

"You've tested it in laboratory conditions?" Torres asked, his voice growing higher. At the mention of labs, Sike flinched, and Bryce glowered.

"The vampires were tortured in labs by the old Bureau," I reminded Torres sharply. "They attacked Bureau soldiers to keep themselves alive, when they weren't being herded into labs for cruel experiments. We have dear friends who suffered unspeakable things. I know you've also suffered, but this is basically us dancing around the fact that two factions who used to be opposed are now working together. You can either choose to get on board or get out of our way."

Torres drew back like a striking snake. "Don't presume to give me orders in my own conference room. We were *something* when we hunted vampires, and now we're... what? A place for you to park your RV?"

Bryce smacked a hand on the table. "Do you want our help or not?"

"I want—" Torres was cut off as Chandry let out a mocking scoff.

"You want us to do our work in muzzles and chains," she snapped.

"I wouldn't say no," Torres shot back.

Chandry sucked in a sharp breath, her eyes growing darker.

I grabbed Dorian's knee underneath the table and squeezed it. Things were starting to get out of hand. We needed to get a handle on this.

"You're a monster calling *us* monsters," Chandry said. "How can you spit in the face of people offering you help?"

"The same way I keep a police dog on a leash." Torres's words blanketed the room in a stuffy silence.

He thought of the vampires as animals. Nothing more than trained beasts to help him in his work. Why was he showing this now, when there was so much at stake? I wanted to call up our government contact and grill them about why they'd sent us here to work in such hostile conditions. If they wanted a skilled team of experts to help in the Leftovers, we needed support to do so effectively.

"I thought humans were better than this," Chandry said, her voice breaking at the end of her sentence. "You sit there, high and mighty, thinking your guns and ignorance will protect you. We have families. We were almost wiped out completely thanks to a cruel dictator in our homeland. We've seen people die, day after day. Don't think your pain is any better than ours."

It was like watching an early memory of the conflict between vampire and human groups play out again. I remembered the harsh reality of learning that the vampires fed on darkness and not being able to deal with it in some ways.

Torres was clearly affected, but Chandry hadn't experienced discrimination like the other vampires had, and she wouldn't know to really expect such blatant prejudice from the head of a Bureau branch. It was the government who hired us knowing that we had vampires, so she probably had no idea what his problem was. She was a new addition to our group, absent during those early days back when The Bureau was trying to wipe out vampires.

Torres curled his lips. "Look, I've seen vampires at their worst. I'll never forget my last mission before we supposedly eradicated your kind. I was assigned to a terrible vampire that I'd been hunting for weeks. He hid himself in the waterways, thinking we couldn't find him. I caught him running away from his last victim, though, and followed him like a dog. He was fresh from feeding, blood all over his face, but I got him."

Chandry shook with anger while Sike's face paled and his hands balled into fists.

Torres grinned triumphantly. "He was in a full hunting rage at that point, blind with anger. I shot him straight in the leg while my colleague distracted him so he couldn't run, and then I sealed the deal by plunging a dagger through his heart. I guess not all of our human notions about vampires were wrong. The heart gets everyone."

The next movement happened in a flash. One moment, Chandry was in her seat, and then she was leaping over the desk. She easily picked up Torres by the shoulders and threw the taller man against the wall.

"If you're going to treat us like monsters, then we might as well act like them," she snarled, showing off her fangs for good measure.

I flew up from the table, stunned.

My stomach heaved with despair as I recognized the sure click of a gun. Torres brought up his firearm and pointed it straight at Chandry's chest. Dorian jumped up from the table, yelling for them to stop. Bryce instinctively went to his own weapon on his belt and froze at the reaction, a shadow of guilt crossing his face. Sike reached out his hand toward Chandry, but whether it was to help her or attack Torres, I wasn't sure.

This was bad.

Chandry was shaking as she held Torres against the wall. She only had one of his arms pinned; her other was reaching for his gun. "You won't get out of my grasp, because guess what? I'm stronger. You need to stop talking about us like we are wild animals without any morals."

Dorian jumped in between them, his chest putting up a wall of flesh and blood between Torres's gun and Chandry. He stared Torres down.

"Not like this," Dorian said.

A tense silence filled the room. Here we were, in a conference room, in a near-shootout with what was supposed to be our ally in all this.

I wanted to jump in, but Dorian was more capable with the vampires.

Dorian eyed them as he said, "Both of you need to stand down. There are too many emotions, and it's blinding us to our real purpose." He pointed at Torres. "Put the gun down. Chandry, back off."

Slowly, Torres dropped his weapon, although his eyes were trained on Chandry's fangs.

"I need you to let him go," Dorian told her firmly. He gripped her wrist, and only then did Torres relax an inch.

"But he said such terrible things," Chandry croaked, her eyes now filled with tears. My heart tore for her. She was so upset about Torres that her hurt had manifested into pure anger. As someone who had once let my anger get a hold of me, during my period with the blood curse fix, I understood that pain well—but I'd had to learn that I was responsible for my anger. She would have to answer for this and her feelings in this mission like everyone else.

Chandry hesitated, but finally, she dropped her hold on Torres. She roughly turned away and immediately went to Sike, burying her face into his shoulder and sobbing softly. Sike seemed surprised and gently patted her on the back, as if unsure of what to do. Our free spirit had officially cracked.

Torres shook himself off and glared up at Dorian, and then me. "I could have her license revoked. You see, now, why I can't trust vampires?"

Dorian shook his head sternly. "All we have to do is be civil with each other until this case is finished." His glacial eyes hardened on Torres, causing the man to stiffen. "If you won't cooperate with us and allow us to run this investigation successfully, we *will* break our contract and leave you to fix this problem on your own. You want to save these kids? So do we. We'll leave you alone and follow your rules, but I'd advise you not to push us too far."

Our alliance was officially on the teetering brink of failure. The Bureau asked us to come. We had to save those kids, whether Torres was going to go along with us or not.

Bryce and I might have to put in a phone call to the big guys in Chicago if things got much worse.

11

Kane

*D*reams of madness found me. I floated against a current I couldn't fight, because I couldn't move. No amount of barking orders to my limbs made my arms budge. I was a frozen corpse, drifting in the sky. Roxy's voice haunted my every passing moment. I heard her calling my name in the distance, but my hearing felt fuzzy. A flash of my mother's face popped in front of me and exploded like a firework.

"Work harder," she whispered, the sound close to my ear.

As if I had done anything but work hard my entire life. What was she talking about?

You're dreaming, fool. Wake up.

But I couldn't fight the invisible bonds. I continued to float. There was nothing I could do, and I hated that more than anything. The world around me went black, and then I was staring down, watching the Immortal Plane drift by with a beauty that I'd never experience.

High above the sky, I flew over rocky purple peaks with wild beasts gliding through the air around me. They paid no mind to me or to the lights in the sky. *Souls.* It clicked in my head as I gazed around at them floating through the air with me. Amber clouds wrapped around me, and the souls prodded me onward to some unknown destination. I managed to turn my head again to see the landscape passing beneath us, violet giving way to black and splotches of red and green that echoed with ethereal power. The Immortal Plane was a savage beauty.

It was, even for me, breathtaking.

And yet... something gnawed at my chest. It was hard to describe, but it felt like a deep longing for something. What? I'd experienced that savage hunger vampires got when we had nothing to eat and pounced on anything with darkness, and this was different. It was deeper. I needed something, but I didn't know what that something was.

My head spun. The flying stuff was happening too fast for me. I hated that I couldn't move at all in this throng of souls. Where were we going? I tried to speak, but my throat tightened traitorously. I couldn't get a word out.

The universe handed all of us certain things in life. It handed me an immense capacity for enduring pain. Some mysterious force or vision wasn't going to set me back. *You can do this. You've always known that you can handle anything.*

Something arose from the ground and pulled at me, invisible forces like the unseen threads of life tugging at my body. It felt like thin strands were wrapped around my wrists and ankles, drawing me down, but the current of souls wouldn't let me go. I had to keep going. *What's down there?* It was forest and rocky valleys as far as my eyes could see.

An unseen cord wrapped around my torso and pulled hard, much harder than the current I moved along in. I dropped like a brick as I was yanked from the lazy stream of soul clouds, plummeting toward the ground. *Am I dying?* If this was Death, it was cowardly for not trying to claim me in battle like a true warrior, but instead sneaking up on me in a dream. I wasn't meant to go this way. My destiny was beyond this feverish moment. People out there needed my help.

The kids.

I struggled against the invisible binds, to no success. My body landed. *Or my spirit?* Whatever this nonsense was, I was on the ground now. I saw that familiar bizarre translucent material that had haunted me for weeks. They called it the Pocket Space—far too quaint a name to describe its annoying nature. Hell was more apt, or maybe Bubble Hell, but I'd take it up with the humans later. They named things strangely.

The invisible force pushed me forward until I came to a nearby intersection I knew well. It was the one closest to the entrance of the big bubble where the monster, the Ghost, had taken me. It was where Roxy had found me. I'd heard her name earlier, but now there was nothing but white noise and fuzzy voices in the distance—voices that sounded familiar. Voices that broke my heart, if I listened hard enough, because I heard the echo of my own desperate youth in them.

I was powerless as the force pushed me toward the corner, closer to the entrance. My hopes skyrocketed as a group came into view, and a teenaged boy caught my attention immediately.

"Ricky," I called, but the young human hadn't heard me... or couldn't. Ricky was a tanned kid with freckles, guts, and not much else. He was sixteen, making him the oldest of the gang of children. They were all there from the looks of it—fifteen, I hoped, although I couldn't get a good count with the force moving me toward them so quickly. My vision blurred at the edges as my brain caught up.

These kids—my kids—were alive.

Ricky, in a torn red T-shirt, sat next to Marvin, another human, who was shaking his head profusely at something. I couldn't hear them yet, although I could tell they were talking. One of the wildlings, a girl about eight years old in comparable vampire years, made plant leaves dance from her long grassy hands, and weepy tears streaked down her green face. She had no name I could understand, so I'd called her Flora. A harvester kid named Lurav sat next to her, comforting her.

Not in their defensive fighting stances, I see. They need a lookout, like I told them.

I'd tried to teach them everything I knew before I left, but some habits were hard to break. They weren't warriors yet. They stood around like sitting ducks with the rest of the kids. A warrior's job was never done, and I'd told them that. I wanted to check all of them over for injuries, but the force reached out to turn my perspective toward Ricky.

It was a vessel I had no power of directing yet, like the strings of control were just out of my reach, but I didn't understand how to grasp them. My hands were so close to a solution, but my attention was focused solely on the kids.

Ricky gestured to his compatriots. His face was thinner than I remembered. Before I left, he'd often cried like the others when he thought nobody could hear. I could. Now, there was a hardened expression in his brown eyes that I didn't recognize.

Next to him, a twelve-year-old vampire named Maz stepped forward to interrupt Ricky. He had a sharp, crooked nose that looked more beat up than I remembered. As he stepped into the circle, I wondered where Maz's brother, Brax, was? I couldn't remember seeing him in the crowd. My stomach lurched at that thought, but suddenly their voices filled the air. I willed their discussion to come to me and grasped at it as the only thing I could seem to control.

"I don't know if it's a good idea," Maz said worriedly. One of the younger kids began to cry somewhere out of sight. "We have the food we found from the buildings."

What wasn't a good idea? The kids were starving, and the idea of a dangerous plan made me sick that they were about to do something woefully foolish.

"Who knows if what's in those old cans is even okay to eat, though?" Ricky asked with an annoyed shrug. These two looked haggard.

Brax usually took the lead in these situations, but he wasn't here. It was Maz who now spoke in his brother's assertive voice. Why did he need to take over, and where was Brax?

Ensnared by those creeps is an unfortunate possibility.

I needed to get back to these kids, no matter what anyone said.

"If we don't sneak back into their lair, then we're going to starve no matter what. The monster is gone, but those people are still getting supplies somehow," Ricky said. He pushed his floppy hair out of his face with a scowl.

When I met him in the beginning, he was a cheerful punk. Frustration at myself ate me alive.

Great going, Kane.

If I had been stronger, I could've helped these kids. Instead, I'd passed out and needed Roxy to come rescue me. What kind of adult did that? Left children to fight for themselves? These kids were starving and planning stupid plots to get food. If I was there, I would've yelled at Ricky that we would eat him if he didn't start making better plans.

But starving kids weren't known for thinking clearly.

Maz tensed abruptly. For a moment, I thought he might've sensed me, but instead he said, "I sense presences."

It must be someone the kids were expecting, given their torn faces full of fear and anticipation. The hooded group, maybe. That's who we always stole from when I was with them.

"They're coming," Ricky said excitedly. "Perfect. Instead of going to their hideout, we can ambush them here. We've got to jump them to see if they're carrying supplies. We're going to starve if we don't. We *have* to do it."

"We can't," Maz insisted, and Lurav entered my field of vision, nodding in agreement. "It's too risky."

"He's right," I urged them pointlessly. "Ricky, you need to be careful with this group." My voice fell on deaf ears. Nobody could hear me. I tried to swipe my hand out to snatch Maz's tattered sleeve, but my body couldn't move. Even in this state, my limits betrayed me, again and again.

"Fine," Ricky snapped, conceding defeat when he found no support. "Then we'll hide. Everyone, be quiet."

The children rushed to hide in a small nook, hushing the crying ones among them. They were probably hoping the mysterious cloaked group would pass them by.

I tried once more to get their attention. "You guys need to be careful. You're not even trying to figure out how fast they're coming or from which direction. I taught you better than that. Listen to me."

Nobody heard me. A pull tugged at me again as the kids quieted, and I was ripped away from them. I cried out for Ricky, Flora, any of them— but I was gone from their world. Some force was yanking me through the length of the Pocket Space. I was going, going, and then gone.

Strong but soft hands gripped my shoulders and shook me gently. I smelled the air of Vanim for a moment, before it gave way to the scent of herbs and fire. My mind spun with images of the kids and Roxy's face, the swimming thoughts making my head pulse.

"Kane," a voice called. My blurred vision cleared as I focused on the world around me. The healer, Maefa, stared into my eyes with concern. "Are you with me?"

"Where am I?" I demanded. My dry voice cracked. The kids had been right in front of me. What happened to them?

"You were calling out names in your sleep," the healer said softly. She had been treating me since they'd brought me back from the Pocket Space.

"They found you passed out on the outskirts of the city. You fell out of a tree. Be gentle—you've fractured your arm."

I stared down numbly at my arm in a finely dressed sling. How did I fall out of a tree? It came back to me suddenly... leaving the city, my talk with Roxy, and then waking up in a crazy wild dream or vision. *And the kids.*

"I must have fallen asleep up there and slipped off the branch," I said, trying to smooth over her oncoming questions. She would be expecting something like that from me, probably. "Those herbs you gave me must have been stronger than I thought."

Maefa threw her head back and laughed, her black curls flying. She laughed for several seconds more than she should've done to humor me. I gave her a lopsided smile, since I wasn't sure how I was going to get myself out of her clutches this time. She was kind, but she liked to fuss over me. I didn't want anyone bothering me as I tried to piece together what had just happened.

That wasn't a normal dream. I had never felt anything like that... right?

The kids might be in danger, but it could've been a dream. I both hoped and loathed that it might be real. The kids were in trouble, if what I saw was reality. The experience had been utterly bizarre. I'd lost control for most of it, until I'd managed to finally tune in to their voices properly.

The gnawing sensation of something missing from these mysterious incidents in my life hit me hard again as Maefa bustled around me, humming and chattering about what had happened while I was unconscious. I was missing a part of the puzzle.

"You know, the whole city was searching for you. We even got a call from the Mortal Plane on the new long-distance communicators from one of the humans. He sounded very concerned, based off a tip from one of your human friends. She was awfully worried. It was big news when the most exciting thing we have going on here is construction," Maefa said and offered me some health tonic. I downed it.

It had to be Roxy. She must have been worried when I'd cut off communication without saying goodbye.

Maefa was pleased when I finished the tonic. She filled up another cup, and I cleared my throat after sipping, hoping to figure out a way to get her to leave. Luck was on my side. Someone called for Maefa outside the tent.

"Lay against your pillows, and I'll keep that tonic coming. I put my special blend of herbs in there for you, so you won't be feeling your arm any time soon," Maefa said with a friendly wink. I felt like she was always winking around me. Weird. Had she woven flowers into her hair today? They were making my nose itch. She hovered beside me, reluctant to go to the person who'd called.

"I'm fine," I assured her gruffly, and thanked her as she left. *Because I may be a tough guy, but I'm not a barbarian.*

I settled against the pillows, happy to have some peace even if my mind was in absolute chaos at the moment.

Roxy, are you there? I called for her softly.

Silence greeted me, along with Maefa's fading voice alongside another person as they walked away from the tent. Maefa was probably going to alert Reshi that I was actually conscious now, so she could report back to Lyra.

I know I've been gone for a while.

Silence greeted me. I sipped the bitter liquid Maefa had prescribed. Its tangy taste was bracing, banishing the remnants of my fatigue. I wanted to talk to Roxy, and now she wasn't answering me. I wondered how long she had called out for me before alerting the others. I'd forgotten to ask the healer how much time had passed, although I doubted the woman knew the hours in human time.

Roxy? I asked. *Come on, I know I didn't make you that mad.*

Silence, again. I gritted my teeth, growing a bit frustrated by the lack of action. I had seen the kids. I needed to tell someone, and Roxy was the one I had talked about it with so extensively. Although, she *was* trying to convince me to sit my ass in the healer tent until I was back to full strength.

I gave my arm a grim look. What was I going to do now with this banged-up limb? Problems liked to pile up on me.

Roxy didn't answer, and I was growing worried, more so than I cared to admit. I tried to emulate the feeling of our call from before. She'd wanted to test our connection. It was a wise decision to practice, given that our connection wasn't perfect.

She could be asleep. I growled, irritated by the circumstances I'd found myself in. If I waited any longer to talk to her, the kids might get into more trouble. I wanted her opinion on what to do. Maybe she would have an idea.

If it was a vision and not a dream, my rational brain reminded me. Whatever it was, though, it must have meant something.

Roxy, I'm here. It's Kane. I know I was gone for a while, I said gruffly and then paused. *Sorry about that.*

To my delight, a mocking, sleepy laugh greeted me.

"Kane, is that you?" Roxy asked. She sounded exhausted, like she'd just woken from a deep slumber. I knew the feeling. In an instant, she was fully herself again. "You idiot, it's been over forty-eight hours!"

12

Roxy

"I'm happy to hear from you, too," Kane replied sarcastically. "I'm safe in the Immortal Plane."

His dry tone made my heart skip a beat. It was such an incredible relief to hear from him after his extended silence. Once Lyra had confirmed that he was okay, I'd managed to finally get some sleep. I'd woken up hearing him calling my name, convinced it was a nightmare.

And now, my heart beat wildly against my chest as I hung on his every word.

Darn him for having this effect on me. This thought, fortunately, he didn't seem to hear. I reminded myself that he might be able to hear me if I was too sloppy with my thoughts. He was alive. Better still, he was talking to me. It was really him. Kane was absolutely safe in the Immortal Plane again.

How could you scare me like that? I lobbed at him, expecting some kind of explanation.

"You just called me an idiot, so excuse me. It's very much my daily routine to be difficult," Kane pointed out bluntly. He had me there. He scoffed, but there was a bite of humor to his demeanor.

I sputtered. *It was a term of endearment.*

Was this really happening? He was doing well. I had to pinch myself to believe that it wasn't a fever dream.

"A term of endearment only between us, right?" he asked with a wicked laugh.

I shivered. It was chilly in my room, since I hated using the heater. My bright alarm clock on the bedside table showed that it was four o'clock in the morning. I had been dead asleep when he'd called, but now I was awake like I had just downed a pot of coffee. *It's two hours before my usual alarm. The least you could have done was call an hour later. I was dreaming about zombies.*

That was a lie. I'd been dreaming about him... but I couldn't let him know that. I was careful not to think too hard about it in his presence.

"Ah, I see you were very concerned about me," Kane joked. "Sorry to take you away from your zombies."

I was. He had no idea how worried I had been.

"Oh, I know. They told me that a concerned human ally called in to check on me." I could practically see his gloating smirk as he spoke. I felt oddly exposed, even if he wasn't physically here. I was only wearing my pajamas—a sports bra and a short pair of sleeping shorts. Had I ever been around Kane in anything less than a grubby uniform? He couldn't see me, but it was hard to shake the feeling of intimacy when he was in my freaking mind. I would have liked to see another woman try better.

"I'm joking. I was happy you were worried. The medic told me all about it," Kane said, and I heard the mischievous grin in his voice. "I thought she was going to insist on staying right beside me when I finally woke up. Guess I looked bad. I do have a killer headache."

To be fair, you probably scared the crap out of everyone after falling out of a freaking tree. I was relieved to hear the warmth in his voice. It sounded... affectionate. *I'm glad you didn't die. I was pretty worried when you just cut off without a word.*

"Don't worry. All of Aclathe knows about your call, or Lyra calling because you asked," Kane said. "I mean, even the healers and makers knew."

I pressed a hand against my face, embarrassed. Thank goodness he couldn't see me. He chuckled, which I hoped meant he was exaggerating some of that.

Well, tell me everything already. What happened to you? And don't leave anything out, unless your medic notices you're spacing out and you have to go.

Kane chuckled. "No worries. She went out. She hangs around here way too much. I don't need another Halla in my business." He had a female healer? If he was comparing the medic to Halla, she probably had that style of hovering over him at all times to make sure he was okay. Kane was someone who needed space.

And perhaps I was the tiniest bit jealous, after all, that the medic could be with him physically while I was stuck in the Mortal Plane.

I pulled my blanket over my shoulders to warm myself as we settled into conversation.

"I *was* recovered, I promise. The healer told me that I was saying names in my sleep. I don't know why I fainted. It might just be recovery from the Pocket Space, but... I thought I passed out in the Pocket Space because I was legitimately starving. I don't know what made me pass out this time, and honestly, I hate that."

I pulled the comforter up even more, exposing my feet. Yesterday, Jessie had demanded to paint my toenails bright green. It was after training so I'd relented, mainly because I couldn't find the strength to peel myself off the mat after our Brazilian Jiu-Jitsu drills. I wiggled my toes in the silence. *You said you don't know what made you pass out. Is it hard for you to remember?*

"Yeah, I can't remember much," he said slowly, in such a sad voice that it made my heart weak. "I dreamt of wild things. I think I could hear you calling me a bit, but I was floating above the Immortal Plane for a while. You won't believe it, but I found the kids after that. They're really struggling. They were trying to get supplies from that weird group. I told them not to do it because it was too dangerous for them, but I'm not sure if the cultists found the kids in the end. I must be dreaming about them because I'm worried, but maybe it was real."

His voice grew more serious. It was hedging on that tone he'd used with me before, when he was determined to rush in and save the kids. And he was in no condition to do any such thing. Honestly, I wasn't sure if his dream was an actual vision or not.

Are you sure? I played with the frayed ends of my blanket.

"I feel it in my bones, Roxy. They're in trouble."

I stilled at his use of my name. *It might just be a dream, though. They might be okay. You don't know that they're in danger.*

"And *you* don't know that they're safe," Kane insisted. He was getting worked up, although his anger wasn't really directed at me. "They were barely surviving when I left them. If it really was just a dream, the reality could be even worse."

Yes, he had a point, but he had just passed out and fallen from a tree for reasons unknown. How was he going to save them in that condition? He might be injured or suffering from some kind of weird Pocket Space illness with all this fainting. He needed backup, at the very least.

"I'm going to find them," Kane declared defiantly. "I think they're in trouble."

I ground my teeth. *Of course* he was declaring a quest from his hospital bed. Of course he was, because he was the most infuriating vampire I'd ever met.

You're going to be the death of me, you know that? I'm begging you to take a break. I stood to pace my bedroom, suddenly restless. *You aren't even healed yet, from the sounds of it.*

"Who cares about my arm—" Kane cut off. I raised an eyebrow at my tired reflection as I caught sight of myself in the mirror in my bedroom.

What's that about your arm? He couldn't wriggle out of this one.

"Uh, well, when I fell, I banged it."

His weak excuse made me roll my eyes.

Banged it how bad?

"Slightly," Kane said. He was lying through his teeth. "It was just a bad bump on the way down."

I stamped my foot, wishing he was here so I could kick him. *Do anything but lie to me, Kane. What happened?*

"I hit it coming down when I passed out. It's not a big deal. I could still get to the kids like this."

He was stubbornly clinging to an idea that was sure to get him killed.

What exactly is your plan? If you really did see the kids, there's still no way back to the Pocket Space. Even if you could get there, you can't expect to save them with a busted arm.

"I'll go to the makers and the vampire scholars of the barrier until we figure something out," Kane argued fiercely. "They can find a way to get me back there, I bet. Maybe we can even find another Ghost. If there was one, there could be more."

Despite myself, a smile tugged at my lips. His passion stirred a deep sense of connection over our similarities and only reinforced how close

I felt to him. I leaned my head against the wall, cursing this handsome, driven vampire and his good heart. He wanted to save the kids. I got that, but he was going to kill himself if he wasn't careful.

I had to tell him this was a bad idea for more than one reason. He would fight me—duh, it was Kane—and he was going to make me feel bad for bringing it up, but I couldn't back down from this. I cared about him too much to watch him get himself hurt, or worse, killed.

I've never been one to hold my tongue.

"Tell me about it."

Shush. Look, Kane, I think your heart is in the right place, but you're simply not well enough to be staging a dangerous mission like this. I paced around my apartment as I presented my argument, knowing I would have to find every good point I could make to convince him.

First, you've got to figure out why you're passing out. You can't go on another mission until you do, since you could pass out in the middle of fighting, and then the kids would really be in trouble trying to protect themselves and you. Until then, you're not going anywhere. You don't want to be a burden to them, do you?

"No," Kane grumbled. He paused for a moment of grumpy silence. "I'm just so tired of my body holding me back. I can't understand it."

Kane had had worries about his health before. This was a side of him I had seen by accident, before he realized I could hear his thoughts. I'd overheard him recounting his childhood.

When he was younger, Kane had worked harder than all the other vampire kids his age just to keep up with them. His healing had always been slower. I frowned, mulling over the bits of his life that I'd seen from afar. Something was strange about the way Kane healed, but there could probably be underlying health issues, even among vampires, that caused such a thing. I figured the medics would've picked up on something by now, though.

How long until your arm is okay?

"She didn't have a chance to say," Kane said with a sigh. "All these injuries are taking far longer to heal than the average vampire. It makes me furious."

I smiled, knowing the feeling exactly. We were so similar that talking to him often felt like talking to another version of myself.

I can imagine. Do you feel comfortable talking to the medic about your healing progress?

"I'm not sure she'll be much help, but there might be someone who could give me more information." His tone held a note of melancholy and reluctance, something I wasn't used to from Kane.

Who?

After a long pause, he finally answered. "Halla. She's always noticed something about me that made her force me to work hard, and I want to know what that was. Looks like we're in for a difficult conversation, because something isn't adding up here."

13

Lyra

*C*am stretched his arms up and yawned as we approached the little burger joint where we'd be meeting Alicia's best friend, Isabella. Torres had already gone over what information they had of her testimony about what happened to her friend, but with the fact teenagers were involved, and likely being secretive, I hoped to get something more out of Isabella with this meeting. Which was why I'd brought out the big gun— Cam.

"Don't tell me you're tired. I know the camper isn't the best place we've ever slept, but I need you to be on your A-game," I told him, though I flashed him a grin.

He rolled his eyes and smirked while opening the door for me like a true gentleman. "What you mean is you need me to low-key flirt with a teenager."

I scoffed as he held the door open for me, letting me go in first. He was a young, fairly good-looking man despite the unique vibrancy of his hair that made him stand out. And he was friendly and chivalrous. Girls ate that up—especially teenagers.

"I don't want you to flirt with her. Just be your regular charming self," I quipped as the server behind the counter greeted us. We found a table and sat down to await the girl and her mother.

There were very few people here yet this early, since the place had just opened. We sat next to the large window overlooking the parking lot, both of us occupying the same side of the booth that allowed us to see the door. The team's RV was visible from this vantage point, as well.

Not that I thought there was any reason for worry at a fast food place with a teenage girl, but as team leader, I always wanted to have my people within my sights if I could. A survival skill I'd been taught early on.

Cam sighed. "Fine. I'll play your game. But can I have a milkshake?"

I laughed. "Have at it."

Cam got up from the seat and ambled to the counter, then returned a few minutes later and sat back down, offering me a paper cup of coffee.

"A brave soul," I told him, gesturing to the giant vanilla milkshake he'd gotten himself. "I couldn't handle quite that much sugar for my first meal of the day."

I sipped my coffee, briefly entertaining an order of waffles and hashbrowns before I decided my stomach wasn't ready for food yet.

The old-fashioned bell on the door chimed as a woman in her early forties entered followed by a teen girl with brown hair and matching eyes that darted around nervously.

Cam must have noticed the sudden stiffening in my shoulders. He followed my gaze and then smoothly exited the booth to greet them and offer his hand.

"Ladies! Welcome," Cam boomed in his most charming tone. His voice was happy. Warm. This was exactly why I'd brought him here.

The girl, presumably Isabella, gave him a sheepish smile, but her mother accepted Cam's shake. She had the same brown, wispy hair but green eyes instead of brown.

"Hello," Mrs. Lopez said politely. Her gaze darted between Cam and me, since I knew she was only expecting me.

I half-stood, still pinned by the table, and held out my hand. "Hi, Mrs. Lopez, Isabella," I added, nodding at the girl. "This is my associate, Cam. Thanks for joining us. Please, have a seat."

At my prompting, Cam slid back into the booth next to me, allowing the two females to slip in on the other side of us.

"Cam," Mrs. Lopez said, as if committing his name to memory. "So you must be Lyra, then?"

"I am. And the rest of my team is out there in the camper." I pointed through the giant picture window at the RV crouching at the back of the lot, and Isabella stifled a laugh.

Cam winked at her and gave her a teasing grin. "Yeah, it's a bit showy for my taste too."

I focused on my coffee and let Cam handle the initial small talk to ease their tension. Especially for Mrs. Lopez, whose shoulders were practically glued to her neck. A server sidled over to take their orders, and I zoned out, staring out the window at the RV and thinking about the team.

I was glad to have found most of them in good spirits this morning, despite the blowout with Torres yesterday.

Sike's smiling face had greeted me first, his teeth flashing bright as he jumped down from the loft. There'd been something about him, a kind of smug glow that I recognized all too well as the look on a man's face after a night of... *fun*.

Chandry was much happier as well, which—on the surface—was good because I didn't want anyone's anger and opinions jeopardizing this mission. Not Torres's and not my team's. Despite the challenges of this case, I needed this win. *We* needed this win to make up for the last loss.

But most importantly, Alicia and the other missing kids needed us to stay and work this out.

However, it seemed pretty clear this morning what took place last night between the two vampires. I worried that jumping into bed with Sike wasn't the best way to cope with her feelings.

In real life, it would be none of my business, nor would I care what two grown adults did with their time. But the fact that she was in the human world for the first time, and trying to learn the ropes on my team, made it my business because what if she didn't deal with this properly and it blew up in our faces later? And what if these coping mechanisms with Sike also blew up in our face?

I guess, *for now*, I'd have to let it slide. At least it kept them upbeat, and upbeat meant no more knock-down, drag-outs with Torres or his team. If a warm body could let her put the Torres thing aside, that was more important at the moment.

And heck—even I was still seething at the guy quietly.

I could tell Dorian had noticed the situation too, since not much got past him, though if he had an opinion he kept it to himself. Bryce, on the other hand, did not.

His coping mechanism with whatever was going on with Arlonne, was to razz Sike about his sleeping arrangements with a little more vitriol than neccessary. When I called him out on it, he went off on me, which escalated to a minor fight. I sent him off to deal with Torres while the others remained behind to pore over evidence.

Maybe Chandry had the right idea, to be honest. Bryce needed to deal with his crap. I didn't want him ruining the mission. If anything, he could certainly take out that grumpiness on Torres. In fact, they could take out their bad attitudes on each other.

Sometimes being a team leader was just being a glorified babysitter.

Cam nudged me with an elbow, drawing me back into the present. I jolted and refocused as I realized Cam was steering us away from small talk and into questioning. As expected, Isabella, started relaying all over again the things we already knew.

Alicia had been talking to someone online and then wanted to meet up with them on the outskirts of the Leftovers. She had then gone to Isabella, her best friend, to tell her about a chance to meet up with this person and get some kind of information. What information exactly was unclear, as Isabella still wasn't elaborating, if she even knew at all.

I tried to watch her body language to catch a hint of if there was more to the story. The girl was closed off, sure—shoulders tense, arms crossed, gaze looking everywhere but at us. And while that didn't necessarily mean anything but a case of nerves, I'd have to wait to touch base with Dorian in the camper. He'd be feeling these two out from afar and would tell me afterward if she and her mother were trustworthy and if there was any darkness about them.

I wanted to know if the two of them could be hiding something. I would have hated to think that either of them was involved, but when it came to cases of missing kids, every aspect had to be explored.

I latched onto something Alicia said and held up a hand to pause her story. "Wait. Alicia was going to ride her bike to meet this person?"

Isabella nodded.

"That would have taken hours. Did you not find that suspicious?" My question was probably a little bit harsh, but I needed to give something for Dorian to gauge.

Mrs. Lopez, to her credit, turned a wary side eye on her daughter, too.

Isabella's eyes darted away from Cam where they had been fixed ever since she sat down across from us and looked at me instead. "I did tell her she shouldn't go. I advised her against it, especially meeting a stranger alone that she met online. We all know that stuff is not a good idea. But she compromised and said she would text me for her safety. She insisted on going. She said she needed this information really badly."

Cam gave her a sympathetic look. "And the text you got from her, the last one, was of a license plate right?"

Isabella nodded, and she looked down at where her hands were clasped in her lap below the table. Before her lashes hid her rich brown eyes, I saw tears welling.

"I'm sorry about your friend." I said, my voice more gentle as I leaned forward and hoped I didn't seem too intimidating. We'd even worn our dressy uniforms for this occasion in hopes of looking less gruff and more inviting. "It sounds like you tried to stop her. To protect her. You did the right thing."

The girl's breathing was a bit erratic, and her tears threatened to spill over. I looked at Cam and nodded, hoping he could defuse a bit of her distress, as well as get in some follow-up questions that might lead her to tell us more.

Maybe more of something we didn't already know.

I suspected that the reason Alicia had gone to Isabella was because she trusted her. And if she trusted Isabella, she likely would have told her what it was she wanted information about. Though, the information we had so far—having looked at the forums Torres had shown us—gave me certain suspicions about what Alicia might have wanted to know. But why?

How many of these instances of strange occurrences and powers were hoaxes or wishful thinking, and how many were real?

Had Alicia been exhibiting powers herself?

But no matter how Cam poked and prodded, we continued to go around in circles.

"You've been very brave for your friend, Isabella," I assured the girl. "We want to find her and bring her back to you and her family. Is there anything more you can tell us about the day or night she disappeared? Or maybe how she was acting before she left?"

Isabella bit her lip and looked back and forth from her mother to Cam. I bristled, though I tried to hide it, as I wondered if there was already some discussion with her mother we weren't privy to, one where her mother had either dismissed her or made her feel like it wasn't safe to talk.

Cam pushed his milkshake away and leaned down, his voice very quiet like he was about to share a secret with her. His voice, though, quiet or not, was serious. "Isabella, I promise you that whatever you say, no matter what, we will believe you."

See, this was why I needed him. I didn't know how we'd operated without Cam before. He'd become an integral part of the team.

When Isabella didn't immediately speak up, he added, "We're just here to help you find your friend, and we've seen some very weird things."

Cam had that right. People-eating, murderous trees was just one of the many oddities we'd run into lately. That didn't include anything before Callanish existed.

Isabella took a deep breath and scooted forward in her seat, placing her hands on the table.

Good, he was making her feel a little safer to speak.

Isabella leaned away from her mother and spoke somewhat haltingly. "Alicia had been feeling and acting strange for a while before any of this," she admitted.

I narrowed my eyes on Mrs. Lopez. *Oh yeah, this woman definitely made her feel like she couldn't share any of this.* My parents had been very rigid, but as long as I was being responsible, they never made assumptions or made me feel like I couldn't say or share anything, even if it was crazy. I didn't think it was just about being in The Bureau either.

But I wasn't here to give parental lessons. I had no place, anyway, since I wasn't a mother myself. I couldn't say how I'd be as a parent.

It couldn't be easy.

"*Feeling?*" I coaxed. "Was she sick?"

Isabella shook her head. "Not exactly. She was having problems focusing in school, which wasn't like her, and then she had all these headaches. We've been best friends for a long time, but she was also getting distant from even me. And her family. She was spending most of her time alone and online close to the time when she...*disappeared*."

Isabella hesitated to say the last word. It must have been so surreal for a 14-year-old to be experiencing the loss of her friend like this. The Leftovers and the confusion about what was going on with the world had to make it a difficult time for youth.

Cam cleared his throat. "You say *online*. We know a lot about a website she might have been on. *Occult Geeks*. Do you know anything about that?"

"It's... a forum. A lot of people were on there talking about things she was having trouble with. There were people, Alicia said, just like her. Having headaches and..."

Isabella looked down, nearly retreating inside herself again. Repeating herself like that, being focused on just the headaches, made me feel like she was holding back.

I pursed my lips and held my tongue. I wanted to say something. Either shake it out of her or tell the mother to leave, but we needed to remain calm.

Unfortunately, questioning Isabella—a minor—away from her mother was out of the question. The red tape alone would set our case load back days.

I usually wasn't on edge like this either, but it wasn't fair there were so many innocents involved and Isabella's mother was clearly keeping the girl from *fully* sharing. Add that to the issues with Torres, and I was ready to burst with emotions I had been trying to keep tampered down for my team.

Chandry might have felt comfy losing it on Torres, but I didn't have that option.

"It's alright," Cam said. "No matter what it is, it could help us find her. Nobody's in trouble or judging. Not you and not Alicia."

As he said the word "judging," I locked eyes with Mrs. Lopez so she knew she needed to let her daughter speak. Though, by the way she wriggled in her seat and sat forward with her shoulders hovering near her ears, I didn't think she'd keep her mouth shut much longer.

Isabella looked at both of us, sizing us up. I remained still, a small smile on my face that I hoped looked encouraging.

Isabella looked out the window for a moment toward the RV, crossing her arms even tighter over her chest until she buried her hands in her armpits. She didn't look at anyone when she said, "Alicia was hearing a voice in her head. A woman talking. She looked for answers online and found... well, you know the story."

Cam and I exchanged glances, but before we could assess or ask any more questions, Mrs. Lopez added her two cents.

"It's clear your poor friend was having a mental breakdown," she chided, directing the statement to Isabella and Isabella alone.

I had to intervene before the woman undid the brief bit of work we'd accomplished.

"We don't want to rule out any options," I explained, doing my best to keep my tone even and respectful. "We have reason to believe that Alicia wasn't crazy. We're here to examine everything, all the evidence. It's why we've been brought on to the case."

Isabella's eyes lit up, and she let out a relieved breath, looking at me with all the happiness of a drowning girl being thrown a life raft. I got the feeling she'd been getting a lot of judgment and so had her missing friend, which certainly explained her unwillingness to be truly open.

Alicia could have been out there, severely injured or maybe even dead, and people were speculating about whether she belonged in a nut house.

"I didn't think she was either!" The words rushed out of Isabella. "I mean...the whole thing sounds crazy, and she was acting weird, but..."

"It's okay go on," I urged with a nod.

"I was with her when she had her headaches and a few times when she heard the voice. She wasn't losing it. Just confused. I'm so sorry," Isabella added, her voice wavering. Cracking with emotion. "I should have said all of this sooner, I just thought everyone would think I was crazy, too, like they think about her."

Cam's face softened and he reached across the table to give her arm a quick pat. This poor girl was about to break. "I understand Isabella. Maybe one day, I'll explain to you some of the things I've seen so you won't feel so alone."

The teen's lips quirked into a small, nervous smile.

Cam spoke up again, laying it on thick with that patented charm. "We appreciate what you're telling us, Isabella. I know it can be hard, but you're very brave. You might even save Alicia's life. Any little bit helps. Do you happen to know anything about the person she was talking to online or in her head?"

"Um, not a whole lot. It was a woman's voice," Isabella confirmed, her gaze drifting over my shoulder as she seemed to think back on things. "She had, like, a code name? That's what Alicia called it. Mother something..." Isabella paused, thinking for a moment.

I hoped she could remember and tell us. A code name could very well match up with a username.

Isabella's expression lit up, and she snapped her fingers. "UniversalMother11! I don't know why the number."

She shrugged, obviously going for an air of ambivalence, but her emotions were all over her face. She felt guilty for holding this crucial piece of evidence back.

Now we're getting somewhere.

"Great job remembering!" Cam held up a hand for a high five, and Isabella giggled as their hands slapped together. Some of her guilt washed away with the move. "Was that who she was going to meet? UniversalMother11?"

Isabella straightened, her shoulders setting one by one in a physical example of her determination. "Yes. I didn't want to say earlier about the... the *voice* and meeting the woman she could hear speaking in her head because..."

She trailed off, and I thought she wasn't going to continue, until the next words burst out of her like she'd been holding them in for days.

"I mean, people might just think she ran away and not investigate! That kind of thing...it happens sometimes around here, even when it's not supernatural, and I couldn't let it happen to Alicia. She's not just some sick, crazy runaway. She's my best friend."

Her voice cracked on that last word, and to Mrs. Lopez's credit, the woman slid an arm around her daughter's shoulders to comfort her.

Law enforcement could be such a big help, but sometimes it was also a pain in the ass, between all the bureacracy plus a shortage of manpower that placed working officers on bigger, more higher profile cases. Miami was full of minorities and impoverished people, often outnumbering what America believed to be the majority here, and those were the first citizens to fall through the cracks. To be looked over. Forgotten.

A kid shouldn't have had to worry about that with her friend missing. She should have felt comfortable going to law enforcement for help but instead, she'd clearly learned a healthy disrespect for the work they did.

Or didn't do, rather.

Isabella continued. "This person, UniversalMother11? She was going to explain everything to Alicia. About the voices, the headaches, what was happening to her, all of it. I tried to get her not to go, but she was determined to get answers. How could I deny her that?"

"Of course not," I agreed. "You did what you should have, Isabella. I promise you, we're going to do everything in our power to get Alicia home safe."

Cam and I stood, saying our goodbyes and *thank-yous* to Mrs. Lopez and Isabella in the diner lobby before we watched them leave.

Once they were headed out the door, I pulled out my comm then keyed up, eyes on the RV. "Dorian, be sure you get a read on these two as they come out of the restaurant."

We had to use every opportunity to make sure we knew what we were dealing with. Though we obviously had two suspects, thanks to the CCTV footage, so it was safe to assume Mrs. Lopez wasn't involved, I still needed to know who to trust here.

"Got it," my husband responded from inside the RV.

Cam and I waited for the woman and her daughter to pull out of the lot in their silver Honda before finally walking out, Cam holding the door for me yet again.

Dorian's voice came through the comm again as we walked back to the RV. "No bad intentions. They're both light souls as far as all three of us can tell. Just a typical teenager and her mother not believing her."

"Yeah, that's how I felt about it, too," I said back just as we hit the door and opened it.

Cam and I hopped up the steps into the camper, and I glanced around at the team. Bryce was still MIA, likely sparring with Torres back at headquarters, but Chandry, Sike, and Dorian were all seated around the lounge area, surrounded by binders of evidence.

I continued my thoughts off the comm. "They were telling the truth then. I don't see any reason for them not to, even though the mom made Isabella feel terrible for what she was saying."

Cam grimaced. "Unfortunately, it sounds like the truth might be of limited use to us."

He was right. Our interview with Isabella still left us with more questions than answers. Even if the username and codename were spot on with each other, it didn't guarantee the ability to identify the person behind it. If they were truly committing a crime, they would cover their tracks.

Our team was good and might be able to eventually trace the source, but that wasn't happening today.

"So, what do you think, boss?" Sike asked.

I noted with a kind of dry amusement that Chandry was sitting close by. Closer than usual.

Ugh, hopefully, the two won't become a problem one way or the other.

I considered my words carefully. "It's more and more likely this is similar to what Jessica said she had been experiencing. We have to assume—now, at least—that the criminals are targeting teens who might have manifested some kind of powers. But I couldn't say what they might do with these kids, even if they did have some kind of new supernatural skill."

Dorian's low tone chimed in. "I think we all know exactly what the possibilities might be, but they might be too horrific to think about right now."

I shivered.

This case was shaping up to be just as frustrating as the last.

Who truly was the ringleader in all of this?

Those beings who took Jessica and her boyfriend in the Pocket Space came back to the forefront of my mind, and I wondered, if not for the first time, what interaction they had with the Mortal Plane or other planes of existence, how they were traveling, and what really it was that they wanted.

Other than to be a problem.

If the two criminals in this case ended up being connected to them, I didn't know what kind of tangled web was being weaved.

Or if we'd be able to unravel it in time to save anyone at all.

14

Lyra

*T*he team ate a quick and easy lunch in the RV while Sike and Cam scoured the forums for some information on UniversalMother11, though nothing much came from it. They submitted to *Occult Geeks* again, asking if they could provide more records. It was a miracle Torres had what he did already, since there were all kinds of legal hoops to jump through in order to get the webmaster to comply.

Social media and cell phone services these days were all about protecting privacy to the point of lengthy and expensive court battles. Even if it hurt human lives in the process.

Torres had mentioned there were other websites, though, and we didn't have access to all of them. That would likely become a battle for later down the road.

I worked silently beside Dorian, flipping through binders and bagged evidence I'd already been over half a dozen times. The hope was, at some point, I'd notice something with different eyes.

By early afternoon, Bryce returned from his sojourn with Torres, looking somewhat more loose and less wound up. A verbal boxing match with Torres had been just the thing he needed to get past his bad mood. For the time being, at least.

Score point for me.

Chandry slouched down onto the bench beside me, her eyes sparking with adventure. "So where are we headed to next?"

I closed the binder in front of me on the table. "I'm actually sending Bryce and Cam out on a field trip."

Bryce scowled. "Not back to headquarters?"

"I take it dealing with Torres this morning wasn't pleasant?" I asked, though I knew it was more than that.

Bryce mumbled something incoherent about men who didn't know their "arses from a hole in the ground," but I let it slide without asking for more details. As long as Torres hadn't wrecked the whole game by sending us packing, I'd let Bryce handle the dirty work with him.

I tapped the red plastic binder I'd been reading. "Based on this, we have a few suspects, though all of them are pretty weak. For the time being, I want to focus on one in particular. Not the woman from the CCTV footage, but the other supposed female." Flipping open the binder, I began paging forward to the location with her information. I'd been over this binder so many times—upside, downside, and sideways—that I could have found her in my sleep.

"She isn't the one from the picture," I went on as I paused at her dossier. "Not the one thought to be taking the kids directly, but Torres and his team seemed to have a lot of suspicion about her which is backed up simply by the fact that she had an account on multiple occult sites. Her username was the same on all, and she didn't hide her identity well."

Cam spoke up. "Does her username match UniversalMother11 in any way?"

"Unfortunately, no," I said, standing with a sigh. I stretched, then slipped from the bench to pace from the living area to the kitchenette and back. "Unless you think 'PsychicAna' could be misconstrued as UniversalMother."

"Not in any obvious way," Cam replied thoughtfully.

Dorian's gaze marked my pacing as he said, "That doesn't mean they aren't one and the same."

Pivoting on my heel to pace back to the kitchenette, I agreed. "We can hope."

Sometimes, being in this thing made me feel like I was a caged lion. But at least it allowed us to save some money and to get to each other easily. To be fair, traveling as a team in an RV wasn't necessarily a bad thing.

Cam placed his hands on either side of the open binder, gaze roaming PsychicAna's known information. "Wasn't she sighted near where several of the disappearances happened?"

"Glad someone was paying attention," I teased, rotating back towards the lounge area. "She's confirmed in the area for several of the disappearances, but it may or may not be accounted for in the fact she calls herself a psychic. We know from experience that those with any kind of supernatural fascination, power, or inkling like to hang around the Leftovers and other suspicious places."

I didn't have to be a genius to know all of us were thinking about Jessica when I pointed out the obvious. I wondered what she was up to at the moment, and if she had so easily become one of the bad guys or if she was regretting her decision at all.

Bryce grunted from his place near the front of the camper. "It didn't seem like there was any concrete evidence, though."

"Good catch. No, there isn't technically the kind of evidence that leads to more than a few suspicions."

Cam agreed. "Circumstantial, at best."

"Again," I went on, "because she claims to be psychic, there could be multiple possibilities why it seems like she was involved. That's why I need Cam and Bryce to go talk to her. To see what she has to say for herself."

Dorian perked up at that. "We have her personal information?"

"She didn't exactly hide her identity. Or at least sucked at trying," I joked.

"And what will the rest of you be doing?" Bryce asked.

Though he conjured up a grin to take the accusation from his words, the gesture was empty. His tone still came out accusatory and irritated.

If he wasn't a long-time friend, and I didn't understand what he was facing with Arlonne, I would have slapped that expression right off him.

Clearly, his tete-a-tete with Torres that morning hadn't been enough to erase all his vampire romance drama.

But I bit my tongue and cut my gaze to Dorian. In all reality, my emotions could run high about my relationship too. When things were rough between us, my head probably wasn't all in it, either.

"We'll be listening in on the comms," I said. And probably avoiding Torres if we could help it, but I didn't say that part out loud. I was sure I wasn't the only one who felt that way, though.

The more evidence we could present him with before we needed him for anything else, the better.

"But we aren't coming *with* you," I went on. "I don't want to be too conspicuous with an RV plopped down in the middle of a residential street. Nor do I want to piss Torres off by parading even camouflaged vampires around a human neighborhood. Not unless we have to. As long as we're in his territory, we gotta play his game."

"Yeah, okay," Bryce said shortly. "Get me the address, and I'll see if we can get a car." Before anybody could bother to reply, he sulked off towards the bedroom at the back of the camper, where all of our suitcases were stored.

Cam shot me an apologetic look for his uncle, scribbled PsychicAna's address on a waiting Post-It note, then followed after him.

As Sike and Chandry fell into quiet conversation, Dorian unfolded from the bench seat and crossed the small kitchenette in one stride. Angling behind me, he took hold of my shoulders and his fingers began to work knots from my muscles.

"You need to sit down and relax," he murmured, his lips so close to my ear that his breath on my skin sent a delicious tingle down my spine. "You know we'll figure this out. You're the best leader anyone could hope to have on this case."

Instead of taking his advice to sit, I slowly eased back against him. As my back rested heavily against his chest, his hands migrated from my shoulders to my waist, and he encircled me, taking some of my weight into his own grip, as if he could hold me tight enough to wipe away the stress.

Sliding my hands over his, I turned my head to rest against his collarbone. "I'm just worried. They're only kids, Dorian. So vulnerable and impressionable. And it's been too long for some of them. What if..."

I trailed off, not wanting to finish the sentence.

His arms tightened around me. "We've done the impossible before, and we'll do it again."

We rarely spent much time being affectionate around the rest of the team, so we only stayed like that for a few seconds. But his embrace was more restful and relaxing to me than if I *had* sat down. By the time we stepped away from each other, I was ready to roll.

Good timing, too, as Bryce and Cam came back from the bedroom in fresh clothes with a messenger bag clinging to Bryce's shoulder. We made sure the comms had working batteries then sent them on their way the minute a Bureau representative arrived with a non-descript, older model Crown Vic.

While we waited for them to arrive at their destination, I gave the rest of the team a quick debrief on PsychicAna.

"Full name Anastasia Fry," I read from the dossier. "Has a degree in secondary education but doesn't have current employment. At least, not that we've found. Lives in a modest Spanish-style ranch in a dodgy part of town."

Sike scoffed. "Psychic*Ana*. Psychic Anastasia. Not very imaginative."

"If she's trying to hide anything, she's terrible at it," I agreed. "An amateur at best, considering her real identity was easily accessible through *Occult Geeks*. Still, she might be able to help us."

I had to have hope that she knew something, *anything*, that could bring us closer to the kids or to the missing pieces we needed to understand these strange, unexpected powers plaguing teens in Miami.

No matter how much time passed, the Leftovers continued to present new problems every day.

It made me worry about what we would find out next. How it would continue to escalate.

How many more lives would be at stake.

Chandry asked, "So, what are her correspondences like on this website? What does Torres think she could have done?"

Though her tone regarding Anastasia Fry was curious, there was a bit of a bite to the way she said Torres's name.

Sike grinned and scooted his laptop closer to her, catching her eye as he purposefully moved closer until their bodies were touching. "I can take this one. Let me show you."

I shared a private, amused smile with Dorian. The two were way too obvious. How long before they tired of one another, though? And what would that do to the team?

As we waited to hear from Bryce and Cam that they'd arrived at Anastasia's place, Sike went over some of Anastasia's interactions on the websites, including *Occult Geeks*.

"She seems overly helpful mostly," he explained to Chandry, seemingly forgetting that Dorian and I were even in the room. "She's very outspoken about her abilities and tells some of the kids she suspects they're psychic, too. She gives some of these powers names like clairaudience and clairsentience."

For all my work with the supernatural at The Bureau, I didn't know much about the occult. My experience remained firmly rooted in the cold hard facts of what The Bureau had experienced, and psychic phenomena wasn't really one of those things. So while I'd heard the terms before, I couldn't tell anyone a whole lot about them.

"Look, she's talking to a few teens," Sike said, pointing at the screen. "Saying she can help them develop their powers."

I leaned over where Sike was indicating and skimmed the few lines of conversation, but there was nothing explicit about meeting up with anyone. She was very active in the forums but didn't talk about seeing any of the kids in person.

I was very interested to hear what she had to say for herself, though. And in what secret information might have been hiding in her private messages.

The comm came to life, and Bryce's voice rumbled through the speaker. "We're pulling up now, Lyra. Let's see if she answers her door. Her car's out front."

Bryce's accent was even more obvious over the comm. I looked at the others and nodded, glad that they'd caught her at home. Better to get this over with and figure out how to proceed. I hated being idle.

Chandry sat across from me with Sike while Dorian settled next to me, and I placed the comm on the table between us so we could listen in.

We heard Bryce's heavy-handed knock on the door. Bryce meant business, and Cam could easily switch into a serious stance, looking every bit as intimidating as his uncle, if he wanted to. He just typically chose not to.

Maybe this Anastasia woman would get the picture and know it was in her best interest to answer the questions they had to get rid of them.

But then again if she *was* responsible, she would be lying. Even without any vampire senses, Bryce would be able to sniff that out. He was experienced in so many ways with the best and the worst of people.

Then a sound like a door opening.

"Can I help you?" A bell-like voice chimed through the comm. There was a tinge of worry in there, considering she'd just looked over the two men in their uniforms and scrutinized what they wanted with her.

"Are you Anastasia Fry?" Cam asked in a voice so cold it gave me chills.

"I am. What is this about?"

It was Bryce's turn to speak. "You're aware of a website called *Occult Geeks* and have a profile there and on several similar occult sites."

It was maddening not being able to see and read her body language. I had to trust that Cam and Bryce could handle that part of things, and I knew they could. I just hated being blind and not in control of such a pivotal meeting.

I gripped the table, my knuckles white, as Anastasia quipped, "Yes, and as far as I know, having an online account isn't illegal and neither is talking to people about the supernatural."

She was a cheeky one. I could imagine Bryce being temporarily taken aback by her response.

"No, it's not," Cam said agreeably. "But we have some questions about your interactions there and some of your claims. There have been some missing persons associated with the website."

"The missing teens. From the news." She didn't miss a beat.

I couldn't tell if she was *too* knowledgeable and trying to give them a hard time or if she was maybe worried enough about the teens and the supernatural happenings that she was keeping track of it as much as she could with as little information as was being put out in the media.

"Yes, sounds like you know about them," Bryce said.

I gritted my teeth and hoped his judgment and bad mood wouldn't chase her off and send her slamming the door in their faces.

"Why don't the two of you come in? I'll answer your questions, but I don't know how much I can help."

I turned to Dorian, my jaw dropping open. His eyes were wide in a similar shock.

"She's letting them in," I whispered. I didn't know what to make of it. In most investigations, even paltry, uninvolved witnesses tended to be supremely unhelpful in interviews.

Chandry sat up on the edge of her seat like this was the most entertaining radio show ever.

The slam of the door came through on the comms, and there were some footsteps and muffled sounds as the group of three got settled somewhere inside Anastasia's house. She offered refreshments, and Bryce declined.

Anastasia was the first to break the potent silence that followed. "I'm assuming the reason you're here has to do with the kinds of posts I was answering. You don't exactly look like typical law enforcement to me."

Perceptive. Was she using these supposed psychic powers she had or was she just observant?

There was a rustle of paper, and then Cam spoke, redirecting the conversation. "Is this you talking on a forum in *Occult Geeks*?"

A mere second passed before she confirmed. "Yes. There are so many people coming into their strengths now more than ever before, and a lot of them are young. They're scared. I've been doing what little bit I can to help. I've always felt it was my job to help teach others."

It was too perfect, but I had to remind myself we had little to go on, barely any circumstantial evidence. And she was linked to more than just those who went missing.

Bryce cleared his throat. "The problem is, a lot of these kids you've claimed to be helping have turned up missing. Have you ever tried to meet with any of them in person?"

Anastasia didn't answer right away this time. The direct question must have stunned her.

"No, of course not," she said haughtily.

"But you've been around the Leftovers a lot."

"They're tempting, especially for someone with psychic gifts. Sometimes just being close heightens my powers. Not that I expect you to believe me."

Her tone was angry.

"Oh, I wouldn't say that," Cam responded, going for upbeat. They were playing the *Good Cop, Bad Cop* card. "So you don't know anything about the whereabouts of any of the missing teens?"

"No. I wouldn't hurt anyone or take anyone. Nor would I push someone so young too far too soon with their gifts. I'm just being encouraging and soothing in online forums. Sometimes I do online sessions and classes but not for anyone under eighteen. It's not exactly something just anyone should be messing with."

I looked to Dorian, my eyebrow raising. I wondered what he was getting from this. He shrugged, and I glanced from Sike to Chandry, trying to gauge their feelings about the situation.

Sike shook his head. "She's kind of weird, maybe standoffish, but I'm not getting conspiracy to commit kidnapping or child trafficking."

Chandry shook her head. "I don't think so either."

"Well, we can't clear her entirely," I pointed out. "There's something weird about her, right? Or is it just me?"

Dorian replied, "She might know more about the Leftovers and the mysterious new powers, but that doesn't make her harmful."

The interview unraveled from there, leaving us with far fewer answers than I hoped for going in. As Cam and Bryce advise Anastasia to stay in town just in case we needed to speak again, I sank back against the back of the bench and huffed out a sigh.

We didn't need to bother her in her own home any further. Not right now anyway. But I felt like we'd hit another dead end.

Just as the interview ended and Cam and Bryce said their goodbyes, my phone began to buzz. Torres's Miami number flashed across my screen, and I was glad he'd called me and not Bryce or anyone else at the moment. I was probably the only one who could keep my temper at bay when dealing with him, and as much as I'd enjoyed setting Bryce on the man this morning, my temper had passed, and it was time to be political.

I could only hope that he had gotten over his attitude or at least realized that he was going to have to work with us cooperatively whether he liked it or not if he wanted to save these kids.

"Torres?" I responded as I picked up the phone. I kept my tone light and professional. "What can I help you with? "

"We actually have a bit of a lead on the stuff you picked up in the Leftovers. It's not as clear as we would like things to be, but I thought your team could do something with it," Torres's harsh voice said over the receiver. "Most of the things didn't match anything. So that was a bust, but the hair band was able to be identified as belonging to Alicia like we thought."

My stomach clenched. It meant that she had been out there in that boat for who knew how long. And nobody knew where she was now. There seemed to be no trace at the moment. Where was she? Where had she been taken?

"What about the knife?" I asked, remembering the bloody knife we'd recovered after Dorian sniffed it out. That had sent my head reeling more than anything considering it meant somebody had been injured.

"That's the interesting part," Torres began to explain. "We did get a DNA match from the blood on the knife. But it didn't belong to Alicia or any of the other missing persons that we've associated with this case. But it looks like we might have to rethink that now."

I squinted in confusion. Who could the blood belong to, then? Was it a suspect?

"He gave us a ping on the missing person's case from a short time ago," Torres continued. "However, this missing person is a young boy. Not a teenager. He doesn't fit the profile for this group that's missing at all. We were able to get the information from the police department."

A child? This was even worse. Could he have been lured out to her, or was there something else going on?

"So, were you able to get details about how he went missing?" I asked, feeling on edge. This case had gotten stranger by the moment. "Is anything consistent with the other missing cases at all?"

Torres sighed on the other line. "His last whereabouts were actually in Everglades City on a family vacation. It wasn't that close to the Leftovers, at least not as close as these other cases, so everyone assumed it was related to tourism. Like maybe he'd wandered off or something like that. But with the fact that the knife had his blood on it and it was found next to Alicia's hair tie, it's now highly suspicious. We should probably be taking over the case." Torres cleared his throat like he might have more to say and felt uncomfortable about it. "I figured it was best to get your team's expert opinion before claiming it is ours."

What he truly meant was *my* opinion, but that was neither here nor there. At least he was communicating now.

"I don't think there's any other explanation for ending up there other than the same people being responsible," I said. "Whether it's related to anything supernatural, I couldn't say. But I think we need to use that to figure out the pattern."

I slid my sweaty palm across my pants, realizing what I was going to have to ask of him next. Just as Torres was coming around to my side of things, I was about to piss him off once more. But I didn't see any other way around it.

"We're going to need to use the vampires' senses to stake out the area and look for patterns of darkness." My tone was hard. I didn't want to be mincing words at the moment. "I don't see any other way to figure this out. We actually went to talk to Anastasia, and that was mostly a bust. There's no clear evidence, and she seems to mostly be telling the truth. We have no other leads, so can I count on your cooperation with this? "

Torres grumbled something that sounded like a reluctant agreement. "In that case, I'll be coming with your team. If the vamps cause a scene in public, I'll be ready, just so you know."

I ground my teeth. This was so childish and ridiculous, but I had to think about the young child now involved. "They won't."

15
Kane

*A*s much as I didn't like feeling like an invalid in the infirmary with the healers, I dreaded going to see my mother even more. But with Halla so close and with the fact that Roxy might be right, that she would have some information on what could be wrong with me, I didn't really have a choice. Not unless I wanted to keep passing out and being completely useless.

I grumbled to myself as I crossed the city. My mother had made it clear that there was plenty of room for me at her new house. That she was saving a room for me. I had been saved from that since I needed to be with the healers, which meant I didn't have to give her an answer right away, but I knew it was one of the first things she would ask about when I showed up. Especially considering she didn't know exactly how severe my situation was. Nobody but the healers and now Roxy did.

The situation between my mother and I was a tough one. On the one hand, she was the only family I had left. I would defend her honor with my life if I needed to, but that didn't mean we got along. I didn't know how to feel about her, and now that I'd been so entrenched in the mortal plane and with humans like Roxy, it made it even tougher to justify giving her the time of day.

I doubted my mother would ever get over her issue with humans. The way that she judged every single human in existence on one incident alone.

If humans could overcome their aversion to vampires in order to work together and learn the truth, see that most of us were good just like most of them were good even with all of the corruption in them, then there was no reason my mother shouldn't be giving them a chance. Especially considering they worked hard to help us out when they realized their mistake. But she was a prideful woman, if nothing else.

My father had been a warrior, though I never really knew him. He was killed by humans when I was just a small child. I assumed that was the reason for my mother's aversion—no, hatred—for all humans. But she knew that they weren't all murderers. And it wasn't like vampires had always been entirely innocent either.

I formed a fuzzy picture of the dark-haired man. All I remembered about my father was that he was kind of rough and strict, as would be expected of a vampire warrior. We didn't talk about him often, but then again, we didn't talk often, so I didn't know if that really qualified as an issue.

After his death, I felt this strong, unexplainable sense of need to protect Halla. It wasn't my place, even though I knew I would grow up to be forced to become a warrior myself. Thinking back on it though, my mother seemed to always be protecting me as well, and mothers usually didn't protect their sons in our society. I didn't find it strange at the time because it was just my normal. But now...

I looked down at my fractured arm in a sling. It should be healed in a few days, but I wasn't so sure. I didn't know if it was my impatience or my unwillingness to sit around and do nothing when the people I cared about were possibly in danger, or if the truth was buried somewhere else.

I could think of several times in which I didn't heal as fast as other vampires. Or at least it seemed that way to me. The healing process was much slower. Not like a human, of course, but just different. Frustratingly so. But to counteract that lack of speed, I had just trained harder and longer in order to prove myself. With my father's legacy and my mother's prickliness, I had felt like a failure since I was so different than Dorian and the others.

"Kane!"

I turned my head to the sound of the voice. A friend of my mother's was waving at me.

I pulled myself out of my thoughts and walked over to her.

Aclanthe, probably to my mother's disdain, was now filled with a mixture of Coalition and vampires alike. Many of them had learned to work together, but she probably stood sentinel outside her house glaring at everyone she felt like didn't belong and resisting any change whatsoever.

I appreciated the Coalition for what they'd done. Vanim had been destroyed, and it had been awful before that with all its corruption. Aclanthe was its polar opposite. The name of the city meant eternal springtime, which it pretty much was. Everything was in bloom. Alana's garden was covered in flowers in various shades that couldn't be found on the mortal plane at all. Several of the Coalition had been ooh-ing and ahh-ing about it when I'd been basically locked up in the vampire hospital of sorts.

"It's good to see you. How are you?" I kept a smile on my face even though I wasn't in the mood to talk to anyone.

I wanted to get to the bottom of this, and the more and more memories that came flooding back, the more I believed that Roxy was right. That my mother had answers that she had never given me. Which in my mind, was pretty close to a lie.

"I'm all right. It's a beautiful day as always. I'm adjusting well. Did that human friend of yours ever get a hold of you?" she asked.

I tried to keep from cringing. News in this town spread. It was smaller than Vanim and with more people in it. Cramped. And everyone was in everyone else's business.

Now everyone knew that I was somehow friends with a human or maybe even involved with her. It was a terrifying thought, and not just because I had some qualms about getting involved with someone, especially a human. I was kind of a lone wolf really, but I also knew that even being friends with someone like Roxy could put her under speculation that she didn't deserve. There were vampires who still hated humans, some living amongst the Coalition in the city here because they had no other choice, and my mother was definitely one of them.

I didn't know if she had gotten word or not about this human friend of mine, but if she had, I was now dreading the talk with her even more.

"Oh, it was just a member of the team that works sometimes with the Coalition. I was working with her previously. She just had some questions and was checking in on my condition for the rest of the team." I gave a casual nod, hoping she would buy it, and then quickly scooted past her. "Take care."

Meadows in rolling hills greeted me as I passed toward the other side of the city where my mother would be waiting. The dread settled in me, making me feel hollow. She was just as stubborn as I was, so I realized we were kind of two sides of the same coin. She'd never talked about my weakness before or explained it to me as a child, so I sincerely doubted that she was going to do it now. At least not without a lot of pushing and a lot of fights.

I had to have hope though. Even she should understand I couldn't keep going like this. She was all about strength and survival, which was why she'd married a warrior. So, maybe she would understand the fact that I needed to get back to work. I needed to figure out what was going on and stop being such a burden. It was starting to get embarrassing.

Now that I was older and the cat was out of the bag that there was something going on, she couldn't exactly play pretend anymore. She'd always played it off like she hadn't noticed anything was different about me, and yet somehow low-key called me weak anyway. I didn't want either treatment anymore. I just wanted the truth. Why was that so hard to get?

When I arrived, my mother, Halla, was scrutinizing me from her porch. Others must have told her the message that her son was coming to see her. Even when she was at her sweetest, her cold gaze had never been kind.

"There he is."

Looked like I was in for a scolding for today. I supposed I deserved it though for pretty much being radio silent with her.

"I had to hear it from others who heard it from the healers that you fell out of a tree. Had me worried sick."

"You remember I'm a vampire, right? I'm fine. Just trying to get better."

She led me inside, gesturing for me to sit down at the small table she had set up in her kitchen. The place was cozy and nice, unlike her.

"Okay, so you haven't been talking too much with your human friend from the Coalition who called for you?" Her tone was accusatory.

I shook my head. "It was just Roxy. Callanish is just wanting to keep an eye on me after everything that happened in the Pocket Space you know." I shrugged, needing to downplay everything with Roxy.

My mother had no idea that I could communicate with her in my head, and it needed to stay that way. She wouldn't be pleased. Roxy didn't need to be the focus of that displeasure either.

I couldn't help but let my thoughts briefly drift to Roxy, though. She'd been the reason I'd come here. It had been her idea, but I longed to talk to her instead of my mother. I would rather grapple with Roxy any day, which was funny considering she was also on the other side of the same coin as me.

If my mother could get over her differences with humans, she probably would like Roxy.

I shook the thought of Roxy out of my head, knowing that I needed to focus on what was in front of me. I couldn't delay getting answers anymore.

Halla put some tea in front of me, fussing over me as she kept eyeing my arm in the sling.

"Look, I came for a reason, and it wasn't to fight about humans and the Coalition and Callanish. It's about me." I slowly began to explain what had happened to me. I needed to start at the beginning and give her all the reasons possible for her to help me. She needed to believe that her telling me the truth could make a difference.

To her credit, even though her face gave several negative emotions away, she listened to me tell her about the fact that I was continuing to black out for hours at a time. And the fact that I wasn't healing as quickly as I should have been.

"What is your theory? Can you think of any reason I would have been pulled into the Pocket Space during the meld or why I'm not healing as fast as a vampire should?"

The question was careful, and I watched her expression change from tense to rage.

"So, you don't tell your own mother about not healing, about passing out and falling out of a tree. Had me so worried. And now you want to come into my new home, see me for the first time in a long time, and accuse me of keeping secrets from you. To accuse me of doing something to you to make you different?"

It was all a deflection. I knew it was. Her attitude didn't make sense otherwise. She was trying to hide something, but I couldn't put my finger on what it could be.

"Look, I do owe you an apology for that, but I'm going to continue to have these problems and not be safe if I don't know why they're happening. Maybe the healers can fix it. But if you know something, Mother, I need you to tell me. I need you to tell me why I'm different. Please. Because I'm going to go back out and work with the Coalition and Callanish again either way, and I don't want to be blindsided if I start to have trouble again."

I kept my voice gentle so she didn't continue to think I was accusing her of anything. It was exhausting micromanaging my own mother's emotions.

Halla put her hand on her hip and pursed her lips at me, but she began to talk at least. Even if it was in circles. "I was told something by the harvesters at your birth. Yes, you were different. I've always known this. But that's why I've pushed you so hard. And I've been protective."

My mood darkened. That still wasn't enough. "Tell me. What did the harvesters say?"

Halla huffed. "I knew you were born to be great, Kane. You have been great, and you're going to be even greater. You had to struggle to get there, and you'll continue to struggle. I made sure that you were ready. That you could be everything that you wanted. And here you are. So why reflect on all of that now?"

I clenched my fists at my sides. I knew the woman loved me. And I could see it even more in her actions, but what point was there, now that I was an adult and needed help, in keeping a secret?

"You should have told me. You should tell me now what it is. I have a right to know."

"And don't I have a right to gratitude? For all I have done to build you into the man that you are? Your father would be proud. Don't ruin that. Don't taint how far you've come."

I suddenly stood up, not wanting to be here anymore. It was stifling in that house. "I'll have to think about all of this."

Her voice softened. "You know you can stay here anytime, but at least for this evening, please."

I couldn't accept her offer. "I have to leave. The healers will come looking for me if I don't."

I stormed out of there before she could try to convince me otherwise. I just wanted to be alone. But I knew I would be welcomed back even with the anger I'd left her with. And the pain in my heart and hearing it straight from her mouth that I was different. That I would never be like any other vampire. But if that was the case, what was the reason?

My head was buzzing while I headed back down the path to where I came from. As I did, a voice popped into my thoughts, one that wasn't my own.

"Holy shit," the voice said.

Roxy.

It seemed that Roxy had been there the whole time, and I didn't know how I felt about that.

16
Roxy

"Look, I do owe you an apology for that, but I'm going to continue to have these problems and not be safe if I don't know why they're happening."

Kane.

His voice was in my head again. *Damn it. I didn't mean to do that.*

"Maybe the healers can fix it. But if you know something, Mother, I need you to tell me. I need you to tell me why I'm different. Please. Because I'm going to go back out and work with the Coalition and Callanish again either way, and I don't want to be blindsided if I start to have trouble again."

I had been sitting at my desk doing paperwork and was now unable to continue thanks to the conversation I was overhearing in my head.

His mother. Kane was talking to Halla. Oh, I shouldn't have been a part of this conversation or his thoughts at all. He was trying to get her to tell him something about why he kept passing out and why he wasn't healing fast, and his head was a swirl of past memories. Private moments. Rivalry and struggles with Dorian and others as well at the way his mother had treated him.

It was a good thing I was in my office alone. At least it hadn't happened at the most inconvenient time for once... at least not for me.

We were going to have to get this part of tuning each other out down pat before so much was laid bare that we resented each other.

"I was told something by the harvesters at your birth. Yes, you were different. I've always known this. But that's why I've pushed you so hard. And I've been protective."

How could I hear his mother's voice too? Was it just because he was projecting it unknowingly through our connection?

His mother was admitting to him being different but wasn't telling him how. Kane was disappointed. Hurt. The information was game-changing if she would just spill all the beans.

Holy shit.

"Roxy," Kane growled through the bond. He'd heard me.

Oops. I'm sorry, Kane. I couldn't help it. I just started hearing your thoughts randomly, and then I could hear your mother's voice too this time.

"What the hell, Roxy? Couldn't you, like, turn it off or something when you realized that it was me talking to my mother?"

I very rarely saw Kane's anger directed at me, and I didn't like it. I cringed in my seat, setting my pen down, my paperwork all but forgotten.

I get why you would be angry; that was a very private moment. It's not like I was trying to listen in or anything; I just couldn't shut you out. You know we've been trying to work on that.

I tried to make it clear by sending my emotions as much as I could through the bond that this wasn't something I wanted any more than he did. On the one hand, it was useful to be able to talk to him and made the world a little bit less lonely of a place, but to know that the privacy just wasn't there, that some of my own thoughts weren't just mine, it was disturbing.

What of mine could he one day accidentally overhear? And then the fact that I could hear what his mother was saying too, I could get why he was upset. I hated it.

"I just don't know how to feel about this right now, Roxy, to know someone else heard that conversation..."

His tone scared me a little. Kane wasn't a vulnerable man. It was part of the reason why we never talked about either time that we'd kissed. He was always strong, but with his walls, I felt like I had to punch through them to get any kind of emotion out of him.

I could feel it plaguing him today as if I were feeling it inside of his body. That, coupled with the sound of his voice, was anguish. His mother had all but betrayed him and lied to him.

I didn't always have the best relationship with my mother, so I could get that part, but I didn't have a whole lot of advice to give him even if he wanted it.

I feel just as badly about it as you do, Kane. I'm sorry.

"I get that, I do," Kane practically roared down the connection. "But it doesn't stop the fact that I'm angry and hurt over the intrusion. It's a lot to process right now. I don't know how to handle knowing that you know all of this. "

I pushed the papers around my desk a little too violently. I would probably regret messing those up in a little while, but now my anger was getting to me.

Sorry you've been a little bit busy healing and passing out for us to work on ways to shut it out. The last time we tried, you fell out of a tree!

"This is not the time for your attitude," Kane quipped back, making my cheeks burn.

I don't have an attitude. I'm trying to be sympathetic here. I didn't mean to listen in on you. It just happened, and then I couldn't stop it. What part of that don't you understand?

I hated it when he was like this. He never saw reason. Only his own ego.

I could practically hear Kane grinding his teeth. "You're asking me not to blame you for the intrusion, and yet you're blaming me for the intrusion because you think it's my fault that I keep passing out. Do you think I want this? That I want to be worried over by a bunch of healers and to be different?"

This conversation was getting nowhere, and we needed to calm down before it got too bad.

Look, I said, *I guess we're both upset. Emotions are high right now. But we need to think about something else here. What does it mean that I can hear what you hear?*

Kane growled, but his tone became quieter. "It's pretty weird. It doesn't exactly make sense for you to hear the exact dialogue unless I was thinking it word for word for you, which I wasn't."

Okay... I got up and leaned against the side of my desk.

"We might need to figure out as soon as possible how to block this off.

It can't be good for either of us."

I scoffed. *I would turn it off if I could. But you're right. We do need to try and take the time and figure this out. We should be able to turn it off and on as needed.*

A calm washed over me that I didn't think belonged to me. It must have been Kane. I settled back in my desk chair, relieved that we weren't fighting anymore. It was the last thing I wanted.

I could pretend that this didn't happen and never bring it up again if that's what you want, I offered, keeping my tone level. *But if there comes a time that you want to talk about it, at least you won't have to explain it to me. I'll already know what's going on and why you feel the way you do.*

I shrugged to myself, figuring that it wasn't going to matter. Kane was never going to share any kind of feelings with me, not really. He was so surface level, never opening up to anyone. The one thing about the mind connection between us was that it was the only way to force something like that from him...and that didn't justify continuing to keep it open to any number of things that we could overhear.

"I guess it is a little relief that you're here for me, even if it's sometimes in the most inconvenient moments."

I smiled to myself, picturing the way he might say this in person, smirking at me. *I know what you mean. Sometimes it's good to know someone has your back.*

"I guess since you're here, I'll get your take on this, but I'm going to need some alone time later on to process things if we can manage." Now Kane just sounded exhausted. He did have an emotionally exhausting day learning what he'd learned, plus he was still healing.

Silence fell over us, but I could feel he was still there on the other side of this connection. He just didn't know where to begin.

So, what made you decide to go in the first place? I threw him a bone, hoping he would bite.

"I knew it was time. She would be wondering where I was and why I hadn't visited or come to stay yet."

There was a hesitation there, something more to it. I didn't want to push, though, because I knew how he was with sharing things. He was finally talking to me, opening up. I wasn't going to ruin it by trying to get something out of him too soon.

Seems like a smart move rather than waiting too long. I imagine that wouldn't have gone well.

Kane chuckled. "No, it would not have. But..."

Here it was. He was going to tell me something real.

"I was thinking about what you said to me that she might know something about me and never told me."

Kane sighed, and I grabbed the seat of my chair, white-knuckled, the thought of him thinking about me in any capacity making my heart race.

Don't send that through to him, I hissed to myself, trying to clamp down on my feelings and put a mental wall around them. We were in two different planes, and still, he had this effect on me.

"It got me thinking about things I remembered from childhood. The way she treated me, and other times when I didn't heal like everyone else. I thought I was just weak, but then maybe you...had something there."

I grinned, knowing he was holding back from saying I was right. He wasn't ready to admit that. My gut clenched for him, though. Thinking about Kane as a young boy trying to live up to expectations that maybe he never could have and was never told about made me ache. Maybe that was why he had such a wall now. He needed to appear like he had it even more together than others to compensate.

Well, I only heard part of the conversation, but it sounds like there was something to that theory. What do you think? I pressed lightly, hoping not to scare him off.

"I had to really push her, Roxy."

Ugh, why did it send a shockwave up my spine when he said my name, even in my head?

"I don't like it. It makes me afraid that I can't trust my own mother. She tried to say she was keeping all this from me for my own good, so I would be strong. but all I feel is weak."

I barely heard the last part, like he was whispering it, trying to push the thought down and suppress it.

Being different doesn't make you weak, Kane. In fact, some of the strongest people I know are also the most unique. Lyra and Dorian definitely came to mind.

Kane's only response was to grunt. Typical.

"But what about this harvester prophecy? What could that mean?"

I had to be honest. *To me, it sounded like she was lying about that part. At least some of it. That woman definitely has a better memory than that.*

"How dare you," Kane hissed, taking me aback. "You were in my head or you wouldn't know any of this. How are you to know how much my own mother is telling me?"

Shit, he was starting to get defensive.

I'm only trying to help you, not say anything definitively, Kane, but you're not the only one with a complicated parental relationship.

That was an understatement.

"Doesn't your mother work for The Bureau?"

I laughed. I couldn't help it. *If you would have told her something like that when I began, she would have laughed, or possibly even spit in your face. She hates the idea of a woman being a warrior or career woman. She has these old-school notions about gender roles and all of that. She's tried for years to set me up with men so that I'd settle down and get married and do all of those things instead. Like going goo-goo over a guy would suddenly change me in some way.*

"I can't even picture you that way," Kane said with a chuckle.

I knew he didn't mean it that way, but it stung a little considering the circumstances.

Here he was worrying that he was the one who was weak, and I had become weak because of my feelings for him and the fact that I didn't feel like I could share them. I doubted that he felt the same, and even if he did, he probably wouldn't act on them.

He was too proud, which was ironic, because I had the same problem.

Yeah, me in the kitchen cooking up dinner every night and smiling with an apron on. I cringed at the idea.

"Oh God, don't ever say that again. I like you just the way you are."

I gasped, trying to hold back any other reaction. *Stop it, Roxy, that's not what he meant.*

My mother and I don't see eye to eye on a lot of things. I also had to help raise my siblings a lot, kind of replacing my dad. It just became expected after a while.

I shrugged as if it didn't hurt me, but it did. I loved my siblings, and I wouldn't take it back for a moment. I helped make sure that they were okay, but it meant that no one had been there for me. I had to do it all myself because my father was so in and out of our lives, and my mother couldn't get it together herself.

"I guess mothers are quite complicated. I hate to admit it, but I guess there is a possibility that Halla is at least still hiding something about what she knows. I need to find answers. So, I guess I'll start with the healers at the hospital to see if they can tell me anything else about this passing-out thing. Seems like a good place to start."

I was kind of glad to hear him say that. The passing out above everything else he was experiencing was the one thing I was the most anxious about. It could put him in a lot of danger, especially since he was so determined to just get back into action. Hopefully, they would have something to say that was useful...

"Also, could you do me a favor?" Kane asked.

Sure, what is it?

"I'm wondering if I should pay a visit to the harvesters and ask them directly about this prophecy thing. Convince me before I chicken out."

I giggled at the cringe in his voice, considering he absolutely hated being around them. He was a big baby about it too, despite being an incredibly powerful person himself. Their weirdness always creeped him out.

I think that's definitely a good idea, even if you think they're so weird.

"That's because they are."

Now c'mon, they're not so bad. This felt better. More like us.

"Hmm, well, I guess if there's going to be somebody in my head without my knowing, I'm glad it's you."

My whole body began to tingle at his statement. It wasn't exactly an admission of any kind, but it was probably as close as he got, other than kissing me. Which I guessed with men could mean any number of things.

We'll have a sit-down next week when we have a chance and try to figure out how to disconnect from each other's thoughts so we don't hear entire conversations involuntarily.

"That sounds like a good idea. I know the one time I seemed to do it when we tried before, it took considerable effort focusing on other things, but I also don't know how much of that was how weak I was either. We could even talk again tomorrow. Maybe I'll know more from the healers by then."

Okay, we can do it in the evening here in the Mortal Plane. I don't think I have anything going on, I told him. It was hard to schedule times considering the Immortal Plane didn't have clocks and the lights didn't change with the time. But he was usually pretty good at figuring it out.

"We can do that. You contact me first. I'm going to try and disconnect now."

I waited what seemed like forever until I made sure I heard no more of Kane's thoughts so that he also couldn't hear mine, then I relaxed, falling back into my chair.

I certainly hadn't meant to piss Kane off or to insert myself into his head, but if I thought about it, I'd kind of brought it on myself.

Right before I began hearing his conversation, my thoughts had drifted to the predicament we were in with hearing each other's thoughts and what might be wrong with him, but every time I thought about Kane, I involuntarily went to places I shouldn't, like the two times I'd seen him shirtless, which by the way—amazing.

There had never been any denying that Kane was incredibly sexy. But then thinking about him shirtless got me thinking about the two times we had kissed. My fantasy was about to take a turn for the more exciting when I'd suddenly heard his fight with Halla.

Quite the unfortunately rude wake-up call. Couldn't a girl fantasize about a guy without being dragged into his private thoughts? But I guessed in my world that was impossible.

The problem presented, though, was way bigger than us just dropping into each other's thoughts. The more we spoke like this, the more I realized I had feelings for him. Possibly beyond just the fact that he was incredibly hot.

I doubted I had any chances with him, regardless of the reason, but I wondered if I shouldn't just confess my feelings in a flippant way. Like maybe if I did, we could just clear the air that it wouldn't ever work, laugh about it, and move on.

I shook my head at the ridiculous thought and began organizing the paperwork so I could finish. The idea that he could even like me, that there was even a tiny inkling, was laughable considering he could have his pick of any vampire girl he wanted. And vampires did tend to have a certain look about them, this eternal beauty the humans couldn't provide. And then there was everything else I had to worry about. I didn't know if dealing with unrequited feelings or the tension of me telling him about them was worth the trouble that would be added.

And what if, on the slim chance he really did care for me, it wouldn't work out? Kane had always said he hated the Mortal Plane, that he would never live here. It was why he was in the Immortal Plane even after everything we'd all gone through with him. And my whole life was in the Mortal Plane.

I had to just deal with these feelings, pull up my big-girl panties, and move on as soon as I could.

I picked up my pen and decided it was best to go back to work. The sooner I could get Kane out of my mind, the better.

17

Lyra

I reached over to the ridiculous excuse for counter space just next to the sink and grabbed the bottle of sunscreen, then squeezed a generous amount into my hand before setting the bottle back down. With barely any room to shuffle around in this tiny RV bathroom, I began to apply it onto Dorian's bare back.

In fact, all of him was bare. We were getting ready to visit Everglades City for a chance to get a feel for the place where the little boy had disappeared, the one whose blood was on the knife we discovered in the Leftovers.

"Why did you want me to do your makeup today?" I asked him as I spread the thick, smelly substance across his back, his ass, and down the back of his legs. It was necessary for the shadows to go underneath the makeup that would cover up the vampires' skin tone from tourists.

As I finished with his backside, Dorian turned around, pressing into me with a grin. "I thought it would be a little fun to remember old times."

I shivered, suddenly wishing he were rubbing me down too.

Dorian was a god among men in the looks department. It wasn't just his work ethic and intuitiveness that got to me, although I loved every bit of those too. But his abs...his ass. Yum.

I blushed as I began applying the sunscreen to his chest, his arousal crowding me even more.

It had been a long time since he'd needed me to do his makeup. He'd learned to do it himself a while ago. I should have guessed he had ulterior motives.

I suppose it was the one upside to the small RV bathroom.

"Give me your arm," I said, smiling but trying to ignore him so I could get the job done. As I stroked his left arm to rub in the sunscreen, his right hand landed on my hip before sliding up and down my body and then cupping my center.

I bit my lip as a whimper tried to escape. We were always so busy. Working together didn't necessarily mean more quality time together. And I didn't have the same unabashedness as Sike and Chandry to do anything right under everyone's noses.

But now...

He looked down at me, a flash of lust in his eyes as he grabbed my ass and forced my body up against him. "This makes me think about when we used to do this. Before we were a couple."

"Mmm," I said, finishing up and wiping my hands off before grabbing the makeup to start the first layer. "What about it?"

"I wanted you so badly then, especially when your hands were on me. I just couldn't admit it to myself then."

I nodded with a smile as I began to layer on the makeup that I knew was incredibly uncomfortable. I couldn't imagine having that much piled on me at once. "We have come so far. We found a way to deal with the curse and everything. I thought for a while that we would never make it."

Dorian placed a finger under my chin and lifted it so I had to look at him. "But look at us now. I want a chance to change that."

He winked, and I melted as he slid his hands over my body again.

Makeup forgotten, I leaned in and placed my lips on his. I could feel his reaction to it against my belly, so I pulled away and slid my clothes off, throwing them on the floor. I was forced to stand on the pile since there was no more space.

"I don't want to burn in the sun, so maybe you could help me out a little too?" I teased.

Dorian smirked and gladly grabbed the sunscreen, motioning for me to turn around.

His hands slipped around me, pulling my back against his body. They began to roam everywhere with the excuse of the sunscreen, but soon they found my nipples and my throbbing bud asking for more than we had time for.

I made a show of rubbing up against him for a moment, moaning softly at his touches before I turned around and let him enjoy looking at me while I finished the makeup that made him look human except under the trained eye.

He gave me one last lingering kiss before we put on our obnoxious tourist clothes—T-shirts, sunglasses, and shorts—and we joined the rest of the group.

"I don't know how you do this all the time. Especially this sunscreen. It smells so bad," Chandry said, wrinkling her nose.

Sike nodded sympathetically. "I don't like it much either. I don't know how humans put up with this. And look at us! We look ridiculous. I don't know how humans think this is blending in. These bright colors and horrible fashions stick out like a sore thumb."

I laughed, and Dorian smiled, leaning down to whisper in my ear, "Do I stink?"

I turned to him and scrunched up my face. "A little, but we all do."

Everyone laughed at that, but the lighthearted moment was over the minute it began as Dorian reminded the vampires how they needed to act. Chandry had never done this before, so I was most worried about her behavior. Could she actually fit in?

"You'll have to slow down your movements. Act like humans and interested in things a tourist would. Keep quiet and follow Sike's lead," Dorian added, aimed at Chandry.

So, he was worried about her too. It was her personality, really. That same bubbly charm that drew people to her also made missions like these difficult when she was involved. She would have to be serious, which wasn't her strong suit.

"Of course," she replied, grabbing Sike's hand. "We can pretend to be a human couple."

I gritted my teeth into a smile I hoped no one could see through, though Dorian shot me a look of concern. As usual, we were on the same wavelength.

"Sure, you're Martha and I'm Kevin," Sike said, choosing the most human names I'd ever heard.

"Isn't Martha an old lady's name?" Chandry asked.

I was glad the two could make light of the situation, but I needed them to focus.

"Can I do a silly accent like I'm from somewhere else?" Chandry suggested excitedly.

"No, you can't do a silly voice. We need to take this seriously, especially with Torres on our backs," Sike told her with a frown.

I left the camper, a fanny pack strapped across my midsection, and the rest followed.

Everglades City was a small tourist town with a boardwalk filled with shops and restaurants as well as the swamp itself. Some seemed to be brave enough to try and swim in the murky water, though many signs warned of gators. Luckily, they would be normal ones. No Leftovers here.

To the west of the dock was a little funnel-cake stand where we were supposed to meet with Torres and some techs since Torres was taking it upon himself to hover, just in case the evil vampires decided to attack the innocent humans, possibly the ones responsible for actual human trafficking.

Torres approached, not fitting in with the crowd in the least. He was too stiff and militaristic. He was so worried about the vampires being caught or causing problems, but it was him who was a dead giveaway that we weren't any ordinary visitors.

I fell back to let Dorian take the lead. I wanted to let Torres know how competent and helpful vampires were, even as the two men tensed at the sight of each other.

I held my breath as they began to discuss the plan. We would scout the area like tourists, and the vampires would be feeling out dark energies and clues while the techs with Torres would look for odd signatures.

In the end, after stilted and ill-equipped dialogue, Torres and Dorian decided it would be best if we split up between two different groups.

"So, now what?" Chandry leaned in to ask, her and Sike still holding hands behind Dorian and me, who were doing the same.

Bryce and Cam headed up the rear, Bryce grumbling about all the romance in the air, or something like that. I would have laughed, except I knew what he was going through. He and Arlonne had to stay away from each other and figure things out—which they might not get as lucky as we had with being together in the end.

I frowned and answered Chandry in a low voice, "We look around, sticking to the places we know the boy was last seen. We act like we're on vacation, seeing the sights."

"Seeing the sights, okay," she said cheerily, "What about that shop over there?"

She pointed to a little souvenir and convenience shop right on the boardwalk. It was nothing special, very small compared to what could be found in Miami, but I could see why Chandry would be curious and drawn to it.

I steered Dorian in that direction, and we went in, splitting up to look at different things.

As we looked through some cheesy T-shirts against the wall, I got up on my tiptoes to whisper in Dorian's ear, hoping it just looked like a couple's moment.

"Let me know if you sense any specific darkness. I think that's going to be our best lead," I said.

He nodded, smiling as if I'd said something amazing, and then he gave me a peck on the cheek.

Chandry and Sike were laughing, Chandry grabbing a little water globe with a cartoon whale inside and a palm tree. I went to see it, acting as if I was joining the fun.

"What about a codeword—gators?" Sike suggested.

It wasn't a bad idea so we could talk freely. It wouldn't be unusual for tourists to talk about alligator sightings or worry about one.

We purchased a few things just for the sake of making it look real, and we let Chandry have the odd globe with the nonsensical palm tree underwater. She kept playing with it as we walked.

"I heard earlier that someone said there were some alligator sightings. Do you think we'll get to snap a picture of one?" Sike asked, utilizing the code for darkness.

"Well, it's pretty common to see a few. I bet we will," Dorian answered, looking at me.

Ugh, I hadn't thought of that. It would be hard to get any head start on this considering it was normal to get mixed signatures among humans.

Most had a small amount of darkness. It was just in our nature, especially in large crowds.

But I supposed we were looking for something overwhelming. Someone who had nothing but darkness, considering this person would be responsible for the kidnapping. I couldn't imagine anyone kidnapping and harming children of any age for any reason.

Our feet clapped loudly over the wooden boards as we passed a sign and a few people gathered for a small airboat tour company, and that was when Dorian placed his hand on my shoulder, stopping me.

"I think we could see alligators this way." He pointed toward the small crowd at the airboat tour sign.

I turned to the other two, and they confirmed.

Darkness.

"Lots of them!" Chandry chimed in excitedly.

Sike's jaw tensed.

Okay, so this could be something.

Past the boat tour, I noticed a man and squinted as he came down the boardwalk.

I squeezed Dorian's arm and acted like I was trying to convince him to get us a tour as I mumbled, "Him, there."

"That's the male suspect," he hissed under his breath.

"The one we haven't visited yet," Sike piped in, noticing him too.

The man shot us a look, possibly noticing our interest, and then walked around to the back of the small warehouse building where tourists were being ushered in for the airboat tours.

Could it be the place where the kidnappers were working out of? I couldn't read dark and light signatures, but something did feel off about the whole thing.

Dorian pointed to an ice-cream stand just on the other side. "How about some cones to cool off?" he suggested.

I smiled nervously, glad he was learning terminology so well but worrying about what would come next now that we'd spotted the suspect.

All of us humans got ice cream and sat down on some benches nearby but not close enough where anyone at the boat tours could hear. We needed to assess the situation as quickly as possible and get a plan together.

Dorian pointed toward a couple of strange birds–pelicans or storks that reminded me a little of small, light-colored redbills. They took off and flew above one of the buildings on the boardwalk. "If I could find a way to get up onto the buildings, I could get a sense of whether everyone who goes in and out of the warehouse is dark or if it's just one or two people."

I shook my head, licking my strawberry ice cream. "It's too risky right now. Too many people around to do it unnoticed. Not to mention who knows where Torres is, watching us like a hawk."

Bryce scoffed. "I'm sick of him screwing up our mission. He needs to get rid of the stick up his ass."

Chandry snorted.

I was about to get onto them both when Chandry came up with an idea of her own. "Why don't Sike and I cause a distraction? Like a lover's spat. We draw the crowd to us, and Dorian can leap onto one of the lower buildings unnoticed."

"You're awfully cheery about having a fight," Bryce commented.

I rolled my eyes. "C'mon guys, stop it." I turned to Chandry. "It's a crazy idea, and risky, but I don't see any other way."

Chandry stood up, bounced in her step, and offered her hand to Sike. "C'mon, boyfriend. Time to have a fight."

"What are we fighting about?" he asked.

"Hmmm." She looked around for an idea as they walked away.

Dorian and I stood up and walked toward a small stand selling cotton candy and binoculars, of all things.

He left me there and waited for the distraction as he approached the building to our left.

Chandry's scream pierced the air, though they were far enough away that I couldn't make out the words. Hopefully, the two of them could be realistic enough.

I watched Dorian about to take the leap when all of us stopped in the face of another commotion.

Alongside the boardwalk nearby, tourists began screaming, "Monster!"

18
Lyra

*W*e didn't hesitate as we rushed toward the source of the sound. The problem was getting through the humans. They couldn't decide whether or not they wanted to rubberneck and see what was going on or if they wanted to panic and run, almost causing a stampede.

Like swimming upstream, we finally made it there even with all of the commotion. And there on the dock, an enormous, Leftovers-style mutated snake with multiple heads, at least four of them, struggled to get itself up onto the boardwalk. It was striking at other people and smashing some of the stalls along the water. The creature was maddened, probably because it didn't belong here. But then it spotted Dorian, trying to rejoin us. Something about him set it off, and it began to make its way toward him.

I paused, with probably no time to do so, as I considered whether or not to keep cover and call Torres in instead. Their team was around here somewhere.

But then I witnessed something horrible—one of the thing's heads tried to curl itself around a tourist. Dorian didn't hesitate. He didn't wait for any orders, just dived in. Getting there before us, he tried to appear human in his movements as he tried to get the snake to release the tourist.

I looked at Bryce, and I instantly knew that he was thinking the same thing as me. We would instantly both choose saving people over saving our identities. Any day.

"Break cover."

We moved in on the snake, no weapons in hand. We had to fight this thing with our hands and feet until hopefully Torres and his team showed up. Surely there would be people screaming and running and talking about this throughout the tourist area. So, they would have to show up eventually.

The snake was hard to get a grip on. Of course, it was gigantic and had many hands, and all of them seemed to be able to operate independently of one another. And they were just as dexterous as a tail so they could easily snatch or wrap around a human.

"We have to evacuate," I screamed as I dodged the tail whipping over me and destroying a shop sign.

"Cam, Chandry, the two of you need to start evacuating everyone now," Bryce ordered.

Despite any earlier qualms, I was glad to see that Chandry responded to action, not taking anything for granted. She and Cam began to round up any humans lingering nearby.

With that taken care of, I felt like it was okay to provoke it more, to risk it, so I went in to support Dorian. I climbed up the massive tail and began to torment the head that was coiled around a woman around my age.

She'd stopped screaming, probably to preserve air. Her eyes were wide and shocked. She'd likely never expected something like this to show up here. It was particularly unusual for any of the Leftovers' monsters to show up in a large tourist area outside of where the Leftovers were. I didn't know what it could have been doing here.

And I didn't like the implications at all.

I kicked, aiming directly toward the head, and got the chin. That seemed to distract it enough to loosen the woman a bit. Dorian reached for her and tugged at her, not hiding his strength in the least as he pulled her out of harm's way.

"Why don't you slide down there, ma'am, and get some help from those two that are evacuating everyone? " Dorian suggested.

The woman was shaking but didn't hesitate.

Cam was able to steady her at the bottom.

"Bureau! Out of the way!" Torres shouted.

I breathed a sigh of relief. Finally, Torres's team had arrived. They would get the rest of the place evacuated, and I knew they had guns. And other weapons.

There would be no taking this thing down without them as it got more desperate with its flailing.

One old lady who was near the water came screaming by, much too close for comfort, a child in her arms. She tripped, and as she fell, one of the farthest snake heads looked at the two of them like they were the best meal ever.

Sike and Dorian both jumped in, putting themselves in danger as one grabbed the child and the other the woman, hauling them up just as the snake struck.

I screamed, unable to help it. We were fighting this crazy thing without any preparation for this. We always knew it was a risk to run into one of these monsters, but in Everglades City, it had seemed ridiculous to even suspect it.

Now, this four-headed monstrosity could easily kill every single one of us and for some reason had really singled out Dorian. Was he conspicuous in a way I hadn't noticed? Had the suspect sent this creature after him in particular?

The snake barely missed them, and I wondered if the snake had venom of any kind. I would have to find out the hard way, with one of us severely ill or dying. It would be quite the unfair advantage, but it wasn't unheard of for Leftovers' creatures.

The vampires were still having to move very slowly, and probably for the sake of keeping our cover, Torres did not hand us any weapons. Instead, he gave orders for us to back down.

Dorian and Sike didn't fall back. Nor would I have expected them to. Chandry looked hesitant, as if she wanted to follow orders and stay with the team but also like she wanted to jump into the fight and rip the snake to shreds.

She was the least experienced with hiding her true nature, so I was grateful for her restraint. Maybe I had judged her too harshly.

Callanish and The Bureau were supposed to be working hand in hand regardless of blowing our cover. Most of the humans were gone other than some stubborn rubberneckers as usual. There was nothing we could do about that.

Weapon-brandishing Bureau members surrounded us, and I at least knew to have faith in their aim. They wouldn't accidentally get one of us, though if they took too long to get this thing at least under control, there would still be loss of life.

The destruction of the boardwalk was already catastrophic.

Finally, the snake went down with a smack on the boardwalk, breaking what was underneath it. Wood splintered all around us.

I hated how slowly it had happened and how much room there had been for injury. We'd got lucky.

I knew it was best to blend in if we could, but I felt like Torres tainted that decision whether or not to go all in. It was frustrating. It felt like he was hindering our job, which was exactly what I was afraid of happening when we'd had our first fight.

Torres and his team of techs went around and reassured the few people still around, letting them know that their official presence was there to keep all of them safe. That seemed to draw attention away from us specifically, and when anyone asked or discussed how brave we were, he had his team tell them that we were actually members of a martial arts club that were here on vacation attending a tournament. That was why we'd been able to fight the snake until the real good guys got here.

To our frustration and dismay, but a necessity, all of us left the area and piled into the RV, including Torres and the techs. It wasn't something I would recommend since it seemed like there was no room to even breathe.

"What the hell just happened back there? Torres asked, both him and Bryce in particular on edge.

Not that I could blame them, because that was about the most unusual situation we'd faced, and that was saying a lot considering we'd been presented with a hell of a lot of strange things over the years.

"I don't understand," Dorian said, pacing around in his little corner of the RV. "A Leftovers' creature shouldn't have been there in that crowd, even if it did decide to leave the Leftovers, which is also weird. It's too far away. "

"It could have been coincidental," Bryce grumbled, "but my gut tells me that it's not. Enough time in this business has told me that there's almost no such thing as a coincidence."

Torres looked shocked. "How would they even get near such a thing and get it to behave?"

I shook my head. "I don't know, but we have to think of the possibility. Have any of us ever seen anything like this before? Have you, Torres?"

He shrugged. "I can't say I've heard of anything like this before either. But that doesn't mean I like it."

"The only thing that makes sense to do for now is to keep staking out the area. I don't know what else we could do since we don't have any other proof or leads other than that we did see one of the suspects. We were going to try to get a read and see what he was up to when the snake came along," I explained so that Torres was up to date on what we'd seen. "He was hanging around that warehouse over by the airboat tours."

"I'll make a note of that," Torres said roughly.

I nodded to him and his team. Regardless of their feelings for us, they had saved us back there. "Thank you for all your help."

Torres motioned for his team to leave the RV. He didn't return my thanks, nor had I expected him to even though, we deserved a thank-you for getting that thing off a human with our bare hands. And the vampires hadn't even given away their identities.

I waited until I knew that Torres and the team were long gone before I said anything else. All of us got some water and a snack and sat down around the small dining table in the center of the RV.

Just like our last mission, this one was full of oddities and suspicious circumstances. We had to figure out where to go from here before it was too late for all of these kids or even more kids who could get taken.

"I have to say, for the first time in a long time, I'm speechless. I have no idea what we should do," Bryce admitted.

It was Cam who spoke next. "How are we supposed to deal with these and investigate missing children and catch the suspects if we're too busy with these wild, raging monsters that someone is possibly dropping on us as a distraction?"

I sipped the coffee in my hand, my version of liquid courage. My veins were practically made of the stuff. "There's no way around it. We can't take care of the monsters that they might throw at us and continue to lead this investigation, especially with the fact that Torres is so unhelpful. He may have saved our skin today, but he hated it."

Dorian's face tightened. I could tell he wanted to say more about Torres, probably wanted to say something *to* Torres for that matter, but we couldn't. We would be the bigger people here. But we would be reporting this problem to The Bureau when this was all said and done and as many of these kids as possible were saved. Torres could lead to a lot of mistakes that no one could afford.

I just hoped it didn't have to come to that and he would get over his prejudices enough to see the kind of work we were doing. The vampires had yet to give him any reason to mistrust them.

"Are you thinking of calling her in?" Dorian asked, practically reading my mind.

There was only one team I could think of that would be the perfect backup for this. I trusted them fully and knew that we wouldn't have to worry about any monsters with them on the payroll.

"I don't see any other choice. I think it's time to invite Roxy and the Hellraisers to sunny Florida."

19
Kane

I was in the sky, a redbill below me to carry me to where the harvesters would be. After talking with Roxy, I'd decided it was best to get this over with, even with my broken arm and my aversion to the harvesters.

The harvesters had one job, always had, and due to their creepiness and normal role in society, I hadn't questioned it much in my youth.

But to be put to work harvesting souls for dark soul energy, magic they could never touch, use, or sell and still live menial lives was awful.

Of course, it was different now. I had been told they were happier, better off where they were. Though, they still had a similar job. But they did it because that's what they wanted to do. It had been ingrained in them after all.

Despite the jarring experience of flying on a redbill, though exhilarating as well, my arm felt all right.

I'd gone early this morning to collect some pain-killing brew from the healer, Maefa. That was what had started this whole thing. Well, I'd wanted the painkiller so I could do this alone, but that wasn't how it turned out.

"Isn't Aclanthe beautiful?" Maefa asked from behind me as she held on tight. She seemed in good spirits, laughing and hanging on every word I said, but I could feel the slight tension in her body.

Flying with a large bird that could kill you if it wanted wasn't exactly everyone's cup of tea, but our relationship with the redbills had become a good one. And beneficial when one needed to cover long distances in a shorter time.

"It is," I answered tensely. There was no denying that, but I'd heard from a few that some vampires had trouble adjusting to it.

I was beginning to regret my morning conversation with her in which I'd explained I was going on a journey to the harvesters by redbill.

She had immediately chimed in, offering to take an entire day off just to give me someone to go with if I wanted her to.

I was ready to turn her down. I didn't need a babysitter or a flirt along for the ride, but I'd stopped short.

Roxy had put fear in my heart with the worry she had. What if I passed out mid-flight? Not only would I be lost and injured on the way out here, but it would also make this trip useless.

And if it didn't kill me, then Roxy would once she found out I'd done it on my own. So, I supposed a solo mission was unrealistic.

I had another option, though. I still could have turned down Maefa and gone. My mother lived so close, and she would've been thrilled I was out on another mission. No humans involved with me this time. But I didn't think I could handle her brand of distractions and arguments at the moment. So, I had taken Maefa up on the offer.

There were advantages to having her with me even if she was irritating me, though.

"What can you tell me about my healing? Does it seem off to you?"

She thought for a moment. "You heal slower," she admitted to me. "But as resilient as the others, I assure you."

The healers knew more and were willing to share more in a few days than my mother in years. It made me hungry for more of what she might be able to give me.

"What about my soul? My blood? Is there anything you've noticed off about me?" I asked desperately, feeling like a weak fool.

"Well," she began. "Your soul is mostly light with darkness concentrated in the bloodstream and in wisps of darkness within the soul like most vampires," she explained.

At least that was a relief even if it didn't solve anything for me.

"The darkness is thinner in you than most," she murmured. "That's all I know."

I'd had both wilders and healers tell me similar things before. Why had I never caught on?

The landscape below changed from the rolling hills to the forests, and then back again as we approached the coastal regions. The land was flattening out, and hours ticked by as I endured the healer's jokes and flirtations. But it was still better than having my mother around.

Patches of green and purple empty fields now loomed ahead, small, simple houses scattered around them. This was the land the harvesters had been gifted now.

They didn't need shelters but had them if they wanted a sense of home of their own, but they spent most of their time harvesting souls, dancing, and telling stories.

In fact, there was a large group of them gathered together below us, singing slowly yet incoherently as they did some kind of shuffling dance in a circle with each other.

This was their version of fun, and they deserved it for all the years they served without complaint and continued to serve as long as they had a patch of green earth and dark souls to harvest.

It wasn't too bad of a life for them now, only I'd heard rumors that people were dropping by, asking for soul energy currency and doing them favors. So, some were still taking advantage of them, but it was better than it was.

The challenge ahead was getting them to talk to me in a way that made sense. I never was sure if their babbling was a secret language or due to days on end doing nothing but harvesting souls and getting nothing in return. A defense mechanism against punishment or because they had little to no education. I didn't stick around long enough to discover the reason since they truly did creep me out.

I thought it was because of their constant contact with dark soul energy. It morphed them into something strange and not like any other being I'd ever known.

We landed, and I thanked the redbill. "You can stay with him, if you'd like," I told Maefa. "I hope it won't be long. I just want to see what they might know."

She nodded and thankfully hung back. I had given up too much of my privacy lately.

Steeling myself with a deep breath, I walked toward those dancing and others gathering nearby, cooking something in a large pot and chanting along to the strange beat.

I didn't know how to get any of them to talk to me. The few who turned their heads to look at me let out that strange babbling language that didn't make any sense to me.

"Excuse me, who would I talk to about a possible prophecy?" I asked, passing several more. "About me?"

A couple of them pointed at me and groaned, reminding me of the human zombie fiction Roxy had talked about a few times. It gave me chills.

Finally, a harvester woman, a man, and several younger ones–teens maybe–approached me.

"Something strange," the woman said, pointing at me. Then she pointed to her head and then to mine.

"Oh, you want to touch my head?" I asked.

Feeling ridiculous, I leaned down, and each of them laid a hand on my head, their eyes closing. They muttered something under their breaths, another strange chant separate from the one the dancers and onlookers were using.

"Plane traveler," the woman declared.

"Belongs everywhere. Can fly," the man said, nodding his head in confirmation.

The teens oohed and awed. "Anomaly. Traveler of worlds."

I sputtered in annoyance, trying to ask them to explain, but they simply walked away. What could they mean?

Frustrated, I barreled through that group toward a small cluster of their homes, wondering if I'd find someone more helpful there. Though, it seemed unlikely.

Plane...traveler...fly. Were they saying I could fly between planes? Like the Mortal Plane and Immortal Plane? That idea was madness.

I talked with a few more harvesters, asking for more information, and they crowded me, practically pushing me toward one house in particular. With no other choice, I knocked.

The harvester who greeted me was much older than the rest. He was slow-moving. I supposed he was like an elder or a wise man. He too stepped forward as the others watched and laid his hands on my head. Chanting something.

He opened his eyes, walking around me in a circle while looking at me up and down. An odd prickle ran along my skin.

"Sir," I said, hoping to speak to reason. "Everyone keeps telling me something about traveling or flying between planes. Can you make any sense of it? My mother—Halla is her name—said there was a prophecy of some kind at birth."

"Yes," he said, nodding and looking me straight in the eye. He never wavered which was unnerving. "You are a traveler. Powers are not developed yet."

I shook my head, trying to get the crazy out. I didn't like the idea of developing some kind of magical powers like in a mortal fairytale that depicted supernatural things in a way that made no sense. It was laughable.

"But if I have special powers, what does that have to do with passing out? Not healing as well as other vampires?" I was getting angry with all the cryptic answers, and I didn't know how much stock to put into it, but then I thought about the dreams. The dreams I wasn't sure were only dreams.

I could "see" into the Pocket Space. Maybe I could see elsewhere too. And I could communicate with Roxy in the Mortal Plane. Maybe I wasn't understanding exactly what the harvesters meant, but there was more to it.

"Stay with us," the elderly harvester suggested. "Stay with us, and we will watch you when these things happen. We can give you more answers."

On the one hand, I wanted all the answers I could get, but I didn't think hanging out with harvesters was the best use of my time. And then Maefa would have to stay to watch over me for an indefinite amount of time or fly back and forth. I didn't know if the harvesters could provide medicine the way she could.

"Let me think about it," I said, walking away from the crowd.

This was complete nonsense. The kind of thing they made fun of at the VAMP Camp in Scotland. If I said so much of any of this out loud to other vampires, they would laugh at me and have my brain checked instead of just my body.

There was something different about me. I couldn't deny that, but the harvesters were barely making more sense than my mother was.

I walked toward where I'd left Maefa with the redbill and told her, only vaguely, what I'd found out and been offered. That I needed to consider staying with the harvesters.

Then, I walked away as far from anything or anyone as I could. There was only one person who could help me arrange my thoughts about this.

I needed to get a hold of Roxy.

20
Roxy

"So, what's next, boss?" Jordan asked in a teasing tone.

All three of us were covered in sweat. We'd been training for a couple of hours, but neither of the twins was ready to stop even though everyone else had gone back to their offices or to have dinner.

I laughed. "Are you sure you want to keep exhausting yourselves?" I asked, but I already knew the answer.

Just like for me, training was their safe space. They could clear their minds and focus on bigger and better things. They also wanted to be on their A-game now that they'd had experience in the field. Their maturity still wasn't necessarily there, but they realized how bad things could get in a split second.

"Well, we do get an epic three-day break starting tomorrow. Might as well make the most of what's left before then," Jordan said with a shrug.

The two of them were pumped, and I knew why. They were taking a break from all the grinding now that we were not on a mission and throwing a birthday party for themselves. They were going all out, as they should.

I smiled, happy about their energy. Sometimes, they were a pain in my ass, but it was times like these when we were all in sync together that they energized me and pushed me to be better still.

"Okay, that's fair. I guess you're going to be ready to drop for your party, then."

Jessie scoffed. "We're not old like you. We can go for days. Though we'll probably take day three to sleep it off."

I scowled at them as Jordan snickered. "I am not old."

"Maybe not in age," Jordan said with a laugh, "but in attitude. It's okay. We like you that way." He patted me on the back as I rolled my eyes.

"Okay, now the two of you are going to pay for that in drills," I warned, only half teasing.

I wiped the sweat from my brow and surveyed the two of them, thinking of a drill I could give them. They weren't stopping until they'd exhausted every muscle in their bodies.

"Okay, how about footwork," I said.

Thinking back to my experience with creatures like the Ghost, *I* could even work on something like that. It had turned out okay for me in the end, but if we ran into another desperate, wild creature of that size, footwork might be the only thing that could save us.

"Perfect!" Jessie said. "I'm so much better at that than you."

"We'll see," Jordan taunted.

I smirked. "Jessie, I want you to try backpedaling. Perfect the bounce and irregular pattern of movement to skirt and confuse your opponents."

Jessie bounced with anticipatory energy as she waited for my order for Jordan. Jessie and Jordan weren't as good at organized defense. The two of them loved to ambush enemies together, but that wasn't always the best course of action.

"Jordan, why don't you work on your diamond step. Use it to fool Jessie into thinking about what direction you're going for. Don't back down. Learning and perfecting irregular movements, fake-out techniques, and retreats that could confuse Leftovers' monsters could be the best way to save the team's life out in the field."

"Oh, this is going to be fun," Jordan quipped, both twins with their fists up and ready.

But then my phone began instantly buzzing against my hip.

"Hold that thought," I told them as I looked and saw it was Lyra.

I knew she and her team were out on a mission. If she was calling me, it could have been about something they'd found out.

"Lyra?" I answered. "Is everything all right?"

"As all right as we usually are on a mission." She sounded tense. not like something terrible had happened, but I could sense there was something off.

"Uh-oh. What's going on?"

"Oh, nothing. The usual. Leftovers behaving in strange ways...missing people. This time kids. And we have a rather uncooperative partner in The Bureau's chapter here in Miami."

I nodded, feeling bad for her. Lyra didn't like things not going smoothly or not being the one in control. If there was another team working with them, the dynamic would be totally different, and if they weren't playing as a team, then...

"How can I help?" I asked, knowing it wasn't just a friendly phone call. I loved hearing from Lyra, but I knew better than to think my phone was ringing for social purposes.

"How do you and the Hellraisers feel about Florida?"

Seriously? She was going to ask us to come to join them there? "Honestly, I hate paperwork and sitting around. You know that."

Lyra scoffed. "That I do."

"So, what's going on there that you need us? I thought this mission was only Leftovers adjacent," I stated.

Florida hadn't had much in the way of the Leftovers' problems up until now. I didn't know much about the case Lyra had gone for other than that people were missing and the missing cases happened to all occur close by to Leftovers' areas, but there had been little to no monster activity reports coming our way about the area. But maybe something hadn't made it down the pipeline the way it should have.

"Suddenly it isn't so adjacent," Lyra said, and I could hear the exasperation there. They had to have been having a rough time if Lyra was showing it, and I didn't think they'd even been gone that long. "The kidnappings may have taken us directly into the Leftovers in the Everglades, and the creatures here..."

Suddenly the hairs on the back of my neck were standing up in anticipation of her telling me what they were like. It had to be especially unusual, to be calling me in like this when she had a full team with her plus the branch of The Bureau they were working with.

"They're different. Think worst nightmare things, and we've got them. The Leftovers seemed to mutate these guys instead of killing them off, and imparting their own special style of taint."

I sucked in a breath. I knew what was lurking out there in the Everglades. Was she seriously talking about mutated alligators and snakes? That didn't sound fun at all, even as much as I enjoyed being in the field.

"That sounds rough, but why do I feel like there's more to it than that?" I pressed.

"Because there is. I'll brief you if you decide to bring the Hellraisers here, but basically, we just faced a giant Leftovers' creature outside of a tourist area. It nearly blew our cover and killed several innocents. Something much more is going on here than we expected."

I nodded through her explanation, taking it in stride. It was incredibly unusual for a creature to travel so far outside the Leftovers by itself and in the middle of a largely populated area. If you came near, you were fair game, but they didn't want to screw with anyone in the normal spots of the Mortal Plane.

I scratched my head, remembering the three-day holiday we were supposed to be getting. "How soon would you want me there?"

"We would be flying you out tomorrow night if you're up for it. We're pretty desperate here, especially with The Bureau here being underfunded and less cooperative than we would have liked."

It sounded like Lyra truly did need us, but I turned to the twins, watching them continue to face off regardless of the fact I hadn't been looking. They had worked really hard lately, taking things a little more seriously. I felt they deserved to have their birthday off and get to celebrate, and I wanted to celebrate with them. They would be devastated if they had to cancel all of their plans to go on a mission.

I couldn't seriously consider turning it down, though. It was our job. They would have to learn eventually. I just hated that it had to be specifically their birthday they would miss.

"Okay, I'll tell the team. We'll come help," I told Lyra. "Let me know what we need to do."

Lyra let out a relieved breath, and I bit my lip, dreading what I'd have to do when I got off the phone with her.

"I'll have Bryce organize everything with The Bureau," she said. "He'll handle the details. You just watch your phone for the specifics. We have the resources to lend you to gear up for the Florida branch. We need special equipment here, and the funding is lacking on the local end."

I took a mental note of all of it. This was going to be interesting if it required special gear, but my excitement was drowned out by the sadness that I would have to turn around and break this news to my siblings.

"Okay, thanks for thinking of us, Lyra. Your trust means a lot to me."

"Of course. You've grown a lot there, Roxy. It's great to see how far you've come. You're my go-to for this, and I'm sure Jordan and Jessie will be following in your footsteps soon enough." There was a smile in Lyra's voice.

"If only I can tame them!" I joked.

"Good luck with that. I'll see you soon." Lyra hung up, and I tucked my phone away, looking at Jessie and Jordan as they tried to beat the other.

Their footwork was pretty good, but they were so alike, ending up on an even playing field. Neither one could get the better of the other.

Noticing I was off the phone, Jessie stopped and looked at me. "Hey, what gives? Was that Lyra?"

Jordan stepped forward a few paces to come see what I had learned. The two of them looked curious, so I wondered if they could feel my tension. I was trying not to give anything away and be professional about it since I needed to set an example, but I had a heavy heart about the situation too.

This wasn't the news I wanted to deliver or the way I wanted to deliver it. It would have been ideal if we had a couple more days' notice, but that was the nature of this job. Missions could come out of nowhere, and it was part of dedicating yourself to such a cause. We went where they needed us when they needed us. And that was the strong front I needed to present.

I relaxed my forehead but kept a tight smile on my face. "Yeah, it was Lyra. They are on a mission in the Everglades right now."

"Trouble in paradise? " Jordan asked, snickering.

I nodded. "Actually, she was specifically calling in the Hellraisers. There's a situation with the Leftovers there that nobody expected. The Bureau location is severely underfunded and uncooperative with Lyra and her team. On top of that, they just tangled with a monster that showed up way outside the typical area and attacked a bunch of tourists. They're not going to be able to maintain the investigation and fight off the monsters. They need our help."

I was sure to look both of them in the eyes so they understood the importance of this. We were needed. That was the message I was trying to convey. It was our job to serve and protect in a way much higher than just the average street copper.

"Let me guess," Jessie said tensely, "we're going to be leaving immediately, aren't we?"

Jordan threw his hands up in the air, unable to contain his frustration. "What's the point of asking for days off if we don't actually get to take the time off?"

"I'm not happy about it either. I was looking forward to it just as much as the two of you to celebrate your birthday with you, but it's our job. We are needed to save lives."

I emphasized every word of the last sentence so they could get it through their heads. It was time for them to grow up. There was no room for immaturity in a group like the Hellraisers. Half the world had to grow up early in this generation as they watched the world change around them.

Nothing was truly sacred anymore, and maybe that was why they thought I was old. I had gotten pessimistic, but I didn't see it that way. I was just being realistic. And on most days, I loved what we did.

"You're getting too wrapped up in all of this," Jordan said, his tone low. "I know you're our leader. And I know that this is important. There are other teams. Maybe Lyra doesn't think they're as good as you, but your personal life should still be there. You're making sacrifices you don't need to, and now you're dragging us to do it with you."

I was taken a little bit aback by that statement. He wasn't yelling or having a fit, which was a good sign. However, he sounded concerned for me. I was used to being the one taking care of all my baby siblings. That job was even more important now that they were part of my team. I never expected them to try to school me.

"We just want balance with our career and our life, and we want the same for you," Jessie added more gently, knowing I was likely going to go off on Jordan for his assessment.

"This isn't about a career right now. This is personal. People were almost killed, and Lyra's cover was almost blown. Do you know what that could have meant for the vampires and The Bureau?" I asked, pacing back and forth in front of them.

I wanted them to really think about how their actions had an impact on others.

"Our expertise is needed, potentially to save lives. Of course we're who she would call. Would you trust someone else to do that? Truly?" I hated that I sounded too much like a mother scolding her children, but I was their boss when it came to missions. Plain and simple. "We must answer the call."

"You don't even understand where we're coming from. You don't have anything outside of this. And I can't blame you for that. You were helping Mom take care of us, but..." Jordan said, running his hands through his red hair.

"You were told what you were getting into when you joined up. You knew you were going to have to structure your life around this job. This isn't just any job. Making sacrifices is a part of it. Hell, that's a part of most of adult life. I get that you're still young. I do. I didn't want anyone else in our family to have to face these realities so fast. But to be fair, you did want this, whether you understood what you were asking for or not."

I huffed, exasperated at it. My past was coming up like bile, threatening to swallow me whole. I empathized more than they realized. Jordan had said it–I had been too busy raising them for much of a social life and had jumped at the chance to be a part of The Bureau. I wasn't like other young women. I set aside fun and relationships for them and then for this. Now, they were having to do it too.

I hadn't thought about it before, glad we were all together. But if I could have gone back and warned them not to do it, I would have.

"I get it, Roxy. I know we're needed. It just sucks," Jessie said, hanging her head.

I looked at Jordan, hoping he at least could accept this.

"I don't have a choice, but I still think you're holding yourself back, Roxy," he told me, his eyes more intense than I'd ever seen them. "You're getting sucked into this life and missing anything else. I don't want you to end up old, bored, and alone because you didn't take any time at all away. Think about it, okay?"

I tightened my jaw. "Fine. That's fair."

I didn't like it. I didn't like that my baby brother was calling me out or that there might be a bit of truth to it, but it was something I'd have to worry about once we got back. Right now, I needed to inform the rest of the team and pack.

"Let's head out. We need to gather the others and let them know, and then we should be packing."

Jessie patted her twin on the shoulder. "I know it's going to be hard to do it, but we can postpone the party. Just reschedule it. We'll work it out."

I was glad she was taking a better attitude on this. I hoped Jordan could see he would get another chance.

"I'll help in any way I can as well. You will have a party, just not yet," I added.

"After the party, I want us to revisit this. I want there to be more boundaries," Jordan said, shrugging Jessie's hand off. "And I want to know you're going to look out for yourself too. You deserve it."

His words squeezed at my heart. I was about to answer, but then there was a tense and loud call for me in my head.

"Roxy. Are you there?"

"Shit," I muttered. "Yes, we can talk about this another time." This was just going to piss them off more, but something was clearly not right with Kane, and I was his only mode of contact, or at least his fastest, here in the Mortal Plane. "Kane is calling, and it doesn't sound good."

"Fine, Jessie, let's get ready."

The two of them slumped off, and I reached back out to Kane.

Let me get settled back at my place. I can hear you, I told him, walking away. My stomach growled, having postponed dinner for more training. That might have to wait too. My body tensed at the feel of Kane in my head. What could it be now?

21

Roxy

$\mathcal{I}$ tried not to look like I was too much in a hurry getting back to my place, but truly I was. And I told myself it wasn't just because I wanted to hear Kane's voice. In truth, it was becoming something to look forward to, but I kept muttering to myself that it was about more than that. It was because he needed my help. It was my job, just like I had told the twins moments ago. Someone was in need, and I could help.

However, removing any emotions from it didn't help the beating of my heart to slow even once I made it inside my door. I went into the kitchen and scrambled through the fridge to find something simple. Luckily, I had pre-made some hard-boiled eggs, and I had some cut-up sausages from the previous night. Thank goodness for that.

I went about making my plate, pulling up the mustard to put over both. Then, I grabbed a bag of salad and poured it into a bowl, then drizzled some Italian dressing on top. I looked at it, and then I drizzled just a little more. I had done some extra training anyway, so why not? And I preferred to drown it in dressing.

Okay, Kane, I'm here, I called out in my mind as I sat down on my couch and pulled up a TV tray, though I didn't turn on the television this time. Kane was entertainment enough.

Don't go there, Roxy, I told myself. *The last thing you need to do is have him hear anything and derail all of this. He won't think he can come to you anymore.*

"Glad to hear it," he said, his voice ringing loud and clear.

So, what can I help you with? I asked him, mindlessly shoveling food into my mouth. It probably wasn't a pretty picture, but after everything I had done today, I felt like I was starving, and I knew it was going to be a long night. I would have to contact the rest of my team, pack, and help Kane with whatever was going on in the Immortal Plane.

I kind of hoped he had answers now and that was what he wanted to talk about. It still made me anxious every time I thought about the fact that he was still passing out for no apparent reason. If we knew why, then maybe we could do something about it.

"So, I took your advice and went to see the harvesters. I'm actually here now."

I scooted to the edge of the couch, very curious to hear what he had figured out. *To be fair, it wasn't my idea. You specifically asked me to push you to go.*

"True, but I figured I'd give you credit just the same," Kane grumbled, but I could hear the amusement in his voice as well. "Make up for the fact that I'm interrupting your night to ask your opinion. But it's kind of pressing."

Yes, because it's so awful having to talk to you, I huffed back sarcastically. *I was just sitting down to this lovely meal of leftovers, and no it has nothing to do with trees that eat people.*

Kane full-on belly laughed at that. "You certainly know how to make a guy feel good."

"I assure you, Kane, that I do," I said before I caught myself.

I panicked for a moment, worrying I had crossed the line. We'd always had a bit of banter back and forth, but that was full-on flirting.

"I'm sure you do, but I need your services elsewhere today. The harvesters are wanting me to stay here so they can watch me and give me more information about what's going on, but they seem to have some idea of what it is."

Do I want to know? I sent down the bond.

"You probably do, but it's like they're speaking in riddles. And if they're not, I'm not exactly amused at the idea."

He was stalling. Something about what they'd said was bothering him, but I didn't detect that it was anything dangerous. If anything, he sounded incredibly annoyed.

Well, out with it, I chided him.

"The harvesters keep babbling something about that I'm a traveler. That I can travel between planes. I don't know what kind of bullshit they're getting at, but it's got to be a joke, right?" he asked abrasively.

I nodded for a second, gathering my composure. On the one hand, it did sound crazy, but what about our lives wasn't crazy these days?

It wasn't actually that hard to believe, but it meant a lot of things, one of them being that it somehow related him distantly to creatures like the ghost. Why would he be able to travel between planes without the usual methods? And if he could, then how come it hadn't happened physically yet?

So you don't believe them. It wasn't a question.

"I don't know what to believe. Look, this sounds like the kind of stories that the vampires used to laugh about in VAMP Camp in Scotland. The way human culture has twisted vampires and our lore for entertainment. I'm just too old for all of this. It's ridiculous."

I could imagine his face screwed up in distaste. I put my hand over my mouth to remind myself not to laugh. Making fun of him wouldn't get either of us anywhere other than mad at each other.

Traveling between planes did seem a bit far-fetched, especially from a vampire's perspective. They always thought the supernatural existed, and that the supernatural had a specific set of rules. Traveling through dimensions certainly wasn't one of those rules.

Kane was entirely rigid in his belief system. I didn't know if I'd be able to change his mind on anything, but it was the best lead we had.

I get that it's easy to push it away and disbelieve it, but do you exactly have anything else to go by? I asked him, pushing him to think a little bit deeper.

I knew exactly what his problem was. It wasn't just about some cockamamie powers he didn't believe in. It was about staying overnight with the harvesters. He would see it as an imposition, at best.

He would be wasting his time, and he would be bored. Not to mention creeped out. I wouldn't exactly want to stay with them overnight either, but they said they had answers.

"No," Kane grumbled through the bond, "I guess I don't. I just don't want to waste my time here, and I'm not charmed by this idea at all. I don't want to develop powers and have to deal with them. Have to learn how to use them like some human fairy tale. I just want to have the same strength as other vampires and do what I'm supposed to be doing. Helping the Coalition and saving those kids."

I sighed at his continuation down this path of thinking. He had to take this seriously if he wanted answers, and he needed to learn patience most of all.

What about the dreams? I remember you telling me about those. We weren't sure if they were real or not, but if you think about what the harvesters said...

"So you do want me to put some stock into what the harvester said?" Kane asked.

You have to explore every possibility, like we already talked about. It was the only lead your mother was willing to give you, so unless you want to march back over to her house and demand, yet again, that she tell you something that she's not ready to tell you, then this is where you're stuck right now.

I cringed at how much I sounded like a mother. I was still stuck in training mode, or maybe it was a motherly love, considering the conversation I'd just had with the twins.

Kane sighed. "I know. I just can't wrap my head around it."

As if it's so easy to wrap my head around the fact that we can telepathically communicate to each other across planes, but that's obviously happening. It could be entirely part of what the harvesters are saying, too.

I heard a scraping sound I couldn't place, but then Kane's voice came back to me. "I don't want you to be right about this, but I guess you could be. I mean both of us have this weird power where we can talk in each other's minds. And there is something different about me. If the dreams were real, then it could be some kind of astral travel. They did say flying, but maybe that's what they meant?"

It would be something interesting to take into consideration. I finished off the last few bites of my food and leaned against the back of the couch. I closed my eyes and tried to imagine Kane and what he would look like right now. What he would be doing.

I knew he was with the harvesters, and he had probably ridden a redbill there. Maybe he was standing next to it, probably pacing back and forth and trying not to lose his cool over what he'd learned.

"So, my spirit is possibly traveling outside my body. I guess I could stay and see if that's what's happening when I pass out. But I don't know how the harvesters would figure that out."

You're right, but that's because little is known about them at all. They've been practically slaves up until now. I didn't know why I was snapping at him, other than the fact that there was a lot of tension in my body.

"Is something wrong, Roxy? You seem tense. More than normal."

What the hell does that mean? I shot back, trying to force my body to relax better. I hated the idea of suddenly being so uptight. I'd already heard that from the twins today.

I used to be so much fun, but now that I was leading the Hellraisers, it was also like I had lost some of that. Which would mean that there was some proof that the twins had been right. I was getting lost in a title and not being myself.

"Siblings giving you a hard time?"

Damn, I had sent that down the bond. *I don't need to bore you with my family problems. I know you're on a deadline to make a decision here.*

Maybe I just needed to talk for a moment about the situation, but it wasn't Kane's job to be my therapist or anything.

Kane chuckled. "You know I consider myself kind of an expert when it comes to stubborn family members. I've kind of been dealing with them all my life, so maybe I could be insightful to you if you want to share what's going on with me."

I didn't know if I wanted to dive that deep into my life with him, especially considering I was trying to detach myself and get over it. Whatever it was. But maybe he could be helpful, if only for distraction.

After the silence lasted for a bit too long, he asked, "Roxy, you there? There's no pressure. I just thought I would return the favor since I seem to be ranting to you a lot lately, whether intentionally or not."

He was right. He had opened up to me, so fair was fair.

I had to have a tough talk with the twins, Jessie and Jordan, just a bit ago.

"Oh?"

I could see Kane standing there while talking to me, raising his eyebrow and responding. It made me smile.

Yeah, Lyra actually called. There is some deep trouble in Florida. The Everglades. It's this big area of swampland that was full of a lot of scary things before the meld. Now it's even scarier, and the creatures are coming out of the Leftovers and hurting tourists. So, they can't focus on their mission without the monsters being taken care of.

"Well, isn't that kind of your job?"

My thoughts exactly, but there's one little problem. The next three days were supposed to be off for all of us because it's the twins' birthday. They planned this huge celebration. It took a lot of planning and a lot of money. Now they have to cancel it so that we can go on this mission and keep people from dying.

While hearing myself retell it to somebody else, I realized I did sound judgmental. Not everyone was as deep in it as I was. Not everyone had the same work ethic or planned not to have much of a life outside of The Bureau. My goals all had to do with my career, and my mother had problems with it before. In fact, every time I spoke to her, she pushed me to pull back from it, take a demotion, and go look for someone to marry. Start a family.

It wasn't like I was innately against those things, but they were on the back burner. I would be okay if I never had them. I would only go for them with the right person, and that person would have to deal with the fact that being a Hellraiser came first.

"It sounds reasonable. But I can also see why two people so young might be so affected."

It was surprising to me that Kane was actually being sympathetic. Most of our conversations were either light and funny or revolved around something to do with work. More than half of our conversations in each other's heads were about how to perfect those conversations. It was nice to share something personal for a change, but the closeness I was feeling with him was dangerous.

Yeah, and I feel bad because I didn't want them to have to grow up too fast the way I did. It was a burden I chose to bear. But on the other hand, this is their job. And they did choose this. I tried to explain, but now they're concerned. Things are tense.

"Concerned? " Kane asked incredulously. "What is there to be concerned about? "

I got up, shaking my limbs out. Trying to relax wasn't working.

Instead, I went into the bedroom, passing by my bed and going straight for the closet. I had to get up on my tiptoes to yank down the duffel bag that I would be using to pack. No need to take too many things. The most important things would be the equipment, which Lyra would provide.

They think that I've been missing out on life, basically married to my career. I set the bag down on the bed and began to fill it with some basic outfits, and I went to the kitchen and grabbed a few dry snacks from the pantry. *They think I'm pushing them into that too and that we're all getting in too deep to have a personal life. Honestly, they kind of sound like my mother. I stopped the conversation to come talk to you, but Jordan won't let go. He's telling me we need to discuss it when we get back.*

"I think both of you feel threatened."

Well, that had come out of nowhere.

Threatened by what? I asked as I zipped the thing up. It hadn't taken as long as I wanted it to. Now the distractions were over, and I plopped down onto the bed, causing it to make a strange squeaking sound. I hoped I hadn't busted a spring

"He's threatened that you're trying to control him and steer him into your life path the same way that your mother's doing to you. You feel threatened because you feel like you love what you do and you wouldn't know what to do without it. Which could be healthy but also unhealthy."

His logic was sound, but it meant that I was basically hiding behind my job to avoid failing in real life. Which would mean that Jordan and my mother did have some points.

I hate being wrong.

"You and me both," he said with a laugh.

His laughter warmed my heart and sent tingles all throughout my body. If only I got to hear it in person.

Shit, did I send that thought down the bond?

I stared up at the ceiling and forced my thoughts to clear again. *I guess we really have similar stuff with our families, huh?*

"With me being a vampire, the dynamics are definitely different, but there are some similarities. By the way, don't count on me to ever say it again, but I'm sorry for the way I reacted to you being in my head and hearing my conversation with my mother. It just took me a lot to go there and try in the first place. It felt like an invasion at the time."

My heart skipped a beat, and I took a deep breath as the rhythm tried to right itself. Not only was he apologizing to me, but he was admitting he had a bit of a problem with vulnerability.

You know what they say. The first step to getting help is admitting you have a problem.

"Well, isn't that the hard part?"

Only because of your big ego, I told him.

I liked this. The easy warmth between us, and just for one split second I thought about telling him how I felt about him. This would be as good a time as any to bring it up, but I clamped that down almost immediately. I didn't need him hearing it, and he was busy. I didn't think he wanted to try and process that in the middle of the harvesters, and I needed to be sure that he did stay and get the information that all of us could use.

"Hey, you know what?" Kane said all of a sudden.

What's up?

"Well," he said excitedly, "If what is going on with me is some kind of astral traveling, then that means one thing."

I waited for him to tell me since he'd left me on a dramatic cliffhanger with his sudden epiphany.

"Maybe I could use that power somehow to get back to the in-between space. I could find the kids and help them, maybe get them out. And I could find out more about what's going on there."

I pressed my fingers into my temples, frustrated that this was a topic of conversation once again. He was going to the harvesters to get answers, of course, but the main reason was so he could stop putting himself in danger by randomly passing out or to see if something could be done about his slow healing.

I didn't expect to come back around to this, an obsession growing once again. I could feel it buzzing in his mind.

I still don't think you're anywhere near being in the field. You have a lot to figure out first, I said cautiously.

I didn't want to upset him, but I couldn't stand the idea of him attempting to use this underdeveloped power to try and get to a place where no one could reach him and get hurt again, or worse.

But I'll admit it could be useful to more than just yourself in the future.

"Yeah," he grunted. "I know even Lyra wanted to get back there and get some answers. Her mission was never fully resolved, and everyone was bummed with the death of the Ghost."

I looked down with a sad smile, remembering the poor creature that was running itself ragged to try and fix something with the dimensions or dimensional travel. It had been a monster by technicality, but it was trying to fix anomalies. It never meant anyone harm.

Its fate had been unfortunate.

"Thanks, Roxy. I think I do need to stay the evening just in case the harvesters really can help me. You have a good night and a safe trip to Florida."

Okay. I got up and started changing into my pajamas, wanting to be comfortable for the long night of phone calls. *Good night, Kane.*

22

Roxy

I crashed into bed much earlier than I usually would. I had already called all of the Hellraisers to let them know to pack and be ready to go because we had an emergency mission. None of the rest of them gave me the kind of crap that Jessie and Jordan had, nor did I expect them to.

It wasn't early by any means, but I was usually a night owl even though I was also up early for training every day. Restless, I rolled over to my side, thinking over everything I'd done and hoping everything was ready to go. My worried mind went over the checklist again and again to make sure I hadn't missed anything.

Lyra had sent me the claim number for the tickets that would be waiting at the airport for us two afternoons from now, unable to get us out sooner as she'd wanted. The flight was going out at 4:00 p.m. to Miami on the small Bureau plane, and then we were to be met with a car. We would be taken to a hotel where we would find all the gear in the room.

I received a map with directions around the area including Everglades City, which was the little tourist town where the incident had happened with the Leftovers' monster. I also started going over the briefing letter Lyra had sent me from The Bureau department there in Miami.

I could see many places where the paperwork was lacking and

assumptions being made. I spotted the problem instantly. The man in charge, Torres, spoke a lot about vampires being the culprit, especially revenants. Both Lyra and I knew that the revenants were no longer really around, and the ones who were were no longer a problem. They couldn't be controlled anymore and were out of the country entirely. In fact, the entire Bureau was supposed to know that. So either there was a lack of communication with this Miami office or there were so many prejudices that Torres refused to believe it.

I felt bad for her and her team because they had three vampires there with them. That would be why he wasn't cooperating. He didn't want to work with them because he didn't trust them.

I hoped he didn't say anything to me, because I wouldn't hold back. The Hellraisers weren't necessarily part of the partnership there but were being brought in as experts—monster experts. So I would have more leeway to stand my ground. And if I could do so with my own mother, I could definitely do it with this asshole.

Still, he was nowhere near the most worrisome thing about the case. The whole thing revolved around missing teenagers and even a child. There was a concern about trafficking and people using the Leftovers to travel around and get away with it, so it wasn't as easy to track them or find those who were taken.

There was a lot at stake with this mission. But now that I was part of it, that made me responsible for the outcome. And now I was going into it with a team that was less than enthusiastic with me.

I tossed and turned, sweat slicking my neck and my hair. I was afraid that the fight with my siblings would get in the way of the mission. It very well could, especially if they continued fighting me in front of the rest of the team. They could undermine my ability to lead.

Even worse, they could completely refuse to follow orders. But I hoped that they had enough sense to show some maturity, enough care for our relationship, not to do such a thing. If only my brain could shut off and let go of the worry about it.

I needed to sleep, but the swirl of thoughts continued. The next thing to pop up in my head was Kane. Kane and his ridiculous obsession with getting back to the Pocket Space so quickly. I worried that he wouldn't even listen to me in the end. As soon as he found out a little bit of something from the harvesters, he might take off on his own and not tell anyone.

Then, he would do something dumb and possibly end up passing out on top of a redbill or getting eaten by some monster and nobody would even know what happened to him. It would happen long before I knew enough to save him, and because I had spoken up against it, he probably wouldn't even try to contact me and tell me what he was doing.

I grunted into my pillow and pounded my fist against it. I wished I could just go to sleep and stop being so uptight. It wasn't like me. I guessed this was the new me.

Then, I sat up in bed with a startling notion. He had traveled all the way to the harvesters, and I hadn't heard mention of anyone with him. Did he seriously try to go all alone? He was still healing.

For a moment, I thought about calling out to him to check but then realized that would just frustrate him and distract him from the task at hand. Hopefully, if something did go wrong, the harvesters had the ability to help him.

I forced my head back onto the pillow, turning over onto my right side. I began to trace random shapes with my fingertip into the sheet to try and pass the time. I found myself absent-mindedly still thinking about Kane and the conversation we'd had.

It had been one of our better ones. It felt like we were getting even closer to something more. This mental connection between us was forming a more emotional bond.

I thought of his deep voice, his stubbornness, and his face. In my head, I traced the lines of his masculine jawline and trailed over his pale skin. I imagine his shirt off again, as I often did. And I realized I had it so bad, it wasn't even funny.

Have I ever felt this way about a guy?

I couldn't recall being so obsessed that I fantasized about someone when I wasn't there with them. There might have been a lack of opportunity, considering I'd been more focused on my career in my training, but something told me it was more than that. There was something real between us, but unfortunately, it didn't mean much. I worried that whatever I felt wouldn't pass, but instead would keep getting stronger and I would just end up getting hurt. And then there would be no way to permanently disconnect our thoughts from each other.

"Can I sit next to you?" a small, high-pitched female voice rang through my head.

It wasn't a voice I recognized. Who was I hearing now? Or had I finally lost it?

"The other side of the fire seems so far away," the voice continued.

"Sure." That was Kane's voice.

How had I slipped back inside his head?

"How are you holding up? A lot of us have been worried about you with your lack of healing and the fact that you are still having these episodes. I really hoped you could get your answers here."

The woman seemed to be scrambling for something to talk about. Wait, maybe I did recognize the voice. The healer, the one that was always so impressed with Kane. But then, what was she doing there? Kane hadn't mentioned that she'd come with him, or that anyone else had, for that matter.

On the one hand, it was smart of him not to go alone. I wanted that peace of mind that he was going to be okay. A healer would usually be the best person in this case, but more than anything, the fact that he didn't tell me that he was there with another woman, especially one who continued to flirt with him, hurt me.

Did he not realize that there were any feelings there? I didn't think he could be that blind. I mean, we'd kissed twice. Even if it didn't mean a whole lot to him, it had to count for something.

"I seem to be feeling all right. I'm just ready for my arm to be out of this cast and to feel freer with my movement. It's better every day but not fast enough."

So, at least he was starting to heal.

"I can have another look if you want. That's what I'm here for." The healer gave a nervous laugh.

I turned over on my other side. I needed to find a way to disconnect. I couldn't be here. If he caught me again, especially at a time like this, I didn't think we'd ever recover.

But more than that, I didn't want to hear this. Whatever could be there between them, or might develop, with the two of them alone by a fire and nothing but the harvesters around, I didn't want to hear it, and I couldn't bear it.

Think about something else, I told myself. *Think about the mission we're about to go on, about fighting with your siblings. Think about what you will have everyone do at the next training.*

I tried everything I could imagine to get out of Kane's head. This was too private.

"Maybe in the morning. Thank you, Maefa," Kane said.

Since I was unable to disconnect, with slight amusement, I wondered where the conversation was going to go. I guess I was just a glutton for punishment because I decided to stop trying to disconnect. I would keep my mouth shut and not let him know I was there. And I would just listen.

It wasn't just about jealousy, but I kind of wanted to know what his reaction would be if he realized what this Maefa was up to.

It was silent for a bit, and I wondered if I had successfully removed myself just when I was resigning myself to having to be privy to it. But then her mousy voice spoke again.

"You know, even though you said you might stay a few days and I could be free to take the redbill back, I figured I'd stay at least tonight to make sure that you're okay. We don't want anything to happen like you falling out of a tree again. And I just feel like I should be taking care of you."

Oh god, could she have been any more obvious? That sentence was dripping with innuendos, and I was somewhere in between being incredibly jealous and laughing about it. If Kane were interested, I was going to be pissed. But I kind of had to know.

Worse to hear though, would be him figuring out what Maefa was getting at and him not being interested. That was going to be the most awkward conversation of his life. Would he send her away or would he try to slip away from her and go contend with harvesters instead?

"That's very thoughtful of you, Maefa," Kane told her, sounding stilted.

Oh, this was so bad. I stifled a laugh into the pillow because I didn't want the emotion to make it through the bond and him know I was eavesdropping on whatever this was.

"I hate being such a burden on you and the other healers like this. I should be out there going on new missions and finding out other ways to help and more things about the Pocket Space."

So he was so obsessed that he was mentioning that to her too. I wondered if she even understood what the Pocket Space was.

"I know you felt a little cooped up," the woman said, "but it's been nice having you around. You're always good company."

I could almost picture this woman cozying up to him by the fire and trying to get something out of him.

I shouldn't be so jealous, mostly because I was pretty sure that if I was the one in the Immortal Plane, Kane would have taken me on the trip instead of this Maefa woman.

Listening more to this conversation as the captive audience, I was pretty certain that Kane wasn't into this woman the way she was into him. I didn't really have something to worry about now that I heard the back and forth with two totally different tones. Though, I worried for a moment that Kane was that daft, not knowing what this woman was up to with him.

Kane didn't even respond this time, so she kept going, painfully making her flirting more and more obvious.

"So, I know you wanted to talk to the harvesters about something. What are they helping you with? I know you seem to be going through something, so you're welcome to pick my brain anytime or just share with me how you're feeling. I am a great listener and can be a good shoulder to lean on."

Oh, I bet she is, I found myself thinking. *Shut up, Roxy. He's going to know you're there if you keep saying stuff like that.*

"It's just a lead on something."

Ha! He was being so vague with her that he clearly hadn't mentioned anything to her about what the harvesters had told him. So, he wasn't close with her at all. She was probably just his best choice so that he wasn't alone. For all I knew, he was doing it so it wouldn't piss me off to find out he'd gone alone and then gotten hurt again.

"Well, I do hope they can give you some answers," she said, trying to get his attention once more.

It was a hard thing to hold, and I kind of felt sorry for her.

"Me too." His voice sounded distant like his thoughts were elsewhere.

"You know," Maefa began, and I could tell that she was trying to sound seductive even though her voice was so high-pitched. She reminded me of a little rodent rather than a woman. "I don't have to leave. I could stay. I don't think it's a secret that I really like you and for more than just your looks. And if you're more of a one-night stand kind of guy, I could always spend the night. I know how to not get clingy. And I could still be here for you through whatever you're dealing with. I'd really love to help."

I smacked myself on the forehead. She really did sound like she wanted to help, but I wasn't quite sure it had anything to do with his health or his powers.

That confession was awkward as hell to listen to, but I was practically holding my breath to see how Kane would respond to it. Maybe it would give me some insight into how he might respond to me if I told him I had feelings. Not that I would tell him in that manner and offer to basically crawl into his bed and be whatever he wanted me to be, but it was as close to an example as I was going to get.

An emotion from Kane hit me like a ton of bricks. He was confused. I guessed the conversation wasn't going the direction he thought. So, he *was* kind of daft. Imagine that.

Could that be why we hadn't had any conversation yet about feelings or our kisses? Maybe it wasn't all just about the fact that he wasn't interested in anything.

He seemed to be taking a moment to gather his thoughts. They were all jumbled together, though, so I couldn't decipher exactly what he might say. It was only clear he was taken aback. So, he must not have known that she was trying to flirt with him before now.

I tried to imagine someone flirting with me when I didn't know it and then suddenly offer to take me to bed for a one-night stand. I'd probably punch them in the face. Hopefully, Kane could handle it a little bit better than that.

"Wow, Maefa, I really appreciate how comfortable you are around me, and I'm incredibly flattered that you would think of me that way. I'm so sorry I didn't realize that there was anything going on before. I've been kind of lost in my own problems. That was selfish of me."

It warmed me inside that he was being respectful to her while trying to turn her down, but I tried to imagine myself in those shoes, and that would hurt to hear. Well, not hurt. It would be incredibly humiliating. But hopefully, it wouldn't be for her. I mean, she had been brave enough to literally offer a one-night stand. If she'd been offering that to anyone else, I might have high-fived her for her boldness.

"That's okay," she responded, all seductiveness in her voice gone.

"I'm also sorry I dragged you all the way out here and then dashed your expectations. But if I'm being honest, I don't want to date right now. I have a lot of other things going on, and I'm not sure if I'm ready for that or not. And I'm just not a one-night stand kind of guy. Absolutely nothing against you," Kane continued.

I rolled over onto my back, breathing a sigh of relief. I felt like I could try again to disconnect. I closed my eyes and tried to think about the Leftovers' monsters I'd fought. I thought about my mother and some of the fights we'd had, but none of it seemed to work. I was still stumped on this controlling the connection thing. Maybe there was no hope for it.

So, instead, I was voyeur to an awkward silence between the two of them. In fact, they were so silent and still that I could hear the crackling of the fire ringing inside of Kane's head. Did he really feel that bad for turning her down? Kane had a tough exterior, but he was really kind inside. He didn't want to hurt her feelings.

Finally, Maefa cleared her throat. "If it's not too much of an imposition, can I just ask you for a reason?"

My body tensed up, hearing her continue, and I felt bad for her. Really bad now. She had a right to know, I supposed, but since he'd been so clear and said he didn't want to date, I would have left it at that if I were her.

"Are you just not attracted to me, or is there somebody else?" She took it a step further. She just couldn't let it go. And I could hear the miffed tone that she was trying to hide and failing.

However, I had to admit that I was hanging by a thread, waiting to hear what Kane said to her. She had blatantly asked if there was somebody else he was interested in. Maybe with his mannerisms, she saw something that I couldn't. Maybe the fact that he just didn't want to date was not the full truth.

After a few heartbeats, Kane said, "Yes, there is somebody else."

My heartbeat picked up so fast that I was sure I was going to have a heart attack and that the flight to Florida was going to be a no-go.

"There is someone I've become very close to. To be honest, I don't even really understand my feelings for her, but there's something about spending time with her. Just talking to her."

His tone was off, sounding more sad or disappointed instead of like he was actually into someone. Was he trying to soften the blow for Maefa, or was there something else? I couldn't even be sure that he was talking about me.

"I'm not really that vulnerable of a guy. I've kind of been taught to be a certain way, to be outwardly strong, and to deal with my own problems. Which is an issue I need to deal with on my own. It's nobody else's problem, but it makes it hard to talk to people and open up. But I've been really opening up to her, and we relate on a lot of levels even though we're from totally different walks of life," he continued.

"That does sound confusing, having baggage like that and trying to work out what you feel for someone," Maefa lamented.

Maybe she thought if she was sympathetic to how he felt that she might still eventually get something out of it. I couldn't really blame her. It was a solid strategy.

"It's more than just that. I get this feeling when I'm around her. I know there's something there. And she's incredibly beautiful and strong in all the right ways, but I'm honestly afraid that it would never work out. That's why I'm really not in a good space for dating right now...of any kind."

I was taken aback at the statement. Was he talking about us or not? And if so, why did he think it wouldn't work out? Of course, personally, I knew the answer to that if he was talking about me. I'd thought the same thing many times. There were prejudices on both sides of the aisle with our families and the fact that he wanted nothing to do with the Mortal Plane unless he had to be here for a mission, and I had no intentions of moving to the Immortal Plane and giving up my position with the Hellraisers. I didn't know if anything would change that, even falling head over heels for someone.

But hearing the possibility out of his mouth, that he honestly thought it was doomed, threatened to bring tears to my eyes.

He can still be talking about somebody else, I told myself.

"Oh, why don't you think it will work?" Maefa asked, perking up a little.

"We're on very different life paths from each other. And if we got together, it would be a long-distance thing for the foreseeable future, possibly even forever. Then there are things about our families that we would have to fight through. They wouldn't exactly approve of the relationship."

There it was. Kane wasn't mentioning my name or the fact that I was human, but I couldn't think of anyone else that he could be referring to at that moment. We were about as long-distance as it got, and we definitely had the issue of our mothers.

"It's probably for the best if nothing ends up coming from it. I just have to get through it."

I felt like I couldn't breathe. Incredulous and in anguish at the same time. I was not prepared to hear his blunt reaction to his feelings for me. I was more prepared to hear that he didn't have feelings for me at all.

I definitely needed to find a way to disconnect now. My emotions were heightened, and I needed to deal with them.

I didn't think I had made any sounds or my thoughts had been too loud so that he was hearing me or knew that I was around, but I knew it could go into that territory if I stuck around.

He hadn't heard my thoughts so far, so why would he hear them now? But I needed to make sure it stayed that way.

I rolled over again, gripping the blanket in my fist. I willed my thoughts to go anywhere else because I couldn't handle the pain right now. I didn't think I'd ever felt such heartbreak. But then again I'd never been so serious about having feelings for anyone either. Not like this.

"Roxy? Are you there?"

No, this couldn't be happening. He couldn't be hearing me now. Maybe he was just feeling my presence in general. At least I could get lucky in that aspect. I couldn't bear to talk to him right now. Not after what I'd just heard. I didn't even want to know if he knew any of my feelings that were coming through.

I imagined a wall over my thoughts. I imagined pushing Kane away entirely. And for the first time, I succeeded in completely severing the mental connection. It was like I had ripped myself away from his head.

I sat up in bed, knowing I would never be able to go to sleep now. So what was I going to do? Now that I knew he had feelings but that he didn't expect it to work or even really sound like he *wanted* it to work?

I didn't know how I'd be able to talk to him again, but I knew that I had to.

23
Lyra

After having a gloriously large cup of coffee, we were all now back at the boardwalk for another day of investigations. I'd been up most of the night along with Dorian and Bryce setting things up for the Hellraisers to be able to fly in tomorrow evening. They were supposed to be arriving around 8:30 tomorrow evening and taken directly to their hotel.

All of their gear was supposed to be waiting for them in the hotel room. It had taken quite a bit to arrange that part, considering the special suits that were needed to go into the water. The Miami Bureau didn't have any more of them, nor did they have the funding to get more. So we had to get a hold of the ones who had called us in at Homeland Security to loosen their purse strings a bit.

Everything was ready to go, but it had left me exhausted. The work didn't stop, because we needed to figure out what was going on with this airboat business's warehouse. It was our best lead yet, and we needed to get on top of it before even more children and teens went missing or got hurt. Not to mention tourists, considering it seemed like someone was stirring up Leftovers' monsters and luring them into populated areas.

I held a corn dog in my hand, though I wasn't really hungry. It was mostly for appearances. Dorian and I were together, the team having been split up into groups of two. We would be less conspicuous that way.

We'd gotten new outfits, each of us wearing something different this time so we didn't look like we were a group. Hopefully, nobody would recognize us from the day before. In fact, maybe all the people that had witnessed the humongous Leftovers' snake would stay away for a while after what they had experienced. But you never did know with people sometimes. Some people became fascinated with the Leftovers and the creatures, which was partially what led us into this case to begin with.

"I don't know how many more times we're going to be able to come here and not be noticed. We're clearly tourists, so it's not like we're locals constantly visiting," I commented. I was in a rather pessimistic mood from my usual.

Dorian placed his arm around me. "We have to follow up on that warehouse lead. We don't really have a choice, but it'll be all right. We always figure things out, Lyra. We just have to have faith that the answer will come to us."

As we passed by the warehouse, pretending we were going for a stroll and admiring the view, I paid close attention to Dorian's reaction. What did he sense?

Dorian leaned down to kiss me on the cheek and muttered against my skin, "It's still occupied by many dark presences. There are a few light ones too."

I shook my head. "It's what I thought. They've got to be involved. I just don't know how to approach this and keep our cover. I just want to rush in and arrest someone or shake them for answers."

Dorian squeezed me tightly, knowing my frustration. When we had gotten up, we had another briefing from Torres. In the last twenty-four hours, two more kids had disappeared. Or rather, they had been reported missing. They had gone missing together but were last seen on the day that we had arrived here in Florida.

It had taken a few days for the police report to be filed and for the information to be passed over from the precinct that was involved with our team. Once they realized that there was a potential connection between this disappearance and the other ones we were investigating, the police handed it over to Torres late last night.

Whoever the perpetrator, they were quickly taking more victims, and that made me even more determined to figure out what was going on and save them. And I was angry. How could someone be so dark as to do something like this? I didn't think I could ever relate. No matter how many monsters I'd dealt with, human or otherwise, I could never understand them or pick their brains apart. It just didn't make any sense to me. And I couldn't fathom how Dorian was so calm about it.

We reached the area we had been assigned and stopped for a moment, looking over the water. We held hands and looked like a curious tourist couple enjoying a romantic moment. I spotted a trash can nearby and chucked the corn dog into it real quick.

"How are you holding up with all that makeup on?" I whispered to Dorian, trying to get into a teasing mood, but it didn't do a whole lot to lift my spirits.

"I guess you get used to it after a while. Poor Chandry though. She keeps complaining that it's too thick and it itches."

I hated that they had to cover up at all, but opinions could be more dangerous than some people realized.

I smiled sympathetically and looked to where Chandry and Sike were, on the bench staked out closer to the warehouse.

"Everyone seems to be in great moods this morning," Dorian observed, being sarcastic.

I shrugged. We all had a reason.

"Like Bryce who's been pissed off ever since we got here."

I cringed. I knew it would come up sooner or later. Dorian was quite observant and probably had been patient in trying to get answers from Bryce or waiting for me to tell him. He surely knew I'd spent some time alone talking to him when he was driving the RV.

"Yeah, that. I've been meaning to talk to you about it, but we never get a moment alone."

Dorian brought my hand to his lips and kissed it. "If you want to talk, we're alone now. Is there any way I can help him?"

"It's about him and Arlonne. You know that their relationship has progressed to the point that the curses set in. And because of it, they're spending time apart. They have to. You know we went through that in the same way."

Dorian pulled me in close. That had been a terribly hard time in our lives, so I didn't even want to say the next part. But I also didn't want to hide anything from him. Dorian was a generous man, and I knew what he might offer. I just didn't know how we got through it professionally or otherwise.

Dorian kissed me on the forehead.

"There is a way we might be able to help him, but it's not ideal, " I explained.

He squeezed my hand, letting me know I could keep going.

"Bryce and Arlonne have been talking to Reshi. Reshi's asking to borrow our necklaces to try to reverse engineer them. There's a chance that he'll be able to figure them out so that he can make more. If he does, it means that Bryce and Arlonne can be together. Until then, they don't see much of a future, so I'm sure both of them are in a bad mood."

I shrugged like it was no big deal, but it was. There were so many worries and things that could go wrong. What if we never got the necklaces back to working again? How would we be together?

And there was more at stake now because, not only were we married, but also we were running the main team at Callanish together. We couldn't just abandon that.

Dorian scratched his head. "I'm not exactly opposed to that idea, even though there are consequences to it. I mean, the ability for other vampire-human couples to work out and not be in pain... I can't really deny that if we are the way to help them, but I do have concerns. What if the necklaces get damaged during the reverse-engineering process, or what if only arbiters can create them?"

His eyes on me were intense, and I knew it didn't matter what worries he had. He was going to suggest doing it anyway. We would just have to find the right timing and the right plan for it to affect everyone the least.

"I know you're right," I told him, leaning into him. "I'm just scared like you are. Plus, I don't know if we can convince Bryce that there's no need for him to make that sacrifice for the sake of us. That his happiness matters just as much as ours."

"Bryce is a stubborn man," Dorian relented. His face turned serious, and he froze, letting go of my hand. "Get the comm. I smell something. It's dead, and it reeks of Leftovers."

We didn't have to go far to track the scent. The smell became overwhelming as we passed by a couple, posh-looking in the fanciest clothes we could possibly imagine seeing here. I would expect such a thing in the dock of Miami but not here in Everglades City. They were pushing a large cooler down the boardwalk toward the loading and freight area. They were moving from the direction of the warehouse.

I called for Sike on the comm first. "Hey, are you guys getting any kind of read on these people pushing the big cooler?" I asked them as discreetly as I could.

Sike instantly answered back. "Yeah, Chandry and I were going to call you. We saw the couple coming out from the back of the warehouse with that cooler. The thing reeked. Bothered both our senses," he explained. "Bryce also just called us too. He and Cam picked something up on the scanner. I know they're a little bit farther out than we are, but they're closer to where they're approaching now. There is a faint supernatural ping on whatever is in there."

I looked at Dorian, not understanding why they would be carrying a dead Leftovers' monster in a cooler. What would be the point in that? But they were clearly doing something with it.

"It's definitely the remains of a Leftovers' monster, at least one if not more," Dorian explained.

"Let's loop Bryce in, then," Sike suggested.

Dorian used his comm to contact Bryce. "There's this couple heading towards you. We think those supernatural signals you picked up are coming from them, or rather what's in their cooler, which might be a dead Leftovers' monster. Let us know your impressions and see if you see anything we don't."

There was something incredibly sexy about when he took charge like that, and I couldn't help but look up at him admiringly. I was going to miss this when we had to be apart without the necklaces.

"Chandry is back with me now. She was actually able to get up on the roof," Sike said through the comm.

Good, maybe we could get information without creating a scene. It wasn't like we could just arrest these people with no cause and then let them go once we had no reason to hold them anymore.

If that happened, they would just start up whatever operation they had going somewhere else, and we may never find them again.

"Did she get anything?" Dorian asked.

"Let me put her on," Sike offered.

Chandry spoke into the comm, explaining she'd jumped onto a nearby building and was able to hear a conversation the couple was having at the back of the warehouse before they started dragging a frozen, dead monster down the docks.

"They were using strange words, but then I figured out it was code," she said. "Cajun poppers, they called them, like they were catching something and making food out of it."

I cringed, alligator tails and the like coming to mind. I wasn't a fan of that kind of Cajun food, but it took on a whole new meaning after seeing the Leftovers' gators. Not something I would have wanted to ingest.

"Were they referencing Leftovers' monsters?" I asked her.

"Yes. It seems they are selling monster parts as a part of their business."

I didn't know what that had to do with the children, or even if it did. We could have been dealing with two unrelated cases, stumbling upon this operation by mistake while investigating. Either way, it was troubling. Who wanted to buy these monster parts?

Collectors? Scientists? Or was it really restaurants?

Ew.

"I think we need to all meet back at the RV," I said.

Dorian passed the message on to Bryce, and we walked away from the docks, not making eye contact with the couple as they made their way back from dropping off the frozen body parts.

We needed to formulate a plan on what to do about these people and move on in the investigation. It was as close to a lead as we had beyond the websites, but I couldn't say if they were only linked to the one missing boy or all the cases.

For all I knew, it was one big underground network that had previously gone unnoticed with the understaffed local Bureau, the only thing to monitor such occurrences beyond the regular ill-equipped and ill-informed law enforcement.

I couldn't sit down once inside the RV, biting my thumbnail as we all thought about what to do next.

"The airboat company needs to be investigated," Bryce said. "We need to know if it's just a front or if something more sinister is going on out on the water."

"How would we do that, though? I'm assuming there's a reason we didn't just walk up to these people and ask what the smell was," Chandry noted.

Dorian snorted. "You're right, it would have gone badly. Put them in defensive mode and made them shut down, if not get dangerous. I hate to say it, but what we need is a disguise. Someone who can go in and pretend to be an interested party wanting to buy monster parts."

I took my thumbnail out of my mouth and pointed at him, shaking my finger with enthusiasm. "Yes, if we did that, the person could be wearing some kind of recording device. We might be able to gather some incriminating evidence. It would give us more cause for warrants and questioning which could lead to us determining for sure if this is also connected to the disappearances," I said, glad we had something we could work on.

The plan might end up failing miserably, but at least we had one.

This was the best part of my team—our ability to work and think together.

"Wouldn't they still be in trouble for venturing into the Leftovers and taking others with them? Not to mention doing stuff to the Leftovers' creatures," Cam asked.

I knew he had recently become more sympathetic to the plight of the creatures plaguing Leftovers' areas across the country. I was sure part of it had to do with the small, spiky rodent he had bonded with that was currently contentedly crawling all over him as he sat at the table.

"It's a possibility, depending on exactly what they're doing and why they're doing it," I said.

"Lyra." Dorian's voice was low, unsettling. He narrowed his gaze at me, trying to get a message across. "We have to make sure that whoever it is, they are human. If these people are used to dealing with the supernatural, they would easily sniff out a vampire." Dorian pointed to our vampire companions.

"The female suspect, assuming we end up finding her here since we've found the male suspect before, has seen Cam and me already. She would know we weren't just customers." I hated to think she would be involved after almost entirely dismissing her, but there was no room for the risk.

Damn. I could have volunteered someone from Torres's team, but I didn't know if I could trust them to do the right thing and ask the right questions.

"It's up to me, then," I said. "I'll have to be an undercover agent and inquire about the monster parts."

24
Kane

I had spent a whole night with the harvesters, but nothing had happened other than them keeping me awake with their strange rituals. I didn't understand them, but they didn't creep me out quite as much anymore. They just had their own way of life. One I didn't understand, and it wasn't fair to judge them based on that, especially considering they were so eager to help me.

After the strange conversation with Maefa, I had learned the elder who was the most helpful to me was called Carrew. It took great effort for him to speak with me, but I was beginning to understand him slowly. He mentioned they had formed their own way of speaking over the years, isolated from the rest of us and not having much time for social interaction when their sole purpose was to harness the dark soul energy.

But something else about the day was on my mind too. I swore that during the conversation with Maefa, I felt Roxy's presence in my head.

I never heard her speak, so maybe it was a good sign that she had somehow found a way to disconnect when she began hearing a conversation between me and someone else again. But what had she heard before she'd disconnected?

Sweat pooled at my brow, and I wiped at it. It would have been a very inopportune moment for her to be listening in because she either heard another woman asking to accompany me to my bed, or she would have heard me talking about my feelings for her and how I was afraid it might not work.

I had worded what I said carefully since Maefa had been so eager but also pissed about my rejection of her.

Those words were not meant for Roxy's ears.

I needed to find out asap if that was the case and do some kind of damage control if I could, but I was incredibly embarrassed at the whole thing.

I also needed to send Maefa home. I hadn't forced her to leave the night before to try and be courteous after I had to let her down, but I couldn't imagine spending another day with her here. I would have to just trust the harvesters to take care of me until I made it back to the healers, assuming I needed or wanted to go there.

I didn't want any awkwardness between Maefa and me, so if that were still there when I went back, I might have to take my chances with my mother.

The harvesters were mostly working right now, so I found a quiet space outside and sat on the ground, closing my eyes and trying to reach out for Roxy. I knew she would be leaving sometime today or tomorrow to head to Florida, but hopefully, I could catch her for just a few moments to glean what she had overheard.

Roxy?

I pushed my desire to talk to her through the bond too since emotions seemed to have a strong response. But it was silent. Not just silent, but empty.

It bothered me, a weight on me as I went about the rest of the day, but I told myself she was just busy. She would get with me at our usual time.

Instead, I went out to find Maefa and prepare her to travel back. I didn't have to say much, though. She was already waiting for me by the redbill.

"How was your sleep?" she asked pointedly, and I suddenly had no more patience for her.

"It was all right. I think it's best if you go and head back. You have more patients than just me to look after, and I am going to be here until they figure something out." I pointed to the harvesters. "I'm sure they have a way of contacting you if something bad happens to me."

I kept eye contact with her so she might get the picture without me having to be rude.

She sighed. "Okay, but please be careful. We don't want you getting hurt again."

"I will. I know better. Too many people to yell at me this time," I assured her.

Roxy and Halla would chop my head off if I let myself get hurt like that for doing something stupid or wandering off again.

I watched her get onto the redbill, a little sloppily, but then she hung on, and I directed him to take her home and then come back for me once he was rested.

When I turned back toward the harvesters' encampment, Carrew was coming out of his hut, searching the area for me. I walked back over to his place. His hand flew up to my forehead before I had a chance to say if it was all right or not. But I supposed they needed to be able to touch my skin to get some kind of reading. They seemed to be a mystical branch of the species, another thing I could check off on the list of cheesy, fairytale elements my life had taken on lately.

"Traveling is locked. Need to expand your mind," he said. "Tonight. We work on it."

It wasn't a question. I had agreed to stay and get their help, so I would do what I was told to achieve that. While I was here, I was in their territory and had to respect their elders. It was the least they deserved after a lifetime of service to the entire city of Vanim.

I didn't know what he meant, though. Not exactly. What did astral travel entail, and how could I use it for anything other than talking with someone in my mind in the Mortal Plane? That didn't seem that useful of a power to have, no matter how much I enjoyed some of our conversations.

I wandered aimlessly through the expansive territory the harvesters called home, counting the minutes and hours until when I would normally meet with Roxy, which was around her dinnertime. Then, I sat back down and reached out.

Roxy, you there? It's time for our meeting. Can I talk to you? I tried to sound as normal as possible so as not to chase her off in case she had heard something she didn't like, but it was radio silence. Where the hell was Roxy?

Now I was getting a taste of how she must have felt when she couldn't get a hold of me when I had fallen out of that tree. I didn't like it.

I didn't like how it made me feel.

A raw panic rose within me, and I didn't know what to do. The Coalition was back in downtown Alcanthe where I left them. The redbill wouldn't be back until at least tomorrow. So, I had no way to contact The Bureau or Lyra about Roxy to see if she was all right and could be reached the way she had contacted The Coalition to check on me.

What if something was wrong with her? I had always seen Roxy as invincible, which was silly, considering she was only human, breakable, killable, much more than I was. But I had been the one passing out and disappearing into the Pocket Space, not her.

She had her team, her weapons, and her intelligence.

But she was one big monster bite away from not existing anymore. That was the first time I'd really thought about it.

What was I supposed to do?

There was an alternative. One I didn't want to think about any more than her body lying cold and dead somewhere, no more warmth in her lips or her skin.

She might have been in my head long enough to overhear the conversation I'd had with Maefa last night. If she heard the first part, she would have heard me alone with Maefa at the fire and heard Maefa trying to get me to realize she wanted something romantic with me.

Maybe Roxy would have caught on much faster than I had.

I'd turned her down, but that didn't mean Roxy didn't disconnect before then. She could have made the assumption I'd taken Maefa to my bed.

On the other hand, she could have heard the other half of the conversation after Maefa decided to pry and ask if there was someone else, demanding to know the reason I didn't want her.

It had made me slightly angry, but I wanted to be respectful. Still, since when did I need a reason not to want to just sleep with someone I wasn't going to be in a relationship with? Or even to just not be attracted to someone?

I shook my head, hating the idea of Roxy having to hear what I'd said about her. It would have been obvious it was her I was referring to. Long distance, parents not approving, and all of that was true.

Roxy did make me feel some kind of way, and most of the time I forced myself to ignore it. Even though we could speak to each other, I couldn't be there with her. Having feelings for someone was hard enough for me. I didn't want to share my past and my secrets, though it was getting easier with every conversation Roxy and I had.

But then to add into the mix, we were on different planes and would be other than the occasional disastrous mission that would force our physical paths to cross, and then we'd have ourselves a full-blown heartbreak. I didn't need that, and neither did she.

So, yes, some of what I'd said had been true. It wasn't a good idea for us to get involved. If I was being honest with myself, though, *I shouldn't* and I *want* were two very different things, and I was still wrestling with the fact that I felt anything at all.

I wasn't used to this. I had kept myself at a distance from almost everyone, trying to keep myself strong and even with all the other vampires. I didn't need to add anyone else into my life.

Roxy deserved someone better than that, in a better frame of mind, and most importantly, someone who was there to hold her and kiss her every day. Not just twice while in moments of chaos.

I thought of her lips, though, and how she might feel if she heard me saying it would never work out. If she had feelings for me too, which she had to at least have an attraction to kiss me back, then she would be hurting right now.

All I wanted to do was soothe the hurt. To tell her it was nothing personal and that if I could handle living in the Mortal Plane and sacrifice everything I had or wanted for her, I would.

We'd both be miserable. That was what kept me from it. She would know she was keeping me from my home, and I would be living a half-life.

It was probably why both of us were single and stubborn to the bone about this. We needed more than just another person to fill our time. We needed adventure, and we needed our quiet spaces. I couldn't find one of those in a world where I didn't belong.

She didn't belong here either. People like Halla would chew her up and spit her out, and I didn't want her spirit that sometimes kept me going even in my darkest places to be gone.

Shit. What was wrong with me? I didn't think we could keep going round and round like this for much longer. We would have to face our feelings one way or the other, and soon. Even if it was awkward and sad, just for the sake of getting over them.

Unless…

No, I couldn't think about the unless. Human and vampire couples had so many struggles. I didn't know if either of us would handle them.

Still, I did need to at least know she was all right.

I concentrated on her hard. I remembered our kisses, our fights, and how she worried over me. I pictured what she might have been doing right now. Maybe packing, or she could already be on a plane and headed for Florida to help Lyra.

Roxy, please talk to me. I sounded like a desperate fool.

A sigh. There she was.

"What do you want, Kane?" The words were clipped, but instead of angry, she sounded exhausted.

We're supposed to be having our meeting, like always, I told her, hoping for some sense of normalcy. *C'mon, didn't you miss me?* I added when all I got was silence.

"I am busy and can't talk." Roxy's voice cracked, and I flinched. She'd heard something. I just didn't know what. "I may be busy for a couple of days with this new mission. I'll contact you, okay?"

All right, I agreed, unable to handle hearing any more of that in her voice. I doubted she was busy, but I hoped she wouldn't stay away forever. I didn't know if I could take that either.

25
Lyra

As I walked toward the boardwalk, déjà vu hit me like a ton of bricks. On the one hand, I was going to enjoy being someone else for once. I wasn't really an undercover agent. Never had been. But I could see the appeal.

This time, it was necessary. This was now the third time that we would be entering Everglades City at the docks and the second time in one day, and we couldn't be recognized. It would set off the alarms of too many of the dark, shadowy humans running whatever operation at the airboat tour warehouse seeing us all there again. Especially after we were able to fight off a Leftovers' monster. I doubted at that point that the story about us being black belts in karate would be believable any longer.

My team had come through for me. We'd prepared quickly, sourcing the tech we needed and finding a disguise for me in only a couple of hours. Dorian had gotten a kick out of the whole thing seeing me have to turn into someone else and be uncomfortable for a change.

It wasn't quite the same as having to be painted from head to toe in several layers of makeup and sunscreen, but it was still uncomfortable.

On the outside, what I was wearing was actually kind of fun. They had gotten me a wig–long blonde hair, curled, and big like all the other women in the South wore. It was made of real hair, so tons of hairspray went into it to keep it up even with the humidity. My outfit was business casual, a pencil skirt that Dorian had admired from afar. It hugged every bit of my curves, what little I had in my small frame. I was sure he would have something to say about that later.

I smiled, and my core tightened at the thought.

I had a button-down black shirt tucked into it with ruffles on the collar and a cute, little half sweater in heather gray to go over it. I wore a pair of boots, chunky but sensible. Whether I was going to a business meeting or not, I wouldn't be walking around the docks in stilettos. Then, I would stick out like a sore thumb in other ways which I didn't want.

I even had a spray tan, but that part I wasn't a fan of. It wasn't really me. And I never understood the need for such a thing

In my pocket was a small stack of business cards that Cam had whipped up on the fly. Bryce had even contacted a local restaurant asking them for permission to use them as a front for the situation. He explained that they would be compensated for any dealings they would have with the suspects and any questions to confirm that I was working for them.

Every detail has been thought of, and all I had to do now was play the part.

I should have been nervous, but instead, excitement burst through me as I headed for the back of the warehouse. I was a buyer from a restaurant. I repeated that part of the persona in my head over and over to ingrain it. I was a fast-talking Floridian woman with a business mind and a feminine side.

The entire time everyone had helped get me dressed and ready, they had me practice a bit of a Southern accent. Floridians didn't have quite the same accent as Texans or Alabamans , but they did have a bit of a twang. I would have to as well in order to be believable. But then, I also couldn't overdo it.

I pulled out my phone, pretending to be a buyer nervously searching for the address. That way, I could wander toward the back of the warehouse and play dumb for being in a place I shouldn't be.

I moved my phone in different directions and tried to compare it to the scenery around me, as if I were trying to get my bearings, all the while moving closer and closer to the back entrance.

I nearly bumped into someone, and it turned out to be a security guard who placed his hands on my shoulders. As I turned around, I forced my face to go from bewildered to a sly, cute smile.

"Well, hello there, sugar," I said, laughing in my own head about this character I was playing. It was kind of fun. I would have to do something like this more often.

A thought struck me that Dorian might enjoy something like this in the bedroom.

"I'm sorry for bumping into you, " I told the guard. "I was just looking for where I was supposed to have a meeting."

"That's quite all right, ma'am, but you shouldn't be back here. Management and special clients only." His warning was stern but kind.

He didn't seem to take me for anything more than a typical stranger. That was a good sign, though it was easier to fool security than those running the operation.

I placed my hand casually on his shoulder, just tapping it. I let out a little laugh. "I understand that, sugar, but I think I'm in the right place. I need to talk to the managers here. About the Cajun poppers," I said, dropping the code word, hoping it would get me in more than anything.

"I understand your needs. However, my superiors are rather busy right now. Why don't you go around front and have one of the tours and then come back later?"

I wasn't going to give them a chance to escape. I needed to get in to see them now. This was a one-shot deal.

"I think they'll want to talk to me. I have a business deal I'd like to discuss with them. One that can bring them in a lot of cash. So why don't you mosey on in there and see if they want to talk to me? Here, take my business card to them." I pulled one of the cards out of my shirt pocket, right over my breast. I didn't miss the fact that he followed my hand straight down to my body and then back up again when I handed it to him.

He snatched it from my hand and looked at it before nodding. "All right, come with me, but I can't promise an audience anytime soon. May be in for a long wait, " he said with a huff. All of his bravado was gone, though.

I wondered if he had specific orders to funnel through those who would give the best deals. He probably got to take a cut from them too.

"Why, thank you so much, " I squealed in delight, following him inside.

He took me to a staff-only portion of the airboat tour company, and there I was met with two people I wasn't familiar with. They weren't the ones I wanted to talk to, not really, but I guessed that they were the ones who would screen me before I could see the big bosses of the operation. The ones who were likely responsible for whatever nastiness was going on behind closed doors here.

"Who have you brought us?" one of the two males said with a smirk. He had dark-red hair and a couple of little freckles on his face. He reminded me a bit of Roxy's siblings.

The other one was a shorter man with salt-and-pepper hair and a mustache. There was something a little cartoonish about him.

"Oh, it's so nice to meet you finally." I took the lead, showing initiative and strength. Two things they might respond to. I didn't want to seem too demure and scared by letting the guard answer for me. I held out my hand for them to shake. "The name's Arlene Powers.".

The little man reached his greasy hand out to shake mine, but the redhead just kind of stared at it until I pulled it back.

"And how can we help you, Arlene?"

I didn't miss the fact that he didn't give either of their names. So, anonymous it would be.

"Well, I gave your guard here a copy of my business card." I pulled out two more to pass to these two gentlemen. They took them with skepticism, looking them over as I continued to talk. "So, I'm the back-of-the-house manager for the restaurant you see here."

It was an upscale Southern French fusion restaurant in Miami. It was actually very popular and had enough capital that it was looking to expand to other locations.

"I actually drove across the state to try to find some fresh, special, gator meat, if you know what I mean. I hear it's some of the best." I whispered the last part, letting them know I was in on the secret. "It was suggested to me that this was the place to come for exclusives. If it works out, I'll become a repeat customer."

I put my hands on my hips, waiting for them to respond to me. I made sure to tap my foot on the ground a few times, showing my impatience for them to look up at me and give me respect. It worked. They both looked up at me at the same time.

There was a light in the eyes of the greasy man with a mustache. "We are actively looking for more customers, the bigger ones. If you can give us as much business as you say, we can make you a priority customer," he said, looking at his partner for confirmation.

The redheaded man shook his head ever so slightly. "Miami, huh? So who told you about us?"

He sounded skeptical. Was he onto me somehow? Though, they probably had to be naturally suspicious considering they were running a very seedy operation here.

"Oh, you know how it is. I have my sources, hon, and you have yours. It's best to keep them happy by keeping them anonymous." I gave a wink.

That was something these two would have to understand. Discretion was the most important thing to these kinds of people. Even over loyalty and money.

"I'm ready to start this relationship today. To buy. I've come with hefty backing from the restaurant. But I'd like to see a sample of the meat I might be getting first. You know, got to make sure it's quality." I made my voice firmer this time, no longer playing the dumb blonde.

All part of the game. Even my persona had a persona.

"Do you mind if I give the restaurant a call and confirm that this is legitimate?" the redheaded man asked.

There was a look exchanged between the two men, and it was clear that the mustache man was not happy about the holdup. He wanted the cash in his greedy hands.

"Of course, go right ahead," I said smugly. "I think you'll like what you're going to hear."

He dialed the phone number to make the call, and after a few rings, I heard one of our contacts at the restaurant answer. They'd been instructed on exactly what to say if any of these people called. They knew my pseudonym I was using and everything.

The redheaded man furrowed his brows, but he was clearly put in his place by the time he hung up the phone. "Okay, you check out. Why don't you come with us, and we can show you samples of what we've got?"

I gave a curt nod, kind of like "I told you so," and then followed them through a small nondescript door at the back corner of the room. It led downstairs, and it was kind of dank. The staircase was narrow, and I felt a little trapped.

But it all turned out okay when we came out into what looked like some cross between a laboratory and a storage room. As we entered, the skulls, teeth, and bones of Leftovers' creatures were the first things I saw. They had bits and pieces of them everywhere, some for product, and others just for display for the hell of it. My stomach turned, but I was also fascinated. A place like this could teach Callanish a lot more than we already knew about the creatures, what types of them there were, what they could do, and their genetics.

I tried to tamp down that level of excitement to keep my cover. As we passed pieces of the beasts, the smell got to me, and my stomach did flips. It got harder and harder to uphold the character I was playing.

"You have a look around. We're going to go grab our higher-ups. I think they'd be particularly interested in you and your deal, Arlene," the redheaded man with freckles said.

It seemed fair enough. They were who I needed to speak to anyway. I knew one of them had to be our male suspect. We'd seen him around too much for him not to be involved with, or running, this company.

I was soon left alone in the room with the bones. I wanted to go off and explore and take as many mental notes as possible. Really, I wanted to relay a lot of information over the comm if I could, but both of those things would blow my cover. A woman like Arlene would be fascinated in a curious sense, as well as in a business sense, but she wouldn't want to look at the information and details of every single creature here.

Since I was left alone for much longer than I expected, I did start to wander through their collection of sorts. As long as they left me alone, I supposed they wouldn't expect me to do anything less.

So far, I'd seen nothing showing any connection to the kidnappings. There were no signs that they were dealing with any teenagers, and I hadn't really even seen any laptops or computers where they would be contacting people through these websites. That wasn't to say that there wasn't a connection. There probably was. I didn't believe in coincidences anymore. Not after everything I'd seen and heard.

It would probably take some time to get to the heart of this and find out more. One visit wasn't going to cut it, so I was probably going to have to keep up this facade for a while. As long as they accepted me and cut me the deal, then that would be fine. The government would easily hand over the money for a time to get to the bottom of this, especially with how big it was getting. Trafficking was a serious deal, and that was what it appeared to be. Even if it was of the supernatural kind.

I couldn't go off half-cocked now just to try to get the information I wanted because I was in a hurry to save these kids. Which I was. We all were. I suspected that soon there would be more missing teens to worry about. Whoever was responsible and whatever they were doing, they didn't show any signs of stopping. But I would have to still be patient.

As the time ticked on, I began to get suspicious. I'd been left alone in here for too long.

Going off instinct, I went for the door. I jiggled the handle, but just as I suspected, the door was locked. This wasn't good. They had locked me in here and left me on purpose. They were trying to figure out what to do with me. I guessed my disguise wasn't as good as I thought.

I might have looked different, and maybe they didn't know who I was, but they must have known that I was not a typical customer. How was I going to get myself out of this mess? I couldn't go begging for help over the comm. I couldn't have them coming in here and getting harmed. Who knew what else was in this warehouse, how many more of these rooms they had, and how many people hid in this operation? We could be far outnumbered.

I was better off staying here and trying to figure it out, trying to work my own way out. I still had my universe powers, so I wasn't exactly the same as a helpless human. Not a vampire, but not an average mortal either. I would have to bank on the fact that they didn't know that.

I pressed my ear to the wall to see if I could hear anything. Sure enough, there was an argument going on nearby. The raised voices told me so. I couldn't tell if it was coming from above or next door or some other room down here. Though, I couldn't make out the exact words.

My best bet was to wait by the door. That way I could be ready to defend myself if needed as soon as they opened the door. They wouldn't expect Arlene to be vigilant about such things. But Lyra was.

There was more arguing, and then it stopped. Only minutes later, the door swung open. I readied my stance, only to be rushed immediately. I lunged forward, using non-lethal ways to take out my attacker, not even looking to see if it was male or female.

My body moved off of instinct alone, using only my combat skills for now. I would pull on my powers if I had to, but I would rather not give the impression that I was something other than what I appeared right now. Just in case they hadn't figured that part out yet. Keeping something up my sleeve could mean life or death.

I'd just passed my first attacker, getting a very weak pressure point on his neck. He dropped to the ground, but more followed through the door.

I whirled and then froze the moment I heard the click of a gun. Instead of staring down the barrel, I followed it upward to the person who held it. It was the female suspect who we had already interviewed. She hadn't set off any alarm bells. We had figured she was only suspicious by association, and here she was.

She had come around my back, almost unnoticed. She was good, whoever she was. I got the feeling the name we had for her was not her real one. Especially if she was working for an operation like this.

The gun was so very close to me, and I tried not to show the tremor in my body as I tried to look as intimidating as possible. But several more people rushed in behind me from the door I was no longer facing. It was guaranteed that they were here to keep me down. Make sure I didn't fight anymore.

I didn't think that I was fooling anyone anymore. They knew who I was. They must have been expecting us. For all I knew, everything we'd seen at the docks, with the posh couple wheeling out the smelly Leftovers' monster and everything else, had been on purpose. They must have noticed us the first time and guessed that we were investigating.

The suspect sneered. "I recognized you the first day you came. I knew I had to keep tabs on you and watch out for you. You're Lyra Sloan."

So, my disguise had been useless. They were expecting something like this.

"I knew you would have to come sniffing around considering you had already sicced Nicholas Bryce and some companion of his on me. International heroes showing up at my doorstep." The suspect shook her head and spat in disgust.

I resented her take on us, but it didn't really matter. What did matter was trying to survive this.

"Don't worry. I won't kill you. Not unless you fight me. You could be useful to me."

All pretenses of innocence with this woman were gone. How had we been so easily fooled? Especially Bryce.

"Now, get out your phone," she ordered me.

What did she need my phone for? Was she going to take it from me so no one could reach me or ping me to find me?

Before I could ask or do anything other than getting the phone in my hand, the barrel of the gun pressed into the side of my skull. My control over my trembling vanished, and I was ready to turn into a puddle of sobs. Facing a gun in a human's hands was way different than facing a Leftovers' monster. Monsters could be unpredictable, but they were mostly primitive creatures. And they weren't necessarily killing to have fun with it. At least I didn't think so.

With this woman, I got the feeling she enjoyed torturing me like this. And she might even have enjoyed pulling the trigger a time or two.

"You will send a text message to anyone who is waiting for you. Tell them you're going to be gone a couple more hours."

I stared blankly at my phone for a moment, wondering how I was going to do that and still save my life. This last command really scared me because it would keep the team at bay and from looking for me. No one would be suspicious.

By the time the team figured out something had happened to me, it could be too late.

"Do it," the suspect screamed, pressing the gun harder against me.

I had no choice. I sent the text message like she asked me to. All I could do was hope that Bryce or Dorian wouldn't buy it. That they would see right through it.

"All communications off of you. On the ground. " I dropped the cell and my wire.

She wasn't messing around, and I wasn't going to play games with my life right now.

We stood still for a moment, looking at each other, and then she backed off. I wondered why until one of those behind me came up and placed a rag over my face. Chloroform.

My last thought was for Dorian and if I would ever get to see him again. I didn't exactly know what these people wanted from me. But it could be deadly.

26

Roxy

I stared out the window of the small plane, easily ignoring the bit of turbulence we were hitting, regardless of the fact that it was shaking us around a bit. These Bureau planes were always too small to not feel it, but it wasn't just because I was used to it that I was able to ignore it.

We were on our way to another mission, meeting Lyra in Florida to kick some monster ass. Normally, I would have had this familiar feeling of excitement in my stomach. Kind of like butterflies but even better. Without the nervousness. This was my jam. I was good at it, and I had no reason to believe that anyone would really get hurt. At least not seriously.

However, a heaviness settled over me. The last-minute preparations had exhausted me, and I had to admit that I threw myself into that more than usual as well. It was all overkill, and I had taken a lot of the job away from Bryce, frustrating him, of course. He was good at what he did, but he also liked to have control.

I'd been practically doing his job for him to keep myself from thinking. But now as the plane ride stretched before me, all I could do was think. It was a dangerous place to be in right now.

I was still running on very little sleep. I hadn't wanted to dream about Kane. It would have hurt too much.

I welcomed this mission in another way, though. I would be able to throw myself into work. I'd have plenty of excuses not to speak to Kane. I was going to be way too busy trying to keep all of us alive and kill these monsters that were in Lyra's way. I wanted Lyra to succeed in finding these teenagers, hopefully alive, preventing any more from being taken. This case was brutal, and I needed it.

I sat a few seats away from the rest of my team. Jordan and Jessie were at the back of the plane playing some kind of game on their Nintendo. Everyone else was doing their own thing or talking to each other. I didn't know if I could handle talking to anyone without bursting into tears or getting into an angry explanation about what was wrong with me. And that just wasn't work-appropriate. I needed to get my thoughts together and get over this so I could focus on the task ahead.

I'd been avoiding all of Kane's attempts to contact me. Which he'd tried more than once. He even tried after I told him I was going to be too busy, not able to take a hint. Did he know that I was in his head for long enough to hear everything? Or had he just realized I was there at the end?

For all I knew, it was neither, and talking about me to the healer had made him think of me. But even that made me sick to my stomach. I responded once to let him know I wasn't dead. As frustrated as I was with him, I didn't want him or anyone worrying about me the way I had about him when I couldn't get ahold of him.

Since then, I hadn't heard any more conversations he'd had, with Maefa or otherwise. While it felt a little lonely, I was thankful not to be in his head and hearing what could possibly be more things that would hurt me at the moment.

I was at least ninety percent sure he'd been talking about me. I knew he hadn't mentioned the details, but why would he? We were still keeping it a secret for most people that we could hear into each other's minds. We didn't know what the implications were or what others would think of it. So, it just made sense that he was talking about me.

But then again, I could have been just being dramatic, my worries spiraling out of control.

The biggest question I had was why it hurt me so much what he'd said. Any bit of what he'd said could have caught me off guard, but really if I thought about it, it was the fact that he'd said he didn't think things could work. What was ridiculous was that I'd kind of said the same thing to myself over and over as an excuse not to tell him how I felt.

The truth was, I had thought I was the only one catching feelings. It wasn't like the curse had affected me at all being near him. Though, I guessed he could have just been developing these feelings in the past few weeks without me around, kind of the same way I was processing my own feelings as they were intensifying with our conversations.

Not to mention the fact that Kane never shared any kind of feelings. I just thought he really didn't have much interest in such things. But now that he had said that he wasn't a one-night stand kind of guy, and in the same breath admitted that he did have feelings for someone, it put things into a new perspective.

So Kane had possibly been walking around with feelings for me this whole time, not only not sharing them, but also believing they weren't worth trying to do anything with.

Because nothing with us had ever come to fruition other than two kisses, I was conflicted. I wasn't sure whether to be disappointed, angry, sad, or just be right there with him. Telling myself to just screw it all and forget it because it wouldn't work. But it definitely wouldn't work if he had already decided that in his head.

I was guilty of that too, but I had never said it out loud. Part of the problem was this–there was a pleasure underneath it all, knowing that he shared some of my feelings. They weren't unrequited. That at least was a comfort, making me not feel so crazy. I couldn't be happy about it, though, not really, because he hadn't even given me a choice in the matter. Even with my own self-deprecating thoughts about the possibility of a relationship, now that I knew there was a chance that he had feelings too, I would have still given him the option to weigh in. So, he had already made a choice about us not working without even telling me.

It was like he wasn't even considering me at all. It made me feel like shit, honestly. And there he was, the one who had kissed me that one time anyway, damn it!

I hadn't noticed the twins get up until they each landed on a seat in front of me and turned around to face me. Jessie had an amused grin on her face as she poked me playfully, but Jordan was cocking his head to the side like he was trying to read my mood. I was being a bit odd, so of course they would notice at some point. I just hoped that they would leave it alone for a bit, distracted by what they were doing and the fact that they were slightly hyped up for the mission as well.

This morning, they seemed to have mostly gotten over the fact that they weren't going to get to have their party. At least not yet. Most everything had been rescheduled in a couple of weeks. We hoped we'd be back and done with the mission by then. Though, Jordan still had an air of disappointment around him. He just wasn't letting it bring him down the way it was me.

"What gives?" Jessie asked. "You're not acting like yourself."

I shook my head, hoping they would let it go. This was all about business. This trip, everything, and I had just given them a lecture about being an adult and making sacrifices and being committed to their work.

"We're not going to leave you alone until you tell us," Jordan said, acting like he was getting really comfortable in the seat.

I let out a sigh, but then I realized I was doing exactly what they were accusing me of. The problem I was having was not a work problem. It wasn't a secret. The twins knew who Kane was and knew that we could talk to each other in our heads as well. This was my family. Even if we worked together, I could still share things with them. We were only on a plane, and it wasn't like I could defeat Leftovers' monsters from here.

I gave them a soft smile. "I don't know if you'll get it, but you're right. There is something bothering me. Thanks for offering to talk about it."

Jessie perched her head over the headrest, her chin getting squished as she anticipated what I might say. It was like it was the most interesting thing on the planet.

Maybe to them, I was, or had been at one point before I threw myself so much into work that I didn't talk or think about anything else. I had started doing that in order to get my promotion, but I guessed I had never left that mode.

I launched into the explanation without giving too many details about what was going on with Kane. The fact that I'd been mulling over feelings for him for a while after the two kisses we shared but knowing that things could be hard if we tried to do anything. And the fact that I didn't want to jump into anything if I wasn't clear about exactly how strong my feelings were.

They kind of understood about the curse, so that made sense to them that I wouldn't have known. Though, Jessie made a couple of comments about how obvious it was that there was something there even if it was only an attraction.

I smirked and rolled my eyes at her.

"But now the problem is I overheard another conversation I wasn't supposed to. This healer who's been taking care of him was flirting with him, and he let her down easy. She didn't take it very well and wanted to know why."

Jordan flinched. "Could have been awkward for all three of you. I would hate if somebody were to ask me that outright and I would have to try to be honest but also stay respectful."

Jessie gave Jordan a playful slap on the shoulder. Jordan was known throughout the team for his romantic behavior. He was kind of a lovesick puppy, falling in and out of love really quickly with all kinds of people. It seemed he was on a date with someone new at least every month, going on and on about how amazing they were, and about how he could see a future with them only to not be able to make it last more than a month. I stopped trying to keep up with who they all were. I figured when it was really serious, we would all know.

"I think it sounds like that girl has balls," Jessie said. "To say in front of him that she had feelings and then to ask for an explanation why he didn't like her for her peace of mind. I kind of dig it."

I smiled. "You would."

Jordan moved his hand in front of her face. "Let her get on with telling us. I want to know what this problem is."

I gritted my teeth at the next part, hating that I had to go through it all over again. I doubted that they would have a whole lot of insight for me considering their immaturity, but at least they could comfort me about it and I wouldn't be stuck in this thought process all by myself.

"He told her that he had feelings for somebody else, and it kind of sounded like me. There were things about what he said that I didn't think could be anybody else. The problem is, in the same breath, he told her that he thought it would never work out. He's never even mentioned feelings to me, and here he is saying it won't work out right off the bat. I don't know how to feel about it."

"I know the two of you can't see each other in person or anything, but what if you just start being really flirty with him, maybe talking dirty to him? Tell him a bunch of sexy stuff. Kind of like sexting but in your heads?" Jessie giggled at the suggestion, but I should have known that she would have come up with a scheme like that.

Unlike her brother who was constantly going goo-goo over people, Jessie preferred intrigue and adventure. She liked to toy with her love interests. Although, they didn't seem to mind so much. Even with her bright-red hair and her freckles, men usually found her to be both cute and beautiful. She never stayed with anyone who wanted to get too serious anyway.

I gave her an exasperated sigh and a sideways glance. "Can you imagine how awkward that would be? Especially for someone like Kane?"

Jordan shook his head and laughed. "It would kind of put you in the same league as the woman that you overheard in the conversation, wouldn't it?"

We all laughed at that, and if nothing else, I was grateful for the distraction. Even for a little while, my mood had lifted.

"Thanks guys," I told them. "But I think the correct route is to actually go the normal route. I need to be honest with him and confront this head-on. I just don't like the scenarios that keep playing in my head when I do that."

Jessie's mouth opened in a shocked O. "Is our fearless leader actually scared? Of telling a boy she likes him?"

I hated the fact that her silly words made me blush. I swatted at her playfully, but I was a little bit angry.

I patted my lap with a slapping sound, a nervous gesture. "Maybe I should just leave it alone," I said, looking at the window again. "I could just get over it. The thing is, he's probably right. There are plenty of reasons that I can't be with him. That it would never work. It just upset me to hear it that way."

Jessie reached out, a frown on her face, and touched my arm. All joking aside, I knew she felt bad for me. "I've never felt that way about a guy, not yet, but I would hope if I did that the both of us could at least try to make it work even if we crashed and burned. It kind of makes an ass of him to decide that without even coming to you first."

I shrugged. "Right, but this is much more complicated than any other long-distance relationship. I mean, we're on separate planes. He won't come here. He hates it here. And I'm not leaving the Hellraisers. Even if I get more of a work-life balance, I can't see myself racing off to the Immortal Plane to live. Then there's the curse and our families. They're not exactly the understanding type when it comes to vampire-human relations. We are no Lyra and Dorian."

Jordan slammed his fist into the headrest of his seat, making me jump. "The Bureau is just a job for you, Roxy. You know that. If you really wanted this for your life, you could do anything you wanted. You could even keep working and travel to the Mortal Plane on weekends or holidays. It's the same as people do when they live in different countries. Love can win out if both of you try at it. I don't see a reason not to give it a chance. Have you ever felt this way for someone else? Do you think it's just gonna come along again?"

It was as if I'd heard my brother for the first time. Apparently, he had been a closet romantic this whole time. His words sounded like they were out of a movie, but then again, my heart soared with hope when he'd said that. He was right. There were people all over the world doing it. I'd even heard of married people with children where the husband or wife was off in the military or going to college in a different town and would have to come and visit on the weekends. They made it work because they loved each other.

I didn't know that I was ready to shout from the rooftops that I was madly in love with Kane. We weren't there yet. But we could be there. We could get there if we tried, and it was such a waste not to even bring it up. That was what Jordan was saying.

"Thank you for that," I told Jordan, giving him the respect he'd probably never seen from me before.

It took him aback for a moment.

Both of the twins patted me on the shoulder.

"You just think about it, okay? You do what's right for you, and don't think about the consequences right now. Just what your heart wants," Jordan said before both of them got up and walked away.

I placed my chin against my hand, leaning on the armrest and looking back out of the window again. We would be in Florida soon. Some of the things that Jordan and Jessie had just said were some of the smartest things that had ever come out of their mouths. It kind of made me feel proud.

I could do it. I could contact Kane right now and start the confrontation. But then, right after the conversation about overhearing him and Maefa, my feelings would show through.

At some point, they were going to anyway, but when we'd had this initial conversation, I needed to keep my feelings under control. I wouldn't be able to do that right now. But I'd have to deal with this soon. I just couldn't now.

As soon as the mission was over. That was what I promised myself. I would focus on this mission, being here for my team and Lyra, and then Kane and I would sit down and have the conversation. And we would either give it a try or we wouldn't.

In theory, it felt like my decision took the pressure off. It gave me a clear plan, which I preferred. But the worry was still threatening to push through. Like, what would happen if we disagreed? Would our friendship ever bounce back from that?

27
Lyra

My eyelids and the rest of my body felt incredibly heavy. It took quite the effort to get my eyes all the way open, and I strained them to look around. I didn't know where I was, but the memory of what happened came back to me. My disguise had failed, and then I had been surprised, taken by Anastasia in that warehouse her group was using for the airboat tours. I also remembered the room full of monster parts.

A roll of nausea went through me, and not just at the thought. My head was pounding, my heartbeat weak. The chloroform. The aftereffects were still lingering. They probably would for at least another hour.

I seem to be in some kind of warehouse, though there were no windows or anything. The walls looked like they had been reconstructed. And very poorly at that. Not that it mattered, because I was chained up. My handcuffs were attached to a long chain wrapped around a pipe that jutted out of the wall. My ankles were also bound, though I had some freedom of movement back and forth. Oh yeah, my captors felt kind enough to help me keep circulation.

There was something more about how I felt too that was really off. Maybe it was just the chloroform, but the sensation was strange. It was almost like being inside of a dream, and I couldn't put my finger on why, but it all felt wrong. A little bit unreal.

In the dim light, I began to make out the fact that I wasn't alone. The others in the room, all children of varying ages, noticed I was waking up. Some of them glared with suspicion or anger. Some looked completely entertained by the pain I was obviously in. While others just kind of looked sad. All of them looked like little street urchins. Tattered clothing hung off of their malnourished bodies. All of them were dirty enough to make me believe it had been several weeks since they'd had a bath.

"One...two...three... " I began to count them in a muttering tone. I couldn't think well enough to do it in my head. "Eight." There were eight children in here with me.

Three of the children began to crowd around me. Two girls and one boy. The oldest, once I looked past all the dirt and grime, I immediately recognized. Her skin was dark, and as she spoke to me, I could see the glint of her braces in the dim lighting.

"Are you all right?" Alicia asked.

She was free to move about, but she was handcuffed as well. Only one other child had been chained to the wall, a little boy with a sad expression. Probably the youngest in the room.

I thought back to Isabella's worry for Alicia. To the grieving family wondering where Alicia had gone. Maybe they would have been comforted to know that the light hadn't left her eyes. The way the other two children flanked her, it was clear she'd become some kind of unofficial leader. They were rallying around her. She had found some kind of space for herself here, no matter how small. Wherever here was.

"I'll be all right. Just some aftereffects from chloroform. Thanks for asking, Alicia," I said.

I wanted her to know I knew who she was. I didn't know if it would give her hope or at least let her know who I might be. If she were a leader for these other children, I might need her in the future when I tried to escape. If I could try to escape. As long as I was weakened and chained up, there wasn't a whole lot I could do. Universe powers did nothing for getting me out of a bind like this.

"So, they knocked you out?" It was a simple and obvious question, but there was something behind it. Alicia was hard focused on me, and I wondered what she was playing at.

Believing she might be trying to get information for everyone, possibly to aid in their eventual escape, I explained the whole story. Well, most of it. The part where I had posed as a customer because I was suspicious and then had gotten captured. Knocked out and brought wherever this was. And then I woke up here.

"Alicia, do you know where we are?"

She shook her head. "No, as far as I can tell. None of us do."

"I was investigating your disappearance, you know. I spoke to your friend, Isabella, recently. We were all trying to find you and the other kids." I looked around, trying to put names to the faces. But some of them were so dirty and malnourished, I couldn't be sure about any of them.

I was able to pick out just a few from the paperwork Torres had given me in the beginning. The ones in the best shape seemed to be the three standing before me. All teenagers.

"Is Isabella okay?"Alicia asked me in a hushed but agitated tone.

It warmed my heart to know these two were still thinking about each other during all of this. They were truly going to be best friends for life.

I nodded. "She's distraught, obviously, but she was strong enough to reveal everything she could in order to help you. Even after her own mother didn't believe her. Do you remember anything about how you got here? Anything at all that could help me? If I could get out..." I leaned forward as I said it, whispering almost. I wanted to get my point across. I wanted to help all of them.

"It all started when I was having symptoms of my gift. It was right after the meld. That's what people are calling it, right?"

I nodded, urging her to go on.

"I began to hear other people's thoughts. Mostly my best friend's. Isabella. But sometimes I would get my parents and things like that too. People I was close to." Alicia shrugged.

This wasn't new to her. She had already accepted it.

Her power made me think of Kane and Roxy instantly. It was kind of like what they were experiencing, only they were experiencing it with each other. Strange how some of these powers were the same and yet different for each person.

"I wanted to look for answers. I felt like I was crazy or like a freak," Alicia continued, and my heart hurt for her.

The real world could be cruel, especially to children and teenagers trying to find their way in the world, without adding some kind of psychic powers to it.

"I didn't wanna worry Isabella, so at the time, I didn't tell her much. I met a woman online who called herself Anastasia. Soon after that, Anastasia began to talk in my head. We formed some kind of connection."

The boy standing behind her, his arms crossed over his chest, began to hiss at her. "Alicia, don't." His tone was a clear warning.

But why? Did he not want her to tell?

Maybe as loyal as they seemed to Alicia, some of them were more loyal to Anastasia and whatever her cause was. I would have to watch my back even here among victims. Anastasia and her cohorts had done their jobs well.

Alicia turned around and gave the boy a stern look, and he backed off, though he still didn't look happy about it.

"The voice in my head, this Anastasia, she was telling me–no, convincing me–that she had gone through exactly the same thing. She was relating to me in a way nobody else was. It made me not feel so insane. She told me that they had a group that met up. They had the place for me, to train me, and people would accept me. You can see how something like that would have been appealing. I had begun telling Isabella about hearing her thoughts and other people's thoughts. I even tried to mention it to my parents. Isabella took it the best, but she expressed concerns, concerns I had been already convinced to ignore. "

That Anastasia was really a piece of work. Though, I doubted that was her real name. Whatever she cooked up was elaborate, and I had a feeling that she had a criminal record before the meld. She knew what she was doing, brainwashing these kids.

"That sounds hard," I said. "I know that you went to meet her, right? And then that's what got you here? Did they take you in the car with a license plate?"

I pretty much already knew the answer to that question, but I needed her to give me as much information as possible. If there were any way that any of us could ever get back or get a message to my team, they could use that in order to find all of us and get all of us out. Not to mention possibly to find Anastasia and those working with her. She needed to be taken down as soon as possible. How many more kids was she talking to now?

Alicia shook her head. "I shouldn't have gone to meet her, but I needed somebody who knew what I was going through. She was the only person not treating me like a pariah. I knew it could be a mistake. Isabella warned me too. But I thought I could outsmart them. My fail-safe plan was to take that license plate picture. It didn't help. They didn't take me by car. It was like they knew that was what I would do. They planted that car there or something. Instead, they took me through the Leftovers. In a boat." Alicia shivered at the thought.

It must have been a harrowing experience, being chucked into a small boat in the water full of Leftovers' creatures like the ones I had encountered in Florida myself. They were enough to give anyone nightmares, even a grown person. Much less a teenager.

"I ended up here. Well, sort of here. Not in this room. We were in these weird tunnels. But it was like they were pulsing or something. Like they weren't quite made of concrete or any kind of normal wall material. I don't know. It's hard to explain, but it gave me the creeps. Maybe it was because I was still mostly passed out at the time."

As the brain fog and dulled senses from chloroform began to clear, Alicia's description hit me with a pang of nausea anew. I knew exactly where we were now that she'd explained her journey.

"We're in the Pocket Space. At least, that's what I call it. It's a space between worlds. It's the best way I can describe it to you."

I couldn't show that I'd lost my nerve, but being in the Pocket Space was not a good place to be. I had no way of knowing how Anastasia and her group were able to get us here. As far as I knew, the only way in and out had died with the Ghost. But they were getting in and out in some way. But I had no idea how I would get back even if I got loose. No wonder no one could find these children.

"What about you?" I asked the boy who still looked mad behind Alicia.

Maybe I could make him see reason. Come to our side of things. Yes, they were all children, but they were children with incredible powers. Maybe those powers could be used to our advantage to get all of us out of here. And then bring Anastasia to justice.

The boy looked around as if I might be talking to somebody else, but then he sighed. "It's just like what Alicia said. I was experiencing these strange happenings and powers. I could...like...walk through things, it seemed, and move really fast. I don't have the mind-speaking powers or whatever it is Alicia has. All of us are different. But it's pretty much the same damn story. We found Anastasia on some online forum looking for answers, and then we all ended up here through the Leftovers. It's just that some of us disagree with whether or not what Anastasia is doing is helpful. I don't agree with being kidnapped, but it wasn't exactly like I belonged back at home either."

I could see the roughness around the edges. This boy had endured a lot before he came here. His life hadn't been a walk in the park. He might have been abused or something by his parents before. Or lived in poverty.

I could see how Anastasia could rally these kids to her cause if they were being rejected elsewhere.

My gaze drifted to the little boy who was chained up. He reminded me of the two children who had been captured by Sempre.

"Is he okay?" I asked them.

Alicia looked pained. "I think he is. It's hard to tell. None of us knows what he can do. He's being kept chained up or taken away in secret most of the time. We do know that he's the youngest here, though. He's only ten."

It made my heart hurt, and I had to fight back tears. This was an injustice I couldn't stand much longer, especially now that I had seen it in person.

What had they done to these kids? Especially if they didn't obey. Something told me it went beyond just chaining them up.

I tried to make eye contact with the sheepish girl behind Alicia. "Hi," I said.

"Hi. My name is Cassandra Solis," the girl responded intensely, though her voice was shaky.

I nodded, recognizing the name among the missing. "Nice to meet you. I'm sure your family will be happy that you're safe. Can you tell me what they are promising you? Why some of you came or what they're training you for?"

Cassandra shook her head and backed away, panic making her breath come in gasps. "I can't. They'll be mad if I tell you anything. Alicia, we shouldn't."

"It's going to be okay now, Cassandra," Alicia said in a calming but firm tone. "This woman... She might be able to help us. I've seen her and her husband on TV. They know about this kind of stuff."

I leaned back in surprise, though I shouldn't have been. Dorian and I had been on TV a few times. We were anomalies even among The Bureau. And with her work with Callanish, we were famous, or infamous if you asked certain people.

Cassandra went back to join some of the other children.

Alicia turned to me and answered the question that I had asked instead of making Cassandra do it. "I don't know how long we've been here. They've been bringing us food and treats though and training us. They keep saying that if we're worthy enough, that we'll be brought to a place called the Citadel Under the World. We will be highly regarded and get the best of everything. That we're being trained to defend the city using our powers."

"Yes, and if you keep telling whoever this woman they don't like about this, it could get us in trouble and then we won't be taken there," the boy said through gritted teeth. "You should know that more than just me that it feels this way. Think about it. If you were us, in our shoes, would you want that too?" he addressed me directly.

I couldn't tell how much of the way that he and the others were acting was because of interest or survival. Though, with him, it was clearly interest. But I would assume there was something in his background that made him that way. Made him not want to go back.

I thought of Jessica and wondered where she was. She wasn't a child, so I supposed she wasn't here. She was either dead or had fit in well with their ranks by now.

"Some of us want to go home. We don't like being in chains and doing what other people tell us to do. Not having nice clothes or baths," Alicia snapped at the boy. "Why don't you go check on Tyler, instead of trying to keep us locked up here?"

The boy looked Alicia over, grumbling, but then did what she'd said.

"Some of us actually tried to escape," she said, sheepishly looking down at the floor.

I guessed the escape attempt didn't go very well.

"We exited into this weird space. It didn't even look like the Leftovers. It was strange, like an alien planet. We ended up getting lost and couldn't find food. Our captors have this monster that they command. It hunted us down and brought us back here. It was just as well, considering we couldn't figure out how to get away. There was nothing and no one out there, nowhere to go. In a way, they're being kind to us by making sure we have food, but that's about it."

It was good to see that Alicia didn't trust them, and several people trusted Alicia. It meant that they weren't all totally brainwashed. There was a way to work with them. Hopefully, she was right and most of them did want to go home. And those who didn't, well, I might be able to work that out later.

I took it all in, noting all of the nuances of the situation. So they were taking children with powers into the Pocket Space somewhere. But of course, none of them knew how they got here. They were all knocked out. Even Alicia, who seemed to have seen some of the Pocket Space while they were bringing her through, clearly never saw how they got her here to begin with. Otherwise she would have known that they were somewhere other than the Mortal Plane. She didn't seem to realize they were on a different plane entirely, other than the strangeness of it.

I steeled my nerves, even more determined as I watched all of them move around like zombies. They didn't have much else to do.

"You tell them, all of them, that I'm going to help you guys escape. I think I know who it is who's doing this to you. I've met the group before in the Pocket Space. Me and some of my friends have been here before."

The picture in my head formed of the people, knowing they were bad news. Their darkness had been so overwhelming that Dorian and the others had been chomping at the bit to get ahold of them. That told me that they weren't good people to be around. They weren't clearly human, vampire, or anything else, and I didn't like that either. Something strange was going on, something even stranger than we'd ever encountered before. Which was saying something.

"Have you had any success connecting to others with your powers, beyond those you've connected with before, like Isabella and Anastasia?"

Alicia's face was triumphant. "Despite the fact that I've been a little rebellious, there is a reason I can still move freely. I've been doing well. Anastasia has been praising my success."

A spark lit behind my eyes. There was a little hope if she could connect to people. Especially if she could do it across planes the way Kane and Roxy could, then I could get us out of this mess. Or rather, Dorian could.

I pulled my chains against the pipe, seeing how tightly they held to the reconstructed wall. Apparently, this wall hadn't been built well. It didn't even seem like the pipe actually led to something. More like it was mimicking a real room or a real pipe. Something like that would make sense in the Pocket Space, if any of it could make sense.

The clanging got the little boy's attention, the one who was chained up, and I saw the first spark of life in him since I had come to. I began to tug my chains through a weakness in the pipe where it connected to the wall. The boy began to mimic me.

In the meantime, I continued to talk to Alicia. "You said that you'd seen us on TV, right? You've seen my husband? Dorian?"

Alicia nodded. Then she blushed. "He's quite handsome."

I thought it was kind of funny that she used the word handsome, probably to be respectful. It wasn't the first time I'd heard it. "He is, isn't he? Well, can you paint a picture of him in your head and maybe try to contact him? He's in the Mortal Plane with the rest of my team that are investigating this. If you can get a message to him, and tell him that his wife is here in the Pocket Space and that all of the children are here too and came through the Leftovers, he might find a way to come get us. No, I know he will."

My newfound confidence allowed me the last pull to tug my chains out from the pipe. It only did so much considering I was still in handcuffs, but I had a lot more wiggle room. If I wanted, I could get up and move around. The little boy was able to do the same. We were going to get out of here somehow. We were going to be saved.

Alicia smiled. It was a faint, ghostlike thing, but it was there. "Okay, I'm going to try. Keep a watch out and tell me if you see or hear anything. I do have to concentrate to do this."

I nodded. Hopefully, she could get that message through before anyone else came for us. I didn't want to end up dead before there was a chance of rescue. Even in chains, I knew I was responsible. I was the person who was going to save these kids. No one else could do it, and if something happened to me, all hope would be lost.

I made sure to keep whispering to Alicia throughout, reminding her of what Dorian looked like, what he acted like, and what kind of things he might be thinking about. I even told her about The Bureau office where he might be or the camper. Anything that could get a picture in her mind to try to hear his voice.

She seemed to be close when the one padlocked door in the room swung open. Anastasia came inside. It interrupted both of us.

Alicia put her head down, skulking away from me. I didn't even look at the girl, as if we hadn't just been conspiring with each other. I didn't want any of the children to get in trouble because of me.

Anastasia locked the door behind herself so there was no escape. She began to eye the children suspiciously, but I called out to her, to distract her.

"Why have you brought me here? What the hell do you think you're doing? What do you want with me?"

My strategy worked because she turned cold eyes onto me. I kept my hands dangling near where they should have been over the pipe so as not to draw notice that I'd pulled them out from the wall. If I played my cards right, we could buy Dorian some time.

"We knew you would cause trouble for us. That, and we wanted to reunite you with your parents."

My stomach bottomed out at her words. Another manipulation, or was there some truth? I wanted to give in, but what was the price of that?

28
Roxy

I grabbed my one bag, chugging along behind everyone else other than the twins who were heading up the rear, as we got off of the plane and headed into the small airport.

Everglades Regional was a small, independent airport. It was barely a spot on the map, but it landed us very close to where Lyra and Callanish were staying. Close to the Leftovers. So, it was the best place for us. Thus, the tiny plane. No large commercial plane could have landed here.

The building was nothing special, very little more than a large office building. We were quickly ushered through security and back outside to the parking lot. Just as promised, a car was waiting for us. I knew it would take us to the hotel first, but I thought it was best to go ahead and get ahold of Lyra anyway to let her know we'd landed.

As the car took off, another in front of us to fit the other half of the team, I pulled out my phone, trying to tune out Jessie and Jordan's conversation. They were going back and forth, talking about the epic party that they would make up for their birthday they never had and what they might find on the mission. Like what kinds of crazy Leftovers' monsters they might get to fight this time.

I rolled my eyes lovingly as the phone continued to ring and ring. Oddly enough, Lyra never answered. I set my phone in my lap and gave it a few minutes. They could have been in the middle of something. Maybe even a meeting with that contact from The Bureau, Torres. He didn't sound like a walk in the park to deal with, so I could imagine them squaring off with each other, especially if Dorian popped his mouth off. He was usually quiet and demure until the time came to defend Lyra, and then he would go off like a rocket ship.

The thought of my friends and being on another mission made me smile. All thoughts of Kane and those problems were pushed to the back of my mind. This was what I was meant to be doing. I was in my element. So, I would be fine. I had a whole mission to pay attention to, and kids to save for that matter. I was doing good work.

I picked up the phone and tried again as we pulled up to the hotel we would be staying at, but it was the same thing—ring and ring, but no answer.

Feeling a little bit odd now, I trailed behind the twins as we went inside. The three of us would be sharing a room, which would be interesting. It always was with the two of them.

The room was nothing special, but it was nice. Everglades City seemed to be a small town, even though it was touristy, so it meant that fancy hotels weren't a dime-a-dozen here. But this was a nice three-star.

Inside, there was a wardrobe full of the gear that Lyra had promised us we would need. Just as Lyra had said, she and Bryce had come through. They had gotten the government to fund more of these suits. I cringed at the idea of having to wear one. I would be covered from head to toe and trudging through gunk full of Leftovers' creatures I could only come up with in my nightmares, but at least we'd be protected from whatever toxicity the water held.

We picked beds, and I found a good place to tuck my stuff. We needed to go meet with Lyra and the others, but we didn't know where they were at. It didn't sound like they were staying at the same hotel as us. I needed to get ahold of Lyra.

I tried one more time to reach her, but this time, it didn't even ring. It went straight to voice mail. The phone was dead.

With a sinking feeling in my stomach, I pulled up the information I had for Torres. After everything Lyra had mentioned about the trouble they had been having with the Miami Bureau location, and after having read his very biased report, I didn't exactly know what to expect when I talked to the guy. But at this point, I didn't really have a choice. We needed to get going.

I dialed the number, and a gruff voice greeted me. "Hello?"

It almost sounded like I was an imposition to him.

"This is Roxy, head of the Hellraisers that Lyra called in to help with the mission. We're your monster hunters. I can't seem to get ahold of Lyra, so I thought I'd call you. Where should we rendezvous?"

"Oh." He sounded a little bit more thrilled now. Maybe he was sick of dealing with the monsters. "If I can use this number to text you, I'll send you the details of where they're staying. I think it's best to rendezvous with Callanish there since they're so close to the Leftovers and where a lot of the kidnappings have happened."

That seemed like a reasonable request. "Got it. Thank you. We'll see you soon."

Shortly after hanging up with him, Torres sent me an address. When I plugged it in, I found it odd that it was an RV park of all things. But maybe they were either trying to save money because of this budgeting problem with Miami or maybe it was because they were trying to blend in. I supposed with it being a tourist area, it would look better with some kind of RV or camper driving around rather than a fully loaded team with cars with tinted windows.

Since we wouldn't be talking to people, I guess it didn't matter for us. We were just here for the monsters.

I texted the others and gave them the orders. We were heading out in five.

The RV Park was a bit off the beaten path, jutting up to a small creek at the edge of town. The grass was a little dingy, despite the fact that the rest of Everglades City was well kept up.

As I approached the camper, I stifled a laugh. It was about the dorkiest thing I'd ever seen. I imagined that it actually belonged to a couple who played golf and tennis with two kids and always wore bright-colored polo shirts. Instead, it was filled with the Callanish team. I imagined Bryce must not have been too happy about seeing the thing either, but I guessed, to blend in, he had to do what he had to do.

Torres was parked along with two of his team members near the RV as well. When he saw us, he got out to greet us. He held his hands stiffly from me to shake. "I see there aren't any vampires in your lot."

I shook his hand firmly, maybe even a little too tightly, and scoffed. What was up with this dude?

"I don't see how that's relevant. My team and I are here to do what we can, though. We're going to keep those nasty monsters out of your way." I put my hand on my hip.

"I assume you've been briefed?" he asked, hitching up his pants. He reminded me of a grandfather, a very military one at that. Stuck in his own ways and habits like a time long passed.

"I have. Seems we've got an interesting situation here." I made sure to match his energy.

He seemed to respect me, which was good, but I could feel the underlying tension. He had some aggression and prejudices over Callanish. I could see the trouble they'd been dealing with.

"That we do," he responded, pointing to the RV. "Feel free to go in and get your orders. You can let us know what's been decided when you're done."

I gave a firm nod of thanks before knocking on the camper door. It was Dorian who greeted me and let me inside. Despite the camper's large size, it felt cramped. Way too many people inside. Everyone popped their heads out from where they were sitting, some of them on bunks in the center of the camper, and waved. I had to leave my team outside since there would be no room for the rest of us.

There was no sign of Lyra, and goose bumps prickled my skin. So there really was something going on.

"What's the deal, Dorian?" I asked him, immediately sensing the strange mood. "Where's Lyra?"

Dorian sat down, rubbing his head as if it hurt or he was exhausted. "Lyra texted me and Bryce that she would be a couple more hours. She was on a sting mission at the boat tour place in Everglades City. The one we think has something to do with the Leftovers and possibly the missing kids. We even saw one of the suspects coming out of there with what we believe to be monster parts." Dorian waved a hand in the air as if all this stuff he was saying wasn't the important part.

"She's been gone for four hours now since that message," Bryce added, his voice grim. "The message seemed off to me. We wanted to give her the benefit of the doubt, though. Didn't want to ruin the sting."

Bryce's matter-of-factness made me think of Torres standing outside. The two of them were so similar, they were probably butting heads. But worse was the fact that Lyra was missing.

"I've been saying we should just go storm the warehouse. Screw the lead. It doesn't matter because she's been gone too long."

I followed the voice back to one of the bunks where Chandry, a vampire from the Immortal Plane, sat. I guessed she had joined the team recently.

"If we go all half-cocked, Chandry, not only could we ruin the sting entirely, but we would ruin the fact that Lyra can trust us. If she said she would be gone, it was probably for a good reason. She's our leader. We should trust her too," Sike said, causing a lot of tension to thrum between him and Chandry. Though, they were sitting on the same bunk, so I could only imagine what that dynamic was.

For only a second, it made me think of Kane one more time, but then I wiped him from my mind.

Everyone was tense, clearly having their own opinions.

"The point is," Dorian said a little louder now, "that we have no idea what to do. We could have a stealth mission with the vampires trying to find Lyra. I could sense her aura anywhere at this point, though I weirdly don't feel her now. I don't like it." He rubbed his head even more, his eyes closed. His face was screwed up in pain or confusion. "Everyone, quiet!" he suddenly roared, which was entirely out of character.

Everyone was looking at him strangely now, but as I surveyed him, his concentration all inside his head, I was almost positive I knew what was going on. I recognized that in my own behaviors early on with hearing Kane.

"Guys, seriously. I think he's hearing something," Sike said.

I hadn't been paying attention since I had been avoiding the idea of Kane, but if I tuned back in to my powers, I noticed that there was something trying to come through. It was a voice...a girl's voice. This was wild. I couldn't make out everything she was saying, because she was trying to contact Dorian directly, but he was definitely hearing something.

Everyone watched with intensity as Dorian tried to decipher what was being said to him. We all waited with bated breaths to see what he would have to report to us. Maybe this had to do with Lyra. What could this mean about the powers I had? What were the true capabilities?

Eventually, Dorian spoke up, explaining what he was hearing. "It's a child's voice. That missing girl, Alicia. She's with Lyra."

Everyone who was sitting on the bunks jumped off to come closer to Dorian to hear what was going on. It was becoming increasingly clear that Lyra was in danger, especially if she was with a kidnapped child.

"Are you sure it isn't a trap? I mean, if the suspects are trying to help these kids learn their powers, they could be luring all of us out by using them," Cam suggested, seeming suspicious.

I could see where he was coming from, but it wasn't like we had any other leads. And I assumed that time was of the essence. These kids had been missing for a long time, and no one had been able to find them. Now Lyra was with them too? We couldn't lose Lyra for that long, especially with as much information she would have now that she was with the kids. We needed to follow this lead as soon as possible.

"Let's hear him out," I said, knowing I was out of my depth since this wasn't my team. But my rank was as high as Lyra's, if compared to the Hellraisers. I had been called in for a reason. Maybe I could help pull some respect toward Dorian. Only Dorian might have more say than me at this point. And I was sure he was erring on the side of finding Lyra, no matter the cost. She was his wife after all.

"Lyra showed up there with her and the other kids. She said there are eight kids and then Lyra. Some group of adults kidnapped them. That part was fuzzy. She was kind of in and out. As if she wasn't experienced with the power. But then again, neither am I," Dorian explained.

"They said there were vampires in the group. The ones that kidnapped them. Lyra showed up and started talking to them, and they all figured out together that they're in the Pocket Space somehow. They were all knocked out after meeting with these people about their powers. Something about the websites and tricking them with cars and license plates. Also unclear."

I placed my hand on Dorian's shoulder for support. I wanted to coax him to give us as much as he could.

"Lyra is chained to the wall as well as another child, and some of the rest of them have handcuffs. They were taken through the Leftovers. So, they're saying there's some kind of portal there. And then I think she was trying to tell me that there's a monster. A monster that these people control. I don't know. She cut off after sounding like she was really scared. I think maybe the captors walked into the room or something."

My heart skipped a beat, thinking about what that could mean. All of them could be in danger right now, being tortured or something. And what of the monster? Could it be the monster that they had tried to send after them from the Leftovers? Could they have control of several monsters? Or could the impossible be true? That there was another Ghost. That would mean the Pocket Space could be accessed again.

Either way, we were going to have to find a way in.

"We need to get to the Leftovers, then," Bryce said, kicking into high gear.

Cam stopped him, putting a hand in front of his chest. He looked scared, having stood up to his uncle, a formidable foe, but he hissed, "Seriously, this could be a hoax. All of us could end up getting stuck in the Pocket Space or worse. And then what would the kids do? What would Lyra do? There's no one who cares enough to come get us out."

Bryce grunted, unable to argue with his nephew about that. It was a risk.

"I doubt they're expecting the Hellraisers to be there. It's not like they have a watch on us twenty-four hours a day. So even if they plan to do something with all of you, I doubt they have enough manpower to do something to all of us. We can overwhelm them."

"The only thing is that we are currently working off of Miami's equipment. We'll have to convince Torres that this is okay. Not to mention, he calls the shots when it comes to what we do in public. We all know that we're going to have to use the vampires' powers for this. He won't like it very much," Bryce added.

I cursed under my breath about the way he was trying to hold up the mission.

"It's up to the two of you to convince him. If he has any care or respect for Lyra at all, he will want to help," I explained, looking at Bryce and Dorian.

"All right, Dorian and I will go talk to Torres, but I'd like it if you brought the twins in here. I don't want them interjecting themselves and ruining this. I could only imagine what they might say to a man like Torres," Dorian said.

I gritted my teeth, tending to agree with him. If they popped their mouths off at the wrong moment, it could doom Lyra as well as the kids. "No problem. Just send them in here to talk to me."

Dorian followed Bryce to the door, looking like he was completely defeated. Shortly thereafter, the twins came inside.

"I'll let them brief you on what's going on," I said, pointing to the others left in the room. "Things got a little bit more complicated. Lyra's missing. I'm going to go help the others talk to Torres."

I hoped that made them feel important enough that they were getting a briefing before the rest so they wouldn't follow me. Outside, Dorian and Bryce were already locked in a tense conversation with Torres.

I walked over to them, listening in before I interjected myself.

"If we let the vampires use their powers, who's to say they won't use them just any time? And for anything? Who's to say they won't lose control of them and hurt the kids?" Torres was asking, getting defensive.

"While I have constantly assured you that that's not an issue with us, you'll just have to trust us on this one. Lyra's life is in danger. And this gives us another chance to save all of the children at once. It's something we have to figure out," Dorian practically pleaded.

"Look, I'll keep them in line. They won't use their powers until we reach the Leftovers, away from civilization. Is that fair?" Bryce was playing a hard game. He was pretending to be on Torres's side.

Torres looked skeptically between the two of them and then looked at me. I saw the resolve leave his face. "Fine. We'll give you suits, gear, the works. But I'm also coming with backup. I may not be a fan of vampires, but these kids matter, and so does the work Lyra does. I think she's our only hope here too. So don't go getting cocky about it," Torres grumbled.

It was clear we wouldn't be getting any sleep tonight as all of us scrambled to get ready.

"I'll take a member of my team, and we'll go back to the hotel and grab all of our gear. We'll meet you back here in about twenty minutes or so," I said.

Dorian nodded and went to bark orders to the rest. In no time, Callanish, Torres, his techies, and the Hellraisers headed out into the Everglades Leftovers.

29
Lyra

My parents? How was that possible?

When we found Joseph, I suspected that there was a chance my parents were in the Pocket Space. Though, we had never found any signs of them. We'd never figured it out. Deep down, I had worried that they were dead. It was the only reason I had been okay with abandoning that mission for the moment. I didn't want to find my parents' corpses somewhere.

This lead from Anastasia was tempting, but I had to know more. It could be a trick. Everything that came out of her mouth was a twist of the truth. I knew that based on the stories of these children.

"How do you know they're alive? How would they even be alive? The Leftovers with those trees who killed eight people took over their base. I never found them." I was rambling, breathless. I was desperate to hear something about my parents. And for now, it was keeping Anastasia's focus on me. The more she focused on me, the less she could hurt the kids. "How do you even know who my parents are? How do you know so much about me?"

Then, it clicked. If Alicia had seen me on television, then Anastasia probably had too. I didn't realize I was such a celebrity, but it wasn't turning out in my favor, for sure.

"You must know I'm not going to answer you. At least not unless you agree to cooperate with us. We need you for something, and now you need us for something. You need us to find your parents. And just like some of these gifted children, you want to be reunited with your parents just the same. No matter your age. You still love them." Anastasia was speaking as if off a script or like she was a robot. It was like she was using logic that she either had fed herself or someone else had been feeding her.

It was kind of sick. Very culty.

"I doubt that'll happen. I'm unlikely to cooperate with you. But just in case, what is it you want from me?" I asked, gaining my composure and telling myself I couldn't be so obsessed with finding my parents that I would ruin this entire mission and endanger all the children.

"Oh, you're quite interesting to us. All of the work that you've done, all the things that you know. You're not exactly one of the Called, but you might serve a purpose for the Evolved. She wants you. So, I want you."

The Evolved? The Citadel? All these new words and terms. What the hell did they all mean? "What is the Evolved?"

Anastasia sneered. "The Evolved? She's our leader, not a what," she commented snidely. "She's the one who's going to get us all to the Citadel and save us. Save the city. Maybe even the world."

Anastasia was spewing nonsense. She wasn't the leader, after all. There was another leader, some woman called the Evolved. I thought back to when Jessica got taken, volunteering herself in the place of Dan. Was the woman who was with those cloaked figures the Evolved?

So, this person was running the show. Anastasia was just another peon down the rung. That was going to make it harder to reason with her. She was just as brainwashed as the kids.

"I think your presence will help convince your parents to come around. Maybe some others. You do seem to be good at talking and getting what you want."

There seemed to be jealousy mixed in there. I was taken aback by that. What was there to be jealous of? Maybe it had to do with acceptance. Me and my team, if nothing else, portrayed this group full of acceptance. Acceptance of the way things were, of the vampires, of everyone. And my parents, part of The Bureau, were doing the same. It was unlike Roxy's mother who worked for The Bureau but still didn't approve of any idea of vampires.

All of these people that the Evolved was preying on were outcasts.

"How do I know you really have my parents? Or that you even know for sure that they're my parents?"

Anastasia clearly followed the news. She probably didn't know who they were, but what if she knew the situation with them missing, learned it, and was using it to her advantage? She could easily just be trying to torment me and get me to do what she wanted. For all I knew, they were either still missing out there on one of the planes or they were dead.

But the biggest question was why. Why was this woman messing with me? What did all these people want from me? Someone like Roxy could be useful to this group. Or Kane, if they could get to the Immortal Plane, but me? Yes, I had traveled to many planes and come back from essentially the void. But other than someone to interview about it, I didn't see how I could be useful at all.

"Would you like me to describe them to you? Would you like me to tell you what they've said and how they behaved?" Anastasia asked, now a cat playing with a mouse.

And I would have believed that was all it was until she began describing my parents in enough detail that there was no *not* believing her. Somewhere, in the Pocket Space, with Anastasia and her group under the leadership of the Evolved, were my parents.

"You'll find out even more if you agree to accompany us to the Citadel. I'm sure these loudmouth children have mentioned it to you."

"I'm guessing I don't really have a choice," I spat at her.

As she shook her head, I glanced out of the corner of my eye and caught Alicia struggling. She was drenched in sweat, her facial features rigid with determination. She was trying to contact Dorian again. Maybe she already had.

My line of vision caused Anastasia to look away, toward Alicia, and I tensed.

"So, you called the leader the Evolved. Are all of you evolved into something new? Not human, not vampire? Who is this group?" I asked my questions loudly, bringing Anastasia's attention back to me. I needed to give Alicia more time. It couldn't be easy trying to contact someone she'd never met, not to mention someone who didn't have these powers. "What are you going to do with us? And where is this Citadel Underneath the

World? I've never heard of it."

"Oh?" Anastasia asked haughtily. She looked me up and down like I might be her next meal. "So, we know something that the great Lyra Sloan doesn't, that The Bureau doesn't. Look at that. You'll find out all your answers soon enough. But I guarantee that every single person in here serves a purpose. A higher purpose. As I said, we've been called."

Just like Jessica, this woman was spouting pure crazy. Alicia probably knew more about what was going on than her. Anastasia had clearly been duped herself.

Knowing I needed to continue to distract her, though, I spoke to the fact that she was clearly a narcissist. "So, then, what's your personal stake in all this? Do you have powers too?"

I made sure to make my tone sound fascinated. It wasn't a hard leap to think that someone like me, in the business I was in, would be super interested in finding out about all of these powers that came from the Leftovers after the meld. Maybe it would keep her talking and Alicia would be done by then.

"So, you want to know my story? I'm happy to tell you, though it seems like you may be like the rest of them, looking at me like a bit of a circus freak. We're all entertainment to you." She motioned to all of the children in the room. "You would think someone like you, married to who you're married to, would be a little bit different in these matters."

I stiffened at the insult. I'd never seen myself as prejudiced and hoped that no one would ever call me that. Was a little part of what she was saying right though? I had judged Jessica and the way she was talking about things. Some of my team had judged Alicia.

"Now that we're going to be good friends," Anastasia said with a sneer, "I think it's time you started calling me Beverly. I always felt I had a special connection to the other side."

Anastasia was grandstanding now, beginning to pace back and forth as if she were putting on a show. I tried to keep myself steady, readying my hands at any moment to free myself to cause more distraction if I needed to. In my head, I begged for Dorian to pick up on what Alicia was trying to say.

"The other side?" I asked, raising an eyebrow. I could only assume she met the Immortal Plane or something like that, unless she meant the

Pocket Space. But could she know about all of that?

"The other planes. Other realms of existence," she said with a bite to her voice, as if she were trying to teach a petulant child. "After the meld, I found that I was one of the Called. I was stuck in the Pocket Space, as you refer to it, this in-between that we're in now. I thought I was never going to get out. Followers of the Evolved found me. They helped me to see my true potential. I've done well for them."

She stopped, staring up at the ceiling as if relishing in the fact. Maybe remembering whatever it was she did to make them proud.

"Once I had worked my way up in the ranks, they sent me back home to continue their good work in the Mortal Plane, as you call it. The place for regular humans, you know. But there are a lot of people there that shouldn't be there or shouldn't have to suffer there. Not the way things are." She sighed as if it were such an exhausting thing to be different, to be special.

She reminded me of one of those privileged, spoiled, rich kids I had grown up at school.

"You see, I'm working my way up even further. Someday I want to have the partaking of the Blood. I want to be in the Evolved's inner circle. That would be the ultimate life goal for me."

The obsessed Beverly had lost herself in her own story, just as I'd thought she might.

She paced closer and closer to me, and I knew it would be time to strike soon. There were nine of us. I was the only adult other than Beverly, but most of these kids were worn out as badly as me. We could still overpower her. All I had to do was make the first move. Then, hopefully, it would get the rest of them to back me up.

Anastasia turned—or Beverly—and looked straight at Alicia. It was too obvious now that she was using her powers. Instantly, Beverly pounced on the girl.

"Using your powers in unauthorized ways is forbidden by the Evolved, girl!" she hissed, going for Alicia.

Fortunately, this created a good enough distraction. I pulled the chains back out from behind the pipe, and I leaped at Beverly. I wrapped my handcuff chains tightly around her neck from behind, choking her and trying to bring her down.

Beverly panicked, scrambling and reaching for the chain around her neck. She scraped and scratched at it, only cutting her own throat more. Despite all of her big talk, Beverly hadn't been trained in combat. She was no good against me, and I might not even need the children's help.

Overpowering her was easy. I took her to the ground and almost knocked her out.

"Everyone, if you don't want to be here, now is the time to escape. Go!" I told them.

But the boy and girl from before looked nervous.

"You're going to get us in trouble. There's no way out of this alien place. This in-between or whatever the heck she calls it," the boy screamed at me. "There's no point in escaping. You're just going to get us in more trouble."

I let go of Beverly, knowing she was down for the count, and I rushed for the door. Five of the others came running with me. All of us slammed into the padlocked door where Beverly had come in.

Over and over, we beat ourselves against it, trying to break it down. The padlock was starting to budge just a little. It spurred us on. We tried again and again. But then we heard footsteps and then felt the door give. It was opening from the outside.

So much for that escape attempt.

Quickly, the children stepped away from me, trying to look like they were milling around like usual. There would be no hiding what I was doing, though.

Four cloaked figures, some of the group that we'd met in the Pocket Space before, burst through the doors. They were either vampire or something other. They weren't humans. These were the same people we'd encountered in the Pocket Space near the Sierra Nevada.

That was across the country, so how did they get here? They clearly had some kind of abilities or help traveling. Either way, I wasn't looking forward to facing them.

Beverly choked and rasped, pointing at Alicia and me. "I caught the girl, the one with mind speak, trying to use her powers. I think she was trying to summon help. This woman was poisoning her." Beverly kept choking, trying to stand up. She eventually was able to. "The group that was with this woman might know her whereabouts."

One of the cloaked figures spoke from underneath her hood. "I will need to send a group to defend the portal in the Leftovers, and I suppose it looks like we need to speed up our plans here. No doubt that one's husband is going to be after us," she said as if bored.

Yet another person here who knew way too much about me and my personal life. I breathed heavily, looking between them. What was going to happen now?

30

Roxy

"*L*ooks like The Bureau has given us extra suits. I guess your wife's contact for these things worked out," Roxy said, unloading more of the suits from the hotel.

When the two groups had done inventory, they found extras. Apparently, ever since Lyra had reported the fact that the suits that they had previously were too vulnerable, The Bureau had been working on an alternative. They made sure to send some for Torres's and Lyra's teams.

"Perfect," Bryce said, coming over and grabbing one. "I wasn't exactly looking forward to getting Leftovers' juice splashed in my face and burning it."

I had to laugh at Bryce. It was good to be back with the team. Even with Torres coming with us.

Soon enough, the fourteen of us working together headed out there onto an airboat. Torres had two techs and a green underling with him. Then, there was Lyra's team, headed up by Dorian. Torres kept giving him a funny look but hadn't said anything bad yet. Maybe he realized that he was finally out of his element here. They were heading into monster territory, and it was completely out of line with anything he'd done. No matter if the man used to fight vampires, this was an entirely new thing. Leftovers' monsters that were mutated from space and alligators. Possibly an entire plane of existence between worlds. No, those weren't on his radar.

Glad to have my suit, but noting that air filters but no oxygen tanks were given, I hoped that none of us ended up under the water at any point by accident or on purpose. So, hopefully, there wasn't a portal down in the water with all the beasties.

All of us piled into the airboats, seven of us in each, fitting a little bit snug, especially in our suits. At least these were more like wet suits. I had seen the ones for a brief moment that the others had used before, and they had been way too bulky. More like space suits.

I sat at the back of the boat with Sike, his machines working toward looking for any signs of creatures or darkness. Everyone was tense, wondering exactly what we were about to get ourselves into. The morale was low only because Lyra wasn't here. It was so strange to be without her. But Dorian was doing an excellent job, probably using the distraction of being in charge to keep from thinking about the fact that his wife was in danger somewhere.

For some reason, Kane and the harvesters came to mind. That wasn't something I wanted to think about at the moment, but then it struck me. The harvesters had kept telling him that his passed-out state had something to do with traveling between planes. Like he was flying or something. I assumed it meant astral projection. Maybe it was, or maybe it was more physical. Either way, he might be of use.

I still didn't know how to deal with my feelings toward him right now. I didn't really want to talk to him. Mostly, I was afraid that my emotions would come through and ruin the bond we had both emotionally and telepathically. And it was for these reasons that I needed to maintain that relationship.

If his soul could truly travel, especially between planes like that, couldn't he help with this? We were dealing with cross-planar travel here. If Kane could go to the Pocket Space to see the children before we arrived, it was worth it to talk to him. I would have to deal with my emotions and keep them in check. I was a big girl, and it was once again time to put on my big-girl panties.

I thought about everybody else in the airboat, wondering if I should tell them that I was about to contact Kane. Then, I looked at Torres and his team and thought better of it. Better to bring up my oddities after I had something good to say about them. Once I learned something from Kane. We didn't need some kind of tiff on the way to save Lyra.

I took in a few deep breaths, steeling myself in order to reconnect with Kane. He probably wasn't going to be happy that I'd sniped at him before when he was trying to contact me or the fact that I'd been ignoring him. And I couldn't have either of us angry at the moment. Emotions were going to have to stay out of it.

Kane. I put out the initial feelers for him, trying to convey the seriousness of this. I knew he might get petty and try to ignore me since I'd ignored him, but hopefully, he'd get over that quickly.

Kane, it's Roxy. I need your help.

"Roxy." His voice was annoyed, cold. But I was glad to hear from him either way.

Look, I'm sure you're pissed at me. I'll explain why I was so weird to you later. I promise you, it matters. It was for a reason. But right now, I need you to do me a favor. Right now.

Please, please, please, I pleaded to myself. *Please be willing to help, Kane.*

"So, you've ignored me for the last two days, and now you want my help? Really, Roxy?"

I ground my teeth together, frustrated that this was coming to a fight anyway. Had he not heard the urgency in my voice?

Kane, I need you to listen. People are in danger here. I really do need you. Can you put your anger aside for just a moment and help me, please?

Like the snapping of a rubber band, I swore I could feel his mood change. He somehow knew that this was really bad. Most of his thoughts cleared, and I could hear his voice even better somehow.

"I can't exactly say no to you." It came out in a mutter, and I didn't even know if I was meant to hear it.

My heart threatened to pitter-patter out of my chest, but I placed my hand over it, willing it to shut up. This wasn't the time to react to his words like that.

The soul traveling, astral projection, whatever the hell you want to call it that the harvesters say you can do, I think it can help us right now if you could figure out how to use it. Lyra went on this sting mission. By the time I got here to Florida, she'd been missing for several hours. Whoever the bad guy is here, they're responsible for missing children and all kinds of things. I don't know what they'll do to her or what they want with her. But they have her somewhere in the Pocket Space. There was a girl there who was able to use powers kind of like ours. She got through to Dorian, and she sounded scared. She mentioned that somewhere in the Leftovers, there was a way through. If you could somehow find a way to get coordinates or anything from Lyra, that would help us. We could save several lives and maybe not just hers.

I knew Kane wouldn't turn down the chance to help the children. He would be just as affected as me that they were even involved. I hated those kinds of people the most, the ones who used children for their own gains.

"This could be related to the children I saw?" he asked, sounding amazed they'd come up again. "Well, I haven't exactly been able to talk to Lyra before when I was unconscious, but then again, all of us always thought I was dreaming."

I let a few seconds tick by for him to gather his thoughts. He needed to be of sound mind in order to pull this off.

"You know what, to hell with sitting here and waiting to pass out. I'll do anything other than just sitting around like this. I'll try. That means I might be away from your head for a while, though, depending on how it works. Especially if it works."

Understood. We'll talk later. Thank you, Kane. You have no idea how much this means to us.

"Lyra's an important part of the team, and it involves saving kids. I think I do. I'm going to go now."

A feeling similar to static hit me, and I realized he'd purposely disconnected. We were getting better at this whole connection thing; controlling it. Maybe that would make things easier once I shared what I needed to share with him about my feelings. Even if he did reject me. If we could just shut it off, then that would make things a little bit more private.

"Everyone, be vigilant!" Dorian called out.

I snapped to attention, coming out of my trance.

"Last time when we were here, a monster moat was basically surrounding that little island." He pointed to a small, raised hill climbing up from the Leftovers' swamp. A jutting piece of marshland. "It was able to create a whirlpool before pulling us in. It almost killed us."

Almost immediately after that, Sike's machine went haywire. All the vampires began to hiss, looking around.

Darkness. They sensed darkness.

"Shit, they might be lying in wait for us," Bryce said.

The Hellraisers clutched our weapons, ready at a moment's notice to deal with any kind of monster that was going to show its face, or its powers for that matter. I didn't like the fact that the monsters had the advantage of being under the water, hidden to some extent. There could technically be dozens lurking right below us.

A tense, tingling feeling prickled my skin all over at the thought. I looked around; the rest of my team were just as ready. This was what we were here to do. The adrenaline was pumping as we started to cautiously cross over the moat, waiting to see if a whirlpool was going to spring up. Or any monsters were going to come after us.

No one spoke, as if the silence were going to keep any of Leftovers' beasts at bay. And maybe it did help because we were able to cross without incident. As soon as we got the boat across the marsh, on the other side of it and past the slope, there were five people waiting for us.

The people were wearing cloaks, like the ones from the Sierra Nevada. The weird cult that made the vampires practically lose their minds because of the signatures of darkness.

One of them turned to me as I got out of the boat. "You're the ones that got away with our monster."

I could only assume that they meant the Ghost. Was that how they were traveling back and forth? Well, they had to have found a better way now, considering they were here so quickly after they had been in the Pocket Space.

Even though this was coming to a fight, it gave me hope. It meant we could find a way through too.

One of the strange cult members sneered at Dorian. "Don't expect to be getting through us. We're here to stop your little rescue party. Your wife is going to help us whether any of you like it or not. A new era is dawning."

The weird, cult speech made me retch.

"Eat dirt," Bryce said, lunging at one of them.

And the fight began.

Dorian and Bryce collided with the group first, and I thought it was going to be a bloodbath. One of the cult members went down immediately. However, I was wrong. Just as we had suspected before when we had been in the Pocket Space against all of them, these people were not wholly human. They clearly weren't vampires either, but they were displaying superhuman powers. It seemed like some of them could guess moves before we made them, while others were simply just as fast or strong as the vampires. We were an evenly matched group despite the fact that there were only five of them.

"On your left!" Holt called out as she let bullets fly at a monster coming up from the depths.

I didn't look at it too long. I didn't want to scare myself.

To my left, to my horror, a Leftovers' snake was coming up, several heads hissing and striking forward, just like the one they had described in Everglades City.

"Holy shit," I called out, shooting at the many heads.

Jessie and Jordan flanked me, helping me take the thing down as each head exploded. But it kept swinging its tail wildly at us, trying to catch us off our feet. It almost swiped Jessie to the ground, but she jumped as if over a rope.

"Good. We've got it," I told them, proud that all the training was paying off. They were really holding their own.

Holt and Torres seemed to be fighting off their own monsters. The gators seemed to be outmatched by those two, but Lyra had warned me, and I'd looked at the briefings. Guessing by the size of it, it was just a baby. The real monsters were the parents lurking below. I hoped none of those came up.

"They're controlling the beasts!" Sike shouted, and my heart pounded.

They were seriously commanding these creatures? How were they doing that?

As more creatures snaked up onto the mound, they began blocking The Bureau and Callanish from getting to at least three of the cult members. They were shielding them.

Jessie, Jordan, and I looked at each other. They were trying to drive us back, but we took charge. We moved in front, shooting and chopping at will. This was the bloodbath.

Goo from Leftovers' creatures flew, and these things kept trying to strike at us. The suit provided decent protection from whatever water was on their skin that might be poisonous. But I hoped none of them tried to bite through it. I wasn't exactly looking forward to spending time in the hospital trying to figure out an antidote to Leftovers' venom.

As we got closer to the cult, breaking through some of the ranks of the monsters, I recognized the feeling that was coming over me. I'd had it once before. A portal. There was a portal that these people were protecting.

Four of the cult members formed a semicircle around the fifth, a smaller, weaker one. That was the one we needed to get to, the weak link. But they were good at shielding her.

I concentrated, trying to focus on the portal. Once there was a break in the battle, we would need to head for it.

"We need backup. Back to the boat!" Torres called out to his techies.

They managed to make it back across the water somehow and took the boat away. That was our only escape since not all of us would fit in just one boat, and I doubted any of us were willing to leave the rest behind. Now we would have to make it into the Pocket Space if we were going to get out of this mess. But Torres was right–his green backup was clearly outmatched here. Torres was exhausted, and he wasn't going to make it much longer.

The small cult member in the center seemed to do something. She was whispering something; I didn't like that.

"Watch out!" I called, not even knowing what we would be watching for.

And then there it was. Tentacles burst out of the water.

"What in the blazes is that?" Holt called out.

Jessie squealed next to me.

It was horrifying. Whatever the creature lurking below was, it was huge, and it was creating whirlpools everywhere. They were so strong that it was sucking some of us off the marshy hill.

This was not going well for us at all. I had been sure that we could outmatch them because there were so many of us, but they had powers beyond our comprehension. Powers the vampires didn't even have. Who the hell were these people?

Jordan, who was standing below, began to slide down, sucked into a whirlpool. I raced to him, hoping I would get to him in time to pull him back.

31

Roxy

*J*ust in time, I reached Jordan and yanked him back to safety, breathing a sigh of relief.

"Thanks," he shouted on his way back into the battle.

That was it? Thanks?

Dorian and Chandry leaped into action, aiming for the airboat. They pulled the two techies away just in time as the airboats went under the whirlpool and got destroyed. The whirlpool monster started toward Chandry and Dorian as they threw the techies back on the marsh to safety. Waterlogged, the two vampires got back into the melee. No time to grieve the loss of our other means of transportation out of the Leftovers.

"I feel a portal," I called out.

I didn't want them to miss the chance to find it and possibly get around these assholes. It could be the best way, to just avoid the rest of this battle altogether before there was loss of life.

Our escape route was cut off. The moat monster was on the prowl. Things weren't looking good if we couldn't find that portal.

"You can feel it?" Dorian asked, blocking a blow from one of the members of the cult.

He, along with Chandry and Sike, kept trying to get through their line to get to the girl in the middle. The one who was controlling the monsters.

New monsters sprang out of the depths, even as the moat monster and the whirlpool tried to threaten to pull everyone in. I asked for Jordan and Jessie to cover me, and I began to dart around the marsh, trying to concentrate on the feeling of the portal. I needed to find it.

"You're one of the Called," one of the cult members said to me. "You work with them, but you don't have to. You should be with us. Join us. You'll be rewarded greatly. Your talents will be appreciated here."

Was she nuts? Why was I even asking that question? She was trying to convert me to whatever the hell they were in the middle of a battle.

"Like hell I will," I said, spitting at them.

She bared her teeth at me then, attacking me with frightening precision. Her strength was otherworldly. She reminded me of fighting in the Immortal Plane. If you were to ask me, I would call these cult people monsters that could think. Pretty dangerous.

I held my own, but we were going to get slaughtered if nothing changed soon. There were too many of us that were just human. Guns and weapons or not, we were still mortal. I had the feeling that these guys were not.

The battle was chaotic. I could no longer make out any clear winners and losers of the scuffles. It was just a barrage, both sides going back and forth. The cult was protecting the portal, their smallest member controlling the monsters, and we were constantly trying to get through. Trying to make them stop. Trying anything. To no avail.

"Tell us where the portal is to the Pocket Space, and we can stop this nonsense," Dorian shouted. He looked rather impatient, which could be frightening if you were on the other end of it.

"Why would we tell you anything? None of you were of the Called, other than the one who continues to be against us," one of them shouted. "It doesn't matter. You ought to give up now. Maybe we'll find some use for all of you instead of killing you. You'll never find the portal."

I gritted my teeth. What the hell did she mean by that? It had to be nearby with my senses on high alert like this.

"Foresight," Cam's voice grunted out over the scuffle. He was grappling directly with a male cult member now, the man's hood falling off from the battle.

It was getting physical, hand-to-hand combat taking the place of the use of guns. Cam's weapon might have fallen into the whirlpool when that monster kicked up.

Its tentacles were still sticking out of the water. It reminded me of some kind of antennae.

"Strength!" Cam's voice sounded again, pointing to another of the strange cult people that Dorian and Chandry were fighting off together. She was turning out to be a formidable addition to the team. Hopefully, this wouldn't deter her from continuing with Mortal Plane missions for Callanish. Not all of the missions were this crazy.

I laughed internally at the thought of the levels of crazy they had all experienced over the years. But nothing scraped the surface of the last two missions involving Leftovers and the Pocket Space.

"What are you doing?" Sike asked, joining Cam's fight in trying to get the man with foresight off of him. He seemed to anticipate every move.

"Telling everyone each of their powers. It could help in the fight." His voice was strained as he fought, both of them trying to hold the man back. His moves were getting desperate.

Our team was smart. But how long before we exhausted ourselves? Especially the humans? And the vampires couldn't fight alone, no matter how strong they were. In fact, they could probably do with a feed to keep up that strength. I didn't know if Torres was allowing them to feed at the moment with his opinions.

We could lose this battle quickly.

"Draw that thing out of the water. We could get in and maybe get away, then!" Evans yelled.

Holt joined and then so did Jones, blasting bullets at the gigantic thing they could only see a part of. Tentacles flailing, it was able to dodge many bullets, and the ones that hit seemed to barely faze it other than pissing it off.

"Jessie, Jordan!" I called. They were the best at playing games, especially in battle. "Can you taunt that thing out of the water?"

"You got it, boss," Jordan said with a cheeky grin.

The two of them began to skirt around the edge of the marsh, taunting the creature. I didn't like how close they were, but it was the best chance we had. If we could eliminate the blockage in the water, we could at least retreat and regroup. The vampires might have been good enough in the water to get back and get new boats, or Torres could call for backup.

The spot with the portal would likely always be guarded like this now that they knew we could feel the thing, but we could always come back with twice the manpower and new weapons that might work better against these. Maybe even more vampires if we had to.

I had the sinking feeling there was more to all of this than just some missing kids and using Lyra to lure us into the Pocket Space. Something big was going down, and it had to do with all these crazy Leftovers' monsters.

With all the distractions, I was free to feel for the gate, my gun at the ready and shooting at every stray monster that girl sent in my direction. But she couldn't pay attention to all fourteen of us. It was just impossible. We were evenly matched, except for the exertion mentally that it took to use the crazy powers this cult member had somehow acquired. It was still no laughing matter, though, as Jessie, Jordan, and the rest of the Hellraisers were in constant danger from bites, slaps, and whirlpools from the monster the cult member was calling on.

"C'mon, little tentacle monster. It's time to come out and play," Jordan teased.

To my left, the tentacle monster was approaching, its tentacles so close, Jordan could reach out and touch them. Unfortunately, that was exactly what he did as well. One move and a loss of balance on the slick marshy moss, and he was a goner, sliding into the water even as I was shouting at him to quit being an idiot.

The tentacle dug into the water, searching for his body to grab. He was being dragged under.

I knew I needed to leap into action before Jessie did. "No!" I told her, blocking her from following before diving in myself after Jordan. "Keep fighting. Be ready to help if we need it. That's an order."

She furrowed her brows in frustration but then nodded. I was glad it was this way and not the other way around. Jordan would have given me much more flack than that.

The water was murky and hard to see through, and as it splashed. I tried to go under a few times to see if I could find and grab Jordan, at least give him a breath of air or two, but my mask began to fill with water. The one which still didn't provide a way to breathe under this disgusting water.

The smell was acrid, but I had to try again.

I took a deep gulp of air above water, preparing myself, only to get pulled down by the whirlpool, stronger now, and my body involuntarily dragged downwards.

This could be how I would die. Jordan and I both. No birthday party to make up for. Jessie could have very well ended up celebrating alone.

Don't think that way, I chastised myself.

As soon as I stopped panicking, I knew. The feeling had gotten stronger. I knew what they were guarding and why they thought we wouldn't find it. The portal was down here somewhere. I was closer than ever.

Of course my dumb thought before had been the right one.

Hoping the creature was nearby, likely something akin to the Ghost and the way it created portals, I stopped fighting. I allowed the pool to drag me down and around the current until I got flung out at the bottom.

I could see it now, the awful thing causing chaos. It was a giant gator, the size unimaginable like Lyra had warned me about. Out of its back and extending down from its stomach was a network of tentacles like what we were seeing on the surface.

The creature was slightly glowing as if radioactive, and I hoped I didn't get poisoned from being down here too long. I spotted the behemoth tentacle snaking around my brother and holding him to the spot. With a longer glance into the murky depths, I could see the creature was sitting on something strange.

The portal!

I needed to grab Jordan and go to the surface now. They needed to know this was here. We could all push through, overwhelm the creature, and get inside the Pocket Space before it was too late. But the moment I took a deep inhale, a tentacle found me, grasping me so hard I thought I was going through a car crusher.

I squirmed as I was being drawn inward toward the creature. I didn't want to be a Leftovers' beast's meal today.

I battled fiercely, kicking, punching, screaming, and going for my gun. I shot at the tentacles, but the movement never stopped as if this creature was unaffected by the violence.

It was of no use as I thrashed and twisted, and somehow, my thoughts went to Kane and how I wished he were here with me.

32

Kane

*A*fter I disconnected from Roxy, for a moment thinking about the fact that I was able to actually disconnect on purpose, I forced myself to lie down in the grass. I stared up at the sky, a typical cloudy day, and tried to go blank.

Going blank would be a lot easier if I weren't attempting to do it on purpose. And of course, after that, I would have to somehow pass out, even though I wasn't tired.

"You've got to do this, Kane. Roxy needs you."

I closed my eyes, finally forcing all the thoughts from my mind. All of the thoughts I had other than the ability to drift away. I imagined that my soul was free from my body and able to move. I imagined sunshine and rainbows. Whatever the hell it took to pass out. But nothing worked.

Frustrated, I sought out Carrew instead. He kept telling me that he and the harvesters would help, so here was a time for him to help and really prove that the harvesters had the ability to. I was growing impatient.

I found them outside his hut, watching a ritual that some of the other harvesters were performing. I settled down beside him and began to explain to the best of my ability that Roxy, the woman who had sent me to him to begin with, needed my help.

"You want to travel," Carrew said.

I wanted to strangle him for the obviousness, but I knew the harvesters had strange ways of doing things. I was currently at their mercy, so I thought better of it.

"Yes," I said, deflated. "I tried clearing my mind and going to sleep, but it didn't work."

Carrew disappeared inside his hut and came back out with some kind of dried herb or leaf. He passed it to me and made a chewing motion with his mouth, pointing to it. "Helps you sleep."

I ground my teeth together. If he had that sitting there the whole time, why hadn't he already given it to me?

As if reading my mind, he reached over and tapped me on the forehead a few times. "Have to have the right mindset. Communication," he said in that strange accent of his.

I swore the harvesters were an entirely different breed of creature. No vampires communicated like this.

Everything was so cryptic and riddling. I sighed. I didn't have a choice but to go along with it.

Carrew instructed me to take it and meet him inside of his house. Then he would be there soon. Whatever soon was, it was unclear by his words.

But as my eyelids began to droop, my body fighting it naturally, Carrew came into the room. I was lying down on a cot he had set aside in the living room.

Carrew came around behind me, placing one finger on each of my temples, and began muttering something. Was he doing some kind of magic? Or was it just a meditation ritual that would help me? I couldn't tell, but it began to work.

Suddenly, below me, was my body. I was flying up above it, able to freely move, and yet my body wasn't with me. This was weird as hell. Roxy owed me for this one.

I used my thoughts of her, focusing my energy toward her. In a strange dream mode that wasn't really a dream, I began to drift farther away from my body. I was being directed toward her, the same sensation of tugging as I'd felt with the children in my last supposed dream. Only this time, that tug felt like it was coming from farther away. Wherever Roxy was, it was still out of reach.

I found that I could take control of this strange dream space. My first thought went to the Immortal Plane and my home.

It didn't make any sense considering she was supposed to be in Florida in the Mortal Plane, but if things were going wonky with the Leftovers and whatever mission she had going on with Lyra, then it was possible she could have landed herself in trouble inside the Immortal Plane accidentally.

I was flying through the sky at impossible speeds, flitting across the continents and toward the southeast.

I felt free and powerful, grateful that it felt different than before. Whatever the harvesters were doing, it was working. Nothing could hurt me, and this whole soul-travel thing began to be enjoyable. However, I knew that Roxy was nowhere nearby. She still had that faraway feeling, meaning she wasn't on the Immortal Plane. Though, I doubted she made it to the Pocket Space either. She was still in the Mortal Plane trying to figure out whatever was going on with Lyra.

Lyra missing. That was something else. She was one tough woman, and smart. It would take a lot in order to abduct her or injure her enough not to come back to her group.

Roxy's location prickled at me, and then the prickle grew to something else. It was almost like a tether. I knew instinctively that it led to Roxy. And the more I thought of it, the stronger that connection got.

My body sped up, becoming stronger, and I began to fly over parts of the Immortal Plane I had never gotten to see before. All types of terrains and lands seemed to stretch on forever. Some looked so different. I knew we had a diverse set of lands here on the Immortal Plane, but I had never gotten to experience them for myself. I had been too busy training and competing. I had been missing out on a lot.

Finally, I was able to stop, a piece of the Immortal Plane calling me. I could still tell that Roxy wasn't in the Immortal Plane, but this was the spot where the connection was the strongest. In this form, it reminded me of all the technology in the Mortal Plane. The way it created these pulses and waves, and when you were at the center, the machines worked best.

A few of Roxy's thoughts passed through, and it sounded like she was trying to work something out. Like a puzzle or an equation. There were also a lot of chaotic thoughts and noise. Very little of anything coherent was reaching me, and I wondered if in this form, I had to physically be there with her to get a good picture and sound. But I had no idea how to break through into the Mortal Plane with this soul body I was traveling in.

I had broken through to the Pocket Space before. Maybe that would be easier. Even though I was being pulled to Roxy, maybe it was best to just go find Lyra in the Pocket Space first. That was my mission. Then, I could try to come back to my body instead to get ahold of Roxy, even though that path seemed rather slow. But something made me linger where I felt the pull of Roxy. The anger and awkwardness from before came rushing back.

There was something she hadn't been telling me, and it was bothering me more than I would have liked to admit.

I racked my brain, trying to remember exactly what happened to me that got me into the Pocket Space last time with the children. I had felt a connection, a pull, kind of the way I did to Roxy right now, and then I'd just followed that pull to the children. I had just not been concentrating on the way it worked since I couldn't tell if it was a dream or not, and then so many people had told me it probably was a dream.

But not Roxy. She had been the only one to believe me.

I centered myself, searching for auras. I could sense them along with the darkness the same way I could in my natural body, only I could sense them from much farther distances. I could sense them across planes if I tried hard enough. But I wasn't as connected to Lyra as I was to Roxy or the children. So, it was a little bit harder.

I scanned for any connection to grasp onto, trying to ignore the strong pull of Roxy's spirit. That proved to be more difficult than I thought it would be. It was like she was screaming at me. And then I realized why.

The thoughts came in shards, and they weren't anything she was trying to send through the bond. It was something I was picking up entirely on my own. She was in a battle of some kind, but I couldn't get the details. What I could glean is that she was underwater. She had been dragged by something, and she was running out of air.

I was frozen for only a moment, trying to compute the fact that Roxy could die on me. Something was going wrong with the mission she was on.

Fear and fury mixed within me, my emotions stronger than they ever had been. Maybe it was being in this ethereal body, or maybe it was the fact that Roxy's life was threatened. She was the only person I'd ever gotten close to, unless I could count my mother, which I wasn't sure I could, considering how many lies she had told me.

Lyra could freaking wait. There was no choice. I followed Roxy's spirit, but it dimmed and dimmed as she was panicking under the water. When I let go and allowed myself to just drift to her, I felt my spirit pulled from the Immortal Plane into the Mortal Plane. I felt the moment I crossed the barrier between them, but it happened naturally. Barely a tug.

I adjusted to my vantage point, seeing everything happening before me. It was a vicious fight to the death. There were Bureau members, Callanish members, and people I didn't recognize fighting the cloaked figures from the Pocket Space. The ones dripping with darkness.

My hunger craved them as their darkness bombarded me, but that wasn't what I was here for. I needed to focus. Off the side of a marsh where they were fighting, a large whirlpool was threatening any chance of escape. I willed myself to go down into the depths, and found in the center of it a most terrifying creature.

It was an alligator, or it had been before it mutated due to the Leftovers, and out of both ends of its body grew long, slimy tentacles. Underneath it, I felt the pull of a portal. Whether Roxy had gotten pulled in or not, I didn't know, but I assumed that that was what they were all here for. But this creature was both creating it and blocking it.

I let myself float underwater next to Roxy who was being pulled in by this alligator. Roxy's fierceness hit me like a ton of bricks, and she was focusing on fighting despite the fact that she was entirely exhausting her body and what little oxygen supply she still had.

Roxy! Roxy! I called out to her a few times, but her thoughts were already starting to get fuzzy and confused.

She was losing consciousness. She had a mask, but it wasn't watertight. Water was leaking in through it, and she had breathed some of it in. And there was no air. Whatever these suits were, they didn't have tanks for oxygen.

I needed to calm her down and let her know I was here, and then I had to spring into action. I didn't know how, but I had to save Roxy's life.

Roxy, it's me. I know you can't talk to me right now, but I want to let you know I'm here. I found you. The harvesters helped me, and it worked.

I hated this. We should be celebrating together that I had figured it out. I could travel between planes. I could astral project just like she'd suspected. But instead, I was watching her struggle to stay alive.

Listen to me. I can see more than you can. I can see everything. I know that there's a creature sucking you in and that there is a gate into the Pocket Space beneath it. The monster is reeling you into its face. I need you to fight just a little bit longer. When I tell you, punch with all your might. You'll get it right in the face.

She didn't answer, but her struggling stopped some, as she searched her suit. She pulled out a single dagger.

Good, it would heighten the chances of injury for the creature. I readied myself, making sure my senses were sharp. She had to do this at just the right moment.

Just as she came close enough, I gave her the go-ahead, and she lashed out with a dagger to hit it in the eye. The creature made an awful screeching noise that could be heard even in the depths of the water. It was earsplitting and enough to set my stomach into a spin. I had seen many things, but whatever they were facing in the Leftovers in Florida, this was something else.

The tentacle let her go, and I noticed on its other side it had been holding another one of them. One of Roxy's siblings? It let that one go too as the whirlpool stunted. Though, the portal remained beneath it. I could still feel the gateway.

I expected the two of them to float back up, to start kicking and swimming back up to the surface of the marsh, but Roxy did no such thing.

Roxy, you did it. Now swim, I commanded, but even her fierceness was gone.

Her body began to sink, her consciousness gone.

"No!" I screamed probably the loudest sound I'd ever made in my life.

There had to be something I could do. I wasn't going to watch Roxy die.

33
Lyra

I stared down the cult members defiantly, and I noted that they were giving me a wide berth.

"What's the deal with this one?" one of the men said in disgust, though he seemed wary, looking me over and assessing what kind of threat I might be.

I ignored the argument that ensued between Beverly, still rasping due to me choking her, and the other four cult members. Instead, I felt my way around the space. The gravity was a little low, just as I remembered in the Pocket Space before. Despite the chloroform and the handcuffs, I was feeling pretty good and confident. The energy was similar to the Higher Plane.

I wanted to smile to myself, but then it would give me away. They still assumed that I was weak, and I needed it to stay that way. If this were anything like the Higher Plane, then my universe powers would be useful here. Even if only for a short while.

They always exhausted me and left me ragged to the bone if I tried to use them in the Mortal Plane. That's why I almost never used them. But if I could summon up enough power, maybe I could free myself and all of the children who wanted to go with me.

I thought of my parents and the anger at how Beverly and the others were using me. Using the information they knew about me to lure me in and try to force me to be a part of whatever game they were playing. That wave of emotion allowed a burst of wind to come forth from me, knocking all four of the cult members back through the doorway and into the tunnel beyond.

Beverly stared at me, mouth agape, but there wasn't much she could do. She didn't have the kind of powers the rest of them had. Speaking into someone's mind wasn't going to save her here, and she hadn't been trained in combat. She wasn't high-ranking enough for that, I supposed.

As she realized I was taking a stand, she ran, probably in the opposite direction of the rest of the cult members. I doubted she ever would move up in the ranks now, assuming we couldn't just nip this in the bud once Dorian and the rest got here.

Feeling a little drained, but nothing like in the Mortal Plane, I addressed the children around me. "I'm leaving. You saw what I can do. Come with me, and you can go home. You can be free again. Surely, Callanish and The Bureau will help you figure out your powers, what they mean, and possibly how to use them correctly. How to control them if you don't want them controlling you. But you have to come with me now."

Alicia and three others came to my side. That included the ten-year-old I'd managed to show how to get out of his chains with the fake pipe.

Alicia turned to the rest, trying to implore them to come with us. But they wouldn't budge. One of them just looked scared.

The boy from before sneered. "I told you, I'm not coming. You'll just lose anyway. There's no use rebelling. It's better this way."

I didn't have the time to turn back. I heard the cult members regrouping, scrambling to come to after being knocked back.

On the count of three, the four of us rushed into the tunnels, coming at them with all we had. We were able to bottleneck them into the tunnel as I fought the first one. It was the safest way to take each one of them out. They were stuck, fighting one at a time or trying to fight through their comrades and possibly hurting them too.

The children were helping every way they could, and I got the first glimpse of some of their powers. The little boy, much like me, seemed to have control over elemental powers. Wind, fire, the shaking of the earth. Though, some of the movements he generated were so violent that it took all of us off of our feet for a few moments.

He had to be careful using them. No wonder they had kept him under lock and key.

"How can I help?" Alicia asked, standing back from everyone else.

Her power was mental, and she didn't do any good in combat. But I knew a way she could help us.

"See if you can get any of the others to come with us. I want to save as many of them as possible. I know some of them came from rough lives, but I'd like to help them. In the meantime, can you also contact my husband again? Let him know what's going on, that we're escaping?"

Alicia gave a purposeful nod.

I understood what it was like to feel useless. In the beginning while fighting next to Dorian, I had often felt like I was nothing. And then even worse when I began passing out from the curse.

Alicia went back into the room to try to rally the rest of them and do what I'd asked her to do, and I went back to my struggles with cult member number one. The little boy tried to focus his strength on the other three cult members, keeping them at bay. It was giving me the chance to take out this one, though my universe powers were exhausted.

I was fighting hand-to-hand with handcuffs. It would be a little bit before I could use anything else again.

Weakened slightly, trying to dodge the powers of the children behind me, I felt safe approaching the cult member, getting in a few good punches.

As I did, Alicia came back out into the tunnel and said, "Your husband couldn't talk, but he said he was much closer than before."

The thought gave me strength. The team was coming for us, and we could get these kids out. We were saved.

It gave me the mental strength I needed to dodge an attack and then land a foot square to the cult member's stomach. With a strong punch, the older boy that was with me knocked her out entirely. She lay sprawled across the tunnel floor.

Alicia came running out into the tunnels, another girl with her. She was able to convince one more, who was previously scared. That was good. Together, it looked like we might get out for a moment. Like we might get them subdued enough that we could go and get a head start, at least until Dorian could find us.

But did I want to run? They had information about my parents, or at least they might have had that. I wanted to go find Beverly and torture her or any of these cult members until they gave me info about them. I knew I couldn't do that and still save the kids, though.

They needed me. They were looking at me with some kind of awe. They saw me as a leader, and I was afraid that if I left them to their own devices, they would never make it out, possibly falling back in with a cult from necessity.

"Where are my parents? What do you know about them?" Punch. Kick. "Beverly said that you needed me for something involving them. Where are you keeping them?" Dodge, block, and punch again. That was my routine, and each time I asked a question, I either got a laugh or absolutely nothing.

They weren't going to tell me anything, and it was frustrating, to say the least.

"Children!" the man who had seemed scared before called out. "Come help us, and you will be greatly rewarded."

No, they couldn't possibly expect the kids to fight against each other, could they?

But with that call, those who were still inside of the room came running, and we were blocked in on both sides. There was nothing we could do to keep fighting, and I wasn't about to hurt children either. Alicia was frantically trying to convince them to stop fighting us, letting them know that whatever the cult was telling them, they were lying. It didn't work.

My energy almost regained, I elbowed the chin of another cult member, taking him down to the ground with the sickening knock of his teeth together.

The ten-year-old recklessly ran past me, trying to subdue the others, but then he was grabbed. His scream hurt my ears and my heart.

"Either you surrender, or we kill him," one of the remaining cult members threatened.

Considering their morals thus far, I didn't doubt that they meant what they said.

Furious, my nails digging into my palms, I realized I didn't have a choice. "Fine. Everyone, stop fighting. For now."

I wanted them to keep their confidence up. We would get out of this; it just wasn't the way I wanted or as soon as I wanted.

More cult members flooded the tunnel, each one grabbing one of the offending children as well as me and tying us up with rope. They wrapped it around and around and tied it tight. It wouldn't be so easy to get loose this time.

"We need to get this group to the Citadel and fast. Our plans must proceed now."

I guessed I was going to find out what the Citadel was sooner rather than later.

34
Roxy

The ripping sensation of the mask being pulled off of my face was the first thing I felt. Then, breathing into my mouth. It wasn't so much that I couldn't use my lungs; it was that they were full of water. My body was pushed over as I choked and gagged, spewing acrid Leftovers' juice onto the marshy ground. Someone was rubbing my back, coaxing me through it.

As my sight and other senses began to clear, I realized it was Chandry. She must have gotten me out of the water.

"Jordan," I managed to choke out, my voice barely there. It was going to take a while to heal that.

If I hadn't been so worried about my brother, I would have been pissed off. Being in this shape, I admitted that they would make me wait at least a couple of days before going out in the field again, unless I threw a tantrum. Which I probably would.

The problem was, inhalation pneumonia was a thing. I wasn't really up for a stint of secondary drowning, especially with poisonous Everglades water.

"I got him," Jessie cried.

I forced my pained body to turn over and saw that Jessie was standing over Jordan. She was doing the same thing for him that Chandry was doing for me. They had managed to get us both out.

The fight was somehow over, though I didn't know what happened. The water beside us was calm, and so was everyone else. I looked around, trying to glean if we'd lost anyone, but as far as I could tell, everyone was okay. Or as okay as we could be.

I coughed up more water, my lungs burning, and Chandry dabbed my face and then her own. She was soaking wet. She had been submerged in the water trying to get to me. I'd have to thank her later, but my thoughts immediately went to Kane. Had I been hallucinating, or was he there with me? I swore he had told me exactly what to do to get free of the tentacle.

Kane! Unlike my physical voice, my mental voice was much louder, pretty much yelling. *Are you there, or have I gone crazy?*

"I'm right here with you," Kane responded, louder than usual. It was almost like he were standing next to me.

Have you figured out how to travel between planes? That's what he was trying to do before everything turned to shit with the fight. But how did he end up with me instead of finding Lyra?

"In fact, I had to find a way to break into Dorian's thoughts. That wasn't easy."

What!? How had he done that?

What about Lyra? I asked

What I could only describe as a snarl came from the other end of the bond. "Are you kidding me? That's your concern right now? You're lucky I didn't go find Lyra first. Instead, I followed the tether straight to you. What the hell was all that about? You almost died, Roxy."

Kane was completely losing it, angry at me. I knew exactly how that felt.

I coughed up more Leftovers' water as I held back a laugh. *I may have almost died, but I didn't. You helped me. Thank you.*

Kane scoffed. "You have no idea how frustrating it is, watching you flail around and knowing there's so little I can do."

I could imagine the set of his jaw, his eyes dark as he scrutinized me. I couldn't believe he was giving me a lecture about having been taken under the water in a whirlpool. It wasn't exactly like I'd called the monster and said, "Here, gator, gator. Come get me."

Are you freaking kidding me? I don't know about that, you jerk? You weren't the only one who can care about someone, even when they're far away and nobody seems to think anything between the two of you can work.

I spit it out before I could stop myself, and all bets were off. Who would have thought it would take me nearly dying and him using his astral travel to save me for me to finally tell him what I was thinking?

I could feel some kind of emotion coming up from Kane, but Dorian interrupted my thoughts.

"Roxy, are you talking to Kane?"

I looked at him sheepishly. There was something about Dorian that made me feel like I was talking to my father or something. Well, not my father but a father figure.

"There's no time for whatever drama the two of you are having now. We've got other things going on."

A loud harumph came from Kane.

I smiled despite myself. "So, fearless leader, what's going on?"

"Cute, Roxy, especially coming from someone who almost just died." Dorian pointed to one of the cult members, completely taken down. Torres was holding the one who had been controlling the monsters at gunpoint while Chandry tied her up. "We made it to rescue you and Jordan when Kane suddenly started shouting in my head that you were drowning under the water. It was good timing because Cam and Jessie pointed out this... person"—he pointed to the one who had been controlling the monsters; he didn't even know what to call them–"who had taken control of the creatures, sending them after us. We were finally able to separate her from the group and threatened her to stop the creatures that were aiding them. When their creatures stopped attacking, the rest of them left into the water and vanished. So those other two, they're gone."

I willed my voice to be more than a rasp the best I could. It sounded more like I was a chain smoker, though. "It makes sense that they would jump into the water like that. While I was down there, I found the portal. It's underwater."

"Do you know how to open it?" Cam asked, looking at me curiously.

"I think so," I said confidently. I had learned a long time ago that "fake it till you make it" could save lives.

Dorian turned his head to Torres and his team. The Bureau members would have a decision to make. I doubted that they would like the Pocket

Space very much, especially considering it would put us in direct conflict yet again with the cult. Much more of them too.

"You're welcome to stay here and call for help," Dorian said. "This Pocket Space, it's an in-between world. It feels very strange, and this is the first time we can get into it without the use of a special monster that we accidentally killed. So, it would be very dangerous. And it's full of these cult members."

Torres was looking at Dorian with what I thought was newfound respect. They had been working together, in tandem, trying not to die. Being in a bind together bonded two people faster than anything else, in my opinion.

"My team and I are coming with you. We want to help Lyra."

I gasped, and several other people were agape at the idea that Torres was willing to risk going to a place like the Pocket Space.

"Truthfully," he added, "I just have to know what it's like. I don't know why, but I have to."

A shiver traveled up my spine, knowing that the Pocket Space wasn't something to be curious about. It was the kind of place where someone could get stuck forever. Everything was strange, and nothing made sense. You were everywhere and nowhere at the same time. I wasn't exactly looking forward to going back.

Remembering Kane, I tuned out of the conversation between Torres and Dorian. They would figure out the strategy and then let the rest of us know what to do. I found that it was comforting for the time being not to be in charge of everyone. Despite the fact that I didn't want to just sit and do nothing and behave like an invalid, I *had* gotten injured. My body was tired, and I took the few moments I had to rest.

Nobody had told me to stay behind yet, likely because with my sensing of the portal, I was too important. I couldn't let them down because my body ended up giving out.

So, I guess you figured out how to travel between planes? I asked smugly.

"I was beginning to wonder if you forgot about me," Kane joked. "Yes, I felt your distress and was able to pass the barrier into the Mortal Plane somehow. It was just automatic as soon as I felt this tether, I guess to you. So, obviously, my soul isn't visible over here, but I can see everything that's happening. I can even kind of zoom out and see an entire scene, if that makes sense."

Fascinating. What about your body? What happens to it?

I could feel the resistance dripping off of Kane. "Honestly, I don't know, but I'm not leaving you here to die again. Sorry, not sorry."

I almost laughed at his use of the human phrase. *Fine, but when we get through the portal, you need to help us fight these people. You know what the stakes are.*

"Hell yeah."

I could hear the smile in his voice. It felt good to have him with me, even though I couldn't see him.

Dorian's voice pulled me away from Kane for the moment. He was ordering the cult member we had tied up to get us down to the portal. Whatever she had said or done before to get the creature to obey, she did again. Whirlpools sprang up all around the mound, but they were strong enough that they left an opening through the water, able to lead us down into it safely.

It was so strange, seeing the path down through the water. I stood up and followed the rest, Chandry still soaking wet in front of me.

"I can't even sense it," Dorian admitted with his brows furrowed. He looked like he had all the concentration in the world, and even he couldn't tell exactly where the portal was. He looked at the other vampires who shook their heads.

They turned to me, so I guessed it was up to me to figure it out.

I put my feelers out there, looking for it again.

And there it was. The gate was pulsing its energy at me.

"Let's do this."

35
Kane

I followed them all down into the water where the portal was waiting. The way into the Pocket Space had finally been found. Or at least, one way. If there were one here in the Leftovers of Florida, could there be more gates leading in and out in strange places like this?

All the vampires tried to sense the portal so they could open it, to no avail. Could they not feel it at all? The signature was so strong it was nearly blinding. Roxy had no problem finding it either, taking over with confidence when the vampires had failed.

"Can you feel it too, Kane?" she asked.

I can. As plain as day. I wonder why they can't.

I couldn't make much sense of it, but it was only us. Yet again, we were the odd ones out. It had to mean something, right along with the fact we could speak into each other's minds and the Ghost had been so interested in us and not the others. But we weren't going to figure it out now.

Roxy approached the portal, looking down as if she might be able to see right through it. "Do you know how to do this?" she asked me, her nerves seeming to get the better of her.

It's pretty easy. Just place your hand over it and feel its energy expanding and inviting you all in. It will open pretty easily, or at least it should.

My lack of confidence didn't deter her from trying. Her mask was off, the clearing in the water created by the cult member allowing everyone to breathe easily. Her hair was wild from having been in the water and almost drowning. She was so brave, just trying anything that came her way and expanding her powers even though most human minds were too small to accept such things. She looked amazing.

She was learning all these crazy things about herself, and it was nothing to her. No big deal. Just another day at work.

"Kane, did you just say something about my hair?"

Shit, how loud had my thoughts been? I might have been a little too obvious. I gritted my teeth to gain my composure, but then realized she deserved to know it.

Actually, I was just thinking that you look like a goddess.

This wasn't like me. I would have normally been happy to change subjects or ignore the topic altogether, except for the fact that only minutes ago, I'd almost lost her. The entirety of existence almost lost Roxy, and that would have been a tragedy. I knew I wouldn't have been able to come back from that, and that when it all snapped into place.

I'd known Roxy was beautiful, inside and out. I'd fought with her side by side. I'd seen her injured and at her peak performance. We'd fought and flirted. And no matter how far apart we were, we found each other, guessing the other's mannerisms and feelings even without every single thought streaming through the bond. Something had always been there between us, and I had been too stubborn to do anything by trying to kill it with my every action because I was afraid of what the consequences would be.

We were welded together now, though. The tether to her had been so strong when I separated my soul from my body I hadn't been unable to ignore it. There was no escaping her, even if we didn't work out or we never admitted anything to each other.

I cringed at the thought of what might have happened had I not tried so hard to get ahold of Dorian. If I hadn't succeeded in getting inside of his head, would they have found her in time? They had been so busy fighting that she easily could have been lost right along with her brother.

I never would have forgiven myself even though it wouldn't have been my fault. It was one of the few times I could say for certain these abilities I had were more than useful. And now they had directly saved someone's life.

Roxy concentrated, her hand over the portal. She strained to get past the wall of determination to let me know that she'd heard me, a lot of it anyway. "Thanks. I guess I do resemble a warrior goddess or something."

Her voice was flirty and sassy, but there was a hint of shock underneath it. I knew her well enough to tell. She hadn't expected me to roll with her punches and be honest. It was good to know I could still keep her on her toes.

A few thoughts escaped into my mind from Roxy as she willed the portal to open for her. Many of the thoughts involved me. I was shocked to see it on full display. I had guessed, especially after her reaction to possibly overhearing the conversation with Maefa, but it wasn't real until now.

"I'm not sure this is the time for all this," she told me, sweat forming on her brow at the level of concentration.

I know, but there's a lot I want to say to you, I allowed myself to say, no longer holding back. Once the flood gates were open, they were hard to shut once more.

The portal opened, achingly slow. Another difference with the Pocket Space I could add to my list of anomalies.

As it did, Roxy was able to address me better. "Look, we will talk about this. Whatever this is between us, we can discuss afterward, but whether or not we can still talk long distance, you're going to have to leave me now."

I should have known it was coming. My original plan had nothing to do with following the feel of Roxy's spirit straight into the middle of a Leftovers' battle where Roxy had almost lost her life. I needed to help them in any way that I could, but the idea of leaving her now shook me.

"I need you to travel ahead of us, into the Pocket Space, and get to Lyra. Report back to us anything you can glean. I'm counting on you for this, Kane." Her voice was pleading.

I had almost forgotten about Lyra, the reason this dangerous rescue mission was underway.

I wanted to be a baby and whine, asking all the why's, but it was simple. It was unlikely that I would be noticed by any enemies in this form. As far as I knew, no one could see me this way. And my soul could travel much faster than they could on foot. To top it all off, they needed someone to find out where Lyra was and what condition she was in so the team could prepare for the best results.

Okay, I'll do it, I told her proudly. *I just don't know if our connection will drop from each other if I go too far out of range. So, don't freak out if you don't hear from me.*

Before, when I was soul traveling by accident, I had passed out and then lost contact with Roxy, but I didn't know if it worked the same when I had already been speaking to her while actively participating in the traveling. I didn't want her to worry if we got cut off for a while as I did what I had to though.

"Okay, thank you, Kane. Go find Lyra, and be careful."

I laughed. *You're the one who needs to be careful, apparently.*

I gave Roxy a final look, unease trying to keep me from turning around, but I did it somehow. I pushed my soul through the portal and began sailing through the Pocket Space to find Lyra. I turned my focus on, looking for anything to cling to in order to find her. I needed to scout her out, by aura probably. Or a signature that would at least point out vampires and humans. There were monsters in this plane just like any other, but sentient beings like humans and vampires didn't belong. Their signature would be odd to find and rare, even with that weird cult of hooded...things skulking around.

My soul was moving through the strange tunnels of the Pocket Space, and in this form, it felt slightly more natural to move through them. I made note of the directions I went in the confusing maze of Pocket Space tunnels so I knew where I had been and where I hadn't. They were winding and expansive, and Lyra could have been anywhere inside of them. Or outside if she had fought her way out somehow.

Through each tunnel, I searched for auras that would lead me to Lyra. I felt human signatures, but they weren't on the path I was taking yet. I would have to keep looking.

Vampire signatures were everywhere as well, much more than what I thought there would be in the Pocket Space. I found myself curious about them but didn't pursue any of them.

But then there were the other signatures. The ones that weren't human or vampire, though they had some similarities of both. They reminded me of something. It was on the tip of my tongue, but if I strained, I still couldn't recall what it was I was thinking of. Regardless, it was strange. I knew those signatures, especially mixed with the amount of darkness pulsating from them. They had to be the hooded people we had met in the Pocket Space before. The ones the kids had been afraid of and ran from.

Anger came over me, and I wanted to tear them limb from limb or feed on them, but I didn't even know that it would be possible in this form. I had done many strange things so far, but that might have been beyond my abilities.

Following the signatures, I was getting closer and came out at the end of one of the tunnels. A boulder outside of the tunnel sat by itself with a woman sitting on top of it. She looked weary, clutching herself and trying to breathe. She must have been injured. A slight signature of darkness came from her, so I didn't mean to linger. She wasn't saying or giving me anything to go by.

Nothing about her was threatening, and she didn't seem to see me. I passed by her, heading for another tunnel where I felt the darkness pulling me to where the strange non-vampire or human creatures belonged. But then there was a voice in my head.

I turned and peered at the injured woman, maybe another follower of that group who had been left behind in some scuffle, and she was sitting up straight now, a smile on her face.

This woman was speaking in my head. She knew I was here but didn't appear to be able to see where I was as she was looking around and not at me. But I didn't like that she'd noticed me. I needed to dodge suspicion somehow.

"What are you, my friend?" she asked me as I allowed the connection to clear. She was human, nothing else, but she must have had some kind of psychic powers nonetheless.

The meld had done some strange things on all planes, including giving humans abilities they'd never had before. What would Roxy's take on this be?

I kept on listening but didn't respond. I was hoping she would give something away. If she'd been in a fight, it likely had to do with Lyra.

"You're clearly powerful. I can feel it. And you're traveling without a physical body. That's something not even I can do yet," she mused as if I were an experiment or on display. "You know, the Called has a place for people like you. They will foster your talents and reward you. We are forming a whole new existence that is better for everyone."

She was babbling like a crazy person, and I was becoming agitated. And what the hell were the Called?

I didn't answer, and since this wasn't Roxy, blocking her from my specific thoughts was easy to do, though pushing her out was something else entirely now that I had let her in. She was strong in what she could do.

"Why are you not answering me? You could be great. You have no idea what you're missing by not joining us. There is no one out there who will accept you like our leader will. The Evolved. She is the best of everything, and she will lead us all to victory and further evolution in the Citadel Under the World. I plan to go with them too. You can join us, friend. No matter what you are, you will be cared for and trained. You will be one of us."

The babbling was becoming concerning, and I realized she had nothing for me. She wasn't going to give away anything about Lyra or the children, just try to rope me into whatever schemes the crazy people in this place were up to.

The Citadel Under the World sounded made up and completely bonkers. To be fair, so did my powers and the fact that the Immortal Plane and Mortal Plane had literally mixed. But to me, this was so far-fetched I couldn't put any stock into it.

I sighed, hoping that if I physically left and tried to shut her out at the same time, she would leave my mind and let me go on my way.

I turned back towards another tunnel, following those signatures again and hoping I would find Lyra with them so I could get back to Roxy. I pushed and pushed at the woman's consciousness inside my mind and then focused on the task at hand. I thought of Roxy and how she looked opening the portal. Worried about her trying to die on me again. Eventually, as I sped into the tunnels, the woman's voice and signature left me entirely.

I was sure she was annoyed by that considering her attitude and behavior, but it served her right for bursting into souls' heads and trying to convert them to some insane cult.

Two figures came into view as my soul flew to them in the tunnels. In a bend in the tunnels ahead, I could hear voices, and the tunnels shook and rumbled. Something was going on.

Two cloaked men were having a conversation. I swooped toward them while also taking advantage of the fast movement of the Pocket Space. It had been the one good thing about that strange in-between space.

As I listened in, I realized they had gotten away from the fight with Roxy and the others. They were going to meet up with some of the others, who must have been the ones making all the noise ahead, and let them know that Lyra's team was coming.

"They are probably headed to the Citadel," one of them hissed, mentioning that weird term again. "But we'll have to stay behind." He didn't seem happy about it.

"To catch the others, yes, but we'll be rewarded for it. Not only will it keep them from attacking the others and taking that woman the Evolved wanted, but we can also grab the beast-speaker for them. They'll like that a lot."

I got the idea that the two of these men were pawns in the grand scheme of things even though they wore the cloaks and gave off strange auras. But who was the beast-speaker...?

"The one who could feel the portal?" the first man asked, his eyes widening. "That's right. You said she took the Ghost from us somehow."

Roxy. They were talking about Roxy. Anger pulsed through me, but I didn't have time to dwell on it as I came around the corner and found utter chaos.

A group of four of the cloaked people were rushing Lyra and a group of children in the tunnels.

The two I had been following stopped, gathering their own strength to join the fray. They were going to be wildly outnumbered now, and even with Lyra's universe powers, they would likely fail.

I noted that a couple of them, Lyra included, were chained up with handcuffs and ropes around their ankles. It didn't make the fight easier either. I watched them fight, and I recognized the teenage boy who was joining in. It was the boy from my dreams, one of the ones I had helped while in Pocket Space.

Joy and worry surged through me as I watched all of them. These were the children I had been trying to get back to and save. If we could save Lyra, then the kids would be all right too. Though, I knew there were more somewhere.

But then I saw them. They came from the other side, ambushing Lyra and the children who were fighting alongside her. They must have been under orders from the cloaked group, but why were they following them?

What were they offering that made these dirty, hungry children fight for them?

The fight was hopeless, but I wanted to see the outcome so I could let Roxy know the specifics. Maybe I could figure out where this Citadel was so that once they kicked the asses of the two who were staying behind to ambush her and the others, they could find a way to follow after them.

A little boy, very small, was the source of all the rumbling and shaking. It seemed he could do something with the elements. Control the very earth beneath them. But he was grabbed, and they threatened him, forcing Lyra to surrender.

I bared my teeth. I wished that I were in my body. Threatening to harm children was the lowest of the low. What was wrong with them?

Defeated, the children and Lyra were tied up by the others so they could be led to the cult's home base. I remembered it from when I was stuck there.

The boy I had befriended got tied up too, and I wanted to talk to him and let him know I was here. Would he be able to see me or hear me if I tried? These children all had special powers of some kind, which was why this group wanted them. Maybe I could get to him.

I had even been able to get to Dorian, so I had to try. Just to let him know.

I followed them and pushed a few times, trying to find the way into his mind. Finally, I felt the resistance end, and there I was.

Don't be scared, Max, I told him. *You can't see me, but I'm here. I can soul travel. I'm helping the others that are coming for you.*

"Kane!" the boy said, excited and surprised. He could hear me!

Yes, it's me.

"We thought you were dead!"

I chuckled. As if anyone would take me down so easily.

36
Lyra

ot tears stung my eyes, but I wouldn't let them fall. Every child was bound up the same way I was, including the little boy whose name I now knew...and recognized. Though, he looked nothing like his picture anymore.

Landon. The boy who had pinged on a missing person's case in Everglades City. The one who nobody had known was linked until Torres was notified while we were in his office. This was the little boy we had been searching for clues about when we had found the airboat tour company and had to fight the crazy Leftovers' snake away from tourists.

The cult members barked orders at us, threatening each one of us to keep us marching our way down the paths of the tunnel. I kept my eyes and mind open, looking for any way of escape. The children they controlled, plus the three cult members since they'd had to leave the one I incapacitated behind, outnumbered those of us willing to fight. It didn't look good, but I had to keep hope alive. At least for the sake of the kids.

The two who had joined at the end stayed back. I had heard them say it was just in case my husband came for me. Was that possible?

I told myself over and over that I hadn't come this far and done this many things in order to lose these kids or for me to die.

Then again, they had told me they wanted me for something. They wanted all of us for something, so maybe that would make them hesitate even if we ended up in a fight again. But how long would they tolerate us not cooperating before they gave up on whatever they wanted us for?

The only hope I had at the moment was wherever they were taking us, I would find my parents and at least get those answers before anything worse happened to me. I had no doubt it would haunt me beyond this life if I didn't figure out if they were okay or not.

The youngest teen, the girl who had been too frightened to talk to me earlier, was having a hard time keeping up. I noted, really looking her over for the first time out of the corner of my eye, that she was nearly as skinny as Landon despite the fact she was at least three years older. Her head was down, her feet dragging along.

She had helped the others ambush us, though I hadn't noticed exactly what her power was. But it had seemed to exhaust her.

I pressed my lips together, wanting to scream at them all. If they were going to use these children to fight their battles and force them to be a part of their cult, then the least they could do was pay attention to their well-being. Sure, Alicia had mentioned that they were fed and brought candy, but how well were they fed? How much, how often, and was any of it even nutritious?

I remembered being in the Pocket Space before, and there had been no source of food at all. Not even vegetation to try and sustain, especially since it might be poisonous. And Kane had nearly died for lack of anyone to feed off of as well. Other than the cult members who were impossible to get close enough to do anything with, this in-between world was empty.

One of the cult members came up behind her and pushed her in the back, urging her forward. Then, they did the same with Landon. Alicia and the boy who had fought with us were on either side of me and slightly in front, leading the group forward.

Cocky of them not to think Alicia would take off considering her history, but I guessed we all knew we were defeated for the moment. There was nowhere for us to go even if we got away, and the Pocket Space was probably crawling with even more of the cloaked people. Beverley was also still on the loose somewhere, recovering.

I turned, narrowing my gaze at the nearest cult member for a moment. If they wanted us all to hurry so badly to wherever they were taking us, the least they could do was help carry the smallest, weakest children. They made such a big deal about fitting in and helping each other, but when it came down to it, they treated the children as nothing more than slaves.

Alicia's pace slipped a bit, and I knew it was for a reason. "Something feels off," she hissed, looking around us. "I don't like this."

I shook my head, letting her know I didn't either. But I also didn't want her to get caught talking to me and be hurt anymore. She was the communication between us and Dorian. I felt guilty for using her like that, but it was our best chance of any kind of escape.

The other teen, the boy, fell in step on my other side. What were these kids thinking?

"Are you Lyra?" he asked in a whisper.

I didn't know if the cult members could hear or if they even cared as long as we were moving along as they wanted us to.

I nodded. "But how do you know that?"

"I'm Max." Then, he said, "Do you really know Kane?"

Kane? This boy knew Kane? I couldn't interrogate him, though. If they heard us talking about somebody else, someone who might be related to The Bureau in some way, it could get us all in trouble. I looked forward, processing the shock of this boy knowing both my name and Kane's. I pretended to be just as much a compliant prisoner as the children.

All three of us were silent for a bit, and then I nodded again, knowing he deserved an answer now that I was composed. "Yes, I do know him."

Max's eyes seemed to light up. "Kane's voice just spoke into my head," he said slowly.

It took everything for me not to stop and gape at him.

Alicia's head snapped up as well, looking at him a little too long.

I cleared my throat, and she looked away, our steps luckily never faltering. But she seemed to be thinking the same thing I was. We had been told none of these other children had mind speak, the ability to hear each other telepathically. It was only Alicia. So how, of all people, was Max able to hear Kane in his thoughts?

"Kane says to wait for rescue," the boy continued in a low tone. He was speaking quickly, making sure he got the message across.

I knew Kane had those abilities just like Roxy and Alicia, but how he had managed to get to the boy or anyone in the Pocket Space I had no idea. How was it possible? He couldn't have come from the Immortal Plane to the Pocket Space. There wasn't a way to, and he hadn't been in the Astral Plane either. I doubted the healers would have even let him with the troubles he was having, last I heard.

"Help is on the way soon," Max clarified. "He said just not to let the kidnappers kill any of us in the meantime."

Alicia covered a scoff with a cough. Easier said than done, I was sure she was thinking. I felt the same, except this gave me hope. Despite me not understanding how this was possible, Max was very confident in what he was saying. It didn't make any sense that he would make it up.

I racked my brain for how there could be a connection between the two, but then I remembered when we had come upon Kane in the Pocket Space before. He had mentioned a group of kids he was protecting while he was stuck here. This had to be one of the kids who had been with him.

Kane had been protecting the kidnapped children from the cult!

I sighed. I didn't want to wait for rescue. It wasn't my style, but I had to trust Kane, and I knew I could trust Dorian. They would get us out. They probably had a plan already in motion. I didn't have a choice but to go along with whatever they were going to do.

"What are you whispering about!" one of the men called out angrily.

We had been caught.

"We were just wondering about the Citadel and what it would be like," Max said, saving face.

I could feel their tense suspicion as they processed whether or not they believed the lie.

"Isn't that where we're going?" I asked, hoping to make it seem more plausible.

"Be quiet," the man barked back but did nothing else, thank goodness.

They all remained tense and on alert, though. There would be no more talking.

The sounds of battle hit my ears from the tunnels behind us where we had left the other two cult members and the one that had been knocked out. She might have come to by now and would join.

If they were fighting, it meant it was Dorian and the others they were ambushing. They had made it! Hopefully, they had been prepared to fight right away upon entering the Pocket Space considering the cult had been lying in wait. I didn't know how many of them would have made it through, but I had to trust my team and the Hellraisers. They had beaten the odds many times. They would do it again. Even with the strange powers these cult members had.

"Move!" the cult members said in unison, pushing us farther and faster.

Alicia's eyes were blazing, looking at me.

When Max and I picked up the pace, she didn't. She hung back with Landon and the girl. She groaned as if she were tired and in pain. She was going to slow us down and give them time. Smart girl. If she wasn't a teenager, she would make a good addition to the team. Hopefully, her parents could be proud of the way she fought here once she made it home.

The noise got louder, and I knew they must have been pushing the cult members into a retreat. We were going to collide.

"Be ready to fight," I gritted out at Max.

I hated that the kids would have to use their powers again. They were likely to pass out after too long, but we didn't have a choice. This was our best chance at getting out of here finally.

Bryce came into view first as I turned on my heel, Alicia, Max, and Landon mimicking me. The cult members began to stop, not paying attention to us anymore.

Then, the best face I had ever seen came into view. Dorian was trailing right in front of Roxy, and even Torres had come. I counted fourteen in all. Fourteen had come to rescue us. Those were good odds.

I was shocked but happy that Torres had come along with his team. It didn't matter that he had been an ass; he was coming through for us and more than capable. His vampire-hunting instincts were kicking into gear and would help him down here more than anything.

The wall of the cult members who had been herding us along with two of the children who still seemed to want to fight with them were blocking us from the others. In front of them were the three cult members who had run from Callanish and The Bureau members.

It was chaos as powers and guns flared. I called upon my universe powers, glad to find them replenished. It was time to do this.

"Alicia, you need to stay back, okay?" I warned her.

Her eyes met mine, and she looked frustrated but obeyed anyway, backing toward the exit of the tunnel. She hated sitting it out, I could tell, but this wasn't her job or her fight. This was our job now.

Max was emboldened, though.

"Landon," I said, keeping a grasp on my powers and building them for the right moment, "I need you to go with Alicia, okay?"

He nodded and ran to her. Alicia enclosed the exhausted little boy in her arms. It was the best I could do.

The girl who was wrapped up with the cult members went running as well, ducking behind Alicia and Landon. It would be another child saved. I would do my best not to hurt the others.

"Max, I am going to do something, and the kids need to get behind me or push through to the other side and get behind my allies," I told him. "That includes you."

Max shook his head. "Let me get everyone untied. I can do it."

I nodded. "I can give you a few minutes." It was all I could spare.

Max, who must have had great strength, but also pyrokinesis, began to burn and pull away the bonds tying his hands. The rope burned and pulled away as sweat piled on his brow. My team was keeping the cult members distracted for now, but I worried that they would turn to us soon to make sure their slaves weren't getting away.

His hands finally free, he went to mine next. As soon as he was done, he took Alicia, Landon, and the other girl, bowling through the cult members with his strength, temporarily knocking two of them over. The others took the distraction and followed, and Alicia tugged one of the girls fighting with the cult along too, despite her scowl.

All they had left was one teen boy, and the rest were ushered behind my team. I faced this side of the cult alone.

They didn't seem to know where to look, and I took advantage of it, the wind power coming to me again.

"Brace yourselves!" I called out to my team. I didn't know if I could control it well enough to not knock them over.

As a wave left me, fast, booming, threatening to rip the tunnel apart, my team huddled together, protecting the kids. The cult members were swept away farther down the tunnel before being thrown about and finally falling to the ground.

They weren't dead, though, and only one of them didn't get back up. It was the one problem with them not being quite human. But at least we had the advantage now. There were more of us, and I could join them.

Fighting away the bits of exhaustion from using my powers again, I sidled up to my team who were getting back in position, the children being shoved behind them again. We could do this. We could beat them.

Having a moment to better survey our ragtag group, I noticed that Chandry was fighting with a handicap...namely a cult member chained to her. Roxy and Jordan both looked like they'd been chewed up and spit out, and Roxy's voice was husky and lacking as if she'd lost it at some point.

"More are coming!" Roxy called out just before giving her team of Hellraisers more orders. "A man and two women," she added.

"How do you know?" I asked her, confused.

"Kane," she replied, and it was all the explanation I needed.

He must have been with us. He and Roxy had powers beyond what we had thought before. That was becoming clearer, especially with the way the cult coveted her so much. It would be interesting to see where that could go and explore it if we ever got out of this mess.

Luckily, we still outnumbered the group even though, just as Roxy had predicted, three more joined the onslaught of attacks from those who were superhuman. They were still no match for Dorian, Chandry, and Sike as the three vampires wore them down, but even Torres, who had specialized in taking down vampires, was starting to struggle.

I needed to keep morale up. We all needed to if we were going to make it out. Two of the cult members moved from the fray, staying back. They seemed to be whispering in hushed tones as if discussing strategy or something. Maybe their powers were more subtle than their strength.

For a horrific moment, I worried they had some kind of mind tricks beyond just mind speak, but then Roxy began giving instructions and warnings about their plans. Kane was listening in to what they were saying.

"The kids. They're going to circle around and surround them to try and get them back."

I gritted my teeth. We couldn't let that happen, but if this continued too long, they were our vulnerable point.

Torres called out to Chandry, "Cover me!" He ducked to the back of the group, motioning me with him. "Sloan, we need a better plan. These kids have to get out of here."

I nodded in agreement, feeling for when my universe powers would return. I pulled from the frustration I was experiencing and hoped something massive would build. "No offense, but the humans are the weakest links. Could we split up a bit? Some of you can have cover to get out and through the portal with the kids?"

I hated the plan. I wanted to stay and defeat these jerks and get information about my parents, but I couldn't keep putting the kids in danger for my own wants or needs.

Torres pursed his lips. "Get them to buddy up with me, the techs, and Roxy. We'll need her for the portal. Otherwise, the rest can stay up front to fight until the last second."

I shook my head. "That'll be too obvious. They'll know what we're planning if they don't already." I tapped my head, worried someone could reach inside of it and pull everything out.

Roxy, Kane, and Alicia could do something amazingly useful, but in general, those powers were frightening if thought about in the wrong brains.

Torres growled at the fact that I was right. "It needs to be Roxy. She's one of the better fighters. She can fall back here with the kids. Send you forward with your"—he looked down at my hands, looking for the right words—"magic. It would make sense as a strategy and distract them from other possibilities. When the moment is right, we break away."

Torres rubbed his head and added, "Chandry will have to come too to keep that one in line." He pointed to the small woman handcuffed to her. "She's controlling the monsters in the Leftovers, including the one with the tentacles and whirlpools."

I stifled a gasp and focused on the possibilities. I went over the plan in my head and couldn't think of any other way.

"Okay, but we'll all have to start a retreat. Some of you will be faster than others." I gave him a pointed look. "Some of the kids are exhausted. You may have to carry them. Spread the word."

Torres reloaded his gun and then went to pass this information up the ranks. I turned to the children, confirming with a nod and a smile that they understood. They were going home.

"I'll make sure they all come," Alicia said.

"Thank you for being so brave."

Torres weaved his way back through the crowd, and I prepared myself. I hoped my universe powers would be back in full swing soon so I could end this quickly. I tried not to think about how, yet again, I would be leaving the Pocket Space without so much as a glimpse of my parents. I wanted so badly just to take off on my own and go looking, but that wasn't the smart thing to do. If anything, it would get me or even them killed.

The signal was being given to retreat. It was time to head back through the tunnels and to the portal Roxy had found.

Like a well-choreographed dance, we began switching places. Some fell behind and others surged ahead. It would look random, hopefully, to the cult members. Roxy and I crossed paths, only meeting eyes for a moment, and I had to put my trust in her to make sure we all made it out of here, the kids first, and all of us alive.

I was glad it was her.

I took my place beside Dorian, fighting at the front as we twisted around, moving back but hurtling blows at the cult members when they got too close.

Chandry's fight was mostly with the cult member she was tied to. I hoped she came through because I doubted we'd survive the whirlpool coming out of the portal.

The cult members gave chase, not willing to give up on whatever it was they wanted, me included, and I looked at Dorian with chagrin.

"They want me, you know. They won't kill me." My voice was quiet, knowing Dorian would never like my line of thinking. My rational brain didn't even like my line of thinking.

"Lyra..."

"They have my parents. I want answers about these people, and I want to find my parents and see for sure that they're alive. You could leave me here. They can't hurt me until I've done what they want."

Dorian set his jaw, and because I could read him like a book, I knew he was searching for the right thing to say, filtering all the possibilities that passed through his head. He finally settled on, "You know that wouldn't be a good idea at all."

His voice dripped with sympathy. He understood. Probably would want the same thing if it were his family.

"I do know," I confirmed as the retreat picked up the pace, and we turned to run.

The farther we got away from the cult members, the farther I got away from ever having the answers my soul begged for. Would I ever get them?

37

Roxy

I gave my orders to my team, knowing I could trust them. I had to trust them. My job was the portal and the children. It was a heavy job.

As the retreat began, I surged ahead, moving to the back of the group but not so fast as to alert suspicion. The children were looking after Lyra as she traded places with me like she was their personal hero. Even bigger shoes to fill, apparently.

Chandry moved in front of me, dragging our lonely friend the monster puppeteer to make sure that our other friend the tentacle gator wasn't going to cause any issues when I opened that portal. We had to get these kids to safety, which became more apparent as the group of cult members surged forward, attempting to break through the line Lyra, Dorian, and the Hellraisers were holding for the rest of us to get a head start. They would sacrifice and stay behind too if that was what it came to.

It was almost time to break away, and I pulled the kids around me as they fell back. Torres was preparing his techs to come with us. We would be grabbing the smallest of them and running. There was no time for these weak children to keep exhausting their powers or run when they were clearly malnourished and dirty. Not to mention just bone tired.

I would have to turn away and run which meant I would lose my vision of what was happening entirely. They needed Kane more than I did.

Kane, you have to go and watch the cult. I need you to get back into Dorian's head if you can. I have to get these kids out, and they need you to give them the breakdown of anything. What they are planning, what powers they have if you can figure it out. They need to win. I want them to make it through with us, I explained hurriedly.

"I agree that they need me," he relented, but I knew a but was coming. "But don't think for a second I'm cutting off communication with you. If you think I am going to let you out of my sight after all this, you're crazy, Roxy."

His voice was deep and possessive.

Why the sudden protective urges?

I expected him to laugh, but he didn't. Kane had never been so serious toward me.

"I just watched you almost die!"

I scoffed because I couldn't help myself. I knew it wasn't the time for this drama, but what I had to say just slipped right out of my thoughts and into his. *Yeah, but you just told a girl you didn't want her because you care for someone else. That someone else sounded a helluva lot like me, and yet you still don't believe it would work?*

I pulled a little boy into my arms. He couldn't be more than nine or ten.

"So, you heard that." His voice was a sigh. "I'm sorry, I–"

I groaned. *I feel the same way, but...*

"There's no time!" Kane said, now desperate and angry.

He snapped me out of my thoughts just as Torres grabbed another one of the kids and swung them over his back. Chandry grabbed yet another. The battle was starting to move too fast to keep our conversation going and concentrate on getting them out. He was right about there not being time.

Fine, Go, I told him. *But you should know since you're so damn worried about me that I have feelings for you.*

A brief pause, and then, "Go with the kids. Get them out. We'll talk later. I promise."

I promise too.

It was a fight to the death, my instincts running the show as we scrambled to get back to the portal before they realized what we were doing.

My mission was clear: get the kids out of here at all costs. I hated the idea of leaving my team behind. I was their leader. It was my job to sacrifice myself in times like these, but I was the only one who could open that portal. I had to take the children with me.

The silence without Kane in my head was helpful when it came to focusing on the task at hand as I pulled my mask back onto my face, ready to go underwater. But it was an uneasy feeling knowing that he was elsewhere, helping Dorian and Lyra on the front lines as we retreated back into the Leftovers.

Yards ahead of the others, Torres, his techs, and I whisked the children away toward the portal. Chandry brought up the rear, attached to the cult member that was apparently able to control monsters. She would need to cooperate to make sure the children didn't all drown.

We made it back, and I approached the portal, Chandry manhandling the tiny woman with so much power in one finger it was almost unimaginable. I would have thought it was crazy a couple of years ago. But here I was, opening portals to new worlds and reading others' thoughts.

I didn't know what to expect, and I kept the children back with Torres and the rest of his Bureau team as I forced it back open again, the strain on me even worse this time. Thankfully, water didn't come spilling out when I opened it, which was a good sign.

"I usually stay on the outside when doing this," the woman said in a squeaky, sheepish voice, but she reached her hand through the portal. I half expected her to start screaming in pain, her hand chopped off by that awful tentacle monster. But instead, she did something and then nodded. "The creature has drained the channel. It's safe to cross."

I put my head through, double checking. I didn't want to risk any more lives for this, and I didn't trust even a captured cult member at this point.

I stood, half in and half out, holding the portal open for the others to make it through.

"I'm not sure how long I can do this," I admitted to Torres.

He nodded, his techs springing into action, "Get over there and call in a helicopter to evacuate out of the swamp. Make sure the kids make it through with you. Keep them safe."

The techs took his orders immediately, passing by me and back through the break in the pool of nasty Leftovers' water. Then, the kids that weren't already in someone's arms followed right behind.

I spared a look back to the tunnels where we'd left the others far behind now. I could distantly hear the sounds of battle but knew nothing more.

Kane, I called out, wondering if he was around or not.

He did say he wasn't going to leave me alone for too long since I'd almost died. The memory made me smile.

"Roxy," he said, coming through, but his words were quick and quiet like he wasn't right next to me anymore. "It's not looking super good with them. Some of them are injured, and the cultists have pressed them into the corner before the gate."

A loud bang startled Torres and Roxy, and they must have burst free of the corner as they came barreling toward Roxy and her group. At least the weakest kids were safely on the other side.

Let them know they only have to hold off a little longer, I told Kane, but as I watched, checking between the Mortal Plane and the Pocket Space for what was happening on both sides, they were all still fighting stubborn cultists, and they were clearly slowing down.

The twins were holding their own well, and I swelled with pride, but even Bryce was struggling to keep back the cultists with powers. They were pummeled with fighting they weren't used to. As much fighting as many of us had experienced as vampires, it had been a long time, and this was different. Completely unpredictable since the powers weren't like what vampires displayed.

The portal lurched, and my eyes widened. I pushed with all my concentration, but it was getting harder and harder.

I turned to Alicia and Max. "Come on. You need to get out. Go," I told them, but they shook their heads.

"We aren't leaving without Lyra," Alicia said. "She tried to help us, and we want to make sure she gets out."

I nodded, lauding the bravery of these two teens. It wasn't every day a couple of kids wanted to be around with a possible fight to the death in an in-between plane just for someone who'd helped them. Lyra tended to bring loyalty out of people, though. There would be no arguing with them.

I stuck my head back into the Mortal Plane and saw the techs were pulling the last child out of the water, their shadows disappearing. I breathed a sigh of relief. They'd be able to call for help now.

A scream caused me to look back into the Pocket Space. An arrow pierced the monster cultist's chest, taking her down. Chandry kneeled by her side, trying to help her in any way she could, but it looked grim.

Dorian tackled one of the cult members with a bow and arrow, his fangs ripping into him. He was dead.

The sound of rushing water came from the other end of the portal. Our cultist and the only safe way back into the Mortal Plane was knocked out.

A beast neared, going insane, and a wall of water was threatening to crash down on us. I didn't even know if the techs and children would be safe on the marsh with this much water.

"Stay back!" I called, hoping they would draw the kids close.

I saw the eyes first, the gator coming right at me. I had to make a split-second decision. "I have to close the portal!"

With no other choice, I let go, and the portal shut, flinging me temporarily to the ground with the force of it.

"What did you just do!" Torres yelled, his rage making him almost nonsensical.

"Unless you wanted to take your chances in the burning water with whirlpools and an out-of-control beast, I had no choice. It was coming right for us. The safe way through is gone," I told him through gritted teeth as I forced myself upright.

The rest of the cult was pushing toward us now. We needed to get ready to engage them again. Our only way of survival was in their demise.

Kane, I called, *can you go into the Mortal Plane again? I want you to make sure the kids and techs make it out and report back to me. Please.*

Hope. It was the only thing I could cling to when there was none. This had to be the most dire situation we'd ever been in.

"Yes, but then I'm coming right back here, Roxy. Do you understand?"

Of course.

"Who the hell are you?" Kane's voice rang in my head, startled and angry.

Kane? I asked. *Kane?*

He was engaging with someone I couldn't see or hear. What the hell was happening?

Kane!

His voice vanished. I couldn't hear a thing anymore. But if something happened to his soul...or his body...if something had gone wrong...

I couldn't handle the thought and bent over, my hand on my stomach. I couldn't think about it right now. I needed to deal with these cult assholes, but if Kane was gone, I didn't even get a chance to really tell him how I felt. For us to decide where this could go.

I am in love with Kane.

If only I hadn't been so stubborn before.

38
Lyra

I struggled to stay upright and to ignore the searing pain across my left arm. There was a gash, slowly bleeding, that would likely need stitches if we ever made it out of here and back to the Mortal Plane. I doubted there was enough equipment with the group to fix me up if we got stuck on this side. Either way, I would probably end up with a nasty scar.

The cult group had grown once more, and their strength was indescribable. Even though we were tired, they didn't ever seem to. Their injuries, just as frequent as ours, either healed fast by some magic, or they just didn't care about the pain. Maybe they had been conditioned not to react to it. It wouldn't have surprised me with the way they behaved.

The closer we got to Roxy and the children, the more I worried this plan wouldn't work. If we rejoined the others, I had no doubt the kids would be taken once more. Escaping a third time was unlikely with them involved, especially with the stamina this group was displaying.

Bryce was tiring, and I watched out of the corner of my eye, forced to keep the woman I was fighting at bay, as the man he was fighting alongside the others broke through the line and pulled out a bow and arrow.

Anguished and angry screams came from all three groups in the fray, but I didn't know what they meant. I couldn't spare a look behind me to find out who the arrow had hit.

I held back tears mixed with beads of never-ending sweat from the exertion of staying on my toes to keep from receiving a killing blow from these superpowered jackasses.

"I have to close the portal!" Roxy's voice drifted over to me, and internally, panic set in.

We were going to be trapped.

"We shouldn't have taken Riley down," one of the cultists said, talking to the one I was fighting with. "She was the best we had to control those beasts."

They glared at each other, allowing me to get a blow in. A punch across her jaw.

So, they had shot down their beast speaker. That was the best I could call her. What a power to have!

Dorian broke free from his fighting stance, barreling after the cult member who'd got away.

The one I was fighting shoved me back. "This base is compromised. We'll have to start over anyway," she screeched, teeth bared like she was a beast herself.

They might have been faring physically better than us, but they were just as lost and sick of this fight as we were. I tried to split my attention, watching the others to see if they needed help, digging for more universe powers that wouldn't show yet, keeping this woman at bay, and listening to what they were saying to one another.

Hopefully, Dorian and Sike would hear as well, and we could find a way around them, through them, to be rid of them. Anything was better than this stalemate.

"Let's go back through the portal. Kill all of this group. Then, we can get the children back. I'll take my chances with that monster for them." This was from a man Holt and the twins were fighting, strong and fast. His voice sounded like the grating of rocks over metal.

We finally met up with the others, Torres standing in front of Alicia and Max. Roxy was in a fighting stance, though something about her expression worried me. The other children had gotten through at least.

"We can't let them get through to the portal," Torres said. He began to fight, fierce as ever, telling Alicia to stay back even though she wanted to help so badly. "Use your head, okay?" he told her.

Another new ripple of respect ran through me for the man. He deserved a bit of credit after all this, and just maybe he had gotten over his ridiculous opinions about vampires by now.

I tried to keep my morale up, but as we clustered together, I could see everyone's injuries. Bruises all over Bryce snaked underneath his suit. Chandry was trying to remove the body of the cultist she was still strapped to, handicapped by what was now dead weight. Holt had a slight limp. The twins had fared the best so far, though Roxy looked well for someone who had nearly drowned.

I moved, determined to get to Dorian so we could strategize. We needed a new plan quickly. We couldn't keep going like this.

I felt my universe powers prickle at me once more, not as strong, but enough to send a blast of flame from my palms. They attached to a cultist's robes and caused her to scream, and she retreated.

"How have you been using your universe powers so much?" Dorian asked, finally fighting by my side.

My body relaxed a little because it felt like home.

"I know you don't like to use them because they drain you, but you should try it. They are easier to use here. Less tiring," I explained to him between jagged breaths.

Torres came up next to us, passing me a knife. "You might need this."

I nodded, grateful to have a weapon for the fight. My powers and strength had been doing well up until now, but I didn't know how much more I could eke out.

Dorian concentrated on the group gathering around us, trying to break through our line to get to the portal. I guessed they had decided that was their best course of action. Then, he leaped in the air, landed on the nearest enemy, and incapacitated her.

Just as quickly, he leapt again and took the man next to her down as well. Both of them were knocked out. His energy seemed to work the same as mine here, though as a vampire, he had a little more stamina than myself.

One of the male cultists pulled back several feet away from the fight, talking seemingly to himself. "But we've got important things going on here."

Someone must have been communicating in his head. Was it the Evolved?

I spared a look at Dorian, three of the group now incapacitated or busy. He shook his head.

"Okay. Fine." The man gritted his teeth but then stepped forward, addressing the rest of them. "We will retreat to the Citadel. We've been summoned to the Evolved."

Most of them stopped fighting but began hurling insults at him. A couple of the cultists continued to fight, though, ignoring the order.

"I said the Evolved needs us. Do we deny her call?" he said. "The woman and her friends will be stuck here anyway. No beast control, no portal, no food or water. We'll find them again soon enough."

They backed away and rushed up the tunnels away from us. The fight was over for now.

I didn't know what the Evolved could want, but at least for the moment, it was to our advantage.

We all began to sit down, breathing heavily. Jessie and Chandry came around to check on wounds, tending to them the best they could with what little we had.

Exhaustion hit me, and it was worse than the pain. If this were the Mortal Plane, I would have been asleep for a long time by now.

I lay back on the ground, catching a wide grin on Alicia's face. "What's that look for?"

"I was able to get in his head. I pretended to be Anastasia while remembering the ways she talks to me. I told them the Evolved needed them to retreat."

Alicia had probably bought us lifesaving time.

"Congrats on the quick thinking. You're good at this."

Alicia beamed, but then her shoulders dropped. "Will we be stuck here now?"

I shook my head, not wanting to lie to her. "I honestly don't know."

"Should we just try to make it back anyway? Open the portal again and face the gator?" Sike asked, sliding into a spot next to Chandry who had finally been uncuffed from the dead cult member.

"I'm not sure I could hold that portal open long enough for that." I twisted to look at Dorian. "Dorian, are you still communicating with Kane?"

Dorian shook his head.

"I lost my connection to him," Roxy explained, near tears. I had never seen her like this. "He was talking to someone, and I couldn't see them. He was angry or confused."

A silence fell over us. Nobody had an answer that could help her, and it didn't sound good.

"I'm glad we got most of the children out," I said, an idea coming to me. More like a spark, actually. "I am sorry we didn't get the two of you out."

Max and Alicia shrugged.

"I wanted to stay until you got out," Alicia admitted.

Max added, "I've been here for so long that I know how to survive. You have to steal from the cult, but I've done it before."

"Thank you," I said genuinely before addressing everyone, hoping they would be on board with me once we had a bit of time to recover. "If we're stuck here, we should go on the offensive. We should find their headquarters and figure out how to take them down. We need to get to the bottom of this anyway. They're well connected, and this Pocket Space spans at least the country, if not the globe. This is our best chance to do it and stop them."

"We have the kids with us, though. I know they can be an asset, but do we really want to put them back in danger?" Chandry asked.

I was surprised at her maturity. Sike nodded in approval, seeming impressed as well.

"I agree with Chandry on that, but I don't see any other way to be done with this," Dorian chimed in. "They will kill us anyway if we don't find some way to bring them down from the source."

"I'm all for taking down these assholes," Roxy rasped out, her voice still strained.

I couldn't help but grin at that, and her siblings chimed their agreement enthusiastically.

"This place..." Torres began, looking around. "It's scary and strange. I have never felt so off-kilter, but I also want to see more. I want to know what's going on so I can take it back to The Bureau. So, I'll agree to it."

I had to grin at him.

"It's not like The Bureau will be able to contact me anyway with comms down here."

Even Bryce broke a smile at that.

I braced myself with resolve. We were going to go after the cult and finish this once and for all, and I would finally be able to get answers about my parents.

39

Kane

I couldn't let Roxy down. I needed to pass back through the Pocket Space barrier into the Mortal Plane and see if the kids made it out of the Leftovers all right. Then, I could come back to her and check that she was okay. The fight they were dealing with was a tough one, and I was afraid there would be casualties. That group of cloaked people from the Pocket Space were so powerful it was insane. It worried me.

Roxy, be careful.

Silence answered me.

Roxy–

"Oh, Anastasia was right. You *are* exquisite."

That was not Roxy's voice. That was for certain. Another female voice had invaded my head, and it was different from the woman I had encountered earlier.

Who the hell are you?

Instead of an answer, my soul was yanked against my will, away from the battle. I tried to push back against the force, but there was no way to resist.

"Don't fight," the voice said, but it only made me fight more.

I didn't know this person or what they wanted. I needed to get back to the Mortal Plane and then report to Roxy.

Fighting back did nothing, though, and I felt the familiar sensation of passing a barrier, but what plane was I going into? The Immortal Plane?

I found myself floating in a forest I didn't recognize. In front of me, I made out the light of another soul, almost like the amber soul-lights, but something was different about this one. And I was certain it was what was pulling me.

Did I look like that in the Immortal Plane as well? In the other planes, my soul seemed to be invisible.

I pulled my thoughts away from myself and focused on the soul, surrounded by dark energy, and yet it was still able to float rather than sink where the harvesters would take it.

"Stay with me," the woman's voice said.

I have to get back to my friends, back to the battle, I argued, trying to flail, to turn away.

But I wasn't even sure how that worked. Movement had been so natural up until now. It seemed impossible to be deliberate about leaving.

"But don't you want answers?" the voice asked, light and enticing.

I didn't have time for this, though. *I don't have any questions.*

It was a lie, of course, but those questions didn't matter right now with Roxy and the others in danger.

"Oh, I think you do. I can give you answers about what's happening to your soul, these new powers. You're special. Can't you see that? Don't you want to know why?"

I did want to know, and it seemed like I couldn't lie to this strange soul. So, I stayed silent instead.

"I think we must be the same kind of soul," the voice claimed before its shape changed, stretching into the shape of a woman with long, flowing hair, sharp vampire teeth, shadows flickering in her skin. She was completely naked.

"You're another like me. The meld separated your body and your spirit," she said, and I couldn't seem to make her stop or leave her behind.

I had to listen to it all and try not to focus on her body as she kept gesturing, sweeping her hands over it as if wanting me to look.

What was with all the women throwing themselves at me like this when there was only one I wanted and wasn't sure I could have?

"I'm not able to talk to normal souls like this," she rambled on. "I didn't even think there was another like me. Yet, given the way your soul is traveling and the way you can talk into my mind, you must be another half vampire, half human."

What the hell?

Rage and anger overtook me at the suggestion. What game was she playing? I knew my father.

This is absurd! I blurted out.

She flew toward me, circling me and examining me with curious eyes. I tried to follow her gaze, wondering what it was she could see. I hoped I wasn't bare before her like she was.

"You woke up in the Pocket Space after the meld. You're passing out and having wild dreams."

I tensed at her words. *You could have pulled that from my head or guessed it based on the powers. It doesn't make me part human.*

A nagging feeling chipped away at me, though. Was there any possibility?

"What about your healing time? Not like a vampire but not like a human either," she pointed out, catching me off guard. "Having to work harder than your peers at everything."

All of my speech and thoughts were gobbled up in an instant.

"The meld was the best thing to happen to the ones like us, you know." She kept flying around me and getting slightly closer each time. "I was able to learn to control my powers quickly this way and discovered that they are almost boundless. I can teach you too, if you'd like. I am one of the Called, and we are creating a new society where what we can do is valuable. You could become as powerful as a minor god."

Her voice was giddy, making these offers to me when I was still trying to process the similarities and what they could mean.

It was like my brain was on fire or about to burst. I couldn't be half human. My mother hated humans. They murdered my father. But yet, what she was describing was undeniably his same story. It could be a trick, but she had similar powers too. Coincidence hardly existed anymore.

I couldn't handle it, though. It was all too much. *No, you're crazy. I'm not going to join a cult. I have to go back and help my friends now.*

I tried to fly away, though my concentration was shaken by her words. I pulled and pulled, but it was like moving through sap.

"Consider my offer," she said as I kept fighting her presence so I could get back. "For now, take some time to calm yourself and think."

My soul was shoved violently, spiraling now at top speed. Still, I had no control, until I was tugged back into my body.

No, that wasn't where I wanted to go.

I woke to the harvesters shaking me.

"Are you distressed?' they asked me. "Are you okay?"

I felt like I had just climbed a mountain, unwilling for a moment to even move my lips. But I needed to get back to Roxy. I had to make sure she was okay and tell her what had happened. She would be worried, and it might make her lose the fight. I tried to tug my soul out of my body again, but the nearest harvester who must have taken a turn watching over me shook his head.

"Your soul must be inside to recover." He poked at my chest for emphasis.

I groaned, no choice but to concede. I couldn't make it work again if I wanted to. Instead, my thoughts and emotions turned back to the idea of being half human. It couldn't be right, could it?

But what if...

What if my father had an affair with a human and that was the problem? That would explain why my mother treated me differently and why she hated humans so much. No matter what, though, I had to get the answer. To this. To the Pocket Space and the children. To the cult. I needed to recover and get back. There were some things we needed to hammer out and some dots to connect when it came to my life.

I closed my eyes, promising myself it would all come soon.

Milton Keynes UK
Ingram Content Group UK Ltd.
UKHW010701201023
430994UK00001B/77